# AWAY FROM EVERYWHERE

# AWAY FROM EVERYWHERE

## A NOVEL | CHAD PELLEY

LIBRARY AND ARCHIVES CANADA CATALOGUING IN PUBLICATION

Pelley, Chad, 1980-
Away from Everywhere / Chad Pelley.
ISBN 978-1-55081-265-7
I. Title.
PS8631.E4683A92 2009    C813'.6    C2009-902809-3

BREAKWATER BOOKS LTD. acknowledges the support of the Canada Council for the Arts which last year invested $20.1 million in writing and publishing throughout Canada. We acknowledge the financial support of the Government of Canada through the Book Publishing Industry Development Program for our publishing activities. We acknowledge the financial support of the Government of Newfoundland and Labrador through the department of Tourism, Culture and Recreation for our publishing activities.

Printed in Canada

  Canada Council
for the Arts   Conseil des Arts
du Canada

**Mixed Sources**
Product group from well-managed forests, controlled sources and recycled wood or fibre
www.fsc.org  Cert no. SW-COC-000952
© 1996 Forest Stewardship Council
FSC

FOR PEGGY,
FOR EVERYTHING THAT CANNOT
BE PUT INTO WORDS.

*"All happy families are the same;*
*all unhappy families are unhappy in their own way."*

— LEO TOLSTOY FROM *ANNA KARENINA*

PART ONE
A LINE CROSSED BECOMES A WALL

# BUT FIRE BURNS

IT WAS THE HARSH CONTRAST of her blood on everything around them that he remembered the most. The warmth of her blood on the cold of his flesh. The dark red handprint on the beige headrest of the back seat, smeared downwards from where she tried to lift herself up off the floor – but fell back down. There was a puddle of it on her belly, too much to soak into her white shirt. When he spun around in the driver's seat to face her, he expected widened eyes and an adrenaline-flushed face, but she was just lying there, so ghostly still and quiet, so deaf to his shouting and unaffected by his panic. Only her eyes were moving, scanning their bodies and assessing the damage. *How are we going to explain this?* The affair, she meant, not the accident.

Hydroplaning felt like a circus ride gone wrong, like having his sense of control gutted and guillotined. All sounds were muffled by the forward momentum, and the car felt weightless as it slid across the highway's yellow lines. He turned the wheel, hand over hand. He pumped the brakes, but there was no stiffness there, no resistance, and the car dove into the forest, snapping limbs off trees. It felt more like the forest was coming at him, from all sides. Like a whir of brown and green was devouring the car, chewing on it. Branches shrieked and punched against the sides of the car: scouring paint, denting steel, busting glass.

It all ended in one dull thud – his body thrust forward, then snapped back into place by a seatbelt. The sulfuric smell of deflated airbags filled the car, and smoke – palpable and salty – burned its way down into his lungs and had him panicked, choking, looking for flames. There were none, and the relentless rain would have doused any fire anyway.

The tree trunk that finally stopped the car punched a V into the hood, and the sudden stillness, the lack of motion, was jarring. It felt like it was raining rocks, that the car was being dented, that the metal frame wouldn't last much longer. Any sounds in the blackness of that forest were washed out by the drumming of bullet-sized raindrops on the bonnet of the car; they even snuffed out his throat-cutting cries for help. It felt like he was screaming under water: futile and exhausting. Hannah made no sound at all. She had been lying down across the back seat before the accident, and the impact threw her to the floor. He turned the rearview mirror down, slowly, afraid of what he'd see. She lay there on her back, in a pile of dirty leaves and busted glass, staring at Owen through vacant eyes. He couldn't tell if she was vomiting blood or coughing it up. He didn't know which would be worse. Which to hope for.

"Hannah! Can you breathe? Can you even *hear* me!"

He reached down behind the seat and shook her, like he could jumpstart her with a vigorous shake of her limp arm. The pool of blood on her stomach felt hot on the back of his hand, and with walls of trees and rain blocking out any light, it looked as thick and black as oil. As they waited for help, he could see life coming and going in her eyes: her soul hesitant but ready to leave. Her charcoal pupils the boundary. She was a beautiful thirty-four-year-old, with messy brown hair, who looked more like a child now than a mother of two.

With each howl of December wind, a cold gush of rainwater barreled in through a broken window like a slap across Hannah's face. That's how she saw it, a slap across her face, punishment for what she'd been doing. He saw that in her eyes, they said it all and more. They were billboards to her emotions, flashing guilt, regret maybe. They said that she was scared to die and aware they'd be found out, and that neither fate felt worth the fight for her next breath. She gasped, her punctured lungs struggling for air, and he knew it was her two children she was thinking of. Not him, not Alex. There was a steady stream of tears, but no sounds.

He gave up on his cell phone: the battery had cracked into three triangular pieces. He turned again to Hannah. She wasn't even blinking now. She never even closed her eyes as the wind threw water onto her face, pressing her hair into her forehead and making her blood glisten a brighter red. Her eyes jerked back and forth between his face and the blood on her hands, her long slender fingers outstretched. She seemed more confused than frightened.

"Hannah!" Only panic in his utterance. Like the word could've been any word. "Hannah, I don't have a phone. We … we … need to find your phone … Hannah!"

Nothing. No response. Just more coughing, more blood. Some gurgling now, and then his own stomach felt weak. She looked like someone punched stupid, beaten into a daze.

He struggled to get out of the car and dash down to the highway, but the door was butted up against a rock. It looked like a shark fin: grey, wet, and bumpy. He tried to climb out the window, but his left leg wouldn't take his weight, and he fell back into his seat. The adrenaline had numbed the pain. Every time he tried to put weight on that leg, it felt more like intense heat and pressure than pain, and he shrieked in a way that hollowed him out. He looked down and saw a snapped bone pressing against his skin, just shy of poking through. An inch below his kneecap, his tibia had snapped from his fibula, and the bones were stabbing him from the inside out like a prong.

"Hannah ... I *need* your phone!" He looked at her face and saw two deep lacerations on her chin: claw marks, like a bear had taken a swing at her. He saw one more slash above her left eye, so deep her eyebrow was disconnected. He knew the cuts would form scars, and the guilt threw tears into his words. "Hannah. Where is your–"

She turned her head, slowly, towards her purse, pointing with her eyes. He reclined his chair, slung an arm over the passenger seat, and hauled himself half onto the back seat. He looked down on her and her eyes were twitching, like she was seconds from a seizure. His tears mixed with rain and snot and dripped down onto her. He wiped hair from her face, tucking it behind her ears, and kissed her forehead.

He dialed 9-1-1, and with the help of the calm, gentle voice on the other end, they scrambled to work out where the car had gone off the road.

"I'll turn on the high beams. And the hazard lights. I'll blare the stereo. You'll find us ... *right?*"

～

Hannah was unconscious by the time the emergency response team found the car. She was lying there peacefully, as if asleep in her own bed. When Owen first heard the paramedics coming, their voices sounded so distant and calm. Then he saw frantic zips of flashlights along the ground like helicopter spotlights, and noise rushed at him as fast and loud as warfare: the shouting of urgent instructions, the suck of mud at their feet. Even the snapping of twigs beneath their boots was deafening. Their urgency was more startling than their presence was calming.

The paramedics pried their bodies from the car and loaded them onto long yellow spine boards. As they turned to head back to the ambulance, Owen heard them sigh and curse the rugged terrain between the car and their ambulance down on the highway. They'd almost screamed it in his ear, yelling through the walls of rain, *We're gonna need a third set of hands on each board! Watch your backs!* They treated him and Hannah like cargo, lifting them over rocks, passing them around trees, ignoring Owen's questions. *Just relax, sir. Just take it easy until we get back to the ambulance and take a look at you both. We have no answers for anyone just yet.*

It was slippery and dank. Tree branches and shrubs got in the way, scraping against the bright yellow spine boards. Rocks rolled under the paramedics' feet, threatening to snap their ankles. Lying there on the spine board, his eyes shut tight to avoid the rain beating down on his face, Owen had an eerie feeling that he should have died in the crash. Or maybe that he wished he had. He was thinking about those few moments before he hydroplaned. The wipers couldn't keep up with the rain, and a thick glaze of water, rippled by the wind, coated the windshield and hazed his vision. The glare of oncoming headlights trickled down his windshield like stars caught in a waterfall. He was watching Hannah, so peaceful in her sleep, when the car lifted from the highway and spun into the ditch. His eyes, not on the road, had been wandering across the curves of her body in the rearview mirror: the lines of her ribcage beneath her tight shirt.

As the paramedics loaded the stretchers into the ambulance, Hannah's left arm fell over the side of the spine board, limp because she was unconscious, and swung back and forth like a pendulum.

Owen grabbed a man's forearm, panicked. "We are heading to the hospital in Sheet Harbour, right? It's the closest, right?"

He wanted to be taken to a hospital anywhere but Dartmouth, maybe check in under bogus names. Say they never had their hospital cards or any other kind of ID on them. That they were just out for a drive.

"Dartmouth General, sir. Sheet Harbour is, at present, not equipped for this ... for ... *surgery*. Just take it easy now, and lie back down." He was fiddling with an IV bag and didn't even look at Owen.

He didn't want to seem desperate, and didn't want to have to explain why. "Isn't Halifax closer than Dartmouth?"

The paramedic shook his head.

"Then can we make it the other one in Dartmouth instead. I have—"

He looked at Owen like he was delirious. "Just lie back, sir. My job is to take you to Dartmouth General Hopsital, and it is in your best interest to let me do my job. Especially for your partner's sake." He nodded towards her.

Owen looked at Hannah: his brother's wife, his sister-in-law. Now that title sounded so incestuous and wrong. His lover, the woman his brother had failed, the woman he loved: that was how he preferred to think of her.

He pictured his brother's face, how bereaved and betrayed it would look when he saw his wife and brother come into his hospital, strapped to stretchers from the same accident. He knew Alex was working all weekend, but in that moment all he had was hope. Even if he'd never seen the difference between hope and naïveté.

He looked again at Hannah and the two paramedics who were working on her. All their attention, the quick movements and taut faces, made it clear how helplessly injured she was.

"Sir, lift your head." They placed a mask over his mouth. "Deep breaths now."

There would be no point in lying. Owen knew that Alex was smart enough to connect the dots and draw the picture.

Owen was not at a screenwriting conference and Hannah was not shoe-shopping in Montreal. Her car would be found not twenty minutes from Alex's cabin, on a stretch of road that led to nowhere *but* his cabin.

"Deep breaths, sir."

He looked again at Hannah, at the paramedics who had done all they could for her. It was only a matter of time now. He looked up at the white ceiling, jostled back and forth by the bucking of the ambulance against the rough pavement.

The paramedic adjusted a knob. "Deep long breaths now, sir."

The periphery of his vision blurred, engulfed by whiteness. He thought of the time he and Alex had run off on their parents at a zoo, each daring the other to stick a hand in the bear cage. They agreed to do it at the same time: the first one to take out his hand was the loser. He couldn't remember who won.

Everything went white.

~

When Owen regained consciousness in the hallway of the hospital, he was wearing a rigid neck brace. He couldn't look to his left or right: just straight up, at the square, dotted ceiling tiles framed by beige metal. He couldn't see if Alex was nearby and had caught on to him yet. He didn't know where Hannah was, or if she was still alive.

Everything seemed blurred. His eyes were overwhelmed, or the lights were too harsh. All he could see were glowing strips of yellow: long fluorescent light bulbs passing him by, one by one, as medics carted him down the hallway. Eleven, then they turned a corner. Seven more fluorescent strips, another turn. The sickly smell of hospital tingled in his nostrils, making the hair in his nose feel thick and wiry, and he could feel dried blood caked against his skin when he shifted his body. All of his adrenaline was long gone now: the broken bones were throbbing, the deepest lacerations felt filled with salt, flames, glass. When three more long fluorescent bulbs passed him by, he was lifted from the stretcher onto a bed, and the fluorescent bulbs were replaced by two large domed lights. They looked like headlights, like a car headed straight for him. Then his brother's long, unmistakable face was peering down at him. Alex's eyes were either questioning or denying what he saw.

*Owen?*

Everything in the room was gone now, except for that look of astonishment in his brother's eyes. It was wild and haunting: a frightened fox wanting to pounce or run. As both brothers struggled for words, a nurse appeared and pried Alex out of Owen's field of vision. She had his arm clutched in her hand, her pink nails digging into his freckled and sparsely haired skin.

"Dr. Collins! The woman in the next room, same crash, she needs your *immediate* attention! I don't know how she's still breathing!" The urgency in her voice wasn't enough, she had to shout, to yell the specifics. "It's bilateral hemopneumothorax. We're sure of it, she's suffocating, and I am guessing cardiac tamponade, and those are just the chest traumas …"

Alex blatantly ignored the nurse because it was his *brother* right there in front of him. But the nurse insisted, she tugged at his arm, sank her nails a little deeper. Creases now, where her nails met flesh. As he was promising Owen he would be right back, Owen grabbed him by the arm so urgently it made a slapping noise. He had to warn his brother, to at least lessen the shock. "Just, wait … one second."

Alex and the nurse turned to him. Their attention, their eyes all over him like that, it made it harder for him to speak, to confess.

"Alex." He waited for the courage to finish the sentence. The pause only made it harder to utter the next few words. There was only the vicious truth. "It's ... Hannah ... in there." He tilted his head, slowly, towards the next room. Hesitant to be so curt. So definite and honest. He fell back into his bed breathless, his heart thudding off ribs.

Alex tore his arm free from Owen's grip. His one hand clapped from the sudden absence of Alex's arm. "Hannah is in *Montreal*, Owen!" His voice quivered in denial, as if all of a sudden so much made sense. As if he understood that curious way Owen stood next to his wife now: like a man fighting against every inch of himself not to reach out and touch her. Not to let eyes linger too long after words during a conversation.

"Alex ... me and Hannah, we ... we were at your cabin ... all week."

He looked at his hands, no longer able to look his brother in the face. Alex refused to believe Owen, so he had to trust his eyes. Owen watched him walk into the next room, dragging feet like blocks of cement, moving only because he had to. He pressed the palms of his hands to those green doors with all the hesitation of a man about to commit suicide, then thrust the doors quickly open.

Owen was stabilized and alone in his room. Through the dead silence he heard doctors asking for more suction, more blood. More light. The shouts and screams were getting louder and more urgent. And then a sustained beep tore through Owen's room. It sank into him like a bullet in slow motion. He heard Alex swearing, then wailing, then being constrained and comforted. Something got knocked over; it sounded like pennies falling, like metal on metal, for five long seconds.

Owen expected Alex moments later. He expected his brother to barrel into the room and grab him by his neck and snap it. To yell, to shout in a way that brought saliva out with the words. He braced himself for it, not to protect himself, just out of instinct. But Alex never set foot in his room.

Owen sat alone in cold silence for days, contemplating life, suicide, love: the intricacies of each, the flipsides. He thought of his place in the world now, without family, without Hannah, without love, and without hope.

# A GHOST, ALIVE

ONE GLANCE OUT HIS WINDOW and he saw it was one of those grey days, maybe rain, the kind of day he could use as an excuse to be lazy, to stay in bed and avoid the world. Mummified in white sheets and propped up against a mahogany headboard, he sat up in bed, sipping bitter black coffee from an oversized white mug, a novel splayed over his knees. He'd paused to stare out the window. Grey clouds clung to a grey sky, like balls of lint on an endless blanket. The same crow was zipping left to right and right to left, etching temporary black lines across the window.

The book fell off his lap and lay front cover down on the beige carpet. He stared at it on the floor. He'd lost his page. He couldn't concentrate enough to read anyway. Every ten minutes he was back in that car.

Another sip of coffee.

He'd placed the filter so carelessly in the carafe that he could feel the grit of coffee grounds against his teeth, and the steam rising from the mug coaxed tears from his eyes. The cold of the day had crept in through his window and crawled into bed with him, so he fetched a black downfilled comforter from the hall closet in a futile attempt to stay warm. Everything about his life felt futile now. Memories of Hannah were constantly batting off his skull like wasps trapped in a jar: buzzing, stinging, and clawing their way to the surface to play out over and over again.

It was the morning of Hannah's memorial service, and he'd awoken to a memory of them at Alex's cabin: Hannah dropping a CD into a stereo as Owen lit a fire in the fireplace. She laughed when she caught him reading the instructions on the store-bought log. "I think you just light them, Einstein. I think the idea is you burn the log!"

He smiled at her sarcasm, as he always did. She never considered herself funny but laughed at herself habitually, and the sound of her laughing always walked right through him like a ghost.

She turned and flashed him a black and purple CD cover: *The Lioness.* "Owen, you'll *love* this album!" She always spoke so clearly, neglecting no syllables in her words. She pronounced album as AL BUM, as it if were two separate words.

She pressed play, wandered over to the light switch, and flicked it off. The room was lit only by the fire now, and the flickering flames had her shadow dancing along the wall. Reflected black onto the ceiling, the glass of wine in her hand looked like a ten-pound goblet. "Most people make music you *hear*, but Songs Ohia play music you *feel*. Do you know what I mean?"

He insisted she drink it, even though he couldn't now, because wine evoked something in her; it awakened her to the world and made her hypersensitive to its emotional landscape. She *felt* everything when she drank red wine. She'd describe those sensations with enough passion and detail that he often made jot notes and incorporated her ramblings, and everything about her, into his writing:

*Have a character like Hannah who uses her hands as much as her eyes to see the world.*

*Lying in bed she says, "Love is most epic between those who cannot share it."*

*Have a character whose smile lingers, just a few seconds, after she laughs.*

*A guy notices cat scratches in the headboard of his mistress' bed, from where the cat climbs up into the window. This bed is also his brother's bed. It took noticing the cat scratches, a detail, never to sleep with her in that bed again.*

He knew this made her nervous, his tendency to spin his own life experiences into short fictitious stories, but she'd told him it was what she loved about his writing as well: the free glimpses into his otherwise secretive personality, guessing the real people he based his characters on, and wondering which passages were drawn from his own life and which he merely imagined into existence.

Owen was still kneeling by the fire when she approached him. She moved so silently across the room, she touched him with such grace and necessity, that he could love her guilt-free. He laid his head back, resting it on her breasts, and could smell her messy brown hair as it spilled over his face: like fresh rain on cement. She kissed his forehead.

Her voice, the calming sound of it, was how he knew he loved her. "I saw this coming, you know, me and you."

Owen was comfortable with the affair by now, the awkwardness had passed, but he was still rendered uncomfortable by that label: *me and you, us.* It too blatantly disrespected Alex, it felt too insensitive, so he never responded to her, and she ran her hand through his hair, knowing how much he liked her fingers as a comb.

"I don't know, it's ... it's dangerous and illogical that we can meet an absolute stranger and somehow relate to them before any words are shared, you know?"

She tugged at the collar of his black sweater, exposing the bright red t-shirt below it. He looked up at her and she nodded her head towards the couch.

They curled up to watch the fire burn, to watch shadows crawl along the walls and take each other in. He fumbled around on the couch, entangling himself in Hannah. They fit so well, so easily together, that it was hard to feel guilty. *Two pieces of a two-piece puzzle* was how she always described it. When Owen fell asleep on the couch that night, she threw a blanket over him and went off to her bedroom because Owen refused to sleep in Alex's bed.

⟃

Owen spent the rest of the day writing in bed, trying to convert some of the scribbles in his notepad into publishable short stories. Writing was his only chance at distraction now, his only means of actively forgetting. It was seven in the evening by the time he stopped to consider supper, and Hannah's memorial service, he'd heard, was at eight. He could have gone, but he had enough respect and compassion for his brother not to show his still-bruised and unwanted face. He stood by his window, holding the curtains back with his right hand, watching a herring gull search for something in the snow-covered grass along the fence beneath the streetlight. There was nothing there. He caught a glimpse of himself in the window and stared at the purple halo around his left eye, and the teeth prints still stamped into his lower lip.

In a way he was content to miss the service. He wanted to forget Hannah's face, the specifics: the wet glistening of her chocolate eyes, and the two lines that formed brackets around her mouth whenever she smiled. He wanted to forget what she looked like because maybe then that lingering image of her, so frail and lifeless in the back seat, covered in blood and guilt, might stop haunting him. He slept with the light on for days after the accident, because darkness only triggered it. He'd pull a sheet over his head to find a balance, a compromise between lightness and darkness. It was her face that stood out themost: the gash on her chin so deep bone was exposed, and the laceration above her left eye so wide that her eyebrow was disjointed. He didn't even have to close his eyes to see it. Her face superimposed itself on his mundane surroundings: a wall, or the kitchen table while he ate. The white ceiling above his bed, or his medicine cabinet mirror as he shaved. Sometimes she was screaming, her throat rattling or erupting blood. Her teeth dripping red.

Since the accident, he'd become a recluse. Leaving the house was too much of a hassle: the shower, shaving, trying to look presentable enough to be out in public, and he stayed in bed so much after the accident that he never got used to walking with his crutches. Inside, he could hide away from the world; he could pretend it wasn't out there. Any of it.

With the exception of his aunt, Lillian, no family members were bold enough to visit him during his stay in the hospital, and on the night Owen was released from hospital, Lillian took him out for supper before taking him home. It was a swank restaurant. The bright white tablecloth draped all the way down to the shiny hardwood floor so that Owen couldn't see his aunt's legs. He kept butting her shins by accident with his cast.

"It's okay, sweetie." She pulled her chair back a little more each time he knocked her shins; the first kick hurt so much she had to massage the pain out of her leg, her taut face contorted into a temporary knot.

The waiter came to take their orders, and she told him that they were waiting for a third person to join them. Owen's head shot up from the menu like a jack-in-the-box, and the anxiety felt as solid as stone.

She laughed as if to apologize to the impatient waiter. "It's my daughter. She'll be late for her own funeral, that one."

Owen hadn't heard laughter in days, it sounded so hollow and contrived.

"You'll have to give us a few more minutes." She flashed another apologetic smile to the waiter.

She peeled back the sleeve of her black top to check her dainty watch. Lillian was a beautiful woman, the kind of fifty-nine-year-old who could wear that tattoo on her forearm with grace. It was a red Taoist symbol that meant nothing to anyone but her. She was a retired architect who looked, ate, and acted more like a typical art teacher, and the sound of her voice hinted remarkably at her kind disposition. She looked at you when she spoke, and punctuated her sentiments with emphatic facial expressions: soft smiles and stitched-together eyebrows.

He asked her, hoping that she would say no, hoping that he'd heard her wrong, "You've invited *Gail?*"

"She's still your cousin, Owen. That hasn't changed. She's in town for ... the service. You two haven't seen each other in a year or more. It's been far too long."

He propped a menu up to mask his anger. "I don't think that matters now, Lilly."

"Don't be ridiculous!"

He shook his head but spoke calmly, to make his point seem more valid. "I'm not being ridiculous. And she knows I am here, right?" He slapped his menu down on the table. "Lilly, you told her I am here, *right?*"

Lillian kept on smearing goat cheese spread over her bun. She looked away from him as she chewed. He didn't force an answer. He was too timid. Instead, he sat there chewing his bun more forcefully than necessary. He knew Gail well, as well as a brother knows a sister. He knew that Gail never kept her opinions to herself, and she saw the world in black and white, in right and wrong. Owen wanted to leave. He wanted to be home, alone. When Lillian had asked him to go out for supper he said yes, but meant no.

Owen had his own motivations for this meal though, and with Gail on her way, he didn't have much time left to press Lillian for answers about how his brother and nieces were taking the loss. He wanted to know what their faces were filled with, their words: rage, melancholy, betrayal? But he didn't know how to word it, or when to ask it. Chewing the bun felt that much more laborious. Concentrating on his wording, and distracted by the weight of those words on the tip of his tongue, he never saw Gail approach the table.

"Are you fucken *kidding* me, Mom?" Her arms sprang from her body for emphasis. Twenty heads turned to face Owen's table and a sudden and pronounced silence enveloped the room. "I almost convinced Alex to take the kids and come join us. What if—"

"Sit down and lower your voice, Gail." Lillian nudged a chair out with her knee. "These people didn't come here to watch you put on a show. And spare me the theatrics. He is still your cousin."

Gail rose from the chair the second she sat down, as if it were spring-loaded. "I'd sit, *Mom*, if that piece of shit weren't here." She pointed at Owen with a quick nod of her head. Arms folded now. She looked at him as if there had never been any love between them, and as her eyes wandered up and down his body, her face puckered up like she smelled sulfur, like she had a mouthful of it, thick and gritty on her tongue.

"He might still be your nephew, but I don't consider him family anymore." Her head shook back and forth in short, quick gestures of incomprehension. "In *fact*, he seems to be destroying our family every chance he gets—"

"You can leave now, Gail."

"My pleasure. Quite frankly, I have better things to do. I think while you dine this piece of shit, I'll go look in on his brother and the kids. I mean ... *Goddamnit!*"

Owen couldn't look either of them in the eye. "Look, I'll go. I'm sorry I came anyway." He slid his chair out from the table, but never stood up. "And you're right, Gail. No one is denying—"

"Shut up. You don't get to act all repentant or noble or whatever you're doing. You're a heartless bastard and you know it! If you care about your brother at all, if you have any dignity left, you'll get out of this city and go drink yourself to death, because that's all you are good for." She bit her lip, hard, and shook her head even faster. "And you know it, right?"

She waited for his subtle nod. And then until he nodded more hardily.

It hurt all the more because, growing up, Gail had been like a sister to Alex and Owen. They had traditions, games they'd play together in the backyard. The way she shrieked joy as they chased her around the yard with the hose, worried they'd knock out her contacts with the spray. It was only a bittersweet memory now, of what was. Of who they had been.

It was a small, ten-table restaurant, booked to capacity. A waiter approached them to silence the scene, but Gail was out the door before he got to their table. Lillian apologized to the waiter and ordered for them both.

"I'm so sorry for that, sir. We'll both start with the featured blue-cheese beef medallions and the Waldorf salad."

"Yes." The waiter fumbled awkwardly, embarrassed by the scene. "Well." He took out his notepad. "Can I get you anything else to drink?"

"Two glasses of the house shiraz."

Owen shot her a quick look, surprised by the order.

"Sorry, one glass of shiraz, and some more water for my nephew. Thank you."

The waiter walked away, and Owen felt every set of eyes in the room peeling themselves off of him, one by one, though they all shot back quick glances throughout their meals.

"Lillian, I love you, dearly. You've been a surrogate mother to Alex and me, but if this is about me being a charity case, if you are here because you feel bad or obligated to Mom ... spare me. Spare yourself from scenes like that one." He nodded in the direction of the door, as if Gail had left a trail of fire behind her. "I am fine on my own. I always have been, right? And I don't want you to be here with me for the wrong reasons."

"Change the topic. You know me better than that." She tore another bun in half, and the irritated tone in her voice verified her honesty. "I wouldn't be here if I didn't want to be here, and we both know it. And you're going to have to get used to being treated like this for a while, but don't worry. With time, things will get ... I don't know, easier." She bit into the bun.

"It's not like I accidently broke a vase in the guy's house, Lilly. I shattered his fucken life. And the kids'." He stopped talking as his voice constricted. His throat filled with sand. He shut his eyes tight, tight enough to numb them.

Lillian acknowledged she might have just lied to him with a quick rise and fall of her face. He was that itchy, old, worn-out sweater that everyone was finally throwing away. The one they weren't sure why they'd ever kept around anyway.

Lillian could get away with an allegiance to both sides because she was a paradox in every way. She grew herbs and only ate vegetables from her own greenhouse, yet she smoked a pack of cigarettes a day. She stocked seven bird feeders with different feeds and photographed the array of birds that gathered in her backyard, but had no interest in their proper names. She was that ethereal person who walked around town with all the unofficial privileges a cop has: using the staff washroom in the public library or poking her nose where it didn't belong, and no one would question it. So, the night Owen was released from the hospital, Alex never resented her when she knocked on his door and matter-of-factly stated she was there for Owen's things, that she was on her way to the hospital to pick him up and take him back to her place. He swung the door open, let her in, helped her gather Owen's things and bag them in Sobeys bags. She stayed for coffee, drew horses with the girls, offered to help Alex in any way she could, and left no less loved and respected. Callie and Lucia were clinging to her right arm and begging her to stay as she pulled the door shut.

∽

When Lillian got home from Hannah's service, Owen didn't have to pry for the summary. She came in, brushed snow from her jacket, put on some coffee, called out to him, assured him that she was alone, and sat him down at her small, round, mahogany table. She burst right into one of her philosophical rants, but all he wanted was the details of the service: Who wept and who stood stoic? Had the circumstances of her death polluted the atmosphere? Trimmed down the attendance? His head was full of uncouth questions he couldn't bring himself to ask. They'd have to sit there like burning embers.

She tore into an obviously prepared speech, stringing sentences together without pause. "I am not going to try and justify what you did, because infidelity is cruel and savage," she said, speaking as matter-of-factly as she always did. "But I know, like you now know, that in an affair people are too quick to blame *people*, because our feelings are out of our hands, and anyone with a grain of sense knows that much." She plucked her earrings out and slapped them down on the table as she finished the sentence. "Your father and I sat around this table having the same conversation one night, Owen." She tapped two fingers on the table, her thick pink nails dinging like metal on wood. "He said love is beautiful in the same way a lion is. Half the beauty is in the sheer power of the thing. The control it has over you. And the chance it might tear you apart."

It was evident she'd practiced this speech in the car on the way home, as a consolation for him, and the need to be consoled, to have his actions justified, made him feel pathetic and irritable.

"Our feelings are out of our hands. We cannot blame ourselves for how we feel. Sometimes it just happens, like rain." She pointed at the window, like she'd just made a genius comparison. "Sometimes it just rains." She was stumbling now, obviously off course in her pre-planned speech.

"What I am trying to say is that sometimes two people cannot ignore something bigger than themselves. When an affair is committed between two people in love, not just two people fooling around for the thrill of it, it's a little different. She must have loved you to physically act on her feelings, Owen, and you loved her, right?"

He shot her a quick look – wide eyes and an open mouth – that said, *I do. Not did.*

"And that is why I am still talking to you. I know you've been wondering."

He picked a receipt up off the kitchen table and rolled it into a ball with two fingers. "I just. I can't imagine being Alex today. It's surreal. I just can't. Most men might not have gone to the memorial service. I don't think I would have. I just, I don't think I could have looked at her knowing she ... you know?" He avoided the description, still ashamed at his role in it all. "Alex has always been the noble sibling, I guess. I've just been his brother, the other son. And now the heartless bastard who ruined his life." He let the balled-up receipt drop back down on the table. It bounced twice and fell to the floor. Lillian bent over to pick it up.

"You're anything but heartless, Owen. It takes more than one mistake to be heartless."

"My life has been a series of mistakes."

"It's only a mistake when it's your fault," she said, getting up from her chair. "Goodnight."

"Thanks for trying."

He meant it.

~

After Lillian had gone to sleep, Owen went into the living room with Hannah's journal. When Lillian claimed the belongings from Hannah's written-off car, on Alex's behalf, her journal had been amongst the items in the bag. Owen went through the bag when Lillian had left the room. The journal wasn't his to claim, but he justified it, knowing she might have written about him. About them. Alex didn't need to hear about the affair, in detail, in his wife's words. But Owen did.

It was hard-covered. It was black, with a red spine, and had a sunburst orange stain on the lower left-hand corner that looked like a sea anemone. The surface was smooth and matted, indented with a long ago completed to-do list. She must have used her journal as a writing surface in bed one night. He ran his fingers over those indentations. He liked picturing her in bed, her purple pajamas loose and resting against her perfect body in a way that made her look vulnerable, desirable. On the inside cover she'd written her name, then scratched it out with a black sharpie marker. Hannah Collins. As if she was unsure, unsatisfied.

He sprawled out on Lillian's slippery, brown leather couch. He put a pillow on his chest to prop up her journal. It was the closest he could get to Hannah now, so he'd savour it, like each entry was a fifty-dollar bottle of wine that needed some occasion to be uncorked.

He let the journal unfold in his lap and read a random excerpt: *The final stage in the evolution of any relationship is the death of intimacy. You can love someone after that point, dearly, but just not the same way.*

He turned a few pages back, and read some more.

*...and worse still is knowing that I could be beautiful, ravishing even, but it wouldn't matter. It wouldn't matter because the world is full of beautiful women. It wouldn't matter because I know Alex wishes I was more of a professional woman, by his definition, and he seems, at least sometimes, to be embarrassed by me when he introduces me to his female friends, who are all doctors, lawyers, and other success stories. Women with televisions in their BMWs, and enough makeup in their purses to sink the Titanic, who travel just to say they've been there and done that, but do nothing when they are there. But who am I to judge, really? At least they've been there and done that. It's just that all his friends are the same person. Only the name changes. Alex knew who I was when he married me, how I am. It didn't seem to matter then. It does now. And the truth is, everything about his life is flawless, so shouldn't I be? These women, these "female acquaintances" of his, they are petty, shallow. But maybe that is what he likes about them. They aren't too deep to drown in. Like me. Their traits are external and evident: bony hips like handles and cleavage even a priest would glance at...*

Owen closed the book and lay down on the couch. He'd read it like a novel, front to back, dog-earing his favourite parts. For the first time since the affair started, he reflected on how it had all begun and traced it back to him telling Hannah all the things Alex was taking for granted: petty, innocent little things, like how good she was with Callie and Lucia, that she made her own mayo instead of buying it, and how she bit her lower lip in a really cute way when she spread it over a slice of bread. Then he started noticing all the complimentary things there were to say to a woman like Hannah.

He loved her need to touch things, how she'd rub the velvety skin of a peach before biting into it, or how she'd smooth her daughter's shiny, jet-black hair every time she hugged her. And then he thought of her delicate, tactile hands as those of a passionate lover. And how weightless his body would feel with her hands on it. His mind would drift as he watched her planting bulbs in the garden, or scrubbing forks and knives in the kitchen sink. And he started picturing her body without those clothes on it: the jeans that carved out the curves of her body and the cardigans she always wore over shirts that cupped her breasts, like hands to be jealous of. He hated it when she wore her grey cardigan with the white tank top beneath, because whenever she bent forward he could see everything he wanted from life and everything he couldn't have.

The image hollowed his bones.

He started picturing her lying on her back in his bed, naked, the fingers of his right hand snaking slowly from her belly to her breasts, to circle her nipples and feel her quiver beneath him. He took that image to bed one night, and couldn't face her the next morning. He'd waited until ten o'clock so she wouldn't be in the kitchen. But she was.

With the girls entertained by the television, she sat at the kitchen table reading a novel. He watched her from the corner of his eye as he searched the fridge, a little too long, for milk. She'd periodically use a finger as a bookmark or just splay the book open on her thighs, and stare out the window – because every cloud was a miracle to Hannah, and it was that very fascination with ordinary things that made her so mesmerizing. He wanted to sit at that table and share meaningless stories with her, or their favourite movies and meals, and dream jobs and vacation spots. He just wanted her voice in his ears. He needed it. Like lungs need oxygen. Like how they're useless without it.

# THE BIGGEST LIE

*June 18th, 2008,*
*Alex, Owen, and I on the way to the cabin.*

*My sister is watching the kids again, or, rather, living vicariously through them. Any chance to babysit Callie and Lucia and she'll take them like they're free gold, because my daughters are exactly what every expectant mother wishes for. The best thing in my life is knowing they could not live without me. Being needed this way. Alex loves our children, but he doesn't know them like I do. Their favourite books and meals and animals and colours and places to go. I am their link to the world, they are experiencing it through me, and I know they are becoming who they are because of me. It is an astounding acknowledgement. I never question my purpose in life anymore, I am my children's porthole to their world. They will become who they are through me.*

*Alex and I are taking his brother up to the cabin for the weekend. Owen is hoping to get a lot of writing done, and Alex keeps boasting about how the place is perfect for that, as if he knew. As if he's written a few bestsellers himself. It's funny, really. I remember watching an interview with Harry Crews, and Crews talked about a doctor he knew who said, "I'd write a novel too, if I had the time," and Crews found that as presumptuous as a writer saying he was going to perform a heart transplant on Tuesday. Like anybody could do it if they "had the time." It's not that doctors are haughty, or that Alex has no appreciation for the art and labour of writing, it's just, he thinks he is in touch with everything, yet he is living on his own planet most of the time. Assuming things, dismissing things. Important things. Because nothing is as important as his life and his needs and his job and the world he knows. Like being a doctor, and medicine, are the apex of civilization, even if one prefers literature or the farming life. Alex assumes a writer and a farmer are those things because they couldn't be a doctor. Like everyone would work ten-hour overnight shifts on Sundays if they could.*

*Owen and I have started to bond over rolled eyes at Alex's expense.*

*It's only just gotten normal having him live with us. I was so petrified at first, balancing being a wife who understands her husband wanting to help his brother, being a good mother thinking about what is best for her daughters, and my own personal feelings on having a supposedly recovered alcoholic, fresh out of rehab, just down the hall from where I sleep and shower. I mean, who wants a roommate at my age? Who wants to stop wearing their one-piece, cozy, purple pajamas to the kitchen table in the mornings? Who wants to have that many more dishes to wash every night? Who wants someone there asking what's wrong when you feel like lying on the couch and staring at the ceiling?*

*But then he showed up, scuffing his shoes off the mat outdoors before stepping into the porch, with his head down and a shy smile from ear to ear. I was expecting some madman to come*

*bursting into the house, boots still on, traipsing mud from
room to room, with a look on his face that said "so what, get
over it." What does that say about me? The cutest thing so far
is how he keeps his laundry, his juvenile boxers, in plastic
Sobeys bags in the corner of his room. Like it'd be pornographic
if I saw them in the hamper in the bathroom. He must wait
until no one is home to wash them. I think it'd be funny if I
didn't leave the house for a week straight, what would he do
then? Go commando for a day? Turn a pair inside out?*

*I feel a little vile for being such a bitch about it at first. If
anything, things are a little livelier around here lately, and
the kids have really taken to him, and that seems good for him.
Even Alex says so. I think Alex himself is surprised at how
benign Owen's presence is in the house. He just sits in his
room, writing away on that little black laptop of his, about a
nun nursing a junkie back to health, but the junkie is showing
the nurse how she's as much a slave to her religion as he is to
his smack. How they are both "just filling holes dug by modern
life." Something like that.*

*He is in that room more than he is out of it, and when he is out
of it I don't mind the company. Truth is, lately anyway, I get
lonely in my big but empty house. Lately the only conversation
I have is with my daughters, four and five years old, and I've
got a lot more to share with people than cookies and fairytales. I
want someone to see what I'm doing in the garden. I want
someone to talk books and movies with. Alex is never home and
has time for nothing but work. He doesn't care about having
something constantly in bloom in the garden, or all of my new
books, or what the kids and me did today. "Oh, that's good,
honey." That's all he ever says: "Oh, that's good, honey." He
can't even feign an interest. I mean, who says "oh" when they
are interested? Nobody! They burst right into their response, so
excited there's no time for any "ohs." But not Alex.*

"Hey, Alex, I took the kids to the mall today."

"Oh, that's good, honey."

Is it too much to say, "Which mall? Did they have fun? What did you buy? Did you get any ice cream for them?" I could scream at Alex for every "oh" he utters. I might start. I will start. I will warn him. Three chances and then the screaming starts. The uttering of threats.

Owen is good company. He has lived in St. John's since I've known Alex, so Owen and I have only met a handful of times, and every time, we've been in a rush or a crowded room, like at the wedding. With him involved in the wedding, nothing could have gone wrong, I remember that much. I caught him checking with the kitchen staff on special food orders, and prepping the emcee for his speech. Before the reception I saw him double-checking that there were enough disposable cameras for every table and asking everyone if they had signed the guest book.

Owen is the kind of guy you get to know instantly because he is open like the ocean and curious like a kid, and I swear no one has wanted to know every detail of my life like he does. I guess it's because he's a writer, maybe, so I am some character and he can't know me until he gets my "backstory" and notices all my defining characteristics, like what I take in my coffee, and how I hold the cup, and if I am scared that the first sip is going to burn my tongue.

Point being, I am enjoying the company, I'm showering in it. I'm making plans for the first time in far too long, feeling like a chicken freed from the coop and other such lame similes. I mean, Jesus, a trip to the beach, why was that once a silly thought? Now all it takes is a sunny day and Owen is loading the kids and me into my car and driving us to the beach, or the park, or even camping – we are going camping on the long weekend! There is something so charming about Owen, he is like watching fire burn. He taught the girls how to make marshmallow-roasting sticks without hurting themselves yesterday, and it was inexplicably captivating to hear him speak, and move, and laugh. Callie says Owen is her new best friend, and Lucia's teacher has asked me who this Owen guy is she's been talking so much about lately. I told Owen that and his smile nearly split his cheeks open!

I think Owen is enjoying his stay with us too. The picket-fenced home, the kids. I think he wants the life his brother has in many ways. He's great with the kids. It'll be a shame if he never has his own family. A real and true shame. He asks Callie and Lucia what they want, and no matter how ridiculous the request, he'll grant it, even if it means being wildly imaginative and building a tree house having no idea what he's doing. He did it though, the tree house. Alex only ever talked about calling someone to come build the tree house. Owen though, the girls asked for it and three weeks later it was built, rubber-tire swing attached and all. He built it on one condition: they listen to their mother more. He fell off the unstable ladder twice, busted a thumbnail open with the hammer, and everything he touched for a full week made him flinch on account of the splinters, but he didn't care. Like I said: father material. He even crawls up there with the kids at night and tells them moderately scary ghost stories before bed. The fresh air knocks the girls out; they've never fallen asleep so easily. I thank him for that every night, and every night he shrugs it off and reassures me he enjoys it as much as the girls do. He says it's the fresh air that knocks the girls out, he says that's how his mother wore him and Alex out. It's odd, Alex never talks of their mother, but Owen never shuts up about her. Alex actually leaves the room when Owen shares a story of their mother. I like his stories. About his mother, about anything. He's experiencing this world in a way so different from his brother.

*Alex has warned me not to pry about Owen's past, to avoid the questions that require the past tense to answer. I see no dark past in Owen though, and I don't understand how Owen could have a dark past and Alex not. They are brothers, but whatever, Alex exaggerates and has a God complex. Everyone is below him. He is a great man, my husband, but … nothing I haven't written about before. Besides, I think people like Owen are simply too hard to understand, so we lump them in with all the other lost causes. People act a certain way for a reason, and it is the reasons we should judge, not the people. Sometimes a person's life just gets off track, that simple. Owen is the sweetest man I have ever met. Period. He is refreshing. He is that guy who would run to the top of a burning building to save a little girl's cat, hamster even. It makes the drinking sad, not dishonourable. He opened up to me once. He said he wasn't running from anything, and he wasn't being a slob. He was just trying to feel alive, and the drinking, before it got out of hand, helped him feel more alive. I don't know what he means by that, by "feeling more alive," because I've never known a guy so in touch with life. So emotionally responsive to it.*

*Ever since Alex bought this cabin he's been saying how much Owen would love it up there. They must have been really close growing up, they speak so fondly of each other. It's sad about their mother and father, but I think all that brought them closer together at least.*

*We're about halfway there. I figured I'd crack open this journal I started last winter out of boredom, because I hate these horrible audiobook CDs Alex buys to listen to when we drive out here. He says it's an intellectual thing, "beats the radio," but deep down I think he does it to avoid the awkward silence. Ten minutes into the drive and we run out of conversation, and that first ten minutes is usually just him talking about some patient of his. Then forty minutes of silence. Nothing pronounces the death of a marriage like silence. It's not that I*

*don't love him, and I know he loves me. But. But there is a
thin line between familiarity and sterility, and a thinner line
between neglect and the excuses he uses.*

*In any case, I know that's why we have these short story CDs,
because Alex doesn't care for fiction, and I know that if I
asked him something about one of these stories later on he'd
remember nothing. He isn't even listening. He just looks out
the window at all the young beauties in their twenties.
Their daring wardrobes that a thirty-four-year-old like myself
cannot wear without rolling everyone's eyes. Their innocent
laughter and eager sexual appetites I cannot match. Their
flashy accessories and technological appendages: iPods and cell
phones and ... God, I'd love to be that stunning, oblivious,
wild twenty-one-year-old again. I think everyone dies at
thirty; thirty to eighty is just one last long breath. I mean by
thirty we've filled our future with far too many wishes to ever
come true. Growing up we are naive and concoct a far too
perfect future for ourselves, so it's only natural that as adults
we are a little let down. The world is not the place all those
childhood fairytales promised us. All lovers are not like Barbie
and Ken, and now I want to burn those fucking dolls for lying
to me! (lol.) They painted far too beautiful a picture to ever
live up to.*

*Sometimes I hate myself for babbling and rambling like this.
What a shame, I'd at least like a solid reason to hate myself.
Not just a long, vague list. It only seems healthy that if you are
going to hate yourself, you should know why. You should be
able to justify it.*

*Why do we hide from the truth when it shows its ugly face
everywhere? Why close our eyes to it? For ourselves or for
others? The truth is, and today I'll finally admit it, I am bored
with my life. I am afraid this is it. I am terrified. I am
trapped in a life that took years to build. I built it so solidly, so*

confidently, that it is like a cage around me now. The marriage vows and the mortgage payments and the family album filled with nostalgic photos. Melancholy is my new shadow. If it weren't for Callie and Lucia, I don't know. I'd probably burn it all down. I realized I was stuck in this monotonous life long before Alex bought these stupid audio CDs. About a year ago we stopped kissing. It feels weird to kiss now. That's when you know it's over. Couples go on fucking long after the love is dead, that's primitive. But a good kiss is how we tell someone all the things we love about them that words could never convey. When we can no longer kiss our lover with passion, we are admitting – in a blaring silence – it is over.

But knowing a relationship is over, and letting go and moving on, these are two very different things. Chalk and cheese, black and white, day and night, pleasure and pain. Birth and death.

# PART TWO
# TO THE WALL

# THE OTHER KID

OUTSIDE HIS WINDOW, OWEN LISTENED in on two kids building a snowman. They were arguing about what to use for a nose – a rock or a carrot – and contemplating the gender, the name.

"Bill!"

"No! It's a girl!"

"No it's not!"

"Yes it is, *stupid!*"

One kid was calculated, practical, instructed the other how to best pack the snow. The other was more concerned with the name, what kind of hat they'd use, how long the snowman would last. Lillian's dog ran along the fence, barking at the children.

He crawled out of bed, just past eleven, wondering what his aunt truly thought of him: a man with no job, a man who sleeps with his brother's wife, a grown man waking at eleven o'clock on a Tuesday morning with nowhere to go and nothing to do. A man stranded in his aunt's house, a thousand kilometers from home. Whatever home meant. He was a burden, but Lillian would never say so. *I'm enjoying the company, dear. It's a pretty big house to be all alone in. And you need somewhere to rest up, someone to look after you til you get that cast off, right?*

It was too obviously a lie. He had nowhere to go, no money to get him there. Not acknowledging that, dancing around it, made him feel even more rueful.

She had breakfast made for him, eggs and bacon between burnt toast, with a side of hash browns greened with fresh herbs, and she'd left the coffee pot on even though he'd told her she brews her coffee too strong for his liking. *No thanks, Lilly, that stuff is going to punch holes in your kidneys ... You know, Lilly, tar is cheaper than coffee beans...*

She'd laugh then, like maybe she did enjoy his company.

Lillian was outside with the dog, urging it to relieve itself so they could go back inside. He peered out the window and saw her topping up her bird feeders. He felt like another bird to her, but something big and ugly, like a vulture, which only she would take in and care for. He put the food on a plate and hurried back to his room to read more of Hannah's diary. As he read, he chewed and sipped and wiped crumbs from its pages. He tried, with a butter knife and then the tip of a pen, to dig up some bits of toast from the crease between its pages. There were lines he read twice. Pages he dog-eared to go back and read later.

He laid her journal down on the edge of his night table and tuned back into the neighbour's kids talking about the snowman. They were fighting now. One wanted to topple it, and the other threatened her not to. They reminded him of himself and Alex at that age. Such opposites, and yet so close. To any set of outside eyes they were nothing alike: Alex was the school president, Owen was the class clown, and they were right. But this was to their advantage: it meant that what one didn't know, the other did. It also forced them to dig so deep into each other for common ground that the roots of their bond were that much deeper.

He thought of school days with his brother. How they'd sit in the back seat of their father's rusted red station wagon and listen to him scraping ice away from the windows. The sound was so loud it was as if the noise was coming out of their heads, not into them, and they had to raise their voices to talk to each other. Each day, as their father's face appeared from behind the ice, a little distorted by the wet windshield, he'd shake a fist and make some corny joke about how they'd never offer to help him clean off the car. *Not even if a hurricane was stormin' up behind us!*

Instead, they sat in the back seat exchanging homework. At the time, the biggest advantage of being fraternal twins was that they were both in the same grade and had all the same homework. Anything non-subjective, like math or geology, they split down the middle and exchanged their answers in the back seat of that car. It halved their workload and freed up more time for them to play video games together. What one of them couldn't get past in one of those games, the other could. They never fought over the controller, they shared it as fit. Owen could still see those nights now, their dark bedroom lit only by the surreal glare of the TV screen, the walls alive with all the colours and motions of a kaleidoscope. Alex always sat up on the edge of the bed in blue pajamas, kicking both legs straight up in the air and holding them there each time the game got intense. And Owen could still see the inside of that car they sat in every morning: the navy blue upholstery, dulled and rendered bumpy by age, and the cigarette burn in the passenger seat. Yellowed cotton poked up from it like an upside-down icicle. His father always jammed it back down with his forefinger, and got mad when their mother plucked it out and threw it away. *It'll be empty in no time if you keep at that!* He could still smell the ninety-nine-cent pine tree air freshener his father put there when they were in grade six. It was still in the car when they were in junior high, hanging from the rearview mirror and blowing parallel to it whenever someone rolled down a window.

Most of those school mornings were similar enough to blend into one memory. All that ever changed was the song on the radio or the homework they exchanged. That may have been why the sudden change in their father's personality, near the end of grade nine, was so marked and poignant. By the end of that school year, he spoke only to answer their questions in the mornings. He'd stopped hassling them to help shovel, and he cleared the ice from the car without making any jokes about how useless they were. If he did speak, and Owen was the first to notice it, his voice was flat. Something was missing, there was no tone, no inflection at the right places in his speech, just a flat line of simple one or two word sentences. His lack of emotion was evident in his now monotonous voice. He seemed more like a body dragging itself around than a man alive. Every morning he fell into the car seat and let out a long, exaggerated sigh. One morning he'd shaved only half his face and didn't notice until he got in the car. He went to work anyway. He stopped styling his hair, and then stopped ironing his shirts, and then stopped tucking them in.

Near mid-May of that year, he started spacing out at red lights. He habitually looked down on his hands whenever they were at a red light, as if fascinated by them. He watched them like a captivating play only he could see. He'd pull his skin tight to eradicate a wrinkle or gently comb the hair on his wrist, and he often laughed a little as he came out of what looked like a daydream. They never bothered to tell him to go, they'd wait for a car behind them to blow their horn.

Owen tried to ignore his father's change in personality, but one night before bed Alex mentioned it to their mother, who explained, "Your father may be losing his job, that's all. He might be a little glum like that for a while, but everything is going to be all right. He'll just have to give up the journalism bit and work in another field…"

They nodded when she finished the story, reiterating, "Everything will be okay, all right?" They were satisfied with having an explanation. Any explanation would've suited them just fine. "Now go to bed."

Less than a week later, they were driving to school and Owen saw his father notice a payphone in front of the courthouse on Water Street. His father did a double-take, as if it were an old friend he'd spotted. The car jutted out of its lane, no indicator, and bumped into the curb before it stopped. Owen was confused, but liked that he'd have a valid excuse for being late. Alex though, he didn't want to miss a minute of math class. Mrs. Saunders always recapped the last day's class, stressing what was most relevant, what he'd need to know to secure the A he was after.

"Dad! What are you doing? We're *already* late!" Alex smacked at his new watch.

It was odd of their father not to have mentioned needing to use the phone, but not answering Alex was even stranger. Instead, he slammed his car door, needlessly hard, as if to shut Alex up. He cast an eerie look back at them as he marched towards the phone: it sliced at them like a knife. His eyes were glowing, bulging from their sockets, as if his eyeballs were swelling and the sockets could no longer contain them. He was on the payphone for ten minutes, flailing his arms and stamping his feet. He slammed the receiver down and picked it back up to yell some more, as if the target of his arrow-headed words could still be on the line.

"Alex! What the hell is this?"

"I don't know, just … just keep your head down, don't look at him, don't make him mad … okay?" He wiped a sweaty palm on his jeans. "Don't look at him and don't say anything … and don't make him mad. Pretend we didn't see anything. Okay?"

Owen forced a laugh. "Jesus, Alex, it's Dad!"

"Is it?"

At school they were given a late pass to bring back the next day, signed by one of their parents to confirm they were legitimately late. Owen had a habit of cutting classes, so the principal was skeptical. When they came home after school that day, they walked into their house, laughing about a substitute teacher's botched delivery of Steinbeck's *Of Mice and Men*, and slung their bookbags down in the porch, having actively forgotten about their father's fit of rage that morning. They were heading up to their room to play video games when they saw their mother sitting alone and strikingly silent in the living room. She was watching the carpet like it was a fire. The TV wasn't on, there was no music on, and she wasn't reading. She looked aged, and with her hands lying on her knees, she looked defenseless against the world.

"Mom? Are you … all right?"

"It's your father." She got up off the brown couch immediately, clutching a white pillow between her hands like a sandwich. "I'm worried about him. His boss called today. He might have quit, we don't know." She turned and laid the pillow back on the couch. "He just … he got up and walked out around eleven this morning," she said, throwing her arms in the air. "He didn't say a word to anyone. Joyce called to ask if he was feeling ill. You know what he's like. Who knows what he was thinking, who *ever* knows what your father is thinking? He keeps everything all pent up, all to himself."

She caught herself growing frantic and calmed herself because Alex started to look panicked when she panicked.

Alex showed her the late slips that needed to be signed. He hauled the crumpled pink slips out of his bookbag and smoothed them. "I don't know what the hell he was doing or who the hell he was talking to," he told her as he sank into the couch, "but it was kind of creepy. He gave me this nasty look when I asked him what he was doing, and then he was going apeshit on the phone!"

"Watch your language, honey, and what phone, where?"

"The payphone, down by the courthouse on Water Street."

They would have been fools not to have seen how the story alarmed her. She looked like someone just shot at in a war.

"Oh, you know Dad ... he ... he probably forgot to use the phone before he left this morning." She forced a dismissive smile. "That's all."

She laughed a nervous laugh, but her mind, behind those flickering eyes, was clearly racing for an explanation. "When your father comes home, don't say anything, don't act any different than you usually do, okay? Like I said, he's just stressed out about finding another job. His newspaper isn't doing so well, that's all." She'd gone beyond trying to calm them now and was trying to calm herself, pressing wrinkles from her clothes and taking quick breaths.

When their father opened the front door that night, their mother was leaning in the porch entrance, waiting to greet him, presumably hoping for a logical answer, one that would alleviate all her worries, one that would make her feel stupid for ever worrying in the first place. But he said nothing. She pried. "So, how was your day?"

Kicking his shoes off in the porch. "Fine enough." He almost tripped over Alex's bookbag as he entered the hallway, brushing past her on his way to the bathroom. His shoulder butted into her breast hard enough to hurt, but she wouldn't acknowledge the pain, wouldn't rub it out. That would mean something was wrong.

Owen sat on the couch watching his mother's mind roam, having witnessed the flash of pain on her face and his father's seemingly lobotomized body stumble up the hall. She saw him watching her and tried to hide the concern on her face. She smiled and headed for the kitchen, claiming that she'd left the pasta sauce on for too long. From where he sat on the couch, he could see a bottle of pasta sauce on the kitchen table, the lid still unopened. It was next to an onion, still sealed in its peel, and a tub of mushrooms still sealed in plastic wrap. It was the first time Owen knew his mother was straightfaced lying to him.

Twenty minutes later, at supper, his father complained that the food tasted funny, as if there was *something in it*. He chewed it with his mouth open, loudly, making a wet sucking noise, and looked around the table for a response. A single strand of shredded parmesan cheese clung to the bristles on his unshaven cheeks, dangling there, like a silkworm from a tree. He asked with an utter urgency, "Is it just me, or is there a funny taste on this spaghetti?"

He was obviously more paranoid than disgusted. He walked over to the cupboards and examined the box of pasta. "Was this sealed when you opened it?"

Perplexed and alarmed, she nodded a slow nod.

He opened the fridge door, grabbed the tub of parmesan cheese, and sniffed it in an exaggerated manner, hauling it away from his face to clear his nostrils between whiffs. He checked the expiry date on the pasta sauce.

"I can trust you, Claire, but I don't know if we can trust everyone you've got traipsing through this house. Not anymore. I don't even trust the phones in here anymore. I've been working on a story for another paper, see. High magnitude. A different paper. But keep that between us, okay?"

They all nodded, shocked, concealing their fear. Owen knew that if he spoke, his father would hear a quiver in his voice. A quiver he felt safer hiding. Alex shot his mother a look: *See!*

"It might just be a funny taste in my mouth from earlier today. The coffee I drank. I think one of the youngsters at work might be poisoning my coffee when I'm not looking. I've tried to catch him. I can't tell you how though. He might be listening. It'll ruin my plan. But I am setting him up. Don't worry. I think he's jealous that I built up my career the old-fashioned way, but he fast-tracked it with some lame college degree ... so he doesn't have the respect and reputation that I've earned. He wants to steal my stories. He can't come up with his own. None as good as mine anyway."

He never noticed his family's collective fright, but talked right at their shocked faces. "I think he wants my job, and I think he'll do anything to get it. All of them. They all would. I had to leave work today. It wasn't safe. I don't know who to trust anymore. But it'll be okay, soon. It'll all be okay once I figure out my plan to catch him. I'll get the police involved when the time is right. Too early and I'll spoil it. He's just about to fall for my trap."

He walked out of the kitchen as he finished the sentence. He stormed up to his room, put on his pajamas, and went to bed at 6:30, as if that were perfectly normal.

The kitchen felt like the inside of an oven, and the silence rang in their ears. They were afraid to breathe, to move or speak, because doing so would unpause life, and they would have to face their new reality. Their new life as a family. Worse still, they would have to deal with it. His decline into schizophrenia had been so slow they could ignore it at first, until that one week when it all came faster than a car crash.

❧

In high school the rumours were true: Owen and Alex had a "crazy father."

Owen resented his brother's shame about their father. He saw through how Alex dove into the books and was crowned valedictorian. How Alex stayed hip and dressed head to toe in logo-visible clothes. It was all to compensate, to prove himself, to seem distinguished, flawless, and above all: normal.

By grade twelve, the jokes about how two brothers could be so different got old fast. *They must have different fathers. One of them must be the postman's son. One must have been dropped on his head.* Each a masked query as to why Owen wasn't more like Alex. Especially since they were twins. Alex was always quick to point out that they were fraternal twins, not identical, so it was *obvious* why they weren't more alike, why would they be? According to his biology textbook, page 501, fraternal twins were no more genetically alike than a normal set of brothers. But the jokes came anyway, and Owen watched as his infuriated brother recited genetic fact to family and friends of the family. The insinuation that he and Owen should be alike just because they were twins trivialized all the conscious effort he put into distinguishing himself from the likes of his brother.

When Alex came home one afternoon, gloating about how he'd been declared valedictorian for their graduating class, Owen saw Alex's elation deflate when their mother advised Alex, in a jovial and good-natured manner, that he *better get crackin' on that speech.*

Right away he turned to his brother. "This speech is how this school – the teachers and the students – will remember me!"

By grade twelve, it was obvious that Owen had inherited their father's way with words. But writing was the *only* thing Alex thought his brother could do better than him, so he wasn't jealous of it.

"C'mon, man, you gotta write it for me. It's gotta be perfect, man. This is a big deal."

Laughing, Owen cut him off. "It's high school, Alex. It's probably the most irrelevant thing you'll ever do in your life. Besides, a rock could graduate *high school* with honours."

"Owen! Stop that right now. You should be proud of your brother and–"

"Oh shut up, Owen! We'll see who's where in ten years,

okay? I'd say I'll be a lawyer, and you'll be a goddamn bum or criminal who'll need my help, shitface. I bet you'll at least need my money–"

"Boys! Stop this *right* now!"

"Calm down. I'll write the goddamn speech. I'll write it if you give me your allowance Friday."

"Owen, for God's sakes, watch your language. At least in front of your mother. Surely that's not too much to ask."

He smiled and nodded, *Sorry*. "It's just that … it's sad. He thinks finding some unknown angle in a triangle faster than the shit-for-brains next to him matters."

"*Owen!*"

Owen wrote Alex's valedictory speech, and it inspired even the adults well past their "carving out a life" stage. He got a kick out of writing it so melodramatically. He thought it was corny, and that anyone even remotely cerebral would see the dark satire permeating the speech. So he was surprised at how well it was received – and the standing ovation. He also got a kick out of lacing the speech with words spelled differently than they're pronounced, knowing his brother would be too proud to ask him how to pronounce them. During the speech, Alex said malevolent wrong. He said mal-vo-lant, and someone snickered. Owen did it to prove to himself that contemporary prestige is a sham, an illusion, and that the real geniuses of the world are the ones who don't play the game of life: the Wordsworthian writers living in small cabins near nature, or the fiery-eyed, passion-infused city dwellers who were capable of more, but satisfied with less. Because, at that age, he felt that money and material things were just things that could be thrown into a fire and burned. They were that meaningless. So surrounding yourself with those things was like insulating yourself against the world.

As Alex walked across the stage, shaking hands and bowing to the applause, their mother wiped a tear from her eye with her bumpy knuckle and leaned into Owen, her dress spilling over the side of the chair. "I know all this means nothing to you, but you should know how proud your father would be of you two. His little writer and his little valedictorian." A whimper, a smile on her face, twitching lips. He knew if his eyes met hers she would tear up, so maybe he would have too. "You've got a way with words, honey. You're just like him … your father."

He changed the topic to keep her from crying. All the while thinking of that silent understanding that had always existed between him and his father. Embracing it. Alex, and even their mother, was almost jealous of that inherent understanding. One night, Christmastime, after far too many drinks, and after the crowd of visitors had left, Owen's father called him into the kitchen and made him promise that on his fiftieth birthday the two of them would take an Alaskan cruise together. His mother too obviously listened in on the conversation as she rinsed mugs and cutlery in the kitchen sink, scrubbing the forks extra long just to linger, because her husband never talked of vacationing. Not with her anyway.

His father was sitting in a chair, but swaying like a man fresh off a merry-go-round. His teeth, and centres of each lip, were a reddish black from all the wine. "We'll get away from everywhere," he promised him. "We'll hear the sound of silence. We'll *feel life*."

Owen nodded, dismissing his drunken father.

"I know you're only in grade eight, but you understand me, don't you, about *feeling life?*"

# WELCOMING WANDERING EYES

*July 18th, 2008,*
*At the cabin, restless in bed.*

*I just woke from the same dream again. My insides are made of garbage and my bones are rusted metal. It hurts to move. My fingernails are cracked and stinging. I dream my heart is burning. I can see my heart burning inside my chest, but I can't bend my arms to put out the flames. I've lost everything and I can't find it. I am in the middle of nowhere and can't find my way back to something familiar. And as soon as I realize I don't even know what I'm looking for, I wake up.*

*Today in the car I saw Owen pretending to read an old magazine while we drove. I wasn't convinced. I know he can't read while the TV or stereo is on, he says it's too distracting, so how could he read while Alex's audio CD was playing so loudly? And he was staring at the same page for fifteen minutes, and I know him well enough to know that nothing in that lame magazine could get his attention for any longer than a minute.*

*I wanted to think that Owen was only pretending to be reading that magazine. That what he was really doing was staring at*

*my cleavage when I wasn't looking. It really seemed that way.
I didn't notice how low my tank top was lying until I saw his
eyes darting on and off my breasts in the rearview mirror, in
bursts he thought were too quick for me to feel them there. I
slugged the shoulder of that tank top down farther, to loosen
the cling of it against me. It's not my fault if the wind blew it
open and Owen was watching. It's not my fault that I felt good
being noticed. I tell myself the diet is for me, and the exercise,
and all the fashion magazines. And maybe I do do it all for
myself, but maybe it's because I've forgotten what it feels like to
be noticed. To feel eyes on you like that – and know what they
want – is empowering, enlivening. Reassuring.*

*Alex is never home anymore, and when he is he has an endless
list of excuses: too tired, too hot, too cold, too busy. Yet there is
more porn on his laptop than on any college kid's computer. He
doesn't even hide it. Does he think I don't notice, or that I don't
care? Am I not beautiful anymore, or is he just too used to me? I
guess it's like eating the same sandwich every day for lunch. I
guess he's sick of me that same way. Him still being attracted to
me after years of marriage would be like him eating the same
sandwich every day for years and pretending to still like that
ham-on-rye. I don't know if I can really even blame him. Blah.*

*But I refuse to be mustard on the tongue. To lack flavour.*

*So I make no apologies for enjoying the desire in Owen's
eyes, because it was the way he was looking at me: not because
they were breasts and he is male, but because they were my
breasts. It made me feel beautiful and desirable, like someone
worth secretly admiring. It made me feel like I've been dead for
years now. His eyes wrapped themselves around me, whispered
everything I needed to hear, and brought me back to life. All
that in ten seconds.*

*I felt his eyes on me like hands. Did he feel me feeling them
there?*

*Feeling his eyes on me felt as good as sex. Better even. Because nothing feels better than wanting. To want something, nine times out of ten, feels better than having it. There is more passion in a shared look between two potential lovers than there is in sex, in my experience. In my experience, we have the most lust, passion, and desire for someone before we start sleeping with them. In my experience, men fuck that passion into oblivion, and wind up attracted to someone else. Then they deny this: to themselves at first, and then to their loved ones.*

*At least we can blame biology, the instincts seared into us by a billion years of evolution. It's easier that way. "It's only natural for the mind to wander." And what is natural is beyond us, like God making marionettes of us. To fight desire is, by this logic, unnatural and exhausting. I keep coming back to Natalie's bold statement last week: "Adultery is only immoral if it is others you are putting first and not yourself. Isn't it wrong to deny yourself?" I disagree if she is referring to sex with a stranger, or a man who means nothing to you, for the cheap thrill of it. That is what cheating is: cheap sex for thrills. But what about when you feel an emotional connection to a man like you've never felt before. What about when you feel that emotional connection like a soft bearhug every day, and your heart and soul are encouraging it, finding reasons to cross paths with the man? What's that called, if not love? What about when a man, who isn't your husband, understands you more, makes your skin alive with a static tingling, makes you laugh more, flatters you and makes you feel distinct, desirable, one in a million? Notices you, the little things that make you you? What then?*

*To be selfless but self-defeating is such a slow suicide.*

*What about when you jump out of bed without hitting snooze even once, because you know you'll be seeing that man today?*

*Thing is, I've seen the way Owen looks at me, like Alex used to. I've seen how Owen assesses our marriage and feels bad for me.*

*He even apologizes for his brother's absenteeism, and takes the kids out for ice creams and walks along the river. The kids' rooms are filled with bugs in jars Owen collected himself. They Google what to feed them, how to make sure a caterpillar will pupate. I know Alex would do all these things if he had the time, but I also know Owen would make the time if he was as busy as Alex.*

*It's the way that Owen treats me that made it okay for me to indulge today. Because I always thought the purpose of marriage was to be satiated, not hungry for desiring eyes. I am starved for attention, and that is not why I married. I married to spend every day loved and wanted and noticed and safe and happy and satisfied and jealous of myself. I should not feel selfish for wanting to be adored.*

*Owen reads out back with me as I garden. He comes with me to the plant nurseries to weigh in on what I buy, and helps me lug it all back to the yard. He compliments my work in the garden, and I teach him stuff about gardening, and I know it sounds so stupid to say this, but that makes me feel useful and intelligent, and though my reasoning is vague, having someone to witness what I do with my time makes me feel relevant to someone. Owen is excited about the tomatoes in the greenhouse, whereas Alex still buys tomatoes at the grocery store even though I've told him they are growing out back. I've told him a thousand times, and that means he never listened to me a thousand times. He only cares to hear certain things, like supper is on the table, I picked up your dry cleaning today, and that yes, I am sure I am all right.*

*I am needy, I need some attention, maybe I shouldn't blame my husband for that. But I wasn't always a hassle, I wasn't always so invisible, so unnecessary. Where do I place the blame for that? The rolled eyes break my heart every time. I am married to a man who rolls his eyes at me. Then I feel silly for thinking he should adore me too much to roll his eyes at me. Childish really,*

*idealistic. But it is how I feel, how he makes me feel, like I want
a man who knows the shapes of my fingers, the shampoo I use,
and how to never upset me enough to make him roll his eyes at
me.*

*Owen and I grocery shop together now, or go buy new books, or
music, or clothes, or whatever. Last Tuesday we lay on the couch,
the same couch, just on opposite ends, and listened to a Damien
Jurado CD. It's fantastic. "And Now That I'm in Your Shadow"
kills me! And the songs he does with Rosie Thomas are way too
beautiful. He's Owen's favourite musician. If Alex has a
favourite musician, I wouldn't know who it was.*

*Owen and I do things couples do together. The things Alex and
I used to do before time slipped in between us and replaced
closeness with this invisible distance. Alex and I do nothing
together anymore. Not even sex. Not even meals. If he is even
home for supper, and not at that goddamn hospital, he eats in
front of the TV, not out back with the kids and Owen and me.
I mean, what did he buy a house with a yard like ours for
anyway? Definitely not for me, I know it was for show.
Everything Alex does is for show, to prove himself to a bunch
of people who really don't give a damn. People are either jealous
or indifferent to the material success of others, so why bother
showing yourself off?*

*I feel like a ghost in my own home. Sometimes I feel like I
could fling a plate of food across the breakfast table and Alex
wouldn't even look up. It's only since Owen came to stay here
that I noticed that and admitted it to myself. Owen is an
Omen: my marriage is dead. Yet I know in his own way that
Alex does care deeply for me. And I tell myself that's enough. So
then why am I writing this? Why did I give Owen that eyeful
today? Was it for him or me? Is there a difference?*

# WAYS OUT

OWEN ROSE FROM HIS BED slowly, hesitated, and climbed the rest of the way out. Bare feet on fresh new carpet, a cheap but noticed comfort. He walked over to the window to check the weather, because changes in the weather were now the only thing that made one day feel any different than the last. There were three yellowed blades of grass poking up through a blanket of white snow. The wind was beating them off the brown fence. A metaphoric mirror.

It was noon when Owen woke up; it was later and later each day now, and Lillian had stopped setting aside half her breakfast for him. She never commented on his life but she didn't have to. The notion spoke for itself. He felt a fool in her house, pathetic. He wanted to be alone, he wanted to be free from the eyes of others so he could fall apart and come back together without a witness seeing how he chose to do so. It would feel like rejuvenation then, not degeneration.

He wanted to be back in Newfoundland. Owen was lost in Nova Scotia, his brother and aunt's adopted place of residence. He was stranded there, financially. Halifax felt like a shaking bed, an itchy blanket. He needed only to secure a job and a place to sleep and he would return to St. John's, maybe Rocky Harbour, but definitely somewhere back in Newfoundland.

Three months before the accident, Owen had taken Hannah to see St. John's. She had always wanted to see where Alex grew up, but Alex never made it happen. She wanted to honeymoon there; she felt it would be appropriate, but Alex bought two tickets to Cuba instead, and acted like she should be pleasantly surprised. She sat bored on a beach for five days while he read medical journals about breakthroughs in cardiology and oncology. The day before they left, she combed the beach for a handful of blue spiraled shells. She put them on the mantle back at home in a pottery bowl she had. Later, she told Owen that she couldn't stand the idea of a souvenir from that trip. *It was like trying to take a joke seriously.*

To rid her of curiosity about St. John's, after months of overhearing her and Owen talking about the place, Alex bought her and Owen tickets. She was ecstatic about the weekend trip, and Owen was ecstatic to have her to himself for two full days. Alex couldn't go, he was on call Saturday night, but Lillian could watch the kids.

She'd insisted on the window seat, and Owen remembered looking over her shoulder and noticing how slowly the clouds drifted past the window, like the plane was barely moving, like time was grinding to a halt. He looked up from his novel from time to time to watch her watching the clouds. When a mass of green appeared in a bigger mass of endless blue, her eyes widened. "Is that it, Owen? Is that Newfoundland?"

She poked her finger at the window. When she took it away, her fingerprint was there: a series of perfect, un-smudged, concentric circles. There was something infinite about it, something so exclusively Hannah.

"Is it? Is that Newfoundland?" She nodded this time, instead of poking at the glass.

He leaned over her and felt her warmth, her body beneath

him, and shrugged his shoulders. He was smiling. As always when she spoke, he was inexplicably smiling. This effort-less effect on him was what he now missed the most: the soul-filling warmth of being next to her.

It was only natural that a woman like Hannah would love St. John's. Everything about the town was so charming to her, especially the people, and the fact that cars yielded to pedestrians, and that young men held doors. It was the bright colours of the rowhouses that struck her the most, and how vivid and alive the town was, despite the grey, fog-shrouded skies. They made her fill her camera on her first night there.

"Why are the colours so vibrant? Why are the houses attached? It's like God spilled a bag of gumdrops all over this city and they all melted together!"

It wasn't a question so much as a statement.

On their first day there, Owen took her to the old battered cannon shelters beneath the Fort Amherst lighthouse. The fog siren frightened her into his arms every time it blared. They could be together like that in public now, and it strengthened their love. More than they had expected it to. There was a loner minke whale. She tried ten times to photograph the whale, but came up short every time and ended up with ten pictures of water and nothing more.

"Here, you try!" She handed him the camera and stood behind him to watch the screen as he lined up the photo. He caught the whale on the first try. Nothing glorious or worth framing, but enough to satisfy her. Enough to show the kids when she got home. She had one hand on his shoulder, the other tucked into his coat pocket on the opposite side. She nodded when he showed her. "Try one more."

But the whale never resurfaced.

He turned to hand her the camera. Saw her sun-reddened cheeks, and the smile on her face looked so right, so impossibly perfect. One second of her time, every word she spoke, the feel of her skin on his, how the curve of her body fit into his. It was all too perfect, so perfect that he couldn't hate himself for loving her. When he wrapped his arms around her that day, he sank into a better world: she was a porthole to something more. But as he looked at her standing there, her hands tucked into the pockets of her hip flannel skirt, her body arced into the direction of the wind – he knew he could never have her. Not like he wanted to. He could never make a wife and mother of her. Their love would have to be secondary to *her* marriage; it would have to be ephemeral, "wrong." He wanted his own children, a wife, a life. Things she could never grant him.

"Are you okay?" She slung her arms around him and rocked him sideways, dancing slowly to the sound of the waves and seagulls. She combed his thin hair back into place with her hand.

"I don't feel guilty anymore, Hannah. And I love you."

They said nothing for a while. They were in love but no one had used those three words yet. So he made light of the situation, but meant every word. "I love this water bottle, just because you've touched it and sipped from it. I love the air in our hotel room, because maybe you've breathed it in–"

She laughed, broke free of the embrace, and gave him a soft, playful slap in the face.

She asked about the tower, Cabot Tower, that sat atop Signal Hill, and she wondered why Alex ever left this place.

"Can we get in there? It looks like a … *castle*, doesn't it?"

"Yeah, we can go up after supper. Have you ever had salt-water taffy? Is that a Newfoundland thing? They sell it there."

They were hand in hand in the open, walking back to their rental car, no longer needing to hide their love. That day at Fort Amherst, they knew, was a day in a life that could've been, if they could just summon the courage to consummate their love, and shatter Alex Collins like glass.

≈

Owen thought of St. John's for the rest of the day: the ever-changing mural ads on the cement walls of the LSPU hall, and the way the city had seemed so much more alive with Hannah there by his side. She was the tourist, but in showing her his hometown, he was appreciating it all more than ever. She brought out all the features of the place: the unique architecture of the buildings, the carved turrets of the courthouse on Water Street, and the coarse grain in the rock of its walls.

Then he thought of his father, locked away in a mental ward at the Waterford Hospital across from Bowring Park – a park where they had picnicked and fed ducks twenty-five years ago, before his father got sick. He remembered his father handing him a loaf of bread and guiding him towards the ducks one day.

"You're everything beautiful this world can be, my son."

Owen was getting too old for those compliments, too old to be at a park with his father, and yet his hand still felt so big on Owen's back that day, and so god-like. Now his father was just a body suspended between life and death, like a corpse perpetually waiting for CPR or a body bag, kept alive by a coin-sized lump in his brainstem that kept his heart beating and convinced his catatonic body to breathe.

By the end of grade ten, Owen's father had fully surren-dered to schizophrenia. He went delusional, then catatonic: a raving lunatic and then a body in a rocking chair that wouldn't have the instinct to flee a burning room; a man seeing people to a man with no use for eyes. It was an unbearable, life-altering year for Owen and Alex, every day of it, especially since the biggest turmoil in any of their friends' families that year was that their mother wouldn't extend their curfew.

It was the week his father was finally and indefinitely committed that Owen started writing. His first short story was about a man in a coma; it was a contemplation on the distinction between being human and being mere flesh and bone. How being alive means being connected to others, invisibly, and nothing more. It won the junior division for fiction in the provincial Arts & Letters competition. He and his mother went to visit The Waterford that same week, and he told his unresponsive father all about it. He left a copy of the story with his father that day, just in case he *snapped out of it* for five minutes. He waited until his mother had turned her back and headed towards the door, and then he laid it on his father's lap so his mother wouldn't see his pathetic attempt at sharing this joy with his father.

Initially his father stayed at home, medicated and more or less house-bound. It was the strange utterances his father made, particularly in the shower every morning, that startled Owen the most. He'd string unassociated words together, almost singing them, and laughing to himself. "I am not the alien who smoked the last Jeremy!" "Candy eater eighty, sixty-seven." The doctors called these "word salads," and said they were one of the defining symptoms of schizophrenia. *Word salads*: the title sounded so unprofessional, so unreal. More so than his father's delusions and hallucinations.

One morning, two weeks after his father was diagnosed, they were all eating breakfast together. His mother and Alex had finished up quickly so they could get in the shower before Owen. It was just the two of them at the table, quietly sipping too-sweet tea and crunching burnt toast. Neither of them was comfortable with the idea of schizophrenia just yet.

Nothing triggered it – no loud noise, no sudden movements – but his father jumped up from his chair, slung an arm above his head, pursed his lips, and started into a word salad. Something about it frightened Owen out of the kitchen and into his parents' bedroom. He dove down onto their waterbed, lifted slowly up and down by the wave, and felt nauseated by the guilt. He felt like he'd just betrayed and embarrassed his father. He held his body still, as if he could pause life, maybe rewind it. He came back to the kitchen with his social studies textbook, pretending he'd only bolted from the room to get the book.

"I've got a final today." He flashed the book. It fell out of his sweaty adolescent hand and crashed onto the floor, buckling the hardcover corner.

His father nodded, knowingly. "I'm sorry about that, Owen. I dunno. I thought it might be funny … I guess." He shrugged his shoulders and slumped his head. "My pills aren't magic, okay?"

⌇

Prior to his father's illness, Owen had never viewed his parents as a couple. He saw them only as two parents, living together, whose sole function was to raise and support their children. It took watching them fall apart, layer after layer, to see them as a couple who had loved each other. A couple who had loved each other in a way that one couldn't persist without the other.

The wall between the laundry room and his parents' bedroom was paper thin; he could've poked a finger through it. One night he heard them talking as he searched for his pajamas in a ball of clothes in the dryer.

"It's the pills, Claire. I'm into this, but I'm just … not … it's a side effect, it's not me … just keep going, here … just keep going, like this."

"It's okay, Roger." A pause. She must've rolled over. "Just get some sleep, we can always try again, the next time you feel ready."

"I can stop taking the pills for a few days and–"

"Roger, don't you even *think* of it! I'm going to watch you swallow every pill now, like you're a fucken baby, d'you hear me? Just go to sleep!"

A slight whimpering then, like she was trying to hold it in, but couldn't.

It was the first time Owen had heard his mother yell at his father and it might have been the first time he'd heard her swear. So who was she now? She'd stopped folding towels and putting them in the hall closet; he was fishing his pajamas and tomorrow's outfit out of the dryer.

As he snuck out of the laundry room that night, he thought of the time his father was committed. Alex, who had taken to spying on his father, caught him outside and looking in a neighbour's window one night at 2 a.m., and ran to get his mother out of bed. Alex woke Owen and they watched the scene from their bedroom window like a movie. Their mother ran outside in her blue-and-white nightgown, looking frantic and disheveled, and for the first time: old. She wept madly, wiping tears away with the flattened palms of her hands as she raced towards him. Owen read it as a mix of fear and sadness. Like she knew in that moment what she had been ignoring about her husband those last few weeks. They watched her run up behind their father, who was going through the neighbour's garbage cans, and haul him back into the house. She dragged him inside; she managed to overpower him as he fought back, livid that she was sabotaging his secret lead. He claimed the neighbour was the kingpin of a nationwide sex slave trade. That he'd been working on the story for weeks now, and his employer was expecting a final draft.

Their neighbour at the time was a seventy-eight-year-old widow named Elsie. She was so innocent, so bored with life, that she made pies and cookies for Owen and Alex on a regular basis. Dropping them over, and coming back for the Tupperware, was an excuse for social interaction.

His mother burst back into the porch, dragging their father by the shoulder like a misbehaving kid. The door bounced off the wall and hit their father as they came back into the house.

The black nylon of his jacket was balled up in her hand. Owen listened in on his parents from the hallway and heard his mother shove their father down onto the couch. She was standing above him, arms folded, waiting for an explanation. They were yelling, then calm, and then yelling. Owen and Alex hid in the bathroom when they heard their parents coming down the hall towards their father's office.

That very night his father shifted from hiding his theories to trying to justify them. He "admitted" that the pizza fliers being delivered to their mailbox were coded, that his supposed employer was leaving them there. He showed her the "codes," a drawer full of pizza fliers with certain letters underlined to spell out a hidden message. Among the lines of the flyer in his hand, EAT AT SAL'S TONIGHT. EAT SMART. TRY OUR REAL SICILIAN CURED HAM. The underlined letters spelled *Elsie's Trash*. What frightened them the most was the four letters underlined in the next sentence: TAKE IN A LITTLE SICILY TONIGHT! He assured them he wasn't there to kill her.

"I'm just the journalist, Claire, don't worry. Anything that serious would be left to other agencies, not the journalist division. I really don't understand what the kill code means, but it is not an instruction for me, and we are not in any *real* danger unless you blow this out of proportion and–"

"Roger, *please!* Think about it. Where are the paycheques from this company? Where is the goddamn *magazine*? What is it called and where can I buy–"

"It's not *that* kind of magazine, Claire. It doesn't need a title, because–"

"*Roger!* C'mon. You're smarter than this." Screeching now, her words ripping out of her throat. "How can you be selling a magazine with no goddamn name?"

He sat there so calm, so unaffected by her emotions. "It's not *that* kind of magazine. It's not the kind of thing you'll find mixed in with trashy celebrity magazines in a grocery store checkout. And it's only being distributed underground to an elite audience, for now."

～

His father spent three months in a psychiatric ward on medication, getting therapy from a young and gifted specialist in schizophrenia. Dr. Erickson managed to convince him that the magazine was all a delusion. At first, Owen's father thought the doctor was just trying to censor and sabotage his magazine by locking away all of its contributors, but the doctor was crafty enough to convince him otherwise. The drugs helped, once they settled on the right pill, CPZ, and a dosage that didn't make him twitch or slur his speech too badly. The doctor recognized that Roger was an intelligent man and used a lot of logic in his therapy. One day he took him to Elsie's garbage cans and let him go through them. He took him inside Elsie's house to meet Elsie and let him root around until he was satisfied it was just some old lady's house. He showed him that everyone on the street was receiving those fliers and took him to meet the men who published the fliers. With a lot of therapy, and CPZ, Dr. Erickson brought Owen's father back to reality.

In November, his mother signed all the necessary papers to get him out. He convinced her he could control his disorder with the CPZ and cognitive therapy. He could convince anyone of anything. And for months, right through Christmas, he was fine.

But, every time he'd stare off into a distance or think he heard something in the middle of the night, like anyone does, Owen was afraid his father was seeing that imaginary employer again. Or worse. Once Owen knew his father's mind could wander, there was no telling how far. Alex told Owen, maybe every night, different stories he read about schizophrenics killing their neighbours, cats, dogs, mothers, fathers, significant others … kids. Each story exaggerated, but absolutely eerie and unnerving. His father's illness, and the stories Alex told him, changed the environment the brothers grew up in. It fractured it. The world was no longer as small and simple as it had always seemed. It was bigger now, unpredictable, too complicated and unstable for them to retain that blind joy all their friends had. Owen felt distant from his parents and – because of differing opinions on their father – wary of of his brother.

By April of that year, their mother had to hide any fliers that came to their house, and write *NO JUNK MAIL* on their mailbox. She had to get out of bed every night and snoop through her husband's office to see what he was up to in there all day long. She found pages and pages of absolute gibberish, filed neatly away in labeled folders and drawers. Every morning, the word salads were getting worse and worse, and one night she overheard him talking to his "old employer" in the basement. As he picked up on his family's wariness, he grew suspicious of them, and talked about how their eyes seemed "redder than they used to be." He talked about how his wife's face seemed to be changing. "You're always frowning at me, your eyebrows are always furrowed." The food always tasted funny. He was given new meds, new doses, Owen's exhausted mother reading up on them all.

When he was at his best, he would cry and beg her not to sign the papers. All the guilt and indecision was killing her, it never got better, just worse. She knew once she recommitted him, he wouldn't be coming back; she'd be essentially sending him off to die. All the while, Owen knew that if his mother didn't have two children to worry about, she'd never even *think* of sending him back. Every night he heard them fight and cry, he thought of her burden, acknowledged it, and felt something akin to guilt over it. She considered sending them to stay with their father's parents while they all waited for the new medication to take effect. He overheard this in a phone call one night, from the laundry room. He needed a towel, and there were none. He dried off with a pair of pajama bottoms that night. He ran the water cold, for the shock of it, to avoid crying, to avoid feeling.

The bad days were punctuated by good weeks, but one night their father came too close to hurting them. They were all sitting in front of the TV watching *The Wonder Years* when a U-haul truck pulled up in front of their house. Its lights blazed in through the windows, and the rattle from the truck, surreally loud, drowned out the television. He shot up from his chair, drew the curtains closed and yelled at his family. "Get down in the basement! Now! We've got to stick together!" He was screaming so loud veins threatened to burst out of his neck and forehead. "They can't tear us apart, not now, no matter what!"

Before they could collectively assess what to do, their father was yelling at the empty space beside Owen, pointing a knife at a man who was not there.

"Stay *away* from my kid, Ted. You said it wouldn't come to– Owen! Don't move like that! I'm done with the work, Ted. Hurting my family won't change that! *Owen*, My *God!* Stop moving!"

While their mother phoned the police, Alex tackled their father from behind, and he went mad then, suspicious and livid about his own son turning on him. He threatened Alex for crossing him. It took all three of them to pin him down and wait for the police.

He was recommitted that very night. When it was all over, what got to them more than anything was the realization that maybe the man had never seen a point in anything but his work. It *was* true in the end, that when he was writing those imaginary stories to no one, he wouldn't even sit to eat with them. He was *too busy*. His delusions about being a revolutionary journalist, his going mad because he wasn't, made them feel not enough. Second to some non-existent magazine.

After realizing he'd threatened his sons that night, he ceased talking, permanently. Within weeks of being re-committed to the Waterford Hospital, he fell into a catatonic state. He sat in a rickety wooden chair, perpetually rocking back and forth and mumbling to himself in a small, dark room. They would go visit him from time to time, but it felt futile. He had no idea they were there. He didn't even look up. Not even when Owen "accidentally" stepped on his foot to try and get some reaction from him, some proof of life. The hospital treated him with a controversial drug, Clozapine, used on "treatment-resistant" patients. It spiked his white blood cell count to dangerous levels. It gave him seizures and never changed a thing. He was gone. A mannequin, not a man. If Owen bent his father's finger or raised his arm, it stayed that way. *Waxy flexibility*, the doctor called it. Like his father was some kind of human doll; a wax figure. Inert.

A month later, Owen came home from school and found his mother asleep on his bed. She was on her side. His baby blue pillow had a few navy drips on it: his mother's tears. The sight of her tears didn't help to share the burden of a mutual loss. It accentuated that loss. The tears never brought them closer together. They simply stated they weren't a family anymore. Just three people coping. Readjusting. Coming out of it as different people.

His math exercise book was wedged between her hip and the mattress and pointing up diagonally off the bed – the one he'd written in the night before instead of doing his trigonometry homework. She must have been reading it, before the tears and the nap.

*When Dad was diagnosed with schizophrenia, I promised us both that I wouldn't treat him any differently. When he was committed to a hospital, I promised myself I wouldn't see him any less. But now that he is catatonic, I don't have any part of him left to hold on to. His body is still there, physically, in that cold dark room, but he is long gone. He is a beating heart in a net of nerves and nothing more. Wherever he went, he took some vital part of me with him. The part of me that could have favourite TV shows and movies, and give a shit about music. The part of me that could smile at a day like today: the last of the snow is gone and it is jeans and T-shirt weather and everyone is finding reasons to be outside. Not us. It doesn't help that Mom is a zombie now too. Just a different kind. And Alex is pretending like nothing happened. And my friends just change the topic.*

*When Alex and I were eight, Dad took us camping. When we registered and paid for our lot in Terra Nova National Park, we were given pamphlets on bear safety. I read that campers were not to leave food out in the open, and should cover any trash in order to avoid luring bears. Desperately excited to see a bear, I left a trail of crumbs leading to our trailer, I uncovered the garbage, I did everything the pamphlet said not to do. I never ate half of my hotdog at lunch, or half of my burger at supper, so that I could lay the remains out for the bear that never came. I waited for Dad and Alex to fall asleep and sat outside the trailer for over an hour, just waiting. Nothing. And I fell asleep disappointed.*

*I only now realize why I could have done something so careless when I was a kid. It was because I felt like Dad could have protected me from anything. Not simply that a father can protect his children, but more specifically that Roger Collins could save Owen Collins from anything. The day Dad tackled me and threatened Alex was the day I lost that feeling of childhood naiveté. I don't think anyone should be able to attribute that loss to one distinct memory.*

# OH TO BE SQUAT BETWEEN
# A WALL AND A LOVER

*July 30th, 2008,*
*Back from the grocery store.*

*I just walked to the bakery for some focaccia bread. The kids love it, and I'm an addict. I've joked with Gene, the European baker, that he ought to put an addiction notice on all his baked goods. He's such an endearing man, always covered head to toe in flour and bliss, always chatting with his customers in his broken English. Bellowing at them as if they were across the room. "TODAY, HAH-NAH, I HAVE JUST MADE DE CHOGOLATE-STRAWBERRY DANISH FOR YOU!" He actually does that clichéd Italian gesture of kissing his fingers and flicking them away from his mouth when he boasts about something culinary: "MOAW!" He is reason enough to shop there. He knows the girls, Callie's sweet tooth. He gives me little treats free of charge to bring her. She makes him little crafts that he tacks up on the wall in the back room: drawings of bakers with giant chef hats, or chocolate chip cookies made out of brown foam and black pipe cleaners.*

*There were couples everywhere as I walked back home. Couples, and me alone. Happy couples, possessed by each other's presence. Basking in each other. New lovers, true couples, they take that enthrallment for granted. To be in love like that is to cease to exist, to be freed from yourself, to be found in each other. Not everyone can say they would let go of everything for one person. Not without hesitation, not without lying. It is a confidence and a thrill for the new lovers only, or those few rare couples whose bond even time admires and shies away from.*

*There was a couple walking their excited German shepherd on a taut red leash. It kept spinning around, getting tangled up in its leash, and jumping up and down, its nails clicking off the sidewalk. It kept turning around and hoisting itself up on two legs and patting at their chests with its front paws in a "Hey! Look at me!" kind of way. They were standing so close together that the dog's left paw was on the guy's chest and the right on the girl's. There was no space between them. They even walked in step. They were used to the dog jumping all over them. Jumping all over them in a way that meant they must walk that dog every night, together. Together. Together, and me there alone.*

*And there were two couples sitting together on a bus stop bench, laughing hysterically, oblivious to the world.*

*There was a young man who had his girlfriend squat between him and the brick wall of the grocery store, in a vulgar public display of affection. He looked like the kind of kid the prissy-looking girl's mother wouldn't approve of. Her with her ready-for-Broadway makeup job and a jacket too pristine to be grinding up against brick like that, and him with his bought-faded-and-torn jeans and styled-to-bedhead hair. There was something genuinely James Dean about him, though. He was kissing her neck and scooping her into him with both hands on her ass to hide, or maybe apply some pressure to, any bulge growing there between them. She was embarrassed but pretending to like it, all the while making sure no one was watching. I mean, what if a teacher saw, or her aunt came out the door with a cart full of groceries?*

*There was an elderly man helping his feeble wife out of their station wagon, the kind with wood panel siding. He held her by the hips as she climbed the curb at the entrance of the grocery store. He didn't mind. Her feebleness wasn't a burden. It was sweet. They moved at their own pace, like the rest of the world wasn't there. I followed them around for a bit in the grocery store, just to see what they bought.*

*I suppose these couples have always been there on my many walks to the bakery, but it is only lately that I am noticing them. To be envious, you have to realize you are missing something in your own life.*

*I am only now admitting to myself that what keeps Alex and me together is what was, not what is. The foundation of our relationship is dated, crumbling, in need of renovation that wouldn't be worth the effort. I married in my twenties. It might work for some couples, but I think the problem with me and Alex is that I was not done growing as a person before we got all cohabitated/married/permanently involved. Alex is the same man he was when we met, but I have changed quite a lot. So much so that Alex almost feels like a stranger now. He is not what the new me would want in a husband. He is not what I would choose to surround myself with now. It's not that I am wiser, just different. I've become who I am in my thirties, but cannot escape who I was in my twenties. I forged myself into that life the day I got married. The days Callie and Lucia were born. I could compromise, accept the better aspects of my relationship, seek them out and shun the others, but I resent doing so for an absent husband. Alex is a great man, a decent father, a dignified doctor, but not the husband I thought he would be eight years ago when I said "I do." When you are made to feel transparent, you start to feel that way. Then your mind wanders to the remedy, to being loved and celebrated.*

*I used to like being alone for the walk to Gene's bakery. Taking in the city sounds and all the people. I'm the type to pet a stranger's dog and get silly with children. To make an adventure out of the walk. Lately though, everything seems like a reminder, an omen, a blatant revelation that my marriage is dead. And I can't help but fear the death is contagious. That it will consume me and I will spend the rest of my life just pretending to be alive. Fantasizing.*

*At least I've got Owen. He comes with me just about everywhere now. I think I'm really distracting him from the writing thing. He says he needs an hour to get absorbed in his work, and then three or four more to be productive, but I'm knocking on his door every half hour with an interruption. I knock on the door with tea and a sandwich, or to invite him along on the walk to the bakery, or to see if he wants to come along to pick the girls up from school and take them to the beach. He'll take the laptop and join us, but he never types a word. He says it's a good thing to have nothing to write about, whatever that means. The other day he got sand in his keyboard, it was Lucia's fault. I saw him messing with the keyboard: the sand screwed it all up. He didn't say anything, not even to me. He just closed it in an "I'll deal with this later" kind of way. Three days later Future Shop called to say Owen Collins' laptop is serviced and ready for pick-up.*

*Tonight, when Alex called to say he wouldn't be home until after midnight, "something came up," I asked Owen to watch the kids so that I could take a walk. The weather was perfect, and everything was quiet enough for me to hear the clap of my sandals off the sidewalk. I love the sound of that. And I love the colour of the sky this time of night. When it's purple and the clouds look black, not white. It's so peaceful; it is the longest and most soothing hour of the day. It makes the book you are reading that much more serene, it makes a walk to the bakery relaxing and not just exercise. It was Owen who pointed that out to me. It's appreciating the little things that makes Owen and Alex different men.*

*I married Alex for all the right reasons: he is a good man, a handsome man, a financially secure man. What I loved Alex for at first was that he saw more in me than other men. I've always had a façade that attracted men, but lacked whatever it takes to keep them around. They all expected some magic from me that I never had. So they got what they wanted from me in one hot and sticky night, and then realized I had no more to offer them than any other girl. Everyone but Alex. That is why I married him. He saw in me the wife and mother I could be.*

*But Owen, he sees it too. More than his brother ever did, and more importantly, now! He needs and appreciates my mothering him, my opinion on things, and he calls me his "agent" now, because whenever he lets me pick out what story to submit to a contest or journal, those are the ones that win. He notices the silliest things about me, like how supposedly oval my wrist bone is.*

*Lately it feels like everyone but Owen is a stranger, including me, just because he brings something to every day that the days we're apart lack. And I'm stronger now that he is here. I'm lost in you, Owen, with no need to be found. I am afraid of what that means. I am afraid of how good it feels. Some might call that love, you know.*

*~~I want an affair,~~*

*I want an affair,*

*with you.*

*Not even an affair. Not the sex anyway.*

*I just want to feel your body against mine. Your warmth, your shape. Your arms around my body.*

*I want an instant where there is no space between us.*

*What is that called?*

# A LOOK LIKE GOODBYE

A LITTLE MORE THAN A year after Owen's father went catatonic, his mother stopped going to visit because it "made no more sense than talking to a statue." She told Owen that their father wouldn't want him staying attached as if he were alive, and encouraged him to let go and move on. Owen knew it wasn't cold of her. He knew that visiting felt like going to her husband's funeral, week after week, because he felt the same way. He overheard her talking to their neighbour one night, from the patio just beneath his bedroom window.

"Looking at Roger now is like ... staring at a mirror that reflects who I *was*, and can never be again, you know? And it's been almost two years, but I don't know myself without that man. I know that sounds pathetic, I know it's time I–"

"No, it doesn't. Okay? There is no proper reaction to something like this."

Owen peered out the window and saw Nancy's hand on his mother's knee. They were sitting in patio chairs. His mother was slumped down in her chair with one leg tucked under her and the other sprawling out over the patio. A mug of tea rested on her belly, cupped by both hands.

"He's been away for well over a year now, and sick for longer than that, but … I dunno … I still roll over in bed at night and expect to see him there. I mean, we shared a bed for twenty-one years. It's a crushing instinct I have, a cruel habit. Some nights I'll wake up and pat the mattress beside me. Some nights I have this recurring dream where my bed is infinitely big. I dream that I wake up and walk for days and never find the end of it, and then I start looking for Roger, calling out his name until my throat and voice are chaffed into muteness. I'm walking and walking and the only thing I can see in any direction is mattress, with the edges blurred by clouds."

Owen watched her pause then and look up at Nancy, circling the top of her mug with a knuckle. "I just haven't slept the same since. You get used to that other body there in bed with you, you know? And it always feels so cold in my room now, even with the heat on bust or when it's twenty-odd degrees out."

She set her mug down on the table and ran a finger along the bags under her eyes. To keep the tears in, he figured. He felt her sadness, her bleak confession, like a cheapshot in the throat.

"I know all about it, Claire. I felt the same thing when I left Dan. The only time I missed him was when I crawled into an empty bed those first few weeks—"

"Exactly! Weeks. *Weeks*, Nancy. It's been the better part of two years for me. I am stuck in time, and I know the kids can see that, and I know that's not good for *their* recovery. And lately I feel like every time we visit him we're leaving a piece of ourselves behind in that wardroom. I can't do that to them anymore, and I don't have the strength left to do it to myself."

So Owen lied. He said he had made the basketball team and either had a practice or a game on Mondays, Wednesdays, and Fridays, but he'd be home by supper. A friend's mother would drop him off. Alex knew it was a lie, and his mother overlooked the fact that Owen was anything but an athlete. He was capable, but uninterested. Owen spent those six hours every week sitting with his father, reading, writing, and telling him about everything he was missing out on at home. Even though his father was entirely unresponsive, Owen let himself believe there was a non-verbal communication at play between them. He let himself feel the words that weren't there. He imagined their conversations.

He always left a copy of Saturday's *Globe and Mail* with his father before he left, and a final draft of any of his own writing, just in case. It was his father's descent into madness that sparked Owen's flare for writing. His stories served as a place to dump all of his emotional baggage, and then writing turned into his sole passion and talent. He longed for his father's guidance and opinion on his writing. He wanted desperately to return to that room and find one of his short stories covered in his father's eccentric and illegible hand-writing. To see a mess of red ink on his pages: Xs, check marks, jot notes, tips and suggestions, brutally honest constructive criticism. A smiley face, right up on the top left-hand corner, where a teacher would leave a grade. He pictured his father reading it; he saw the pages buckling under the grip of his large and chapped hand, the other hand using a red pen to prop his chin up like he used to do in his office while reviewing his own work. Sometimes, accidentally, it was the pen tip, not the pen cap that he'd prop his chin on, so it was common to see his father with red or blue streaks of ink on his chin. It drove his mother mad, always scouring her husband's face with rubbing alcohol. He'd just laugh as she tutted. A hearty laugh, like a man who appreciated his wife's taking the time to groom him. Sometimes he'd haul her into him for a kiss, or the kind of intimate hug that made Owen uncomfortable.

Owen always drew the curtains wide open as soon as he walked into the room. As wide as they would go, and then he stretched them some more. They were dusty and floral patterned, and he tied them up with the drawstring in a way that annoyed the staff. He did this because sunlight seemed to put some life back in his father's eyes, and he thought that maybe the sudden blast of light might wake him up. Some day. To Owen, it had to mean something that whenever he started rocking the rocking chair, his father would keep the motion going by himself. But never a word, never a look or a nod, just the occasional snickering outside the door from nurses or graduate students.

The secret trips to see his father cut into his lunch money on those three days a week, because he needed bus fare. After the hour-long visits with his unresponsive father, he would go sit at the bus stop bench next to Bowring Park. The park was always overflowing with father-and-son pairs. There was always a plethora of fathers feeding ducks with their kids, or pushing them on a swing, or warning them not to do a thousand different things. But it was never jealousy he felt, nor sadness. It was something much more profound, unfair, and inarticulate.

∽

Owen's neighbour, Nancy, had made his mother's recuperation a pet project of hers, and he loved her for it. Maybe she was a benevolent woman, or maybe she was a lonely woman, as sad and broken as his mother, looking for a friend in a neighbour. It didn't matter. She was the only person Owen heard his mother talk to about his father. Most of their conversations happened beneath Owen's window over tea, so he'd turn off his TV or turn down the music every time they'd get together to talk.

"… I'm not saying it's due time, Claire. I'm just saying you should let yourself be open to the idea of a new relationship is all. *If* something happens organically, go with it."

She laughed, and Owen smiled for her. That she could laugh now.

"It's not that I loved Roger too much to remarry, Nancy, my dear. I just can't entertain the idea of being with another man and losing it all again. And the truth is, I don't have anything left to offer a man. Roger took it all with him wherever it is he went."

"Oh c'mon, Claire. I mean—"

"What? It takes years to build a solid and meaningful relationship, and that long haul of firsts and fights and accepting each other's flaws … it's … it's just too exhausting. I just can't see myself going through all the motions and getting myself that far into a relationship again. Besides, there's nothing a man could offer me that I have any need for anyway, as an over-the-hill woman and mother of two, with an ill mother—"

"Oh poor you, Claire Collins. Boo-hoo! You're still a gorgeous woman and a wonderful person despite it all, so quit talking like you're dead. Why don't we start there? I mean look at *me*, Claire, I'd kill to have your face and your skin and your hair … and that body. I'd have me a man in no time!"

They laughed like they were old friends then, not just two single mothers trying to get back out into the world.

"I don't know, Nancy. We're out of the game." A school-girl chuckle. "I haven't been on a date since the sixties … *the sixties.*"

"Shhh!" They laughed like cackling hyenas. "I don't let myself go there, girl. Truth is I wouldn't know what to do with a man if I had one in my bed tonight anyway, I suppose—"

"Ah! I'd be a nervous wreck. I'd make a fool of myself, I would. I mean, when you're in a relationship for too long you get used to some safe but sterile routine with a man, you know? I mean, sure, it's mechanical and to the point, and the passion is gone, but at least you know what to do with each other."

"Hah!" Nancy cracked her mug down on the table so hard it echoed over her laughter. "You too, hey?"

Owen ran to his window to shut it. He wound the handle until he heard the wood creak against the frame and threaten to crack. He locked it, like that would make the glass more sound-proof. He hit play on his CD player to drown out their chattering, the specifics. He preferred to think of his mother as a mother, not a woman. Not a friend of Nancy. Not a woman who talked about *that* kind of stuff over tea.

But he didn't get to the window in time to spare himself the worst of it. He saw his mother winding her wedding ring around and around her finger, and heard one last sentence. "Besides, Nancy, I'm still a married woman."

She held up her hand with a brutal mix of bleakness, hope, futility, and unconditional love.

⌇

His mother missed her husband. He and Alex weren't enough. They'd go to sleep and she'd be in her room alone, with only infomercials and books as company. They'd go out to movies and parties, and some nights Owen pictured her home alone on the couch, watching a movie, laughing, turning to share the moment, but no one was there.

She started to bury herself in distractions. Monday night was movie night with the kids, Tuesday night was grocery night, even if they didn't need groceries. She joined a book club and a cooking class. She eventually found salvation in volunteering all her spare time away. Having no spare time meant she never had to evaluate her life, or compare now to then.

There was a battered women's shelter three blocks from their home that needed a woman who could spare them twenty hours a week. "It's a perfect match, it's fate!" She told Nancy all about it and explained her role there to Owen like she'd just won the lottery.

Helping out at the shelter initially distracted her, but over time she developed a genuine sense of purpose in being there. She started to feel alive again, and relevant. She befriended and almost mothered her assistant, Abbie Darenberg, and despite the two decades between their ages, they brought each back to life through their insightful, almost therapeutic discussions. She'd sit at the kitchen table, elbows on knees, with the phone in her hand, twirling the cord and laughing at Abbie for an hour or more each time she called. Owen would sit on the couch in the next room, pretending to be watching television, but not so secretly eavesdropping, smiling every time he heard his mother's from-the-gut laugh.

Within a few months, she was offered a full-time salaried position and took it. Owen was infinitely thankful to someone, or some*thing*, somewhere, for how her job had rejuvenated her. He noticed her shopping again, letting a few bright colours slip into her wardrobe. She'd stopped watching TV and started reading again. She started cooking nice meals, buying thick hardcovered cookbooks by the armload. Some nights, she and Abbie went out to the movies.

When Owen and Alex got their licenses near the end of grade twelve, they begged and pleaded to be able to drop her off at work, so they could be one of the few kids who took a car to school. She agreed, largely because of the frequency of vandalism in her parking lot – the car was safer parked at the school – but also because she liked to grant her sons' wishes whenever she could, as a sort of compensation for what had happened to their father. Every night, when she called them for a ride home, they'd flip a coin or argue about who had to go to pick her up. But the coin tosses and arguments died off after Owen met Abbie.

Owen was waiting impatiently in the car, flipping through a CD leaflet, when he looked up and saw his mother waving a hand to him, signaling him to come in. He parked the car and she buzzed him into the building. It was a moderately secure building, since the boyfriends, husbands, or fathers of the abused women often showed up, demanding to speak to their "loved" ones. The door was a deep burgundy with chips of paint dangling from it, exposing the silver beneath. It was also spotted with dents left by the feral men it had successfully kept out.

"Come in for a second, sweetie. I'm sorry, but we just got a new lady about five minutes ago, and I've got some paperwork to fill out. Wait in my office, have a cup of tea, and I think there's a few donuts left in the Tim Hortons box on my assistant's desk."

The second he walked into his mother's office and saw Abbie, he decided that if she were going to be around whenever his mother needed a ride home, he would be the one to pick her up. He started showing up early, hoping for the chance to see her.

Abbie was older than him, but not old enough to write the desire off as a fantasy. Her auburn hair blew like grass in the wind when she opened the window that day, and she never once tried to constrain it. She let the wind and sun do as they wished to her body. She bucked fashion and it worked for her. Her clothes, the way they clung to her, the way the wind tugged them against her, Owen could tell that what lay beneath was worth pursuing. She was warm: a close talker without invading personal space, the kind of girl you can befriend in one sitting and have forever as a friend. Three tattooed swallows flew up the soft vanilla skin of her right forearm. Green and red birds, the first tattoo he knew a person would never regret. They meant something to her, defined her, spoke for her. She had that esoteric, unconventional beauty that made monsters of supermodels.

She turned from the window to greet him. "Hi!" She said it so jovially, like someone everyone's always falling in love with, so he didn't have to feel pathetic. "Your mother always talks about you guys. Are you Owen the intellectual or Alex the genius?"

Her voice shattered him. That one look at Abbie, through his adolescent, hormone-soaked eyes, had him sitting by the phone every day and waiting for his mother to call, hoping Abbie would be working that day. It had him filling tissues at night, and filling the shower drains in the mornings.

When he confessed his crush to Alex, stating that they didn't need to flip that coin anymore, Alex mocked him. "You're pathetic, and she's like five years older than you. That doesn't matter later in life, but we're still in high school. The last thing you need–"

"Ah, whatever. High school is over in a few weeks. And you haven't seen the girl, man, I'm stunned stupid when I'm around her. It's not the kind of feeling I can ignore. I was sitting in Mom's chair the other day, leafing through a Hemingway novel she'd just finished and offered me a loan of. She was standing up, sort of beside me but behind me, with one hand resting on the back of my chair, sort of around me. I could just feel her there, you know what I mean? Like, if I was blind I'd still know how beautiful she was, you know? It was all I could do not to lay my head onto her belly and pray she wouldn't mind ... and ... I dunno, that she'd comb my hair with her hand. And ask me to marry her."

He shot his speechless brother a look that said, *Yeah, I know, right?* And laughed at himself. "I think I'll head over there now, pretend I was over to a friend's house and driving past, and didn't see the point of going home and coming back again."

"It's a two-minute drive, Owen, and Mom isn't off for

another forty minutes. It'll be a little obvious, don't you think? I mean ..."

His brother was still talking as Owen pulled the front door closed.

Every day Owen had an excuse to be early, in order to linger in her presence. One day she handed him a bottle of water, and when her fingers slid across his hand he felt something he hadn't felt since he lost his father.

The time he spent away from Abbie was agony, there was far too much of it. So he had to ask his mother over supper one night. " I like it there too, Mom, it's a great place, doing a great thing for the community, and I think you might need a few male employees there, for when those abusive men come by, screaming at the door, like last week. Abbie told me about Jim Croaker kicking another dent in the door. I'd like to volunteer there too."

She was stirring a pot of pasta, not even looking at him.

"Sorry, sweetie, but it's against policy to have men working there. Besides, no offense, but you'd do little to scare off the violent men we get beating on that door. Jim Croaker isn't even scared of the police, Owen."

She laughed as her son's true intentions came to her. As she laid a plate of garlic bread on the table she shot him a knowing smile. "She's a charmer, Owen, sweetie, I'll give you that."

His brother and mother laughing at him like that. The awkwardness of love exposed. He could only smile and play stupid, and maybe stop showing up so early for a few days.

One day, well into his pursuit of her, he joined Abbie outside as she finished a cigarette on her break. They were talking music. She offered him one of her earphones and introduced him to Nirvana. He reached out for the earphone, but she stuck it in his ear herself. The way her fingers ran down his earlobe convinced him that she felt something for him too. He felt the elation of knowing his courting her these last five weeks was working. As for the band, Nirvana, there was something fresh there, something new and so totally their age. And if she liked them, he'd go out and buy the album that night, just to be that much closer to knowing her.

∽

July third, to Owen and Alex, became a day as significant as their birthdays, as significant as Christmas Day and New Year's Eve. They had just graduated high school. It was a balmy summer's night – shirts clung to sweaty bodies and they had three fans going in the living room. They were watching TV, eating a chicken and rice casserole they'd eaten far too much of since their mother was always *so busy now*. When she called for someone to come pick her up that night, she was particularly cheery.

"Hell*ll*-*o*, lovely! Momma's ready when you are."

As always, because of Abbie, Owen went to pick her up. He dropped his fork, the plate still half full, and pulled on his shoes as he chewed his last mouthful of rice.

He headed for the shelter, desperately hoping to see Abbie waiting outside with his mother. He daydreamed of her confessing her love, or at least asking him to a movie. *Sure.* He'd say it nonchalantly. He practiced a warm-but-not-desperate tone. He pictured himself calling her, contemplating the opening lines, the options: *Hello* or *hi*, or *hey Abbie? Hey Ab?* Maybe *hiya.* You can come at some girls with a *hiya*, he figured. Girls like Abbie anyway.

But as he approached the building, neither of them was outside. They were both inside the door, trying to tug it shut as a man tried to force his way in. His arm, from the elbow up, was trapped between the door and the door frame, and he squealed in pain as they rocked the door against him.

Owen parked the car and met his mother's frightened eyes: the blue cast out of them by the black of her dilated pupils. She shook her head and yelled, bashing a palm off the glass of the window. "Owen! *Stay!* Stay in that car, Owen! Owen, you stay in that *CAR!*"

Adrenaline made the man look more manageable, less dangerous.

"Owen, *don't!* Stay in the car, lock the door! The police'll be here any minute! Owen, the police are on the way! Janine's on the phone with them."

Only in hindsight was it obvious that Jim Croaker – drunk and reeking of stale whiskey – could *never* have pried open that door.

There was something disgusting and inhuman about the shape of his face: the features so small and indistinct and rat-like. And the way he ground his teeth. His faded jeans were stained with blobs of motor oil, some fresh and some set, and his black track jacket reeked of sugary, cheap whiskey. His jacket was only half zipped, and a gold chain disappeared into a thick mat of chest hair lining the edges of his white tank top. Owen recognized him as Jim Croaker from Abbie's description: "A badly groomed mustache and hair so greasy you want to vomit." Jim had been desperate to get inside the shelter for over a month now, to apologize to his fiancée with his fists and insincere words. The last call to the police station had only kept him away for a week.

"*You fucken whores!*" He tugged at the door, and both of their bodies rocked with it. "I'm going to kill *both* of you sluts! Do you hear me! I am going to stamp your skulls into dust, right fucken here on this pavement!" His pasty white saliva sprayed on the window before their faces.

Owen figured he could easily take Jim down from behind, since he was pinned in the doorframe and obviously drunk. He wrapped an arm around his neck so tightly that Jim gagged and crashed his head back into Owen's face, smearing his greasy hair across Owen's cheeks and mouth. It tasted like rancid fish. Owen jabbed his hip into Jim's and swung around, taking them both to the ground. All two hundred pounds of Jim fell on Owen's chest, squatting the air out of his lungs. Within seconds, Jim was on top of him, his knees and elbows boring into Owen like screws as they struggled against each other's bodies.

It was already too late when Owen realized Abbie and his mother had had Jim much more secured than he did now, and that look in their eyes as he approached the door, a look of paralyzing and throat-clenching fear, registered as an omen that he'd made a mistake in tackling this man all by himself. Their lack of confidence in him was contagious.

Owen was not yet twenty. Jim was forty, drunk, and coursing with adrenaline. He belted Owen with three solid punches to the face, not the kind of falsely depicted punches Owen had seen in movies, where two grown men can slug away on each other. They were three unobstructed, powerful shots that had him scared for his life. Each one felt like a car slamming into his face. His head bounced off the ground with each punch, and the recoil hurt as much as the blow. His left eye swelled, clouding his vision and making him feel even more helpless. His nose had made a distinct popping noise before he felt liquid warmth spilling over his mouth and down his neck. Jim fired one more, before wrapping his bony, sweaty hands around Owen's throat.

"Still feel like being a fucken hero! Huh? I'm fucken talking to you, kid! How about I crack your neck? How about I choke you until your brain pops out your ears?"

Owen's arms were pinned down, and he was already winded before Jim had started choking him. His face was getting hot, and his ears were ringing, and then he heard the door open and saw his mother and Abbie dive at Jim. They took an arm each and tried to free Owen from his grip. He groaned and rolled off Owen and onto Abbie. He grabbed her wrists, pinned her arms down, and stared down at her, laughing maniacally. A string of drool fell onto her face.

"Now what, you little *bitch*? Huh? Now what?"

His mother looked down at him, sobbing, and Owen imagined himself physically deformed by those four blows. They both got up to go help Abbie just as Jim sank his head into her chest and bit viciously into her left breast. She shrieked and squirmed beneath his weight. They kicked at him and pulled at every limb, but it was futile. Owen threw himself down on Jim and tried to pry them apart, but couldn't without hurting Abbie even more. She screamed all her pain, unintentionally, into his ear as he fought against Jim. The neighbours kept their distance but were shouting at Jim like he was a rabid dog, reassuring them all that the police were on the way.

Jim crawled off Abbie when he saw the police car storming down the road. She rocked back and forth, crying, hurt badly, violated. She didn't even look up. She just rocked back and forth, her arms in a V across her chest.

As the police approached, Owen saw the look on Jim's face change in slow motion: furrowed eyebrows slowly unclenching and rising, an open mouth. He looked more panicked and flighty now than he did vicious, spinning around in one quick circle like he was being surrounded by a firing squad. When they were within ten feet of him, he grabbed Owen's mother and held her down in a headlock.

"Back off! Now! I'll snap her neck. I swear it! Back, the, fuck, up, now! Go get me Janine out of that goddamn building and let us go, or I'll fucken snap this bitch's neck." He was nervous now and watching his back. "She fucken deserves it, after nearly breakin' my arm like that!" His eyes darted around like a wild animal's. Like a cornered fox.

An officer called out, his words slow and deliberate, "Sir, you are not going to hurt her. You are not going to hurt her because harming her any more than you already have is only going to add to your charges. You don't want that. End this now, before you get yourself in even *more* trouble."

Owen was nervous about how the cop was handling the situation. He knew what they didn't know: Jim Croaker was no more human than a shark. He was drunk, violent, and irrational. He'd hurt her to prove a point, Owen knew it. The policemen were making all the false assumptions he'd initially made. And it didn't seem right to threaten the man. He'd only hurt her to prove that *he* was the one in control.

Jim stepped back against the building with a new surge of anger, like a tortured rodent just let out of a cage. He looked over at Owen and Abbie, now side by side and holding each other. He squinted at them in a cold, hard stare. "You think you fucken bitches won, huh? Is that what you think?"

"Sir—"

Owen stepped in front of the police officers and put up a hand to interrupt them. "Listen! This isn't about winning, okay? And even if it was, you won, look at my face." He tilted his neck left to right and back again to show Jim his swollen eyes. "This is about you getting what you want, and I'll give it to you. You let my mother go, and we'll let you in to see Janine." He turned to the police. "Won't we?"

The policemen looked at each other and changed the wording a little. "The *only* way you'll see Janine is if you let go of that lady, *right now!*"

Jim looked down at a football-sized rock by his feet. "Okay." He feigned defeat. "I'll let her go."

He said it so sarcastically it unnerved them all. He released her and stepped towards the police with his hands up, but swiftly bent down, picked up the jagged rock, and swung around. With all his weight and strength, he brought the stone down across Claire's head. Her skull cracked, she fell slowly but with a thud of dead weight, and Jim dropped the rock. Stared at her. Shocked at the damage. He took off running, not once looking back. For five seconds, even the policemen were silent statues: taken totally by surprise before gathering themselves. One of them called an ambulance as the other took off after Jim.

His mother had fallen like a building: slowly, until gravity took hold and ripped her down. There was a noise to it: a thud, a slight bounce, then her heels clapped. She convulsed, twice, maybe a third time. There was a lot of blood, but it was all contained in one giant pool at the back of her head. Like a pillow.

Owen felt all the weight in his body leave him. He had to consciously draw air into his lungs, and he couldn't get them full. Her eyes were still wide open and staring at him as he ran towards her, crying. He checked frantically for a pulse – his fingers fumbling around her wrist, trembling – but didn't know where to try and feel for it. He was squeezing her wrist too tightly anyway, feeling his own pulse, not hers, as he begged her to speak. She didn't say a word. He cried harder and shook her more vigorously, as if he could bring her back with the right jolt or tear-laden plea.

Abbie lay lengthwise along Claire's body and rocked her like a baby, combing the hair out of her eyes, crying violently, skipping breaths. His mother looked peacefully absent. It was the same look of goodbye he'd seen in his father's eyes, the day he went catatonic.

Owen turned to charge at Jim Croaker with the very same rock, but he was gone. One officer had apprehended him and taken him away, the other waited at the scene for an ambulance to show up, and, when the time was right, to collect a few witness statements.

By the time the ambulance showed up for his mother, her head was sunk into the ground and covered with flakes of soil. Bits of dirt rolled over her face with each gust of wind. She looked fake, like a mannequin. Abbie wept as wildly as Owen while the paramedics loaded his mother onto the stretcher, and they held each other the whole ride to the hospital. With everything happening at once, there was nowhere to lay it all except on each other.

~

They washed, numbed, then stitched his left eye and lower lip. Owen felt no pain, just a dull tug of thread and the impossibility of having to tell his brother about their mother. When the doctors were done, Owen borrowed change from Abbie and phoned Alex. The black receiver of the payphone felt greasy and slippery in his hands. He put in two dimes without hesitation, but held back on the nickel until he was sure he had the right set of words ready.

"Hello?"

Alex spoke like he knew: slow and soft and ready to be shattered. It had been two hours since Owen left to get their mother. Owen tried to talk in a tone that didn't reveal the news before the words, but even he didn't recognize himself in his voice. He laboured over every detail, and standing in that hospital hallway, under the harsh fluorescent lights, it struck him only then why it had all happened. It wasn't because Jim Croaker was a violent mule, and it wasn't because their mother had taken that goddamn job. It was because he had gotten out of the car, and she'd pleaded with him not to.

"C-can you come get me ... then?"

"I don't know, because, what if there's some news about Mom and I'm not h–"

"Do you h-have any money in your room I can take for a cab then?"

"Take it from Mom's piggy bank."

"Wha—"

"The second drawer in the nightstand on … on … Dad's side. It's full of change, but there's some bills too."

"She's still alive, right? Right, Owen?"

"They took her into the ER, so, that means yes … right?"

Abbie sat with Owen as he waited for his brother to show up, and her being there made it all more bearable somehow. They leaned on each other. The scent of her hair on his shoulder — rainclouds and wildflowers — made him feel like *something* was still okay. She held his hand and shared his pain; she took some of it out of him. The bench was hard and too long front to back, so he couldn't recline and get comfortable, other than against her. The whole scene with Jim Croaker had removed any unfamiliarity between Owen and Abbie, because two people cannot live through something like that without being bonded by it.

In the black of the night, through the rain-streaked window pane, Owen recognized his brother's hurried gait before he recognized his face. He leapt off the bench and burst out through the hospital doors to greet his brother, his hands in his pockets and his head slung down. Immediately, in each other's presence, Owen felt a slight but pronounced sense of relief. They exchanged a look, not words, and Owen guided him to the bench where a nurse had told them to wait for some news about their mother. An old woman across the hallway, in a paper-thin black trench coat, coughed and wheezed incessantly.

They sat there for hours that night. After the initial forty-five minutes of silence, Alex finally spoke, "I am only going to say this once, Owen, for the rest of our lives. I promise. But I do need to have said it, for my own sake, and

I am sorry ... but you could've stayed in the car. You could've stayed in the car, Owen." His bottom lip twitched as he repeated himself.

Owen didn't respond. He couldn't. And Abbie didn't interject, because it was true. And if Alex was going to say it only once, then fair enough.

# THE FELLING

THEIR MOTHER DIED IN HER coma, not long after the accident. Neither brother could remember exactly how long, those few days were a long blur of inseparable hours, but it was less than a week. Owen was sitting right there beside her when that distinctive, sustained beep howled from the machines leading in and out of her.

Owen was watching the rain on the window, watching raindrops flutter across the pane and connect to each other and fall away. The sound came out of the machine like hands wrapping themselves around his throat, suffocating him and holding him in place, stopping time – until a barrage of doctors and nurses stormed into the room and pushed him aside. They ravaged his mother's body with a defibrillator: her body jolted up off the bed with each futile shock. Her arms tensed and contorted; her fingers looked like they were snapping out of their joints. The commotion of people yelling over each other and the medical equipment and the weather on the window: it all blended together into one sonic assault on Owen, ripping the tears from his eyes and sucking the air from his lungs. The sounds echoed and bounced off the walls as he stumbled backwards out of the room – until his back hit the wall of the hallway. He slid down the wall, cracked his tailbone on the floor, and closed his eyes. The pressure of his shutting lids thrust a stream of tears down his face. He covered his ears and shrieked as if he was witnessing her murder.

The floor was cold and white, with flecks of black and grey. Stars of reflected fluorescent light flickered on the linoleum floor and disappeared into the shadows of people walking by. He stared at them blankly, in a way that told nurses and passersby not to bother him, to leave him there, undisturbed. No condolences would matter. He closed his eyes and pictured his mother, just a few nights earlier, laying her chicken and rice casserole in the oven, shutting the door with her hip, and laughing into the phone about some comment Abbie had made. She covered her mouth when she laughed, and tucked her chin into her chest, like a shy and nervous kid. It was the only time she ever looked defenseless, or at ease with the world.

A clamour of footsteps came towards him; he saw a flurry of feet rush past him, green scrubs falling onto an assortment of white and black shoes. He didn't have to look up to see and know: she existed only in memory now.

When he opened his eyes and looked up, Alex was sitting on a bench down the hallway, watching him. They stared at each other. They blinked, and people walked through their fields of vision, but their eyes stayed locked on each other. There were no words, but the familiarity and shared distress were vital, so they just stared at each other, one waiting for the other to say this was all too unreal to be real. And then Owen shot up and ran down the hallway like he could outrun the moment. Leave it all behind. He crashed through the hospital door and dove into the first empty cab he saw. He'd take Abbie the news of his mother, and then the rest of his life would be a mystery.

He felt like he had abandoned Alex in that hospital, but he knew one of them had to un-pause life. One of them had to break that stare and make it all real. Taking off like that was the only way he could do it. To leave his mother and to be near Abbie in as short a period of time as possible.

~

It wasn't an ideal courtship, but his mother's fate brought Owen and Abbie together. Abbie was twenty-two with the demeanor and wisdom of a caring, fifty-year-old mother. Owen needed that. He needed the soothing tone in her voice, and that hand on his knee as they talked. It smoothed the roughness off the reality of the words. It planed off their sharpness so they'd pierce a little less. *Dead. Alone. Guilt.*

"Jim Croaker did this to your mother, *not* you."

Abbie lived alone, and let the brothers spend all the time they needed in her apartment, cooking for them, driving them wherever they needed to be, helping them pack the last of their stuff up at their mother's. Abbie packed most of Owen's stuff for him, and chatted with Alex as she did so, to distract him while Owen aimlessly wandered the house. He was acting without thinking. He stuck a foot in his mother's fluffy black slipper, lifted bottles of hair products off her dresser to sniff them, their lilac scent stinging his nose. He lay in his bed, one last time. He opened a cupboard door in the kitchen and just stared at the pile of bone china they never once ate off. Why was it there? A never-used wedding gift?

They were staying with their father's parents now, and their grandfather was looking after all their mother's affairs: the will, the fate of their home, the car. Their mother had waived life insurance, and the brothers only now understood how much she had struggled financially. They'd falsely assumed she was receiving financial assitance from the government for their father's being institutionalized. If she was, there was no record of it.

Their grandfather had no legal title to their house, so the bank repossessed it, sold it, in a down market, and after paying off her credit card debts and outstanding loans, Owen and Alex were left with close to four thousand each. Not even enough for a university degree.

Owen and Abbie were eating supper one night when Alex knocked three grim, spaced knocks on the door. She let him in and took his jacket. "Quit knocking, Alex. It's never locked, just come on in, okay?" She spilled some pasta onto a plate for Alex, and excused herself to go read in her room. As she spun from the table, the waft of her hair had a warming, sedative effect on Owen.

The brothers sat on Abbie's couch all night, talking themselves through it all. It was a bright purple couch, covered in white cat hair, in a small living room. On her black walls, she'd painted a white cityscape mural with birds on telephone wires and buildings crowding each other. Owen found the room soothing; Alex found it strange. There was an old mahogany grandfather clock in the corner. Its tocking sound accentuated the somber silence. It made the tears heavier, fuller. They sat sharing stories and memories, sometimes with twenty long minutes of silence between conversations.

"I like how Mom covered her mouth when she laughed, as if laughter were as rude as belching."

A few minutes later. "I always laughed at how stern her voice sounded when she yelled at the characters in her favourite movies, you know? Like ... do you remember how she'd flail her arms around and jump out of her seat and slap at the coffee table?" Alex got off the couch to imitate her and laugh. He wiped a tear with the back of his hand and sat back down.

"Yeah. Dad hated it, hey?"

"Yeah." Alex said it skeptically, like he wasn't sure, and after a minute of silence, "Sometimes I don't really remember Dad, you know what I mean?"

"That's why I still go and vis–"

"That's not what I mean! I mean, how he *was*, you know? I don't want to forget Mom like that. That's all. Do you know what I mean?"

"Yeah, but, I think the fact that we can sit here and talk about her like this, it's a good thing. She made time for a movie a day. She laughed weird. At least she was a woman we can sit here and describe and reminisce over for days on end. I think we're lucky there. She can never cease to exist because we'll always be able to recollect her, you know? It's not the same with Dad. He was always so ... I don't know. He was such an enigma."

"A what?"

"A mystery, unknowable."

"Or crazy."

Alex laughed, Owen didn't. And an hour later Alex fell asleep on the couch, too stubborn and proud to come right out and say he wanted to be with his brother that night. As much as Alex had always needed camaraderie, he never could admit it, not even to Owen.

They slept sitting up on Abbie's couch that night, with their hands on their laps and their heads tilted to the left as if their necks were cracked. They looked slain. They looked unconditionally devoted to each other, the way a tree depends on its roots. They had the synergy of soil and rain: trivial apart, but together they nourished something bigger than themselves.

Abbie woke at 2 a.m. and covered them with her only comforter. She woke Owen by accident doing so, and sat back on the coffee table to watch him come to. Eyes squinted, lips licking his mouth free from the seal of sleep. "What ...

is … is everything okay? It's okay we're here, right?" He nodded to his brother.

She didn't have to answer that, and looked a little offended he'd asked. She stood up and looked down at Owen and his brother as if she admired them as much as she pitied them.

"This is rough, Owen, but at least you two have each other. I can tell, just from looking at you, that nothing will ever tear you two apart. Get some sleep. I'll be back home by twelve tomorrow, if you two need a ride anywhere. Okay?"

She sprang up off the coffee table to walk away as Owen nodded. He tugged his legs up onto a cushion and laid his head down onto the arm of the couch. "Thanks, Abbie. Seriously. You've been—"

She put a finger to her lips. "Don't wake your brother. Get some sleep."

Her feet made no sound as she walked away. He loved her for it. He loved her. He could taste that love in the meals she made him, and feel it in the way she put that blanket over him.

~

Their father had never been close with his parents, so to Owen, his grandparents were just two more strange faces around the table at Christmas dinner. He was only close to his mother's parents, but *her* father was long dead, and her mother was lost to Alzheimer's, and just as helpless and alone as Owen.

His grandparents were strict, devout members of a small, esoteric, and extreme Christian denomination. They were contemptuous of anyone not living *God's way*. Their condemnation immediately fell upon Abbie, and formed an instant source of tension between Owen and his grandfather.

"She's an outcast is what she is, and I don't want her callin' and I don't want her comin' over. I'll cut the phone lines and bolt the doors shut before I has a neighbour seeing us associatin' with the likes of her. You hear me, boy? Her and her blessed tattoos and her hair all coloured like that."

"What, three little birds on her arm and a streak of red in her hai–"

"And she was makin' a heathen out of your mother, last goin' off. Yes, she was. Them goin' out every night of the week. Had her dressin' like a reckless tramp too, she did."

A few weeks after the brothers had moved in, Owen's grandfather found him in the basement digging through old boxes that belonged to his father. They were filled with yearbooks, hockey cards, pictures of high school crushes in cheap plastic frames, Beatles and Bob Marley records. He was opening a box full of his father's high school newspapers when his grandfather charged across the room and kicked the box back into the closet.

"Shouldn't you be at work, boy?"

"I quit my job when ... you know ... because of Mom, so–"

"Yet your brother's at work today, right?"

"Yeah ... but he's back to work for show, because he's afraid people might think all this makes his life look even more screwed up and–"

"And there'll be no mention of that father of yours in my house, are we clear on that? Stop rootin' through all his stuff. I ought to burn all this is what ... but your grandmother won't allow it. That's where the man got his weak heartedness, his mother, not me!"

The way his grandfather stood there above him – Owen wanted to hit him the way he wanted to hit Jim Croaker. He wanted to transfer the undealt rage.

"You think of him as you wish and I'll do the same, but let's not share those thoughts, because he's brought me nothing but shame. Everything about the man is despicable. Never bringin' his kids up to the church, because he was too busy writin' them vigilante articles, I suppose. And now look at him, up in the friggin' Mental!"

He saw his son's schizophrenia as divine punishment, not a neurological disorder. God was mad at his heathen son and had punished him. His ignorance infuriated Owen, as did Alex's tolerating and defending their grandfather, because he was so clearly scared of having nowhere else to live.

"We can stay at Abbie's, man, she's already said so. We don't have to live here like two little fucken orph–"

"Oh yeah, sure. And get full-time jobs to pay rent instead of going to university, right?"

Owen stared at the ground.

"Owen, I know it sucks here, but it's temporary, and pissing the guy off isn't going to help."

His name was Baron. He always wore a cheap cardigan over a white dress shirt he insisted his wife iron for him first thing every morning. Owen guessed he probably beat that loyalty into her. Baron smoked a pipe in the house and it stank like mould. It made the house dank and dreary. There was no cable, the radio was always tuned to AM, there was no CD player, and all the books were non-fiction. He was a man who would just as soon kick a troublesome kid to the curb. He was a man too militant to distinguish between grief and devilishness.

The house itself reigned over Owen and his brother with its own unprecedented form of abuse. The walls bullied them in a way they could explain to no one but each other. Owen wrote a lot, and Alex checked the days off his calendar. In a few weeks he'd have a student loan and would be able to move into the campus residence up at Memorial University. It was already arranged: he'd be living in Bowater House on Elizabeth Avenue. Every morning Owen watched Alex roll out of bed, walk over to the calendar, and X off the day before. He said it was bad luck if he didn't wait until the day was officially over. In the top, right-hand corner of each day, he'd write in the number of days left until he could move into Bowater House. Something about the countdown, about seeing the numbers, something about his not having a countdown to something for himself, made Owen anxious.

Alex was equally concerned and contemptuous over his brother's lack of plans. They shared a room at their grandfather's, and one night before bed he confronted Owen. "So, like … what are you going to do … when I'm gone … like … in the fall? School-wise, or work-wise or whatever?"

Owen had full intentions of going to university, but needed more time off to absorb his mother's death before he could devote himself to carving out a new life. He didn't want to rush this transition and come out of it stunted somehow. But he didn't know how to share that.

"I don't know. I need to be more sure on a major before I start university, you know? Making the wrong choice, and locking yourself into a career you end up hating, that's suicide really."

"Most people don't know what they want until they're in there taking courses, Owen."

"Yeah, well, most people are only there because they think they have to be. Most people are in there wasting their time and money and scraping by with 50s and 60s, and I am not one of those people. Besides, it's not like I'm *not* doing anything. I'm writing, and writing is where my heart is, at least right now. And if I'm doing what feels right, how can that be wrong?"

Alex rolled his eyes and didn't respond. Owen changed the topic. "So what are you doing anyway? What courses are you registered for?"

"Biology major with a biochem minor. It's a good pre-med undergraduate route. And I start volunteering at that AIDS place in September too, so that when I apply to med school in a few years it will look like I've always been into volunteering. Most people are stupid and leave their volunteer experience until, like, a few months before they apply, and then it's obvious to the interviewers that they were only volunteering to look all good and noble and doctor-like in order to get accepted."

Owen had no comment on his brother's admittedly un-altruistic motivations. And he could tell that Alex was eager to move on and start a new life for himself and to forget all about his childhood, *their* childhood. Something about the disparity between their fall plans made Owen feel distant from his brother, but his reasons were convoluted and vague. He figured that Alex was going to be a doctor because nobody questions the past or character of a doctor, or if they do, any adversity they faced was admirable, not crippling or tainting in any way. Not like it would be for a struggling writer like Owen.

Owen started packing that very night. If he was going to *find himself*, or *reinvent himself*, he'd have to do it in a more nurturing environment, like Abbie's house. She'd already told him he was more than welcome, and at this point they couldn't stand being away from each other. They were ripe with the passion of new love and fully content with the notion of never leaving her bed. It was everywhere on earth, the only place they needed to be. No lights, no TV, just soft music and intimate, probing conversation in between sex. The floor of her room was littered with condom wrappers and used tissues, but that didn't look vulgar there in the flickering candlelight. When they had to be apart, they were talking on the phone until 3 a.m. about nothing and everything and feeling each other in their blood and guts and bones as they spoke. All the coincidences and *me toos* came up in those conversations, and the defining traits that bonded them. They made plans to turn her spare room into an office for him to write in. They had paint chips picked out, grey-browns that evoked poignant literary fiction.

When he knew he was about to move out, Owen took the time, out of an allegiance to his father, to provoke his grand-father, to challenge his archaic views on the world, to prove some point, if only to himself. Night after night his grandfather would turn red, hit walls, and scream his tonsils dry at Owen as Owen deftly pointed out why gays should be able to marry, why the environmental movement wasn't *hogwash*, why war was anything but noble and necessary, and how money spoke to everything *but* a man's character.

"You, Owen, you're what a parent fears their child becoming. *Nothing*. Worse than nothing. Just like your damn father. And look at you there, smirking like that was a compliment. Smirk all you want, boy, because I seen that same smug look on your father's face and I'll promise you one thing: this world is going to bend you out of shape til it breaks you. I guarantee it. It'll snap you like it snapped that father of yours. And then we'll see who's smiling, won't we? People like you. People like your father. There's just no place for you here in this world. This world is going to eat you alive, boy, and I pray I'm still here to say I told you so."

Baron wasn't sad to see Owen go, just five weeks after he took him in. He verified Owen had a job at a record shop on Duckworth Street and somewhere else to sleep, and then let the door slam shut behind him.

The brothers were ready to move on with their lives the day Owen left their grandparents' house, but that meant moving apart from each other, something the two brothers had never thought of before Owen left that day. That first night at Abbie's he tossed and turned in bed, ravaged by an ill-defined anxiety. Abbie turned on a lamp and sat up against her headboard. "You're really going to miss Alex, aren't you? Is that what's wrong?"

"Not *miss* him, no, it's not that. I don't know. It's just weird to think about him not being here ... tomorrow, or ever. I don't know. Does that make sense?"

# TURN AROUND,
# TURN EVERYTHING AROUND

*August 12th, 2008,*
*At the cabin, just Owen and I.*

*This is dangerous. This is exciting, liberating, terrifying. My sister is watching the girls again, and Alex is at some infectious diseases conference down in the States. In Atlanta. It is only the two of us up here for three full days.*

*The obligate silence between us is unbearable now. I want to scream it and relieve myself: you feel this too, right? I almost hope not, <u>almost</u>.*

*And the need for no space between us: he feels half a world away, sitting beside me on the couch. I want nothing between us. I want to hold him, just once, so close that there isn't even any air between our clothes. I want us pressed together that tightly. I want his warmth to seep in through my pores. I want to feel his chest against me as he breathes.*

*I can't be still standing next to him now, whether we are in line buying snacks at a gas station, or at the kitchen counter cutting vegetables for supper. I am alive with him and he is my blood, my skin and bone. Where gums meet teeth and the bend of my elbows. He is adrenaline coursing through me.*

*And he is not my husband. He is not the man I married. He is the biggest complication in my life. He could destroy everything for me. He might not be worth it in the end. He is nothing, by title: brother-in-law. It even sounds so distant, and formal. He is a tidal wave and I am not running for cover.*

*In fact I am diving in. Or wading at least. Dipping a toe in, a little deeper every day. And it is weird to think of Alex as the shark, not the warm sand coaxing me from the water, back to the safety of the beach.*

*Today we swam. His body is somehow symbolic of his utter disregard for vanity. Alex pays fifty dollars a month to have his chest waxed, and more than that on a gym membership. Owen is moderately hairy and twenty pounds overweight, and wears it all like a shield, like one more reason a woman couldn't, or shouldn't love him. Although he laughs at himself, he talks like he's not worth a woman's time, and yet, in another life, he could have all of mine. He could have all of any woman's, and he really doesn't know it. It's almost sweet, but the levity-laden self-deprecation pisses me off.*

*I ran a finger along a C-shaped scar on his back and asked him how it got there. "Lost a fight," he said. "There was broken glass on the ground, and three men stamping me into it." Then he laughed a little. "Funny thing is, losing the fight sort of led to me ending up living with you and Alex." And he told me the rest of the story. How he wouldn't be here, on this wharf with me, if it wasn't for that scar I'd just asked about and run my fingers over. How and why it got there lead to leading him here. To me. He didn't say "to you," but it was awkwardly apparent that's what he meant.*

*I could have changed behind the bushes today after our swim, or in the boat shed. Instead I asked him to turn around and close his eyes. I did this to be naked in front of him. Safely. No adultery. No throwing away an eight-year marriage, stability, a good man, daily visitation of my two children, half my belongings. I had a chance to be naked in front of him and I took it as a compromise. I asked him to turn and close his eyes while I got dressed. I took off my bathing suit, a new one bought just for this trip, and stood before him a good long thirty seconds before slipping on my clothes. I'd never felt more a woman in my life. Even the shadow I cast had a life to it. It made an object of me, something beautiful, desirable, useful, natural. It reduced the complications of this thing between Owen and me. We are only human after all, and love makes us weak. Weak, not wrong. Love makes us weak so we will succumb to it, give into it.*

*My bra was filled with insects and spruce needles and dirt, so I left it. I left it there on the ground for him to see, maybe. My best bra. Why did I pack it for a trip to the cabin? I wore no bra so that later he'd notice how perky I am without that bra. So that later, if I felt like innocently bending over the salad bowl at supper, he'd see my breasts and I could feel his eyes on them. I could imagine what he'd do to them. I could imagine how he'd roll his tongue around my nipple, how it would grow hard in his warm mouth. I thought about all this, I planned all this as I stood naked in front of my husband's fascinating brother. I didn't even feel bad. Just noticed, appreciated, respected. Simple things no man in years has made me feel. Beautiful.*

*I felt a little let down he could resist turning around.*

*I am seducing him now, flirtatious rather, I am guilty of that, but I am not crossing any lines. No physical ones anyway. If we are to make love, give into this obvious mutual attraction, it will be at this cabin, maybe right on that wharf. We both feel liberated and alone here. We feel ourselves here. It's another world, distinct and separate from the life we lead in the city. A world where the things you truly want, for all the right reasons, need no apologizing for. If there is one thing left stopping me from choosing Owen over Alex, it is having to explain myself to everyone. It's not guilt that is stopping me. Guilt has no place where the intentions are all right.*

*It wasn't me who let this marriage die. I married to wade in the feelings Alex once gave me. The ones Owen now lathers me up in. There is a reason they call it falling in love. It always happens by accident, and it's always too late once it happens. You've already fallen, you're already stuck. Right or wrong.*

*I want to be that ethereal, impossible girl he so desperately longs for in all of his stories. I want to be his non-fiction happily ever after.*

# ONCE IS ALWAYS ENOUGH

OWEN POURED TOO MUCH OLIVE oil in the pan and had the temperature too high. He flung two steaks onto the frying pan and a geyser of hissing steam and oil shot up off the stove and seared his forearm. It felt like a nail punctured his arm. He jumped back in pain, clutching the wound and cursing.

Abbie didn't even look up.

He thought of how differently she would have reacted years ago, even months ago. How she would be in the bathroom right now, running cold water over a facecloth and calling out to him, worried that the burn would blister. He pictured how she'd scrunch up her face as she tended his wound – pursed lips and a long inhale would prove her sincere sympathy.

Now he could set himself on fire and know that she wouldn't look up from that goddamn textbook.

She had just gotten off the phone with Alex. Owen heard her asking all about the complexities of muscle contraction. He could tell from his brother's rapid-fire responses that Alex didn't even have to pause to think about the answers. He explained the roles of actin and myosin and Z-lines and calcium pumps, and her pencil scratched and hurried across the page. His brother would get her through that physiology course, and something about that placed him and Abbie in two different worlds.

Something about that made him feel like what he chose to do with his life was wrong.

He tried again, with a playful kick in his voice, "Hey, Abbie, you're pretty much a nurse now. C'mon, what do I do with a burn? Abbie?" He waved his arm in her face.

She looked up at his slightly reddened arm. "I wouldn't call *that* a burn."

He let it go. He ignored feeling like a fly on the wall she didn't have the heart to swat. He went to get the cold facecloth himself, and when he took it away from his arm, he felt vindicated by the blister. He rushed out to the kitchen to prove her insensitive, or wrong, or something more vague and important than that.

She was flipping the steaks. "You've got them charred, Owen!"

"I burned my arm! What's your problem?" He waved a forearm at her from across the room.

"You! And don't get snotty with me! I worked nine to five today, and I have a physiology midterm tomorrow. You were off all day and you can't even make us supper? You *forgot* to go out and get garlic and mushrooms, then you *char—*"

"I was busy today too, and I'm sorry I forgot."

"Busy what, writing?" The way her eyes rolled and her head slumped substituted all the words she kept on the tip of her tongue: *Writing doesn't count as being busy. Wake the fuck up already.*

She slammed down the metal spatula. It jangled and flung steak juice across the counter and onto the sleeve of her white shirt. "I'm sorry, Owen … I… I'm sorry." Trembling lips now, and glossy squinted eyes. "You've burned your arm and I'm yelling about the steaks, and I'm sorry for that ... but we both know it's not about the steaks. And. I'm sick of pretending ... about us."

She was staring at the floor, not him. She folded her arms across her chest, and he thought of the J-shaped scar on her left breast, in the fold of her cleavage, there since the day Jim Croaker attacked her and killed his mother. Nine years into their relationship, that scar still took him back to that day. In the summer, if she wore a low-cut top, she'd smear some foundation on it to camouflage the pink. Her conscious effort to conceal the scar was what made Owen's guilt and culpability no less potent as the years went by. He thought back to how their relationship had started: two people with nothing but each other, and no need for anything else. He shot forward to how this would end: two people needing something more than they could offer each other.

He thought of the first time they made love, not even a month after his mother died. They were on Abbie's couch, and the way she kissed him vibrated through his lips, rattled down through his ribcage, and massaged him from the inside out. He was shy and awkward and a little embarrassed by the hard lump now squat between their bodies, almost painfully pressed up against the denim of his jeans. She only giggled, scissored her hands, and slid her own pants down. She took her shirt off and asked him to do the same, but he never heard her – the sight of her body had deafened him. He was all eyes and hands now, and she was the only thing on earth. He was still taking it all in as she tugged at his pants: the delicate pink folds awaiting him, the way her breasts fell away from each other, the arch of her collarbones. Even the way her bones pressed against her skin and shaped her transfixed him; the out-jutting of her hipbones and her outstretched arms made a net of her, something to fall into. She pulled him into her herself, guiding him into the welcoming warmth and wetness that dropped and hollowed his jaw. The soft clench and tug of her against him now, her seemingly endless depth, relieved his every want and need. He exhaled his every sorrow and then filled himself with the sight, sound, and smell of her.

That day was the only time he'd ever been aware of his own heart beating in his chest and the architecture of his every muscle. He kissed her, and felt some part of him leave his body, enter hers, and come back to him better than it had left him. He watched her finger rub tiny circles just above where he was inside of her, and the sight was so potent he had to look away or finish too soon.

A cloud must have shifted, and a bright beam of light burst in through the living room window. It poured itself across the floor, crept up her left leg, crawled up her smooth white belly, and illuminated her bare chest. It made the scar on her breast glisten red. It was the first time he'd ever seen it. He ran his thumb gently across it – it felt glossy against the smoothness of her skin – and his face exploded into tears. He fell into her arms and wept without explanation. He didn't have one to offer. After a few minutes, she plucked the deflated condom from his flaccid penis, threw it on the floor, and shimmied back onto the couch to better cradle him, combing his hair with her fingers and humming *shhhhh shh shh shhhh, shhhhh shh shh shhhh.*

She tore him back into the present. "It's a charade, Owen, a lie. We are lying to ourselves now … and that is tainting this beautiful thing we had. It's just. Every day of this takes away another memory of how it was."

She looked up from the floor and met his eyes. "I don't want to come out of this relationship with more bad memories than good, and I want to think fondly of you, Owen. You know I'm right, right? This has to turn itself around or end."

At this point, neither of them cared enough for another argument or conversation about *it/that/us.* They had spent eight and a half years together in utter bliss, and then another half year pretending, faking bliss, clinging to what was, and ignoring the inevitable signs of their demise. They were going to bed at different times and only selectively listening to the details of each other's days, and they seemed cold and indifferent to each other when one of them burned an arm on a hot pan or had a bad flu. Their problems were redundant now, and the fighting seemed habitual and unproductive, yet they loved each other enough to be crushed by knowing they were drifting apart. Residual love and a plethora of fond memories made a mess of them: they were a composite of yesterdays too intricately woven to be pulled apart.

She stormed off to their bedroom and slammed the door shut behind her. Although Owen never knew what it was he was doing wrong, it still pained him to hear her in tears behind a closed door. It was a heartache he felt in his throat and teeth, like a dry cry. She wept so wildly at times that she hyperventilated, and one night he heard her throw up, violently, as if she were throwing up her heart. She was precious, too precious for tears, and every sob she wept hacked into Owen. Blows from a rusted axe. She said it was his lack of presence in their relationship that got to her, but he didn't know how to make himself more *there*.

He stood on the other side of the door and listened to her haul a dresser drawer open, as she always did. She'd always dig out a small scrap of paper Owen had given her when they first met, some prose on how much she'd meant to him. She'd throw it in his face like it was a lie, like he'd deceived her, on purpose. Like he never once meant those words. *You made me feel invincible, Owen … and perfect for someone … You made me believe in, in … you … and us … and ….*

The only difference on this night was that he could hear her tearing the note into a thousand little squares, and the sound of it felt like she had scissors shredding their way through his heart. Each rip was so definite and final and symbolic of her commitment to move on and find what he was denying her.

He grabbed the door handle.

"*Don't*, Owen!" She grabbed the handle on the other side of the door and pressed all her weight against it. He heard her nails click off the hollow wood of the door, and he placed his hand where he imagined hers to be. Her fingers still killed him: so thin and feminine they bent at each knuckle.

"Just ... leave me alone, okay? Just ... go ... for now."

He walked back out to the living room and threw himself down into the computer chair. It slid a few feet, and the wheels against hardwood rolled like thunder. For weeks now, he'd exhausted himself trying to pinpoint why they were falling apart, how something once so flawless was now nothing but flawed. He wheeled himself back over to the computer and flicked the mouse to turn off the screensaver: a slideshow of photos on their computer, years literally flashing before him. What he saw was a photo of them on a three-day hike in Gros Morne National Park, running away from everything in the world but each other. Her with a thin, bright blue scarf wrapped around her head like a veil to keep the insects out, him the same, in an extra scarf she had. A pink one. *Any chance we can swap colours?* She giggled and shook her head. *You look too cute in pink.*

There was nothing that day but the crunch of detritus beneath their feet and immaculate, unspoiled scenery. They hadn't seen another person in forty-eight hours. There was something about seeing her all rugged there ahead of him on the trail, ravaged by the elements – frizzy hair and a sunburned face – and still trucking through the trees with an oversized backpack hiding everything but her legs. A frying pan, tied on to her pack, slapped gently off the backs of her thighs with every step, except when she'd turn around and smile at him, maybe every tenth step, just checking that he was still there. A smile and a look that meant she needed him to be there.

He wanted to run down the hall and ask Abbie if she remembered that trip – how he'd convinced her to take a *roll in the wildflowers* with him that day, and they laid a blanket down, and when they took it up off the ground forty-five minutes later there were three colourful butterflies squat dead beneath it and she was mortified. But he stayed in the chair, he stayed away like she'd asked. He opened his computer, because writing was the only way he knew how to process his thoughts. To write them out and see them for what they were:

*How, and why, has love taken what it was supposed to give us? The fire is still there between us, endless beautiful memories make it flicker, but with no wood left, no fuel, what keeps fire alive? With no hope for the future, what keeps love alive? Memories aren't enough.*

*I love the Jason Molina lines:*

*"We are proof*
*That the heart*
*Is a risky fuel to burn.*
*What's left after that's all gone*
*I hope to never learn.*
*But if you stick with me*
*You can help me*
*I'm sure we'll find new things to burn.*
*Because we are proof, that the heart, is a risky fuel to burn."*

*What is left when it's all gone? What is left of me now?*

*Madly in love with Abbie Darenberg, I let myself believe nothing else mattered. There was nothing on earth worthwhile but her, and us, wrapped up on the couch watching a movie. And now, free-falling out of love, suddenly everything matters. Painfully. The job I don't have, the degrees I never finished, the family we'll never have. If she was everything to me, what is there without her?*

*Take the bones from a body and watch it fall useless to the floor. I put her where my bones once were, in my veins and arteries as my blood. Life happens so slowly that we never feel ourselves changing until we've changed so much we cannot recognize who we once were. It's all there in that picture of course, us in pink and blue scarves and alone in the world, but those two people, that moment, it's all dead and gone and alive only in a photo – a deceitful piece of glossy paper.*

*I won't know myself without her. I will have shattered who I could have been in being with her. I want nothing but who she was, when I was who I was. How does time spill in between two people like that? Put a stream, and then an ocean between them?*

Abbie was thirty-one, and their age difference was rearing its hideous face. She was envisioning a future and Owen was revealing himself as more of an obstacle than a part of that future. When she saw a cute little girl in a coffee shop now, or watched a proud new mother pushing a carriage, she thought of having her own children. He knew it in the way she clutched his arm, smiled, and nodded at the child.

She'd gone back to university *to get a better job, so I can provide for a child,* and at this point she had just about finished her nursing degree and she resented him for dropping out of university two years ago *to take his writing more seriously.*

"You were loving geology, you were getting letters from the department congratulating you for the straight A's, and you were all giddy about it. Remember? I don't get it! You have a closet full of goddamn rocks in plastic cases. Labeled.

You'd tell me the differences, why rose quartz is pink not white, and why shale breaks so easily. You loved it. People don't just–"

"Lov*ed*. I *loved* it. And now I don't. Well, I do. I have an interest in geology, but not in a *career* in geology. I'd have no time for writing, and I'd be away too much, you know?"

"You've got to think about your future, Owen. If you can't see into your future, you're never going to get anywhere."

"I am thinking about my future! I'm trying to avoid locking myself into a fucken cage of a life."

"You're such a kid sometimes, you know that? Look at your brother, he's happy, he's getting a life set up. He just got married and is quite excited about–"

"If you think my brother is a happy man, you're an idi ... you ... you don't know the guy."

"Oh, what? Just because he doesn't hate the world or quote from *Walden* he doesn't know what 'true happiness' is? Is that it?"

Owen raised his eyebrows, like, *Well, yes. Sort of.*

Shaking her head, furious, taking her supper out to the computer desk to eat it alone. "This isn't about Alex, you always steer the conversation off track to deflect me!"

He shouted at her back, "Actually, you're the one who brought up Alex."

"It's not about Alex!" she howled. "It's about me being stuck in a relationship with some dispirited kid!"

He felt the barrage of exclamation marks.

"Why can't you just admit you only want me to stay on the geology track for the money? Admit it, and I will. Admit it and I'll play the fucken game and get buddy-buddy with all the right people and name-drop my way into an *ideal* job and buy you a wedding ring that puts all your friends' to shame. Just fucken admit it and I'll throw my goddamn life away for a backyard swimming pool and gaudy, oversized wedding r–"

She threw her fork at him, a bit of steak still attached. It knocked a picture frame off the wall and the glass shattered, the image no longer visible beneath fractured shards. They spent the rest of the night in different rooms. It was journalism that Owen really wanted to do, but that was offered only in Stephenville, a ten-hour drive away from Abbie.

They went to Blockbuster to rent a movie. What one of them picked up, the other rolled their eyes at.

"Let's just go home, I'm sure there's something on TV. We'll have some Jiffy Pop and root beer?"

He smiled and nodded. He knew he still loved the girl by the way her adoration of Jiffy Pop and root beer made him laugh. The specifics of who she was. The familiarity he couldn't let go of, for fearing of losing himself along with her.

When they crawled into bed that night, Owen sensed the sort of paused silence that meant a serious conversation was coming. She was merely organizing her thoughts and arranging the words into a short punchy order. She couldn't accept his abandoning university and had lost interest in his writing when it became clear he might never earn a living from it. Then it was just a waste of time he should be spending on a degree, or at least a better job. It came up in bed that night.

"I'm a writer, Abbie. My day job is secondary, and the more time I spend writing the better quality–"

"Are you?" She finally let herself say it. "What have you published, Owen, besides some shorts in a few lit journals that you never even got paid for? Call yourself a writer when you start earning a stable income from it, okay? All right!"

"Not everything's about money. And maybe one in a thousand published writers actually make a living from—"

"And life isn't a fucken fairytale. So keep your head in the clouds, Owen, try your little heart out, but don't consider yourself noble, consider yourself a fool."

She rolled over and hauled all the blankets off of him. The room was cold, but he didn't bother tugging some back. Her sudden lack of support silenced them both. She cried herself to sleep again, and Owen waited for her to fall asleep before reaching for his notepad and heading out to the living room. If they were going to break up, he could at least fuel his writing with the emotions and insight into love that their demise evoked. But she rolled over as he was getting up, and she spoke with no reluctance, spieling it all out in one rant.

"When I look at you, I see a dispirited kid going nowhere. Another dark wannabe writer. Definitely not husband and father material. Your depressive nature has become a chore, a flaw I falsely assumed I could fix, or something I initially attributed to your mother's death that I assumed you'd get over, like ... like Alex has. And, initially, you had this refreshing, quixotic, and atypical approach to life that was endearing. Now, at our age ... or my age, I guess ... it's just pathetic. You're in no position to provide for a child, and don't seem to be heading in that direction. It's not like we haven't tried or fought for us, Owen, but I just can't picture us five years from now. I can't see you tucking our daughter and all her friends into a minivan and taking them to the movies."

∼

A few weeks later, after they'd broken up, he walked over to the university to buy a newspaper and to sit and circle apartment ads. There was a lost, first-year blonde sitting on the same dated, burgundy-carpeted bench. She was cute, an awkward and shy studious blonde, not the supermodel type. She was drawing cats and flowers in an exercise book next to a math problem she couldn't solve. She doubted herself, he could tell. She could figure it out if she tried, but lacked the confidence to bother with it.

Sitting there on that bench, surrounded by eager students, academic jabbering, and posters recruiting students to study abroad or volunteer for psychology experiments, Owen questioned why he'd ever left Memorial University. He thought it was as simple as no programs that interested him, but in that moment he realized it was something more profound. Indifference. An indifference to something those hundreds of students hovering around him were so mindlessly dedicating their every thought to, like bees at work in a hive, questioning nothing.

And maybe it was an even more profound revelation that he wasn't one of them. And maybe his grandfather had been right that day, about him and his father. *This world is going to bend you out of shape until it breaks you ... there's no room for your type here, boy.*

As he walked home, he found himself fixated on Abbie's "new friend at work," Adam Fleisher. Weeks ago, Owen pulled up in front of the hospital and watched them laughing together in the porch, her hand on his shoulder fit perfectly into the groove of his collarbone, like hands that knew where they lay. Days later it was, *Oh, it's okay. Adam can drive me home. You needn't come get me.* Three nights back she was explaining her situation with Owen to Adam on the phone, not too quietly. *No. I've told him he's fine here until he finds somewhere new. No, I haven't seen him try and find a place, Adam, but that doesn't mean he isn't looking! You don't understand, we have a relationship that extends beyond ex-boyfriend-girlfriend.*

He got home and turned the key to what was now *her* apartment. He started supper, and as the peppers fried and the chicken seared, he dialed a phone number he'd jotted down off a telephone pole he'd noticed on Water Street while he was walking home: *Downtown Appt. Available Immediately.*

Available immediately was all he needed to see. He was done torturing himself with the awkwardness of sleeping on Abbie's couch while Adam slept in her bed. She had given him a reasonable period of time to get out of her apartment before she started letting Adam spend the night. Sometimes he heard them moaning, and the bedsprings grinding into the bedframe. The images interfered with his breathing. Rage, coated in a sadness that made a pulp of his lungs. He pictured how she looked seconds before an orgasm, so free and lost in a place only he could take her for those nine years they were together, her eyes open but shut, silently screaming. And now Adam was that man.

He thought of how she was a link to his mother, at least in some small inarticulate way. He would miss her most in the mornings: how cold the room would be and how warm her body was. He wrapped himself around her every morning to warm himself before crawling out of bed. The days would be that much colder now without her. He'd miss that little purr she made when he wrapped his arms around her to wake her on Monday mornings. She slept naked and looked so pristine and innocent as he kissed her forehead and crawled out of bed. To Owen, nothing was more attractive than a woman comfortable in her body like that.

He thought back to that overheard conversation between his mother and their neighbour ... *Nancy?* How it was the empty bed that got to his mother too, as it now would him. There would be an emptiness now, a physical nothingness beside him. Shouting. A longing and melancholy that would nip at him like a pest every time he rolled over and she wasn't there.

# A PLASTIC SMILE

*August 19th, 2008,*
*At the cabin, restless in bed.*

*I think Owen resents me for it. When he sees me take money from Alex, when Alex opens his wallet and counts out some sum of cash or hands me a card, I feel like a bratty teenager getting her allowance. Not a wife. Not a woman. But only since Owen has come here.*

*I chose it. I quit my job and I'm comfortable with it, but it's an awkward place to be really. I resent the ditz stereotype of being the stay-at-home doctor's wife, the girl who can buy the fancy shoes because of her _husband's_ job and not her own. It means everyone assumes I don't have a brain in my skull, a university degree, any ambition. That I am a sex-toy, a maid, and a mother only. A living slap across the face of the hard-working professional woman. I resent myself for having given into it. For being guilty of it. For throwing away all my own personal and professional goals to be the woman who irons his shirts and makes everything secondary to him. But I chose this life, that's what people neglect to consider, and nine days out of ten, I regret nothing. But lately, and today, searingly, I hate that I have to question if every loving wife is so quick to pick up her husband's dry cleaning or if there is a silent understanding at play here, the perks of my easy life come at the cost of a split role: wife and servant.*

*Because of denial, uncertainty, the vagueness of memories, and the complexities of love, I'll never know how differently I'd feel about my husband and our marriage if he was flipping burgers at McDonald's and I was the doctor. I'll never know if he looks down on me for my lack of professional integrity, or whatever you want to call it. I do know Alex finds it an attractive trait when a woman is ambitious and well-off through her own accord. What does that say about me, his wife? It is one definite thing he can't find attractive about me. And can he really not resent me for having to pay the full bill on our vacations, mortgage payments, and nights out?*

*I'll never know if other people, like Owen, think about this as much as I do. I'll never know how much it alters my sense of self and other people's perception of me. I've heard Alex talk about the girl who left Owen because he was "going nowhere," and I automatically assume the girl made a mistake and regrets it. Daily. I automatically assume she's a shallow bitch. And I automatically can't help think I am no better than she is. No more right or wrong. Whatever she turned out to be in leaving Owen. Sure, Owen has the capacity to be a great partner, a great husband and father. But the truth is, it's there, in the back of your head, no matter what: he'd be a father to a kid whose friends have nicer clothes and the latest toys and technology. He'd be a great husband whose love would balance out the lack of luxury, but you'd still dream about seeing France and Italy as you lie in bed in your modest house.*

*I am accepting of things I shouldn't be so tolerant of: Alex's lack*

*of attention, his jokes about how easy the housewife life is, and
an insecurity he is messing around on me. It's probably
nothing, but sometimes, when he is away, he calls less than he
does other times, so I imagine another woman – a more
professional woman – sharing his hotel room on those trips
when he doesn't call, or calls to say he probably won't bother
calling later. It's probably nothing, but I find it hard to believe
doctors have to work so many overnight shifts and overtime in
general, and I've seen some of those woman, some of those
ditzy girls, he works with. It's probably nothing, but someone
calls here all the time, and hangs up when I answer. It's
probably nothing, but that scarf haunts me, and he'd be naïve
enough to think all women would like the same scarf.
"Which of these scarves is the nicest?" I pointed, giddy, like this
meant I was getting that scarf for Christmas, only I didn't.
So who did?*

*It's in the back of my head, the humiliation, that if he is
cheating on me I might have to turn a blind eye to it. I am
financially dependent on him, he is a living paycheque. It's a
weird trait to attribute to the man you love. To need him for
the wrong reasons. Is it an occupational hazard of the
housewife? Am I required to try extra hard to please him,
sexually, domestically, and otherwise, and still keep my chin
up and respect myself?*

*And I'm trying so hard to love him like I used to, but I'm
finding that consciously trying only makes things worse. This
lifestyle of mine. People are envious of it, but those people
aren't me. People are envious of it, but it's all an illusion, I
guarantee it. Like how watching a magic show isn't so
exciting when you know the rabbit was in the hat in the first
place. The supposed magic of my marriage is all illusion. Why
do some people, who know no better, think that being a doctor
makes a man the ideal husband? A doctor can neglect his wife
as much as anyone, more really, when you consider all the*

*hours they work. And a house this size, after the novelty wears off, really just boils down to having one more bathroom that needs cleaning. I am married to a kind and attractive doctor, but the perfect life and the perfect love are two different things. Owen's right, it's no wonder we're all so goddamn unhappy.*

*I am aware this isn't real anymore. It's a bad movie getting undue praise. Lately that thin line between housewife and wife is blurred, scrubbed clean off the floor. I am not sure how much we mean to each other anymore, how necessary we are to each other. I feel like his roommate most days. Not the woman he's thinking about all day at work. When this started, I felt him thinking about me when we were apart. I wasn't being naïve.*

*And spare me the perks. The more I fill my life with shoes and bullshit, the less I feel I have. I get bored lately, I pace the halls, I feel like a fat waste of life, convincing myself a lot of daytime television is educational or somehow lifestyle enhancing: the gardening tips, the cooking shows. Since I realized I am lying to myself, since Alex stopped squeezing my shoulders when we passed each other in the hall, all I feel is emptiness, and nothing could feel worse or more persistent. There is no logical origin for this feeling, but it's there like the oceans. Vast, obvious. A fact of my existence. Owen, he fills that emptiness. He fills it full and asks nothing in return. He gives meaning to the simplest of things. When I am with him, I am not just smiling, I know why I am smiling.*

*I can't say for sure that I am in love with Owen yet, those are big words, but I do think these feelings are something even more important than love. I feel reborn; rebirth is surely a bigger deal than love.*

*I do love Alex, so I hate to say this, but lately I feel that he is simply the blanket hog who owns my house. The father of my*

*children, the brother of the man I really want. Everything*
*Alex says ... it's like I try to read the book, but all I see is the*
*end. Everything he has to say is so boring and predictable.*
*Halfway through every sentence he speaks, I lose my attention.*
*Is that because Owen is here? Is that Owen's fault? If Owen*
*never came would I feel this way?*

*Three nights ago, I asked Owen what he wants in his next*
*relationship. He shrugged, he didn't even think: "I want*
*to love the way she looks in her underwear, just sitting there,*
*reading, or looking for the right skirt in the closet on some*
*rainy Monday morning. I want the couch to feel different*
*because she is sitting on it with me."*

*Alex wouldn't get that. The utter lack of physical descriptors.*

*I want Alex to notice me, to comment on what I'm wearing.*
*I want Alex to change how I feel lately, not provoke these*
*feelings. I want our home to feel like it used to, just because we*
*were in it, together. Wanting all this, and not having it,*
*makes me feel like a whiny, pathetic, unloved mess. A pouty*
*teenager who fell for every girl's dream in marrying Alex,*
*only to wake up in adulthood feeling out of touch with the*
*world, because every day is the same. Saturdays no different*
*than Mondays. I have to check the TV to see what day it is*
*sometimes. But Alex's shirts are always pressed just so. I resent*
*the devotion being reciprocated financially only, like I'm a*
*fucking maid, and not emotionally, romantically, lovingly, as*
*if I were his wife.*

*I can speculate until my mind is a swirling mess. But I am*
*certain of one thing: the way he used to look at me, the way we*
*used to talk and laugh together in bed at night, it's gone, like*
*last year's snow. Like it never was. We still have our moments,*
*our good days, but it's not enough if I gave up my life for this*
*man. For the way he used to crave me in the shower, palms*
*sliding across steam-lubricated walls, and for the way he used*

*to rub my back until I fell asleep. For the way he used to know just what to buy me for my birthday, instead of giving me his Mastercard, a pat on the back, and a loose limit on what to spend. I should've cut that fucking card in half, but how is it his fault if that made me feel like a whore?*

# ALONE BESIDE YOU

ALEX HAD A FIVE-DAY break during his first year of surgical residency in Nova Scotia, and flew home to visit Owen and help him get settled into his new apartment. He never made a comment about Owen's new place – the cupboard doors askew and the worn-away carpet – other than "You should really make sure the landlord adresses that leak by the window there," and nodded to it to be clear. "It could lead to structural damage for him, and potential health issues for you. Mould. You know? It's in both of your interests. Stress that, okay?"

"Ah, whatever. I won't be here long enough to worry about it. I just needed out of Abbie's for now, you know?"

"You two seemed so good at the wedding last summer." He looked down at his ring. "What happened?"

"I don't know. Sometimes nothing happens. People change. Things change …"

Owen promised himself the place would be a temporary stopover as he collected himself, again. Other than his clothes and computer, he hesitated to unpack his boxes.

His one ambition was writing, but he couldn't concentrate in that house. He needed to fall into the story, forget about his surroundings. It took alcohol and nothing but the sound of his *own* music, but whoever lived in the apartment above his had bad dance music constantly blaring and thumping down through his ceiling. All too lively to write dark fiction to. Not that the distraction mattered. Whenever he sat at his computer to write now, every time, Abbie's pragmatic reasoning echoed in his mind.

"Statistically, Owen, getting published and winning the lottery are comparable. Read your last rejection letter. They explained that they get about a thousand submissions a year but only publish fifteen of those, and of those fifteen, four or five are typically books by current authors of theirs. So do the math: a publisher publishes less than one percent of the books submitted to them! And, I mean, even if you do get published, only one in a thousand published writers can make a living at it. And even for the greatest published writers, I dunno, it all depends too much on chance, and marketing. Literary integrity will get you published, sure, but once your story is a book, well, a book is a product, just like Pepsi and tennis shoes, dependent totally upon consumer behaviours and buzz. On whether or not bookstores decide to put your book on those *special tables* and discount them. It's not practical, Owen, your little dream."

Living in that apartment changed the way he saw himself: his goals and plans for the future. It deflated quixotic into pathetic, idealistic into a living joke. He was a cliché, why everybody didn't *follow their heart*. Comfortable, in Abbie's brightly lit, well-decorated home, with their children named and their vacations all planned, his life was a great fantasy. Looking forward now, all alone in his dingy apartment, he saw a harsh reality, a wakeup call.

Some days he'd consider finishing the geology degree. He'd look up the coming semester's course offerings, see what was available, but years had past and he felt like he had forgotten it all: the differences between the chain and ring silicates, how to plot compositional changes in sedimentary rocks caused by weathering. He couldn't even name all the minerals he kept in those plastic tubs in his closet anymore. He remembered that trip he and Abbie took to Gros Morne, how he filled his pockets with stones as they hiked, naming them as he went, showing them to Abbie as if they were nuggets of gold. They got to the top of the Tablelands and he explained the unique geological significance of the place, fervently, and with much hand gesturing. The way she looked and laughed at him, he could tell she respected and adored his passion. To her it was just a strange, breathtaking, yellow mound: *Like a chunk of Arizona plopped down in Newfoundland somehow.* That was only a few years ago, but the specifics of his little lecture that day were hazy now. It had something to do with two continents colliding, but that was all he could remember about it.

He tried to reassure himself. He plucked an old textbook from a box, flipped it open to an end-of-chapter question and read it: *List the reasons why a shale might have a higher content of $Na_2O$ than of $K_2O$.*

He tried the next question: *Consult figure 11-1. What would be the composition of the first melt if peridotite was partially melted to produce a water-saturated magma of 20 kb?*

He couldn't even speak the language anymore. Years away from it all had clipped his tongue of it. Years of writing, striving for some recognition, made him turn his back on it all. And all along Abbie had been right: he could've done both at once if he wasn't so obsessive over his writing. And only in hindsight was it obvious how much he had neglected her for his writing as well. All that time spent behind the closed door of his office, hearing her pacing around, trying to amuse herself after a long day at work.

∽

Whenever his apartment got too intolerable – ignoring the earwigs, the plops from the leaky kitchen sink, the music falling down on him from above – he'd go to sit with his lifeless father at the Waterford Hospital and be strangely calmed by the cool, silent air of the cement-walled room. The dimness of it muted his emotions. He could focus exclusively on the white sheets of the story he was revising. It was a great getaway except for the limited visiting hours.

One day, frustrated, fed up, wanting a father back, he threw a pencil at him. A sharpened pencil, like a dart. He threw it at him, and it never occurred to him until that moment that he was entitled to feel resentment towards his father. It wasn't warranted or right, but it was an option, and on that day it helped. It helped to hate his father for abandoning him. It helped to believe that if he had never lost his mind, his mother would not have starting working at that shelter. She never would have died. He never would have met Abbie. If his parents were still around he'd have their house to stay in *for now*. Until he got back on his feet, he'd have his old bedroom back. The room he discovered music in and grew up in and where he carved *Nirvana* and *Owen loves Maggie* into the closet wall.

A nurse poked her head in the doorway, the pencil still rolling across the floor. "Visiting hours are over in a minute, as you know."

He nodded to her. It was the cold and bitter nurse he despised. She had a mannish face no man could love – patches of wiry hair on her blotchy chin and cheeks that would grow a beard if left alone, a large droopy mole on her forehead that hung down like a cocooning insect, and a witch's crooked nose. Owen figured she held the world in contempt for the face she was born with. He thought maybe he held her in contempt for his father's condition, even a little. It was inexplicable how much he hated her and that dusty pink cardigan she always wore that was three inches too short in the arms to make it to her wrists. Something about how haphazardly it fit her, how it flared out in the back and was missing buttons, said she didn't care about herself, or anything, including some guy visiting his father, needing something familiar and physical. She was always too pleased to announce that visiting hours were over, five minutes before they technically were.

He pulled his chair in front of his father's. He squeezed one of his father's fingernails as hard as he could, trying to startle him back into existence – the purple of the flesh beneath his nail cast out and replaced by a bone white. He let it go; the purple leaked back in. He looked his father in the eye and begged, spilling his words as quickly as he could, knowing that bitch of a nurse would be right back.

"Dad, if there is some part of you left in there, I need you back. Now. More than ever. More than when I was a kid and they took you away. More than that. More than I needed you to teach me how to walk and talk and ride a bike, or make a fist or add and subtract, or shoot a basketball or hold a knife. I don't know what I am anymore, Dad. If I am right or wrong. You'd understand. I can't find any meaning in anything. I can't force myself to try and–"

The nurse opened the door and sighed. "You need to leave now, sir."

He hoped she hadn't heard him. Saying the words out loud like that, hearing them, the core of his despair, he felt pathetic. Adolescent. The nurse pulled on a gaudy jacket and looked at her watch, and stood in the door until Owen left. She smelled like greasy takeout as he brushed past her. Like bacon fat.

He left his father that day and went to his mother's grave. Anywhere but back to his appartment. It was mid-February, and walking along that snow-covered sidewalk, he felt just as cold. He was practically skiing along the icy, unsalted pavement. He refused to go back to his apartment because he couldn't stand acknowledging that he didn't feel at home in his own home. And he knew the first thing he'd do when he got back that day was open that bottle of Johnny Walker Red, and he refused to drink alone while the sun was still spilling through his windows.

It wasn't Abbie he was missing at home, not anymore anyway. Not her specifically: her banana pancakes, or the way she tapped pens off her fingernails as she processed thoughts, or the smell of their bathroom after she showered. There wasn't a word for what it was *about* her he missed, no matter how long he thought on it. It was needing that female presence in his life. Someone confident and motherly, with his best interests in mind. Without any plans now, any goals, he could feel the future dragging him towards something dark and vague.

By the time he got to the cemetery on Waterford Bridge Road, cars had him wet with the spray of slush. Cold wet slaps to the knees and hips, and twice to the face, a stinging left eye or a taste of salt. The sidewalks weren't cleared and he had to walk along the margins of the road beside dirty mounds of grey snow. He could tell which drivers were innocently inconsiderate and which just didn't care. It was in the brief flash of the brake lights, a sign the driver was taking in the damage in the rearview mirror, maybe cupping their mouth or screwing up their face in remorse.

He found his mother's headstone amongst the sea of others – unpolished black marble with worms of grey running through it – and realized he hadn't been there in over a year. He wasn't the type to find comfort in talking to a slab of marble, and leaving flowers next to her grave didn't feel like connecting with her.

Standing there above his mother, he didn't know what to

say, or do, or think, or why he'd even come there. He expected some vague feeling of relief or comfort, but got a flash of guilt and anger instead. An isolated memory from Jim Croaker's trial filled his blank mind. He and Abbie had been lying on her couch, reading, when Alex burst into the house. He was just getting back from the trial. Owen wouldn't go. He couldn't go. He couldn't be in the same room with the man, couldn't *not* bring a knife or a rock of his own along to the courthouse. Couldn't stand having the weapon confiscated before he could use it. Couldn't stand having his image of the man refreshed. Or his guilt renewed. In his mind he was equally worthy of being on trial for his mother's death, so he couldn't sit beside his brother with that reality there between them.

"He was bawling, Owen, crying his eyes out. Saying how sorry he was. He never meant to kill her. He kept saying he only meant to hurt her, as if that was okay in itself. *Because she hurt his arm and took his Janine away.* He sounded like a whiny, dumb kid. And his lawyer was playing up the sympathy card to go along with his theatrics. Going on about how he was an abused kid with a drunk for a father. What's that supposed to change? He had a shitty father so *our* mother had to pay for it?"

"So ... how did it, like–"

"His lawyer pushed for manslaughter, but the policemen who were there with you ... that day ... who seemed like they felt a little guilty, played up the willful disregard for life card. That's how the lawyer nailed Jim with second degree murder. His *willful disregard for life.* Yet the motherfucker was allowed to kick on that door, day after day, uttering threats, with a *willful disregard for life*, until he managed to drag Mom out the door."

He looked at Owen, added, "Or whatever," and looked down at his feet.

"Until I dragged Mom out the door *for* him, you mean?"

"Owen, no. The time for that is over now. Jim did this. Not

you. I'm sorry for what I said that night. It was in the heat of the moment, you know?"

Just like that, the memory was gone.

It was cold, so cold his hands were numb even though he had them gloved and tucked deep into his pockets, yet he felt better there than anywhere else in the world that day. He felt away from everywhere. Invisible walls surrounded him. His breath hung like clouds in front of him with each exhale.

He sat beside her gravestone, leaning on it, feeling the grain of the headstone tug against his jacket. He rested his head against it and stared at the branches of a birch tree swaying in the wind. Rhythmically. With each gust of wind the branches swayed in a way that filtered the light like a kaleidoscope. It made the ground beneath the tree look afire with dancing sunlight. Lines of blue and grey and yellow criss-crossing each other at random. Almost like TV static now. He reached for his notepad:

> *What is it about light that has this tree in front of me ten feet tall and still reaching, still growing, still stretching towards the sun? I want to want something like that. To be that salmon swimming upstream, to be that determined. To be Ghandi, to care enough about something to starve myself. This indifference. I am not alive, I am not dead, I am something worse.*

Minutes later, there was something about that ephemeral dancing light, how a cloud could soon end it, could soon block out the sun. And there was something about the stark-but-calm cawing of the one black crow in the whole graveyard, hopping along in the flickering light beneath that tree. How the wind blew snow and covered its tracks with each exhale, like the crow had no past to turn and contemplate, or the past didn't matter: a statement that there is forward movement only. There is nothing to be gained by dwelling on a past that is ultimately gone, buried, invisible and intangible. It made him reach for a pen. Everything looked equally symbolic of life and death, endings and beginnings. He wrote his first poem and rushed home to type it up. He was working on a collection called *Home*, trying to write short pieces set in every major landmark in St. John's, knowing a gimmick like that can help a book get published, or at least act as a marketing strategy.

He would've liked Abbie to be there when he got home. To share his first poem with her. Everything was starting to feel insignificant now that he had no one to share it with. He missed calling her into his office to read out a line or two, or to ask for her opinion on what to do next in a story he was working on. *Should I cut this story off here, or add this last paragraph?* He was only ever sure on a piece after she'd calmed all of his concerns and agreed with all his choices. He liked the way her hand clutched his doorframe as she listened, thought about her answers, and shared them. He liked her hands, the way the hair fell away from her face. He liked the impression of her chest beneath her sweater, the cling of it against her. He liked seeing her this way. It wasn't a sexual desire, a mere attraction, it was simply a comfort, or an appreciation of something graceful, right there in front of him and tangible.

❧

Owen was sinking deeper and deeper by the day; something was swallowing him whole. One day he took the kettle off a red hot burner and felt like he could press the palm of his hand on the burner and it wouldn't hurt. Everything had lost significance. It concerned him enough to go to his doctor.

"I'm not depressed, but I don't care if I live another day. I am not psychotic like my father, but I don't feel in touch with reality. I feel like, if someone attacked me on the street, I'd just lie there and take the beating, submissively, and not even feel the pain. I feel like my actions don't have consequences, like I could walk in front of a bus and survive it. Like I could witness a murder and not feel emotionally connected to the scene."

Given his father's history, the doctor looked into Owen's complaints. Weeks later, after a barrage of interviews and a seemingly childish questionnaire, he was told he had depersonalization disorder, and that there was little that could be done for him, for now.

"Medications are in the works," the doctor told him, "but like any disease or disorder, pharmaceutical companies tend to focus their research on conditions that millions suffer from, like cancer and diabetes, so they can get rich off the medications they invent." He shook his head, genuinely disgusted. "When it comes to something as obscure and unpopular as DPD, well, there's no money in that."

The doctor laid his clipboard down and took a seat to deliver some of the worst news to Owen. "I've got a pamphlet to give you on DPD, and a few websites you might want to check out too."

He handed Owen the white and green pamphlet: a poorly drawn cartoon of a depressed-looking teenager staring at the light at the end of a tunnel. He'd wait until he left the doctor's office to throw it in the garbage. It would be rude to do so in front of him.

"But there are a few things I want to give you, a sort of heads-up on in person." He cleared his throat and brushed his bulbous nose with an index finger. "People suffering from DPD are prone to relationship issues, Owen, because intimacy can feel foreign when the disorder peaks. And drug dependency and alcoholism are common, because drugs and alcohol can make a DPD sufferer feel 'more alive,' as you say, when they are feeling detached from themselves. So I need you to be honest with yourself if you find yourself drinking, or worse, and come to me, okay? There are a lot of good programs I can turn you on to."

Owen smiled through the whole summary. Alcoholism and bachelorship hadn't concerned him, schizophrenia had. Owen was simply relieved he wasn't succumbing to the schizophrenia that consumed his father. Alex had mentioned– his concern for himself and Owen in his voice – that most research indicates schizophrenia is hereditary. Owen didn't need to hear it. Didn't need to know that. There were no steps to take to prevent it. There was no way to screen yourself for it, like a simple blood test. It just reached out its hand and grabbed you when you were at your weakest.

In those weeks before his diagnosis with depersonalization disorder, a rabid fear of schizophrenia sometimes kept him up at night. It made his mind wander as he lay in bed; that noise outside the window, *maybe* it wasn't really there. Maybe he was crazy for wondering what the noise was, for picturing scenarios in his head. Was it a tree branch? A person? Any man's mind can wander like that at night, he knew that, but he also knew that a schizophrenic's mind can wander so far it gets lost. That fear of schizophrenia was the last thing his father had left behind for his sons.

He got home that day and started to read the pamphlet. *At its worst, on the bad days, DPD sufferers can feel detached from themselves. Most sufferers describe the feeling of detachment as not feeling emotionally reactive to what is happening to them, or not feeling present in their body, as if they are watching their life as a movie, and yet they can carry out all their daily work and social responsibilities just fine ...*

By the end of the first paragraph, he'd crumpled it up and thrown it away.

*... typically caused by childhood traumas, witnessing something traumatic, or ...*

The words, the causes, it all made him feel weak, pathetic, and he didn't want to know what it all meant, or how long it would last, or why Alex never had all these problems.

# IN NEW SKIN

*August 22nd, 2008,*
*In the garden, desperately in need of fresh air.*

*The danger of being human is our ability to justify our actions.*

*It's been happening for a while now. We started exchanging looks a long time ago, biting into each other's souls with hungry eyes. Not even lewd glances, just a desperate but denied gaze. Wanting the new beginning. The escape, from the world before now.*

*On some nights, those eyes feel more like invisible hands, a soft embrace. A physical manifestation of hope, of how it could be, sort of massaging me into a weak state, a lapse of judgment, so that I might lay my body beside his.*

*And then we moved on from there, having to satisfy the body's need for contact, for touch, the one sense we cannot, literally cannot, live without.*

*Or deny.*

*We started finding reasons to brush past each other, to touch each other. Even if I've seen it a dozen times before, I'll say "nice shirt," and rub his shoulders a little, pretending to examine the material, but more truthfully rubbing his shoulders in a way to let him know that I am good with my hands. I deflate when he touches me. I slip out of my skin. He seems to tense up. I like to think of it as him being struck stiff, erect and aroused. But sometimes he'll almost haul away, like he can't take it.*

*Today was too much.*

*Owen was particularly "alive" today, as he says, and he was tangling himself up in the monkey bars with the girls, and dizzying himself by spinning them around and around on the merry-go-round, charged on by their laughter. So I couldn't just sit there on the bench reading like I usually do. Watching them all laughing like that, I wanted in on the fun. They all headed over to a red plastic tunnel connecting a set of monkey bars to the slide. "C'mon, Mommy, come get in the tunnel with me and Callie and Uncle Owen, pleeeease!"*

*She didn't have to beg. The four of us ended up in the tiny tunnel. It was hardly big enough for four kids, let alone two kids and two adults. It was claustrophobic, we were almost stuck in there, but the girls loved it. They pretended we were all trapped, and made Owen and me pretend as well. They shimmied and squirmed until me and Owen were lewdly squat together. Sandwiched in a way that went my leg – Owen's leg – my leg – Owen's leg. He was in cloth shorts, and I was in a thin, loose summer dress; we could barely feel the clothes between us. They had me pressed down on him so hard that my breasts were pancaked on his throat, and we were more or less hugging each other, my palms flat against the bottom of the plastic tunnel. My lips closer to his lips than they've ever been, and some primal magnetism drawing them closer and closer until I felt his warm breath jacket my lips. I got close enough that our noses touched. And untouched, and touched again. We both pretended not to notice. I could feel him, IT, against my inner thighs, and we pretended not to notice. As Callie and Lucia jostled around, swinging their arms, telling their animated stories about how we were trapped in a submarine, they rocked and squirmed to simulate a sinking ship. Their movements had me rubbing it with my thigh, and I caught myself adding a more sensual motion to how they had me rocking against him. And that's when I yelled at my daughters to stop what they were doing and get out of the tunnel. Even Owen jolted at the tone of my voice, though he looked relieved. Relieved and something akin to embarrassed.*

*That was the first time I've ever unjustifiably yelled at my daughters. We all crawled out of the tunnel and Callie's lips were trembling. She was hurt, but too frightened and taken off guard to know it yet. Lucia stood behind Owen, pouty and baffled. Owen pretended to comfort her so he wouldn't have to look up at me.*

*"You were hurting Mommy's neck and elbows was all. I'm very sorry I yelled, I was hurting and I panicked. Mommy is sorry, okay?"*

*Maybe it was the first time I lied to them as well? My neck was just fine, slung down over Owen like that. I liked my hair on his face. I liked it too much. If today wasn't a line crossed, I don't know what will be. If my daughters weren't there I would have kissed him. Kissed him in a way that said I loved him, and kissed him in a way that would have led to sex.*

*And now we're almost avoiding each other, as if that was sex we'd just had. And despite the clothes that lay between us, it was just as thrilling as sex. The erotic gnaw of not touching each other. The way he was breathing, how his inhales would lift my body. I rose and fell against him, slowly, soothingly.*

*Now I just feel dirty. Alex will be home soon. The three of us will sit around a table, small talk and pork souvlaki. At no point tonight will I feel as alive as I did in that tunnel today. And at no point tonight will I rid this guilt. It's in my pores now, too deep to scrub out or ignore. I fear I wear it like a dress everyone can see.*

*It's all changing the way I look at my children too, my daughters. Less confidently, like I am denying them a secure parental unit and lying to them somehow. Denying them something different from, but equal to, safety: the only definite motherly duty. And I am, or some part of me is, the sole cause of what I am doing wrong to them. A part of me that has nothing to do with being a mother, but everything to do with being a woman, yet I can't separate the two without literally tearing myself in half.*

*Falling in love is so easy, so natural, so romantic. Falling out of love is so painful, so hard, so sharp that it cuts into you with every breath. I feel trapped in my life before now. Fenced in by it. Caged in. Denying myself something the world is offering, quite readily, and won't stop until I take it.*

# FATE AND MISFORTUNE

SINCE THE DAY HE SCRIBBLED that poem at his mother's grave, Owen took to sitting and writing at her headstone for the rest of the winter. When spring came, the snow began to melt and made a wet, muddy mess of the place he once sat. So he bought a collapsible camping chair and brought it along with him. He knew it was an odd or even morbid setting to write in, but sitting under the shelter of the city's tallest birch tree was serene, and the isolation made him productive. The fresh air was stimulating and the sunlight that filtered through the evergreens was calming. It all kept him focussed. The only sound was the distant hum of traffic, the soothing hiss from the taps and hoses the cemetery left running for people who wanted to fill planters and flower pots on gravestones. There was also an occasional fluttering of finches and dark-eyed juncos in the trees above him. The birds got used to his presence within a few minutes of his arrival every day. If he didn't finish a granola bar, he'd fling it to the birds. He tore the crust off his sandwiches for them.

It was quiet in the cemetery. It was loud in his apartment and he hated it there. Everywhere else he could go felt like hassling reminders of feeling lost in life. On rainy days, he'd sneak into the university library, but the busy footsteps of all those students around him made him feel like he should be heading off to a class himself. And he'd grown sick of working around the visiting hours at the Waterford, only to sit and stare at that shell of a man who used to contain his father.

At his mother's grave though, the world felt a little farther away and life hassled him less. If someone did come around, they didn't bother him, because people keep to themselves in a cemetery; the most they'd burden him with was a hardy nod of the head. Nothing existed except the story he was writing.

Some days there would be funerals. On one miserably foggy spring day, the mournful sounds of sobbing and one woman's guttaral cries of goodbye caught his attention, and he tuned into the Brooke family's funeral. Some people seemed so devastated, one woman bent at the waist to let out gut-wrenching howls. Others seemed merely obligated to be there, standing tall and biting their fingernails or blankly watching traffic. Some held each other, and others held themselves. Some were dressed in well-fitted suits; the teenagers wore the best outfits they could throw together: black jeans and a borrowed dress shirt two sizes too big. When they lifted their arms, it looked like they were budding wings.

It was the beloved grandfather/father/brother/husband Thomas Brooke who'd passed away. From the family's reaction, from each of their individual reactions, Owen spontaneously started to create a fictional life story for Thomas Brooke. With the exception of the wife, there wasn't much crying, so he assumed it was a long drawn-out death, cancer maybe, since no one had that loud shrieking cry that meant someone has been taken too soon, too unexpectedly. But by the words shared, by how long people lingered, by the quote Owen read on his headstone after the family left, he could tell Thomas was loved. He could tell Thomas was loved by the way no one knew what to do with their hands when they spoke to each other. Thomas seemed like the glue that held the family together. It was definitely his house where they all got together at Christmas. He was definitely the man who fell asleep in the chair at the hospital waiting for each and every one of those grandchildren to be born, so he could be the first to see them. But there was one girl, mid-twenties: why did she stay back, listless and biting her nails? That's where the story lay, why this girl was the foreigner in the family.

Owen took it from there. He had his laptop with him and wrote the story of what the grandfather did for that girl that no one else in the family could know about. How it was so profound, so selfless and inconceivable, that it meant she died when he did. That she was in that grave with him.

The story he wrote, "Thicker Than Blood," won Owen the recognition he'd been waiting for and opened the door to a modest career in writing. People called to congratulate him on the good news, people who once considered writing a juvenile waste of time and awkwardly changed the subject whenever he talked about his writing.

The story earned him five thousand dollars, but more importantly, a contract to write a novella for a literary magazine called *Tether*. It was a thick magazine released quarterly, and they wanted to divide the story into four instalments and drag it out over the year. Overall, he got the initial five thousand for the short story, and another twenty thousand for the novella, which he agreed not to publish elsewhere.

He gave them *The World Before Now*, a forty-thousand-word manuscript he'd written years earlier. Something that had been rejected by seven publishers. The editors at the journal loved it though, and marketed Owen as "a grittier James Salter." A reviewer in a national newspaper had written: *Collins has written a story that will reach its hands into you and pluck the heart clean out of your chest. He has written it so magically you'll feel that pain and love him for it.*

The money meant he could finally get a more comfortable apartment, and budgeting his spending to a thousand dollars a month allowed him to take the next two years off to write a novel. Start from scratch. Begin again.

He moved into a quiet, clean, two-bedroom apartment on Gower Street, five-fifty a month, heat and light included. That left him with four hundred and fifty dollars a month for food and alcohol, *to fuel the writing.* He used one bedroom as an office, and loved the old fireplace in there, the exposed brick along the entire wall.

Above the toilet in the bathroom, there was what looked like a door to an attic. Within two weeks he had to satisfy his curiosity and open the latch. He dragged a chair into the bathroom, climbed it like a ladder, opened the door, and braced himself for a hailstorm of insulation and mouse droppings. But it wasn't an attic. The latch opened to the roof: a black sky, some stars, barely shining behind black clouds, and the glow of the moon spilling across it all from the left. He crawled up and took wary footsteps, afraid the roof would cave in and swallow him whole.

A previous tenant had built a make-shift patio up there, with a table and two wooden lawn chairs, all painted blood red. It became his new writing nook, and all September long he watched huge cruise ships squeeze into the harbour through two walls of rock locally dubbed The Narrows. Every time a cruise ship left the harbour, Owen thought of all the places he could've gone, of all the different people he could've been. Each alter ego budding a new story to write.

When he was younger, but old enough to have conversations with his father, Roger had made him promise that the two of them would take an Alaskan cruise on his fiftieth birthday. His father was always fascinated by the North, by snow and icebergs, how they could *stop us invincible humans dead in our tracks.* The sheer age and immovable nature of glaciers and icebergs, he said, reminded him of *how short-lived and insignificant we humans are in the grand scale of things.*

His father was turning fifty-three in October; they were already three years too late. If he could have afforded the cruise, Owen might have checked him out of the hospital that year, stolen him if necessary, and booked that cruise.

"We'll hear the sound of silence," his father had said. "We'll *feel* life. We'll be away from everywhere. Because there is no room left in the world for people like you and me, Owen. I know because I've searched and not found it."

∽

Owen's savings lasted roughly two years, as planned. He had a collection of short stories written by the end of it, titled *Four Letter Words*, and his publisher would have it out in stores for the fall of 2003. So it was important to him to find a way to make money from home, where he could favour writing a novel over his job. As a sort of congratulations for his first official publication, Alex fronted Owen some money and he started an eBay-inspired website called buyitlocally.ca. He maintained the website himself, and charged ten percent on any sales made through his site, where people could sell anything from couches to original thousand-dollar pieces of art. What really made his business catch on, at least in St. John's, was selling local music and art on the website and cutting out retailers, so artists got the full twenty dollars a CD or full price on their artwork. He wanted to start doing the same with books, and eventually he had businesses and artists buying ad space on his website. He was averaging not quite a thousand dollars a month, but that was enough. When it wasn't, he used his MasterCard and squared up on a better month.

Some people were jealous of Owen's new lifestyle; even

Alex envied all that free time. It bothered Owen how people always overlooked the labour that went into his writing, the hours it took to sharpen his sentences until they cut like knives, and the sheer mental exhaustion of hauling a fictional world out of his mind and making it feel real enough for a reader to fall into. He wrote at least eight hours a day, the same amount of time most people sat in their office chairs, and the days he worked ten straight hours were a hard-earned testament to his ambition, but still, everyone assumed he *had it knocked, never having to go to work.*

Yet these people were right to say that he spent his days in a way which, for Owen, ate away at his identity and how he fit into the world. The cost of no social obligations, of having nowhere to be at any specific time, of having no family, no significant other, made him lose track of time, of what day of the week it was, and soon one day slipped into the next, stitching identical days together into identical months. He had to check channel nine from time to time to see what day of the week it was. He barely even left the house, and carried an extra fifteen pounds as proof. He felt every pound of it in the extra effort it took to haul himself out of a chair. The soft recoil of gut on gut.

He started feeling more and more detached from himself, from the world. He'd putter at hobbies, in between writing, and go for walks. He rented a lot of movies and taught himself to cook and grow herbs. He even adopted a black lab from the SPCA. But something was missing, gnawing at him. He worried the depersonalization disorder was tightening its grip. He ignored it. There was no way to fight it off anyway.

What started out as an interest in red wine turned into him needing that sensation in the back of his throat every night. It wasn't the drunk he needed, it was that ethereal transcendent feeling that red wine gave him. Red wine and red wine alone. It made him feel more alive, more aware of himself and his surroundings. More in tune with his feelings and the world around him. He saw it as medication, it was waking him up, breathing life back into him that the world had sucked out. Then he noticed how the wine was evoking something in him that made the writing come easier, and that what he was writing had so much more depth and beauty to it. Sentences spilled out of him more freely, more vividly, more honestly. He could only capture things, up to his standards, using wine as a lure to coax the right words out of him.

It was winter, and nothing of interest was in walking distance. The thirty dollars a day he'd spend on wine meant an extra nine hundred dollars a month, which was more than his rent. It was an assault on his savings, but he justified it by saying that if it helped him write, and if writing was how he made a living, then it was worth nine hundred dollars a month. He saw it as an investment in himself, in his writing. Even if it made him irritable and forgetful at times. Even though he was getting confused by simple things like instruction manuals now. Even though he was developing a chronic dull pain in his guts and growing increasingly anxious and depressed.

He'd think of his father from time to time, of his genetic predisposition to end up like his father if he kept drinking. He kept an old pamphlet on schizophrenia in his dresser, one a nurse had given him. He'd read it from time to time, as a sort of check on himself: *Schizophrenia often merely needs a trigger... substance abuse is common in over 40% of schizophrenics-to-be.*

He ignored it all. The wine helped.

One by one his friends all moved away for jobs, or graduate schools, or went into seclusion with their partners, getting married and having kids, or they just gave up on him. But Alex came home from Halifax for Christmas one year and stayed with Owen, and Owen watched those few days startle and crush Alex. It took that to realize how lost he was in it all. One night at the supper table, he watched his brother struggle with where to look and what to say. Owen tried to be discreet about rounding the corner to top up his wine, but he couldn't make all the bottles around the house invisible. And he couldn't correct the slurred speech, or keep attentive and tuned into their conversation. He couldn't stop himself from passing out on the loveseat during the movie they were watching.

They were in the airport saying goodbye when Alex blurted it out. "I mean, I know you're not an alcoholic. The drinking is just a side effect of the depersonalization disorder, I'm sure of it. So it's not your fault. But I think you should go talk–"

"It's possible I'm just a drunk, Alex. It's possible I'm just an alcoholic."

"No!" He shouted it, then looked around, a little embarrassed that the people in the seats behind him, or the blonde flight attendant walking her luggage down the corridor towards them, might have seen his outburst. He turned his back on the blonde and said, more quietly, "We're not alcoholics. It's the depersonalization disorder that has you like this. You'll be fine, just go talk to your doctor about–"

"We?" Owen laughed, sardonically, shocked. "Is that what this is about? You're yet again ashamed of a family member? Rest easy, man, we're in two different provinces now. No one has to know you've got a drunk for a brother. You can tell them I'm a rich lawy–"

"Fuck off! My plane is going to be here any minute, I don't want to leave like–"

"Look, if it helps, why not just write me off like you did with Dad? Okay? I'm giving you permission."

Alex fidgeted then, like a scorned kid. "I'm just saying, you need to talk to your doctor." He looked down at his feet as he spoke.

Owen felt bad after he'd said his piece, and he knew his brother had to leave St. John's with a clear conscience. "Look, Alex. I'm sorry." They were both looking at their feet now. "You're right, and I'm getting testy and defensive. Denial is step one." He lied to comfort his brother. "That's what my sponsor is always reminding me of. I'm already in AA, on doctor's orders, and it's really helping."

Alex was visibly relieved. He let out a big sigh, a weight shifted off the sunken shoulders and his posture straightened. He looked up and met his brother's eyes again. There was a moment of hesitation there, a look of *Honestly? You aren't lying to me?* But then it faded away, like maybe Alex was letting himself believe the lie. The same way they'd all let themselves believe their father wasn't mentally ill all those years ago.

⌒

He loved the sound of it, the hollow pop of uncorking a bottle and the clugging sound of the first pour. He threw the cork in the garbage, and stared at the blank screen. The blinking cursor. The empty page. This was always the hardest part. Page one. And he was too drunk to keep a train of thought. He'd write two sentences and have to re-read them to come up with a third. There would be too much lag time between his modest critical praise and the completion of his new manuscript for any publisher to care about him, and he knew it. He never had the attention span for a novel now, and he knew why. He'd scrapped three already. Blamed a lack of substance and appeal, not alcoholism.

He'd started his newest novel ten different ways before settling on the opening scene. His character was driving his mother home, but ran a stop sign, so she died in his arms. It was a visceral paragraph describing a tooth in a black cupholder, and the surreal sensation of feeling his mother's warm blood and hearing her last words stuttering out of her. His obvious guilt for not waiting at the stop sign, and how the rest of his life would trace itself back to that moment. His novel started that way until he decided he'd have more of a story to work with if it was his child and not his mother. The opening scene being his character having to tell his wife that he'd just killed their daughter. It was important to drop a reader's jaw on the very first page. He was about to revise it all when the phone rang.

"Hey, man, how's the writing game going?"

Owen was shocked by the question, the sudden interest, and taken off-guard by the voice. It had been six months since their conversation in the airport.

"What? Good, I guess … Is that you, Alex?" Owen was drunk, and it broke his heart he couldn't hide it from Alex.

"You're … okay, are you?"

"Yes, yeah. It's just … you know what today is, right?"

Silence. A sigh.

It was the day their mother had died. A humid, windless July third just like it.

"I was thinking, Owen, since you've got such an imagination and a way with words, that you should write a crime novel, or a horror or something. I just saw this great suspense movie on TV and couldn't help think *that's* what you should be writing. *That's* what most people want to read."

Owen was touched that Alex had thought of him, but jarred by Alex's years-long refusal to talk about their mother. He'd just throw up a wall no one could climb over. At least if Owen was in the room. So he let it go and explained what seemed obvious. "I write *literary* fiction, not genre fiction. Switching over for the sake of more money would be like selling out."

There was a pause before his brother responded. A pause of frustration, like he wanted no bitter tone when he responded to

Owen. "Selling out is something kids talk about, Owen. The whole concept of selling out is childish. You could write a publishable thriller, and we both know it. You have to eat. You've said yourself that your website is dying off, and you should start looking for a *job* job."

"Being a starving artist ..." Owen trailed off on a drunken and irrelevant tangent, "doesn't so much refer to a lack of income. I need something more meaningful from life than you do, Alex. Something more than a job and money. Something more meaningful and intangi–"

"Owen ... grow up, man. And spare me, for once, this holier-than-thou artist bullshit. You're not a hero for turning your back on money and society, and you don't sound or act like a man with much meaning in his life! You know that's why Abbie lef–"

"And just because you're a surgeon who can buy a three-storey house and a BMW doesn't make you a hero, Alex. It makes you sad, and empty. Basing the worth of your life on the stuff and things you surround yourself with. You've got no more idea of what it means to be happy than I do, and we both know it. We're just messed up in our own little ways!"

"I'm not the one fucked up. My life is well on track."

Owen slung his head down. "I'm not talking about your life. I'm talking about you. And let's not shit ourselves about why you're a doctor."

"Whatever. I was only trying to help when I called. I've got to go now." The commitment had left his voice.

"I know, and I appreciate it, okay? It's nice to hear from you. It is. And I'm melodramatic, and I know it, and I'm sorry. But I'm never going to understand you, you'll never understand me, and we're both going to try and make sense of this life in our own different ways, okay?"

"Yeah, I gotta go. This is not why I called. And good luck finding some *meaning* in life when you are so goddamn bitter and drunk all the time. I refuse to reason with you when you're this drunk and depressing. Talk later, Owen, take care. And you can be the next one to call. And make sure you're sober, too. You woke Hannah when you called last week, and hung up without saying a word. What was that all about? And you woke the kids. It was 2 a.m. here. I mean *God!* I fucken golf and ski with *her* sister, but what are you to Hannah? My creepy brother?"

He slammed the phone down.

∽

Three weeks later, his telephone was disconnected and there were two unopened disconnect warnings on his coffee table from Newfoundland Power.

He only ever woke up because of the dog. Holden would prod Owen with his snout every morning for food. Cold, wet streaks across his forehead. Owen could forget about the occasional supper, but Holden wouldn't let noon come around without insisting on a full bowl of food. He fed him well to make up for being such a bad owner. If he barbecued steak, Holden got the better of the two. It was the guilt he felt over the dog that made him aware of his drinking problem. Some nights Holden would just sit there and watch Owen. He had a strange posture: he'd tilt his head diagonally and just stare into him, his eyes prying for a reason why Owen was ignoring him. Sometimes Owen would get overwhelmed with guilt and stop what he was doing and take Holden for a walk, drunk, his landlady peering out the window at him as he stumbled down the street with the dog, talking to it more than a civilized sober man would, not avoiding traffic like a sane person would. His relationship with the woman got awkward. She lived below him and they got along great at first. After seeing him like that though, she clearly stopped feeling comfortable around him. She pretended to be looking for something in her purse whenever they crossed paths, or she'd look down at her toes when he gave her his rent. She'd watch him from the window whenever he took the dog out back, and if Owen looked back at her, she'd quickly fling the curtain shut and hide behind it. The curtains were red, with brighter red circles all over them. They made a slow-motion ripple when she pulled them shut, and then she peeked out more subtly when he turned back around. So he stopped throwing an extra burger on the grill for her, and he stopped having the driveway shovelled for her when she got home from work. He couldn't stand to look at her, the shame, the acknowledgement that alcohol had consumed him like that.

He eventually gave the dog away too, feeling that Holden was the kind of dog who wagged his tail too much to live alone with an alcoholic. He deserved some family with a kid to maul him all day long, and a fit soccer mom to take him out for a daily jog.

He was surprised at how much he missed Holden. The ball of warmth jumping on and off his bed at night, or curled up at his feet as he wrote. Or even just the excuse to get out of the house. Without the company of his dog, however, he found himself calling Alex more – in the mornings though, when Alex would be around but Owen was still sober. It had gotten to the point where they were talking only five or six times a year. Throughout his bout with alcoholism, it made life easier on Owen that Alex was okay, "happy," successful. Having a brother so far ahead in life somehow made him feel a little less behind. And if his father ever did snap out of it, he'd have at least one kid worth boasting about.

One night, sleepless, the room spinning, he crawled out of bed, stumbled down the hall to the living room, and watched a documentary on haunted homes. He went to bed with the notion that it was possible his mother was a ghost he couldn't see, watching him. She'd be frowning, crying, shattered by it all. He thought about putting her out of her misery.

⤚

Alex tried one last time. No interventions, no guilting him into it, no clichéd motivational *you-could-be-so-much-more* speeches. He flew home and stuck by Owen's side, unshedable as a shadow, until it got unbearable and Owen broke down and started pouring the drinks, which gave Alex the chance to give him that judgmental look. Alex asked him out to breakfast, and Owen had to acknowledge he'd be too hungover to enjoy himself. He asked Owen to a movie one night, and the first thing Owen thought was that he was usually drunk by the time a late movie started. Too drunk to go stumbling through the cinemas in the dark.

He hated it the most when Alex would come over, look around his apartment, and look at him without saying a thing. It was the looks in people's eyes more than their words that got through to him. The look in Alex's eyes that night when he dropped Owen back home and watched him drop his keys trying to open the front door.

When the weekend was over, Alex pleaded with Owen to come back up to Nova Scotia with him. Owen refused. They settled on a deal. Owen would mail Alex his AA chips, to prove he was attending meetings regularly and getting better. And for the next year he did just that. Except he bought the chips off eBay, stuck them in an envelope, and never once went to a meeting. He marked on a calender when to send each chip – 30 days sober, 60 days, 90 days … the anniversary chip.

# HEAR ME, WITHOUT WORDS

*August 30th, 2008,*
*Beside him and alone in the world.*

*There were a million moments this could've happened between Owen and me. What made today the moment?*

*We were swimming again. He had turned around and I was getting dressed. I let myself go. I gave into that voice that's been screaming the truth at me for weeks now: we belong together, no matter what. No matter what that means. No matter how that screws everything up.*

*I walked towards him. He heard the rocks rustle beneath my feet and he tensed up, curious. To relax him I lied. I told him to be still, there was a wasp in his hair. I kept walking towards him. I pressed my bare breasts against the warm curves of his back. I slid my fingers under the elastic of his shorts and filled my hand with it, felt it throbbing into life. Limp softness replaced by a rigid stiffness so quickly it meant he'd been waiting months for this. Forever maybe. With the other hand I circled his nipples as I kissed his neck, tasted the sun there, the summer's heat. He tore his shorts off and it slapped off my thigh as he turned to face me, and I laughed about it. Nervous, I guess. Elated. We were naked and alone and possessed by each other's bodies, wild with action and movement. His hands cupped the back of my neck, and he pulled me towards him. He had a thumb on my cheek, his hands in my hair. The lightness passing between us. The lightning. Indescribable really. Like my tingling lips were all of me. Like I'd never been so sensitive, my sense of touch so alive. It was so right, so perfect; there was no room for guilt. Just pleasure. Ecstatic pleasure.*

*At the wharf, with just the shade of fragrant evergreens to clothe us, it happened. Water dripped from our hair as our hands explored every inch of each other's bodies. Fingers behind the crooks of bent knees, and roaming hands wanting it all at once. We rolled through pine needles and pebbles, and settled against the splinters and warmth of the sun-soaked wharf, and it was the best sex I've ever had, if only because of the wait, the passion, the build-up. Hell, the view, the sound of the water slapping off the wharf, the look in his eyes, how he looked at me. Like he could cry about how beautiful it all felt. Like he knew it would all end and it saddened him to think about it.*

*The only guilt I have is the guilt of feeling no guilt. It was too right, too perfect to feel guilty over.*

*The rest of the day felt equally comfortable and uncomfortable. At night the alcohol helped remove the discomfort of the day's actions. He joked about me being an enabler, and we made love again. We made love, we didn't just fuck. How is it possible for two brothers to approach a woman so differently? Alex makes me feel like a sex-toy, but Owen is selfless and knowledgeable and brings some passion to the table that his brother never had. My God! I can compare brothers: who's bigger, better, cleaner, nicer to look at and work with. What does that make me? And now I've felt him shuddering there against me, in those precious last few seconds. So vulnerable and all mine.*

*It's been so long since I've seen another one of those things, let alone handled one. But something took over and knew just what to do and … look at me! Glowing with a splinter in my thigh! How can I have a sense of humour with this? I am so very schoolgirl giddy right now. There are so few people who can do that to a grown woman. For years I've felt so unseen. But tonight Owen was all eyes and I was everything he saw. He is the dream a girl crawls into bed and waits for.*

*He's made a little girl of me. Like the thrill of it all is too much for me and I have to share it, to dole it out to other girls, as we scream and shriek and lock hands about it all.*

*I can't tell him I love him because those are words for a husband, not a mantress. That's what I'll call him, my mantress, because I don't know what the term is for the male equivalent of a mistress. He is asleep beside me as I write this, so beautifully defeated by life. I want to know how he got that star-shaped scar on his side; I'll ask him when he wakes. For now I'll just wonder, I'll just imagine the imperfect life this perfect man has lived. Whatever hell he has endured has given him character, if that's any consolation.*

*Owen cowers from life. He has given up on life, on everything, without having tried a thing. Why? Everything he writes is so goddamn sad. He keeps talking about his past but never his future. He keeps talking about "getting away from everything," but the sad thing is he has nothing to run from. No one and nothing. So what is it you are running from, Owen?*

*Actually, come to think of it, what he says he wants is to be "away from everywhere," whatever that means. I don't think*

*he knows even what he means by that, and I think that's his
problem. Owen is brilliant, and could have anything he
wanted, yet he is forever with his back to what he is looking
for, running from it. Heading "away from everywhere." I
worry sometimes. The way he thinks is mesmerizing, but often
equally frightening. He can isolate himself from the world and
exist in his own.*

*I held back on saying what I felt lying next to Owen tonight.
I held back because statements lose emphasis if you say them too
often. I don't have to tell him I love him anyway. What our
bodies shouted to each other tonight was more than words
could ever convey. For some things there are no words, just
actions that say it all and more.*

*Touch me,*

*Without hands*

*See me,*

*Without eyes, without light, in the dark*

*Hear me,*

*Without words.*

# FROM NOTHING TO NOWHERE

IT WAS JUST AFTER MIDNIGHT when he got to the bottom of his last bottle of wine. He threw the empty into his recycling bin and cringed while it was in mid-air, expecting a shatter. There wasn't one. He checked every cupboard twice for another bottle, opening each door slowly, as if that increased the odds. Rarely, in his last few years of alcoholism, did he not have another bottle to go open, but he couldn't even get that right anymore. Especially now that he wanted out. Now that he was trying to sip cola or brew coffee instead – sick of the hangover, the subdued ambition, the pointlessness of everyday life. The absence of passion he couldn't even get from writing, because he couldn't even write anymore.

Earlier that day, he was in the liquor store. He picked up a second bottle of wine, and laid it back down. Picked it back up. He pretended to read the beige label so that the pretty blonde in the tight black dress wouldn't look at him and wonder why he kept picking up the wine and putting it back down. He was moderately sober and thought it might be a good idea not to buy the second bottle, so he could start getting used to the idea of getting drunk and leaving it at that. Not needing to keep drinking for the sake of it. Because he was awake and bored. Or writing. Or just lying there, reading, always habitually sipping.

He was drunk now, and hated himself for his earlier resolve. His faith that he could wean himself off the wine. He was hating himself for searching through the cupboards, so desperate he never trusted his own eyes.

There was no wine in his house, but searching through the kitchen, he found the cheap bottle of rum he'd never finished because it tasted like rubbing alcohol, and he spent ten minutes digging through his freezer, refusing to accept that there was no ice there, and below it, in the fridge, no mix. There were no stores open where he could go buy mix. He couldn't stand the taste of watering it down. It would only make it worse.

He needed that mix and thought his solution was brilliant: he'd walk to a McDonald's drive-thru window and order an extra-large coke. He stuck a foot in his shoe, but the sudden shift in balance toppled him over and he caught the heater on his way down with the palm of his hand, tearing it off the wall. He just stared at it: the jagged white line separating the beige paint of the wall from the bare gyproc where the heater had been attached.

Ten minutes into the hour-long walk from Gower Street to the McDonald's on Topsail Road, he realized he was wearing only one glove. He took it off to stuff it in his jacket pocket but it wouldn't fit, so he threw it at a garbage can. He missed. He kept walking. It started to snow, lightly enough that he could've dodged each oversized flake. He thought of his father, how he'd sit with a cup of tea at his office window and just watch the stuff fall, be pacified by it. Alex always found it weird, but Owen wondered what he saw in it all. He'd watch his father watching it. One night his father turned to him. *C'mere.* He patted his lap. *What if it never stopped, Owen? What if it kept falling and falling and buried us a hundred feet deep? Tell me what you'd miss the most out there.*

*Out there.* Owen kept on walking down the endless road, his body tense from the cold, arms tight against his sides, realizing that he'd grown into a man who spoke of the world with the same contempt his father had. *Out there,* he'd called it, like it was somewhere worth avoiding. All of it. Like the plague, slowly rotting us all away. It had been ten minutes since he'd walked past anything but commercial property adorned in signs and pushing products: hamburgers, clothes, booze, porn, electronics, gas for cars. Cars. *Out there.*

The snow and ice-covered sidewalks had him stumbling along like a man fresh off a merry-go-round. A young teenage couple were walking towards him, but chose to cross the street rather than walk past him. All of a sudden he was that guy now. The disheveled guy you notice and avoid. It might have bothered him if being that person didn't make life so much easier.

He was about halfway there, and a blue car full of kids drove past him, music blaring from the open windows, an indistinct buzz and thumping bass. They each threw a snowball at him. The sudden onslaught toppled him over, and laughter soared out of the car. He was too cold and drunk and irritated to laugh at himself. He was the dumb drunk who gave bored kids something to do. They circled around again and teased him this time. They drew back to throw the snowballs and feigned throwing them over and over. They laughed each time Owen braced himself. The first real one missed, but he slipped trying to dodge it. He stood up and they pretended to throw some more, but he wouldn't give them the satisfaction of running. The second snowball was packed so tight it was ice. It felt like a baseball when it crashed into his face. It pushed his bottom lip deep enough into his teeth to draw blood, like a jab from a two-pronged fork, and he let out a guttural moan that seemed to earn him some sympathy from the kids. The throbbing fat lip added to his anger and justified, in his mind, his next move. But as he was scouring the ground for something to throw, a rock or a bottle, the car sped off before he could decide if he'd actually throw it. He kept a rock in his pocket just in case they came back for round three. He filled the half-inch cut with the tip of his tongue. Tasted the metallic blood there. Felt the warmth of it filling his mouth, enough to let it collect before spitting it out.

Pressing a lump of cold snow into his throbbing lip exaggerated his previous feelings of despair. The run-in with the kids meant he was sick: a pathetic drunk too weak to clean himself up.

The walk and the fresh air, and the encounter with those kids sobered him up some, but he still startled the girl behind the drive-thru window when he staggered up to it and rapped his knuckles on the glass. She didn't want to serve him, she was visibly scared and threatened to get security, but he persisted.

She yelled through the glass, "Sir! It's our policy. We can only serve people in cars, for your safety and our safety, and for health regulations." Her breath against the window condensed, blurring her tired-looking face. Frizzy spirals of hair jutted out from under her cap. She looked equally irritated and sorry for the guy staring in at her.

He saw his patchy beard in the window, his hair woven together at all angles, like a worn-out rug. There were headlights on him now, from a car behind him. Beeping the horn. Throwing confused hands and shoulders in the air.

The commotion caught the attention of two other kids working that night. They looked about nineteen and found Owen's story hilarious and admirable. To a nineteen-year-old, a guy who walks an hour for mix must be the life of a party. They must have pictured him coming from a house party bigger than they'd ever been to, and gave him two extra-large cokes, free of charge, and a pat on the back. When he went to walk back home, one of the guys offered him a drive back to his apartment in exchange for an invite into the party. Owen nodded his head, no words.

When the kid dropped him off, Owen apologized, looking down at his feet, "Shit, man, I'm sorry. Thanks for the mix and the drive, but the party must be over." The kid sped off, more pissed off at Owen than sorry for him.

He was too worn out to take his shoes off, and streaks of slush and dirty water followed him as he walked through his cluttered living room to his kitchen. He laid the cokes in the fridge. Somewhere in the last hour and a half, the urgency for the mix had diminished and the whole act seemed pathetic. He blamed the look that kid gave him when he dropped him off. It was always the looks that got to him. He remembered his fat lip and touched it, to double-check whether that whole scene had actually happened. There was a blueberry coffee cake in the fridge he didn't remember buying. It wasn't uncommon not to know how certain things, like the coffee cake, ended up in his house.

All the dishes were dirty; every last piece of cutlery he owned was spread out across a pile of plates and bowls falling into the sink and begging to be washed: black and brown globs crusted onto everything like a colony of insects. Too much effort to wash off. He hated himself for it. For where he ended up in life, for the life that got away. For the alcoholism. Tonight was the first night he blamed the alcoholism for what he'd done with his life, and not the other was around.

He took a steak knife out of the knife block and went at the cake. He diced it up into cubes and used the knife like a skewer, but on the third cube his drunken grip sank the knife deep into the roof of his mouth. So deep that the knife was *stuck* there after he flinched and let go of the handle. His eyes burst open wide enough to tear the skin surrounding them. The salty taste of warm blood rained down on his tongue and added to the shock and pain. In front of the hazy bathroom mirror, he could barely watch as he plucked the knife from the roof of his mouth. The knife did more damage coming out than it had going in. The cut was deep enough to turn his stomach, deep enough for stitches. The flesh splayed and hanging open. Blood pooling and dripping.

He stumbled five blocks up to St. Clare's hospital, and the lady behind the glass treated him like a drunk who deserved whatever injury he had. Like she was sick of *his type* always taking up half the waiting room. She didn't even look up when she asked for his hospital card or what his problem was.

He waited on a stiff bed behind a green curtain for what felt like an hour, bored, contemplating just leaving, hating that he was so obviously drunk. But then he heard something distinct, familiar. It took him a second to place it. She was drawing back the curtains as it came to him. It was the way she was clicking a pen against her nails, like she always did, absentmindedly, when she was studying. It was Abbie. He hadn't seen her since they broke up and he moved out, yet he sensed her there, almost recognized her silent-but-deliberate footsteps, the dainty throat-clearing cough. He had forgotten that she worked there, and then he heard that clacking of pen against nail: two on the index, two on the middle, two on the ring, and two on the pinky. About a second-long pause between each two taps.

What surprised him more than seeing her was how thrilled she was to see him. She tossed her clipboard onto the bed to free her arms and splayed them wide for a hug, her raised eyebrows an inch above her eyes. She seemed electrified and flirtatious; she was alive like she was on the day he first saw her, sitting by the window in his mother's office. She was alive in a way that made him feel alive. There was energy there, he could feel it, like heat pouring out of a heater.

In a seductive voice, with a Marilyn Monroe curtsy to drive it all home, "So? How do you like me in the nurse outfit, Owen?" She ran her hands down her body, showing it off for the trophy it was. The body he loved for so long, the body he'd mapped, and knew right where to lay his arms when they slept so that they'd both be comfortable. The body with a soft brown mole on the left ribcage. Her body was more toned now, a gym membership maybe. He heard her white sneaker squeak off the linoleum floor and thought about how he'd always tease her about her tiny toes, every time he saw them, the biggest one not even an inch long. *So, do you ever just tip over when you lean forward too quickly?*

She leaned over him in a way that might have meant she still loved him. A warmth falling down onto him. Some natural, distinct, and calming smell taking him back to a better time. The power of scent, so undervalued until a moment like this when you are alive with it.

"Oooh. You'll need stitches there for sure, but it's nothing serious. The only problem will be the awkwardness of stitching the roof of a mouth. They'll probably have to use a few staples on this sucker, O." A smile like *Don't worry, won't hurt too much.*

Being in her presence, even for those five short minutes, made it clear why he'd fallen apart since they'd broken up years ago. It was the way her warmth dripped down on him as she hovered there above him. That buzz in the room that muted out everything but the sound of her voice, the mothering, the feeling connected to something more through *her.* Solely and entirely through her. He had to consciously keep his hands by his sides. It wasn't love; it was necessity, needing one more chance with her. Or maybe not even her, just what he had with her. Something definite and meaningful in a world with no real meaning.

Abbie was fiddling with paperwork and his bed sheets, seemingly lingering in his presence. The words were there, on the tip of his tongue, heavy as lead. He spat them out abruptly. "So … how did things work out with that Adam Fleisher guy, Abbie?"

He wanted to hear a long, horrible story. Instead she didn't even have to speak. She took his hand and laid it on her pregnant belly. "I'm due in seven months! I'm thinking it's a boy, but Adam puts his ear to my belly and pretends he can hear a girl's voice in there." She laughed then, like *How cute is that?*

She let his hand drop and it fell like a stone. "I hope it is a boy. We already have a girl, Kaylen. I've always wanted a boy *and* a girl." She looked down on him like she was only now remembering why they'd broken up. "Well, as you know, I guess."

She was glowing. Her life was working out, just like she'd planned it, just like she'd wanted it to on all those nights she fought with Owen. With his hand on her belly, everything inside him had deflated. He felt pinned to the bed. He felt his lungs drag in each breath of solid, heavy air, and he knew that she was right to have left him. She reached into the pocket of her nurse's outfit and plucked out the ring.

"We got married two months ago. We honeymooned in Prague. You really would love it there!"

He couldn't swallow it; he couldn't stop his face from contorting like that in front of her. He felt his jaw twist to the left and only then realized he'd been grinding his teeth. Maybe to pin his tongue down, or to divert his pain to something more physical and manageable.

Her words trailed off as she saw that he still loved her, years later, or that he at least suddenly needed her in a way she couldn't offer up. It was there in the twitchiness on his face. She eased off on exuding her happiness, for his sake, and he felt appalling for it: snuffing out a blushing bride's happily-ever-after story with that unmanageable, tortured look on his face. Truthfully, he hadn't loved her all this time, but the very second he felt her warmth, her arms around him, he felt like all those years between then and now, and all the reasons they didn't work the first time, were gone. Irrelevant.

Abbie took a step back, not rudely, just to put a little more space between them.

Despite the news of her pregnancy – the finality, the *she's not yours* of it – every minute they spent together that night helped to alleviate all of Owen's repressed baggage that he seldom acknowledged he was carrying. The guilt, bitterness, shame, and piles of excuses that got in the way, in between him and who he could be. It was vague but it was there, in the glistening of her lips, the softspoken words, the warmth of her presence, and the meaning of their connection: the why of it all. The why of what had happened to him and the why of why we're all here, any of us: to be connected to others in some meaningful way. And then the rest of it doesn't matter. Is secondary. All of it. The past that shattered him and the world he rightfully or wrongfully despised, for being so full of men with Alex's values and none of his own.

"Want to hear the funniest thing, Owen? A while back now, I found myself at Claire's … at your mother's grave. It was the day of, you know." An almost shy or nervous look spread across her face. "And then, that very night, I read a review of your book in the paper! I was so proud! What they said was exactly what would matter to you. I wanted to call, had the phone in my hand, but I didn't have your number."

He'd been too busy getting drunk to follow up on *Four Letter Words* and make a name for himself, but she didn't need to know that. And it seemed malicious, in that moment, to remind her that his dedication to writing infuriated her. Or had it? Was it the time he spent behind a closed door, or was it where he ranked writing on his priority list? The notch or two above her, above a "future" he only now saw meant *their* future.

He was back at home by 2:30 a.m., stitched up and cast back out of Abbie's life. When he walked into his suddenly smaller apartment it felt filled with thick, impenetrable silence, like he had to push his way through it. So much silence that there was almost a noise to it. An energy.

He went straight for the cheap rum. He needed something to help wash down that run-in with Abbie. That baby in her belly that could've been his. All along she was only considering what was best for him too, and all along she was right. His being jobless and single in his thirties, living off a credit card, meant that his chance for a happy little family of his own was impossible. That window of opportunity grew smaller and smaller through every year of his twenties, and now, at thirty-five, it felt smashed.

Truth was his whole life was shattered, useless, and he could trace it all back to watching his mother die on the day he put his hands on Jim Croaker and overestimated what he was capable of. Jim being a man not far off the man Owen had let himself become, because of those splinters of guilt that festered in the wounds he never dealt with. Never plucked out and let heal, because he was too busy hating the world for not being some Thoreauesque, idealistic utopia.

Now he wanted that life he'd thrown away: a wife like Abbie, two kids, a boy and a girl, and a dog to chase them around the backyard. To be a father, he only now realized, would give him that sense of purpose he'd been looking for his whole life. Alone in that silence in his apartment, he couldn't handle that realization blaring as loudly as it was. Against the starkly contrasting silence, it was like a casket closing over him. A quiet darkness.

With no destination in mind, he wrestled a jacket on. It came to him as he felt a few bills there in his pocket: get a drink downtown. Get out of the house. Blair Harvey and Mark Bragg were playing at The Ship. And then other intentions came to mind. At first a woman, some physical sensation for a mental distraction, and that release, that twenty seconds when you're not on this earth. It wouldn't be hard to find, especially not if he ventured onto George Street: every second girl pretty and willing. Normally he'd comb The Ship or CBTGs for that kind of company when he was desperate for it. Even in his lowest moments there was some uplifting salvation to be found in the right kind of beautiful woman. The way they hit him like a soft train. Finding something unique in each one, and letting her know about it. Letting her know how well she worked those boots or that scarf, or that charming laugh. To take one of them off-guard and make her laugh and acknowledge she is something worth noticing. When and if it led to sex, every one-night stand he proved a point to himself: we're all literally fucking romance to death, wondering where it's gone. Tonight he despised himself for that kind of decade-long pessimism about the world: hating himself, but thinking his values above everyone else's.

So that night he came up with different plan. He pulled the door shut behind him and held the knob in his hand for a second, hesitating on his resolve. It would have to be the right person he was looking for that night, in order to justify his actions.

It had rained that day. The water in the slush-rimmed puddles looked blue, or purple. The glare of streetlights ran through them all like yellow streams. He wanted that clichéd life now. He wanted a cubicle and bad ties. He wanted to bring Tim Hortons to co-workers, and to get stuck in traffic twice a day. He wanted a son and a daughter full of defining idiosyncrasies, and a dog that ruined all his furniture, and a wife who knew he was having a bad day just by looking at him. And he missed his mother: her from-the-gut and contagious laugh, the way she hummed to herself as she baked or waited for the kettle to boil, the way she skimmed the newspaper every day even though he never once saw her stop and read a single article. Before this night he never missed her, just mourned her. There's a difference, and he was feeling it for the first time. He let the guilt go and could finally cry for her the way he did for his father at first. The unfairness of it all. The potency and irrevocability. He held two palms to his eyes like he was keeping water from spilling through a hole in a dam. The same way he did in junior high, hiding it from his mother, who didn't need to see just how bad he wanted a father back. *His* father. The man who watched snow fall, and propped his chin up with pen tips as he wrote. The man who made his mother who she was.

All hope fell out of him in that one long, dark minute. That domestic life that he wanted now, the wife and kids, the dog and the bad ties, his one last shot at a meaningful life; it all seemed impossible, more out of reach than the sun. Less likely than a career in writing. And Abbie was right, there was nothing noble about what he'd done with his life. There was nothing dignified about a man drunk, with tears in his eyes and this kind of plan in mind, mourning the life he never had to mourn. And there was no point dwelling on a past at the cost of a future, but he'd been doing it for years now. It felt too long to undo. A knot untangleable. He needed someone to tear him apart.

He rounded Water Street, heading to George Street, and saw exactly what he was looking for at a chip truck on Adelaide Street. The guy's hair was too perfect, like a helmet laid flat on his head, and his black shirt looked painted on. A gold chain looped around his neck, his sleeves short enough to show notable biceps. His goatee obviously groomed daily. There was ketchup in it, and he shoved fries into his mouth ten at a time as he insulted the Asian kid serving the fries, too obviously as a way to get the attention of the girl behind him. He muttered something degrading in a fake Chinese accent, laughed at himself, and looked at her. The guy couldn't tell she would smile only when he looked at her. She jerked away from his chip-greased hand both times he put in on her shoulder. Shuddered a little. He'd butted back in line. "Are you deaf? You speaky English? Me want more ketchup!" He turned again with that dumb laugh, and it was perfect.

Owen stepped right up in his face before the kid could answer. "The bottle is right there, asshole. You blind? Dumb? Here!" This would work only if Owen was extreme about it. So he picked up the bottle and emptied half of it unto the guy's fries, globs of red spilling over onto his hands. And then he squirt a line up the guy's shirt sleeve and into his face. He threw the plastic ketchup bottle at him when he was done. A physical exclamation mark. "All good?"

It was like a car slamming into his face, and his vision blurred. The second blow knocked him to the ground. Two of the guy's friends helped pick Owen back up, and they all dragged him into an alley. He wasn't defending himself, just provoking them. One blow and he was back on the filthy ground: pizza boxes, mustard packets, puddles of puke, a used condom. The street sludge smelled like wet newspaper. They all kicked him rapid-fire and the pain was unbearable. It was perfect. It winded him, his heart was an overworked motor. One kick just under his eye, and what felt like a bubble formed above his jawbone. Skin literally tore, and bruised. He was flat on his back now and they were stamping him. Padded hammers laying cold wet spots of street grime. When they stood to walk away he propped himself up and threw a half-empty bottle of beer at them. The guy in the green shirt turned, grabbed him by his jacket, slung him into the wall, his head cracking off it, his tongue nipped deep by his teeth. The blood warm, briny.

He heard a girl's voice screaming at them all, in between telling someone else on her phone where she was calling from and what was happening, blow by blow. "They're going to *kill* him! And I think he wants them to! He's … he's just crazy!"

One guy was behind Owen now, with Owen's arms held back. His whole body jutted forward from the pressure at his shoulders, the blades arching off his back like wings. He saw flashing blue and white lights. The biggest of the three guys stepped back, lunged three steps forward, and his fist was a ball of steel. Owen fell to the ground, not breathing, not able to catch himself. Heard a car door slam, heard sirens, tasted salty slush, saw feet running down the other side of the alley. Blinking through it all, not sure if he was even breathing still, he saw policemen's pants, then knees, and then a face. The other cop asking the girl what happened. Her telling the cop that Owen wanted to die. "He wouldn't *let* them leave him alone! *Gawd!* It was … too sick. He's sick. He wanted to die. He begged and taunted them, and spit at them, and cried and laughed and yelled … it was … sick."

⌦

She must have thought he was asleep, not just ashamed and hiding behind shut eyes. When she wasn't looking, he'd open the lids enough to watch her. He saw her with a phone book, sitting in a chair, half the book on each thigh, a poor speller taking the extra minute to find the name. And then he watched her hesitating. Dialing three numbers then hanging up. All ten, then hanging up. Pacing now, no longer sitting down.

Her voice was quivering. "Alex? It's Abbie … Darenberg. Fleisher actually. Owen's ex, your mother's old assis–"

She paced around the floor, running a hand through her hair, like she didn't know where to start. Like she wished she had rehearsed a speech before calling him. Like she had no idea what Alex knew of Owen's life these last few years.

"Have you been talking to Owen lately?"

Silence. He could just barely recognize his brother's voice, tinny in the receiver, but not the words.

Minutes later. "We don't, that's the thing. He's in hospital … St. Clare's luckily, and in my care. He's in bad shape, but he's okay overall. I–"

Silence, just the sounds of her pacing the floor and listening to Alex and intermittently explaining, she herself confused.

"The police are saying he started it, and there was a witness saying he wouldn't even defend himself, or back down, so he … I dunno … did this to himself? He seems worse than ever, that's why I asked if you've been talking to him lately. He seems so defeated here, Alex. It's … sad."

Silence. A sigh, a shaking head.

"It's Saturday, Alex. Monday isn't soon enough. He can't be alone right now. This has to be his rock bottom and he has to get help and change *now*. Or it's going to be too late. It's that simple and that urgent."

Biting her lip now, rapidly, subconsciously, over and over, waiting for a solution, for an answer to what they were going to do with him. "I can see to it that he's kept overnight, but they'll want that bed by tomorrow afternoon, and I really don't think he should spend another night alone."

More silence. A deep exhale, thirty seconds long.

"There isn't a rehab in the province, Alex. And I don't think he'd go if there was one. It's not that easy to convince people–"

It burst out of the phone: "Oh, he's fucken going, Abbie!"

"Alex, this isn't going to happen that easily."

Her pager went off then and she read the number. "I have to run. My old phone number at home is the same, and if you don't have it, I'm in the phone book under Adam Fleisher. Or you can call this number back if I'm not there. I'll do what I can to have Owen kept here until you show up, but I can't promise you anything."

She sat next to him now, the mattress sagging just slightly with her weight. Owen slammed his eyes shut. She was close enough that he could hear Alex now.

"I appreciate it, Abbie."

"Yeah, well ... like I said, Alex, Owen's troubles run deeper than alcoholism. He'll need one of those therapy-based programs while you're looking into it, okay? He needs to leave this hospital and go straight there. Tonight needs to be his rock bottom."

Alex was silent for so long she had to check that he was still there. "Alex?"

"Yeah, sorry. I'm just–"

"I know, Alex. I know." Her pager went off again. "Listen. I'm going to play the *he is a danger to himself* card to keep him here against his will. That'll buy us forty-eight hours. You'll be here by then."

"Thanks, Abbie."

"Take care, and leave talking to Owen about getting help to me, okay? I know these aren't your kind of conversations, and we both know he'll put up less of a fight with me."

"Abbie ... are you sure?"

"I'm sure. I know how to appeal to him a little better too, I imagine. You just take care of the arrangements. I can do this much for your mother's sake, if not for his."

She hung up the phone, turned to look at Owen, and caught him with his eyes open.

"Oh! Hey you! Feeling any better?" She was too forcefully jovial, too obviously cheery. It made him feel pitiful.

"Abbie ... why are you doing this ... for me? Really?"

"Because a man can lose his footing sometimes. That's all this is for you. You lost your footing. I care about you enough to do what I can, and maybe I'm doing this for your mother as well. And a woman *can* love a guy in a non-romantic way, Owen. But I have to go. I've been paged, like, four minutes ago. I'll be back though, by your side until you're dismissed."

He watched her walk away and pull his door to. He saw the doorknob stay twisted for five or six seconds, then she let go and sped down the hall, like she needed five seconds to shift gears between sympathetic ex-girlfriend and friend of the family to a nurse five minutes late on a page.

# LIFE AFTER DEATH

THEY SHIPPED HIM TO VANCOUVER. That's how he felt: shipped. And it all started in less than twelve hours, the tell-tale shakes, "sweating it out," and the headaches that send most alcoholics back to the bottle, but he had nowhere to go. Being in that clinic was like being locked in a room on fire, there was nowhere to run, no way to end the pain, nothing but time ticking slowly and indifferently by. It got worse from there. He was vomiting and retching enough to temporarily distract himself from the shakes and headaches, but never the cramps. His body was writhing with a stiff, sharp pain. He'd lost all control over his own body. When the nausea was at its worst, his vision was distorted and the colours of everything seemed hazy and vibrant. There was always a bright blue or blazing orange halo around the edges of things, especially his windowsill.

He wasn't expecting it to be that bad. He thought he was having a bad reaction to the pills they were giving him, until they told him the pills were only Ativan. He felt continuously on the verge of a seizure, maybe even death, and he couldn't pry himself from the bed, not even for food. He just rocked back and forth in bed, wanting to fall asleep, dying to sleep through the rest of his withdrawal, until he started having nightmares, visions of his mother on the day she died.

The worst was realizing that he wasn't dreaming; it was more like he was hallucinating. He was in too much shock and discomfort to assess whether he'd gone mad, but he was seeing his dead mother's body in the corner of his room. His frantic reaction was upsetting people in adjacent rooms, and a staff medic had to examine him when the tremors and hallucinations peaked. The medic stepped around the puddles of puke in Owen's room, jabbed Owen's arm with a needle, explaining, as if legally obligated, not emotionally involved, "I am administering Haldol. You are going through a serious complication of alcohol withdrawal. Delerium tremens."

Owen begged for alcohol, just a little at a time to get him through this before his body shut down on him. He was left throwing up and locked in a cage of a body that was attacking him, exacting some revenge on him for years of abuse. When it got worse, the medic administered some heavier sedatives. Every few hours he was being stuck with needles or chewing up chalky pills.

~

Looking back on his forty-hour detox, Owen preferred to call those hallucinations "visions." It sounded less dramatic, and that made him feel less pathetic. In those visions, somewhere between sleep and lucidity, somewhere between this world and another, Owen was staring into his mother's eyes as she lay on his bedroom floor. She was slowly dying, all over again. He didn't want to look but had to. Like there was something to take away from it.

The night the withdrawal finally let up, he fell asleep for thirteen hours. He dreamt that he and Alex were playing the dollar game with their father. It was game they played as kids where his father would throw a dollar on the ground and the three of them would wrestle for it. Whoever held the dollar had to try and keep it from the other two. It was essentially a wrestling match, but their father manipulated their bodies to minimize contact so that no one ever got hurt. The dream played out until they all lost sight of the dollar and couldn't find it. Then he realized that he and Alex were grown men in the dream, but their father was a younger version of himself: before the schizophrenia, before the Waterford Hospital, before the grey hair and crow's feet. His father stood up, waved goodbye, and walked out the patio door into the bright distance.

When he'd disappeared, Owen looked at Alex and they both agreed there was no use looking for the dollar now, or playing that game without their father. Then the room started shaking, like an earthquake, and it was no longer their childhood home. Seconds before the room started shaking, Alex looked at him and said, *We should go now*, and took off running, wondering why Owen wasn't following him. It was ominous the way he said it, but Owen never followed his brother. Even if he wanted to, he could tell the corridor his brother ran down was too narrow for them both and that the ground behind Alex was crumbling with every step he took. He sat down and could hear his brother calling out to him, his voice growing more and more faint, the room filling with dust. At some point, the room transformed into his old apartment, and he was surrounded by dirty dishes, rusty serrated steak knives, and piles of empty wine bottles. There was a snowbank in the corner of the room where his computer should've been. When the shaking stopped he stood up to walk outside. It was bright when he opened the door, too bright to see where he was walking. In that brightness there was nothing to see and nothing to fear. There was no past to run from and no future to cower from; there was only the sound of his feet clapping off the pavement beneath him. Nothing was pushing or pulling him, his mind was clear. He stopped walking when he felt like he was where he had to be. He took a deep breath and felt calm. With each breath, he was sucking up the brightness and about to reveal where he stood, where he could go to feel as away from everywhere as he did in that dream. He woke up. He felt weak but revived.

Full days had escaped him, and he had no recollection of that lowest point in his recovery, but the world seemed more subdued now, and his room looked more detailed. He felt himself in his body now: before it was just a shell that housed him. Now he could feel his tongue between his teeth, the sensation of his fingernails across the backs of his hands as he scratched himself.

Over the course of his forty-two day rehabilitation, Owen let himself fall apart. He brought everything to the surface and dealt with his issues one by one, dwelling on each until there was nothing left to ponder, or at least until it was clear there was nothing he could do about it now. At what point had he let his life go? Why? He thought about what it means when there is no more for a man outside of a rehab clinic than there is inside. The place encouraged him to journal. Anything that came to him. So he did. He also researched the course details of a few culinary school programs. He could love to cook for a living, for his wife and kids. For his brother and the two nieces he barely knew. He'd get to know them when he left this place. He was sure of that much.

# ALEX

AFTER READING ALL ABOUT THE horrors of alcohol withdrawal, Alex flew to Vancouver to be there for Owen as he went through the worst of it, but the clinic had a strict policy that no visitors were allowed for the first few weeks, and Owen wasn't in a state to be visited anyway. Alex understood and left a message for Owen that he would check back in three weeks, and that their Aunt Lillian wanted to come along as well, if that would be okay.

Before he left, he pleaded with the clinic director that his brother be treated with a drug called Librium. He said he'd write the prescription himself if someone could administer it. The staff patronized him: he wasn't the first doctor to come in and tell them how to do their jobs, and Alex left knowing he'd be ignored.

On the plane back home in February, Alex considered inviting his brother to come live with him and Hannah for a while, so that they could keep an eye on him to monitor his recovery. He figured being submerged in a new and positive environment would have to help, but it was a lot to ask of his wife, and could be a lot to subject his daughters to if things got bad.

On a Sunday in March, Alex went back to Vancouver. As he walked towards the doors of his brother's clinic, the idea of Owen coming to live with them came back to him.

He knocked on his brother's door, heard a "come in," and was surprised by the luxury of the room. The television set. It looked even nicer than in the brochures. Real hardwood floors, a stylish bed, modern colours on the walls.

"Hey hey, little bother! How's the luxury life going? Jesus. This place is nicer than my house!"

"Yeah, well, we sort of graduate to different tiers of the building as we get better. Maybe it's some kind of reward system, I dunno." Owen looked sheepish.

"So, how is it going now then? How are you feeling? Did they mention I was by last month? I brought some books for you. Hannah is an avid reader. The modern literary stuff, just how you like it. She suggested a bunch of titles to bring to you."

He laid four books on an end table and Owen examined them right away.

Reading a back cover. "This is very kind of her. I'm touched, seriously, be sure to thank her, and tell her I was impressed with the choices. I thought by now she'd see me as some family burden who was stealing you away."

"No, not Hannah. She says everyone has a story. She says you can't judge a person until you've weighed their story against their character to see how it all lines up. And she insists that anybody can get off track." He caught himself then, felt like that was a degrading or accusatory comment. "I mean ... not that you're some kind of walking tragedy or anything, that's not what I meant. Just that ..."

Owen laughed a little at his walking on eggshells. "I know, Alex, calm down. And listen, I'm glad you're here. I've been wanting to apologize. I've been a prick and a burden and I am sorry for that. This isn't the part where I talk about seeing the light and really turn my life around, but it's the part where I can accept a lot more than I could before, and feel like I have the energy to start from scratch, and you got me here. I appreciate that. The booze made a mess of me and I made some horrible decisions. Things just, I don't know, weigh on you a little more heavily when you're drinking, like you can't see around them. I mean, Jesus Christ, you've got two daughters I've only seen in photos. What kind of brother was I during these last few years? I am sorry for that. And I can't say I feel like I can just spring back to life now, but I know that all that dark shit I had trapped and festering in my head these last few years, I've gotten rid of it all or accepted what I cannot change. You put up the money for this place, and you saved my life."

These weren't the types of conversations Alex was comfortable with, and his brother was all over the place anyway. He nodded once and sat down in a recliner near Owen's bed. "She'll be glad to know you liked the books. She'd be pretty excited if you called her sometime to talk about one of them too. I think she's going stir crazy lately. Too much time around the house doing nothing. She could use a friend if you need one." He rolled his eyes. He pulled the lever and reclined back in the chair. "So?"

"Sooo."

They laughed.

"So what do two brothers talk about in a rehab clinic?"

"Yeah … wanna take a walk around the place, grab a few soft drinks and play catch up?"

"Funny thing is I've seriously been having this craving for a Mountain Dew these last few days." He cocked the recliner back into place. "Let's do it. You can try and explain to me how all this started in the first place."

Rising up off his bed. "You wouldn't understand."

"C'mon, you know what Momma always said." They both

laughed. "I don't have to understand to listen." Alex held the bedroom door open for his brother.

Walking towards a vending machine. "Well ... it was actually this thing Baron said, when we were living there. How there is no place left in the world for people like Dad and me. I couldn't see around that notion for a while. I could only see two things clearly: how the world is and how I didn't fit into it. And I imagined there were only two kinds of people: *successes* and those who fail to succeed. You have your CEOs, doctors, lawyers, that type, living in three-storey houses, plasma screens in the bathroom, three cars in the garage, and then you have the people who have tried and failed, or who just don't have the capacity to achieve that sort of life, so they spend their time feeling bitter, dejected, and jealous about it. But then there was me, not fitting into either of those descriptions and not fitting into the world. I got bogged down by it all after Abbie and me split."

They were at the vending machine now, and Owen put in enough for two Mountain Dews. Handing one to Alex. "I weaned myself off the booze and took up a real sweet tooth for soft drinks in its place. There's something about the burn of soft drinks that makes them a readymade substitute."

They sat on a windowsill, almost hidden behind the huge potted plants on either side of the window.

"And then I guess at some point, I got to hating myself for having thrown my life away trying to get a book published, putting that before everything, and hitting thirty with no solid career, no foundation set up to settle down on with someone." Owen plucked a leaf off a tree, rolled it in his fingers, threw it back in the pot. "Anyway. Once I noticed how the wine was helping me write, it was all over then, because I could justify it."

⚓

Before Alex left Owen's room that day, he pulled five sheets of looseleaf from his brother's garbage can and stuffed them into his briefcase while Owen was using the washroom. He'd seen his name on them and curiosity got the better of him. He'd read it on the plane ride back home, if only to pass the time.

He was hoping it was just another story, that the character name was a coincidence. Another one of his brother's dark and depressing stories, flirting with the boundaries between fact and fiction. Alex always admired Owen's honesty though, and his lack of concern about how people perceived him. Everything Alex did, he did to prove himself flawless, or at least respectable to the world. He was envious of the freedom Owen must have felt in expressing himself so openly, in not caring what others thought of his life. Owen found a liberty in mocking himself, in acknowledging his flaws; it meant there was nothing to hide from. Alex hid all of his flaws and lived constantly on edge, always worrying someone would see through him and all his achievements like Owen could. And he was always jealous of the simple places Owen could find pleasure and meaning, like in his writing, or even simpler, in a hike with a camera around his neck.

But this time around, his brother's honesty on those pages he was reading was too intimate, and it wasn't even a story. It was an essay, or a journal entry, or whatever it was that clinic was encouraging him to write, and his brother was putting himself out there on display like some bizarre sculpture in a museum. The one no one gets. The one people stick their chewed gum under and question the value of. Every line of those five pages was filled, front and back, with Owen's childlike and urgent scribbles. Alex was desperate to know what prompted his brother to write this, but would never ask.

## *"Reflections on Guilt" Assignment*

*We are not as strong as we'd like to believe. We are frail and ever-deflating, but lie to ourselves and act strong. Those scars from our childhood get infected and burn bright inside us, begging to be dealt with. They want closure, they want stitches and to heal. But how? How do I bury a memory, how do I bury a lifetime of haunting memories that have made me who I am, without burying myself along with them? They are a part of me, and there's not much left of me to bury.*

*I can still see that look in my mother's eyes, in everything I see around me. I dream of it, every twisted incoherent dream sequence leads me back to that shelter, staring into my mother's dying eyes and watching all the life in her escaping. Each breath was laboured, numbered, each breath left her body more and more motionless and empty, until there was nothing left inside her. A doll now, a memory. It was the longest and most helpless minute of my life; I suppose that's why it stands out more than any other. I can still see those flakes of soil blowing on and off her face, and that pool of her crimson blood that her head lay on like a pillow. By the time they took her body away, that pool of blood had seeped down into the soil, and my childhood had drowned in it. I wondered what would grow there above it. Grass, dandelions, nothing? Her favourite wildflowers in St. John's were always striped toadflax. It grew like weeds around that old shelter. I could hope for that. It felt like both a morbid and peaceful notion.*

*I saw forty-three years' worth of memories seep out of my mother in that one minute she lay there between life and death. As they fled from her, I imagine them all as being pleasant, except for those last few years with Dad losing his mind and all. None of us truly recovered from that, we just carried on. There is a big difference.*

*As I think back on her now, I can't help but wonder if it was all those pleasant memories she had that made her a better person than me, because I believe we are a product of our experiences, not our genes. I believe that we head into each new day as the construct of all memories preceding that day. I think this is why my brother and I are so different, we have kept or discarded different memories. I think maybe it is my brother's ability to erase the same wretched memories I have that makes him a more stable person than me. We are all born equal, they say, and at birth we are all blank slates, no memories, no identities, no ambitions or desires. But that all changes the second we take our first breaths. That all changes with everything we see, taste, touch, smell and hear until the day we die.*

*My mother, the day my grandfather died, told me that my grandfather wasn't really dead. I never really understood her at the time, but she promised that someday I would. What she meant was that he had an impact on far too many people's lives to simply stop existing the day he died. He would live on in memory, in how he influenced who my mother and I were. What she said was: all that remains of us is in our children. We live on in our children.*

*What does that say about me? Am I really my parents? The best of them? The worst of them? A random mix? In any case I feel a terrible let-down. It's that notion, that statement of hers, that makes me feel depressed and felonious, not simply that I am a mess or a failure. Because if it is true that all that remains of my mother is in me, in who and what I am, I have disgraced the most beautiful woman I have ever known. I have also disgraced my distinguished and benevolent father and his family name. I am nothing, and that speaks so poorly to their character. Thank God, or whatever made us, for Alex.*

*When I get out of this clinic, maybe I can work towards a better life. It's a sad realization: there is no more for me outside of these walls than there is within them. I have wasted my life, at least a decade of it, and it might be too late for me. Our whole lives Alex and I have knocked how each other lives, what the other wanted out of life. We were both capable of greatness in whatever fields we chose. I guess the difference is he chose, I got distracted. By alcohol, and the whole quixotic writing thing. Or was it the lousy childhood, something so obviously simple and Freudian? Our past was like a tumour inside of us, but mine was a cancer and his was benign.*

*I have no trouble accepting the blame for where I've gone wrong. I've taken the blame for plenty of shit growing up, even when it wasn't even my fault, and I have never resented or regretted doing so. Take the incident with Greg Evans' mother. She was there for us during all that shit with Dad going away. So when her ex-boyfriend started making her life difficult, we thought we were helping. The idea was to leave a note threatening him to back off, and to light his compost bin on fire. The fire got out of hand though. We'd used too much fire-starter fluid, and Alex took off, leaving me with the decision to let the guy's house burn down or get caught. I suppose there was no point in both of us getting in trouble, and as always it was understood that I was the one who should take the fall for something like this.*

*The stalker guy opened his patio door as I was hosing out the fire with his sprinkler. He had called the cops the second he saw me. I thought I got away with it all, since I took off over his fence before the cops showed up. I jumped his fence like a hurdle and never looked back. I guess he*

*recognized me as a friend of Greg's. I imagine the note
helped, and he knew what school we all went to. The next
day the cops questioned me, and well, convinced me not
to lie, I guess. Given my age and motive, I got off with
some community service. I was cleaning up litter and
planting flowers as punishment while Alex sat at home
playing our new video games. This meant he was always
a level or two ahead of me and ruined any surprises, so I
stopped playing those stupid games even though they were
the simplest and easiest source of joy in my life at the time.
They sort of distracted us from the silence in the house since
Dad was sent away. I remember hating Alex for that, and
wondering if the hate was ill-placed.*

A stewardess came by with a drink tray as Alex read the
last line, as if he'd mentally summoned her, empathetic
telepathy. He asked for a double scotch on the rocks, tilted his
chair back, and was thankful there was no one sitting beside
him. He twirled the glass in his hands, listened to the ice cubes
clink off the glass, and let that piece sink in. Did Owen harbour
any subconscious unspoken resentment of him? If so, was it
warranted?

He brought the glass to his nose and sniffed. An odd habit
of his was to smell any food or drinks before consuming them.
The smell of alcohol unexpectedly turned him off. To drink it
suddenly felt like siding with the devil that had done his
brother in. It was alcohol that had made a bloody mess of him.
He set the glass back down in the oversized cup holder and
stared at the clouds.

Alex realized the most significant differences between him
and Owen had always revolved around their feelings about their
father, before and after the schizophrenia. Growing up, Owen
never complained about their father's shitty station wagon the
way Alex did, and made do with their allowance, even if it
wasn't as much as their friends got from their parents. Alex was

always sure to let his family know they were poor, relative to most of his friends. Their mother's never-changing retort: *Well you must have some rich friends, sweetie, because you've got your own bedroom and want for nothing!*

He thought of their Uncle Ross, his father's only brother. He remembered that Ross always flew in to see their father, at Christmas and over summer vacation, but his father never traveled to visit Ross. He later pieced it together that Ross had ten times the money his father had, and that was why he was the one to absorb the travel cost of seeing the other. Ross had a home in St. John's, and another in the Caribbean somewhere. On one trip home, he offered to buy their father a new car to replace that *shitty old thing you're driving.* The old, dated car Alex hated so much. Alex couldn't believe his uncle's generosity, but their father refused, muttered something about character, and *it does the trick, point A to point B.*

Alex never spoke to his father for weeks, and one morning he took his father's toothbrush and smeared the bristles along the inside of their toilet bowl. The whole situation surrounding the car made Alex think that Ross was superior to his father, and that money was a testament to a man's character and inherent worth. From that point on he was convinced that a man defines himself not through education or spiritual enlightenment, but through what he owns and earns. You couldn't look at a man like his father and see philanthropy and depth of character, but you could look at a man like Ross and see his money. He assumed that his father rejected Ross' offer because he was jealous of Ross. Alex admired Ross, his money, the smell of his cologne, the hem and fit and price tags on all his suits, and that second home down on some island he could never remember the name of. He admired Ross, but Owen admired their father. Alex thought this made Owen ignorant and beneath him.

*You grow up and be like Dad then, and I'll grow and be like Ross. You can be a poor boring dimwit driving a crappy car, and I'll be the one to come and visit you in my Porsche. Let's make a bet right here today. Twenty bucks says I'll be happier at thirty living like Ross and you'll be as boring as Dad.*

He sat up in the seat on the plane feeling like he owed his brother twenty bucks. Owen might be the only person who knew it, but Alex was never happy. He always wanted more: a bigger house, a better car, and at times, a prettier wife. A more professional wife. A wife that didn't need "warming up" before sex, because he didn't have the time and energy for it anymore. He wanted a son but had two daughters, and as much as he loved them, they weren't cognitively years ahead of the other children in their class like he imagined *his* children would be. He was a surgeon, but the hospital he was working in wasn't cutting edge enough for him, wasn't ranked as one of the top ten in the world.

He picked up his drink, the ice cubes had melted. He emptied the glass in one quick gulp, and wiped the corner of his mouth with the sleeve of an Armani suit. Used it like a napkin. He set the glass back in the cup holder and decided that when Owen was released, whatever was left of him should come stay with him and Hannah for a while. For however long it took to get back on his feet. He was looking forward to it. And it would do Hannah some good to have someone in their spare room so she could start seeing it as a spare bedroom and not what it was intended to be. And maybe having Owen around would liven her up a little. Get her out of that funk. That years-long funk she'd been in.

PART THREE
AWAY FROM EVERYWHERE

# IF FISTS COULD SPEAK
# OR WORDS COULD HEAL

OWEN WOKE TO THE SOUND of a viciously hissing kettle and his Aunt Lillian's motherly voice talking someone down on the telephone. The kettle stopped whistling and he could hear Lillian's graceful hand searching the inside of a tin can for one of her chamomile teabags. That kettle squealed every morning as if it felt the pain of being burned. It was the noise that woke him every morning since she took him five and a half weeks ago.

"One thing at a time or we'll get nowhere at all!"

Lillian was talking to Alex, Owen could tell. Alex had been calling more and more frequently for help with the girls. Any fatherly instinct he once had was thieved from him by grief and despair. It didn't help that he had never been much of a father in the first place. He wasn't a bad father; he just wasn't an inherently good father. He was an absent father too preoccupied with work and his image to discover the simple joys that lay in spending time with his daughters. In hearing them laugh, in pushing their tiny excited bodies on a swing at the park, or in hearing their unlearned thoughts on God and life and insects. Hannah had listened to her girls explain why *they* thought spiders had eight legs and found their theories and reasoning fascinating. Owen would help the girls collect spiders in mason jars, and search the Internet for what kind of food to give a daddy-long-legs spider. Alex, however, just assumed that his girls hated spiders because they were girls, or because there is nothing inherently interesting about spiders.

In the weeks after Hannah's death, Lillian would come back home complaining about how messy Alex's house was. *Filthy, not fit for them kids to be in. The garbage didn't even get out, there were fruit flies. All the dishes were dirty and strewn around empty bags of take-out and pizza boxes.*

Christmas that year was brutal, exactly three weeks after Hannah died. It was staged, faked, lived through with fleeting smiles and bursts of happiness snuffed out by the reality of their new family life flashing at random. Lillian wrapped the girls' gifts that year, not their mother. Lillian did whatever she could when Alex called, and she was spending most nights at Alex's house now, because Alex had forbidden her to bring the kids back to her house because Owen was there. She taught Alex how to use his washer and dryer and felt it was chauvinist of her nephew that he had left so much for Hannah to deal with. He couldn't even prepare an edible meal for his daughters. He poured their baths too hot and never pestered them to finish their meals. He figured extra dessert was fine since it meant a full stomach. Over a period of about three weeks Lillian had pretty well straightened him and the girls out. They were all clear on what the girls were used to eating for lunch and what channels their favourite shows came on. She thought he was going to be fine until the phone rang that morning.

"Alex, rambling on like this isn't changing anything. I'll be over in ten minutes. You're due at that meeting with your boss at nine. I'll be there at quarter to nine to watch the girls. While I'm there I'll find a nice daycare for them to go to after school, and when you get home, I'll go into their school and ask the teachers about making up lost time."

She was trying to calm Alex. Owen looked across the room at the telephone sitting on his bedside table and wanted desperately to pick up the receiver and listen in, but to be caught would be too awkward. He worried about Callie and Lucia. They knew he was staying with Lillian and knew that she was on speed dial, number 2.

Days later, while Lillian was shopping for bird feed, they called him. They were crying too hard to get their words out, their throats too constricted. It was Callie on the phone, with Lucia shouting queries at her and into the receiver.

"How come only Daddy loves us now?"

"Callie, no ... it's ... that's not true, okay?" The words simply weren't there to explain the mess to them. Their vocabulary didn't include adultery and betrayal, and he didn't want it to. Not yet.

The words didn't need to be there anyway, Owen did, to wipe the tears from their freckled faces, but he couldn't be. The circumstances of their mother's death meant they had to lose their uncle as well, but there was no way to express that. Every word those girls uttered into the phone felt like shears slicing into his heart; the longer the sentence the deeper the cut.

"Ask him if he still loves us, Callie. Tell him Lucia said we got hamsters for Christmas but Daddy keeps forgetting to buy us a wheel. Ask him if he can get us the wheel. Tell him, Callie ... what did he say?"

He was as surprised as they were when he started crying. He didn't know what to do with the tears as they wet his face, he wasn't expecting it to affect his speech like that. *C-Callie, t-tell your s-sister...* All he could do was reassure them that he loved them, but that didn't matter to two little girls who needed physical contact with him, the warm comforting blanket of a hug and kiss on the forehead.

"I ... I'm just really busy with work now, like Daddy always was before. But maybe sometime soon we can go for some ice creams at that store you like so much, okay? We'll see. Be good girls for Daddy now, won't you? Promise me? And your Aunt Lilly too. Okay, girls?"

"But all the bugs we collected together are dead now. Even the pretty black-and-orange butterfly. Even the caterpillar you promised would turn into a butterfly if I took good care of it."

"It's winter now, Callie. There's no bugs to hunt, right? Ask Aunt Lillian for the hamster wheel okay? And ..." he hesitated before lying, "maybe next summer we'll go butterfly hunting. At the cabin."

He hung up wondering if she would grow up and consider him the man who killed his mother. They man who made a promise and never spoke to her again. The man who built a treehouse in her backyard, or the man who destroyed her family.

⌒

Minutes after Owen got off the phone with his nieces, he found himself walking to Hannah's grave, thinking he could temporarily escape it all by hiding out there. Her white marble headstone a brighter white than the dirty snow. It was still totally unweathered by the elements, except for smears from a few rotten, soggy leaves clinging to the base of it, some frozen into the inch of snow climbing up the stone. It was quiet enough that he could hear the wind, and bits of litter – empty chip bags and coffee cups – slapping off headstones.

He was sitting at Hannah's grave by noon and was still there at three o'clock when Alex arrived with the kids after school. It was as if the graveyard was designed in a way to provide for such privacy: Alex could not have seen Owen sitting at his wife's grave until he ascended a hill and was within ten feet of him, and Owen never heard them approaching on account of the traffic, and the fact he just wasn't paying attention to the world around him. Then he heard Lillian clear her throat, intentionally. And he heard his nieces, giddy and excited, their tones indicating they never really understood their situation. *Uncle Owen?*

Owen stood, paralyzed, barely even breathing, speechless. The girls were trying to run towards him, but Alex had them clutched at the wrist by his gloved hands. They were an arm's length away from his body, tugging against their father and trying to get free, but Alex's hands were like chains clamped around their wrists. The heel of his black shoes dug into the snow so they couldn't jerk him forward. Lillian took Lucia up in her arms then, and Alex did the same with Callie, all the while glaring at Owen.

Owen knew what was coming. It was clear in Alex's eyes what his intentions were, and Owen knew he'd have to stand there and take it. That it would hurt. That it would hurt even more because it was a man he loved who would be inflicting the pain. A man he loved had good reason to close his fist and bust open his jaw, drive skin into bone, draw blood. And he'd have to watch the whole thing, hopeless and repentant.

Owen watched Alex dump Callie on Lillian, and watched Lillian start to panic, but he still couldn't move. He wouldn't move. He just stood there, waiting.

Five sprinting paces and Alex was right there in his face. Owen dropped to his knees to take it, and halfway down he felt a foot pressed against the back of his head, and saw Hannah's gravestone coming forcifully towards him. He heard Lillian and the girls screaming now, fear thick in their pitch, and felt the thud of her headstone against him like a gunshot. Felt his neck almost snap as his head met the stone at a sharp angle, and his brother's boot kept it there, sliding his forehead across the stone. He hit the ground then, looked up and saw a drop of blood in the indented C of *Here Lies Hannah Collins*. There was blood collecting in the hair of his left eyebrow. It was warm. He looked to Lillian, knowing he couldn't fight back, and saw that her first instinct was not to haul Alex back, not to choose sides, but to shield the girls from as much of this image of their father as she could. She was trying to spin them around, turn their backs on it all, cover their eyes. They fought against her, trying to shake themselves loose.

Owen was on his hands and knees now, like a dog. He'd fallen face first into hard, crusty, ice-glazed snow. It was sharp: a bed of needles pressing into his cheeks and eyes. He rolled over onto his side and looked up to see his brother standing over him. He pressed his shoe down on Owen's face as if it were a giant fetid insect he wanted squat, forcing his face into hard, crusty ice. The wet footprint on his cheek was cold and soothed the sting. He could taste the snow in his mouth now, and it was a mild distraction from the pain. Alex stamped his chest and Owen felt as if his ribs had cracked, all of them. He panicked and gasped for air and got none, and his lungs felt filled with fire. And then a pop, a ringing ear, the lobe split from the pressure of the kick.

Owen tried his hardest to whisper, "Not now, Alex, c'mon. Not here, not in front of Callie and Lucia. Not in front of Callie and Lucia."

The girls were frantic, screeching so loudly their throats sounded raw and bloody.

"Not in front of the girls? You think you own them now too? Hey? Talking like *you're* their fucken father ... at *my* wife's grave."

Callie broke free of Lillian's grip. Lillian just wept, and threw her arms up in the air, and looked on and then away from the scene, again and again.

"It should've been you that died in that car, you piece of shit drunk, because at least no one would miss you. But no, it's like Mom all over again. Here *you* are and there *Hannah* is." He pointed at her headstone, only now noticing Owen's blood there.

Alex looked betrayed that the girls were pleading for their father to stop beating on Owen. They grabbed at their father as he swatted their hands away like flies.

"Alex, it's not the right time for this."

"Here, why don't you take them too?"

He grabbed Callie by the arm, hard enough to hurt her, and shoved her down on top of Owen. It was too much. Owen finally stood up and comforted Callie, told her it was okay, that Daddy was sorry and didn't mean to upset her. Owen looked up and saw Alex staring at his daughter now. Unsure, with a slight trembling of atonement about him. Alex saw only his daughter now, what he'd just done to her. He turned and saw Lillian appalled, Lucia afraid of him. Both of his daughters feared him now. He swung his head around the scene like a man deeply sorry and deeply ashamed, totally silent now, and yet there was that look of relief and vindication that strangely meant he was only human.

When two policemen approached them, Owen waved them off and assured them all was well. He had an arm around Callie and used her like a crutch. He pressed the fingers of his other hand into the cut near his temple to assess the damage. He ran the backs of his fingers over the bump on his head.

❧

The police drove Owen home from the graveyard, and at the first red light they broke a ten-minute silence. The one who spoke was a stereotypical, fat-but-fit mustached cop. He spoke to Owen by meeting his eyes in the rearview mirror. "I would encourage you to press charges, sir. Frankly, any man who would get violent in front of his children like that ... well ... I have to question not only his parenting, but if he is abusive himself ..."

Owen only laughed, sardonically. Shook his head. Saw the officers look at him, then each other, perplexed. Why bother telling them that they had it all wrong, that they had shown up too soon and that he deserved much worse a beating. Instead he simply laid his head against the window and followed telephone wires with his eyes, up and down and up and down between poles. An occasional bird on a wire. Clouds ready to rain.

As the police car pulled into Lillian's driveway he sighed with relief. Her house was covered in ivy and surrounded by trees, which made it appear hidden from the world. It gave the sense that he could crawl into that house and disappear from the world, or at least be protected from it. He wanted a house like this for himself now, in a much smaller town back in Newfoundland, or maybe Alaska, that mystical place his father talked about so much. Maybe Italy, the one place on the globe he'd ever cared to visit. But the balance in his bank account was no more impressive than a teenager's, and his reality reflected that. He had no alternative to staying with his benevolent aunt and being stranded in his brother's town, unwanted.

He got out and tried to shut the car door, but it wouldn't close because the buckle of the seat belt was hanging out. He didn't bother to deal with it and kept walking towards the house. He wanted to be hidden away in his room when Lillian got home.

The officer in the driver's seat hopped out to fix the seat belt. Owen threw his arm up to wave them off. He checked his pockets for his keys and they weren't there. He'd have to sit out back and wait for Lillian.

✑

That same night Lillian woke Owen around midnight. She was careful to find a part of his body not bruised or cut, and squeezed him gently from his sleep. He rolled over and saw Lillian's tired face illuminated by the orange glow from the digital display on a small black portable telephone. She slowly extended her hand to Owen and almost cringed as he reached out for the telephone, like it was a blade he was about to squeeze in his hand. She left him alone with the phone, but stood close enough to his bedroom door to listen in on the conversation.

It was Alex, Owen knew it. He recognized something in the silence. He couldn't decide on the tone of his hello and breathed deeply into the receiver, waiting for the courage, for all the right words to come to him.

"Owen?"

"Alex?"

"Owen, it's Alex. I'm sorry about today."

The sound of his brother's voice evoked a smile: his emotional and physiological responses confusing each other.

Owen cut his brother's apology off abruptly. "Alex, listen, I deserved it ... I deserved worse. You don't get to feel bad here, and–"

"Don't talk! I don't want to hear your goddamn voice, okay? Not right now anyway. This is my turn to talk, you might never get yours, and really, you don't deserve it. You do deserve an apology though, and I am truly sorry. That was not how I wanted to end things between us. I was possessed and overrun by something bigger than me. Nobody deserves to get beaten like that, and that's not what I wanted to do to you, okay? I don't hate you. I love you. That's what makes a mess of all this, and my actions today are not how I wanted to end things between us." Alex paused briefly, like he didn't want to ramble on like this and talk in circles.

"I don't want to physically hurt you. I don't want revenge. I just want to move on without you in my life anymore. I forgive you because I know you never meant to hurt me. It was out of your hands, for both you and Hannah, whatever developed between you. The same way my emotions were out of my hands today." He paused, like he sounded too forgiving now, but he let it slide, if only to be done with the conversation as soon as possible.

"So this is it, Owen. Goodbye. And I am sorry about today. I gave Lillian a cheque for you. Twenty grand. It's enough to get you back to Newfoundland and out of mine and the girls' lives. Maybe you should go to Dad's old cabin for a while. Maybe you can look Abbie's number up. Whatever. Just, for me, and you owe me this: leave. Forget about me and Callie and Lucia and Hannah. I took more out on you today than you deserved. It was about more than Hannah, it was years' worth of pent up–"

"I know, Alex–"

"Shut up, Owen! I can't take hearing your voice right now. I asked you not to talk, didn't I? *Fuck.* Can you just shut up and listen only?"

He tried to curb the anger. Thirty seconds passed before Alex spoke again. He filled that silence with a clicking noise he made from plunging his tongue down into the floor of his mouth. It wasn't so much a nervous twitch as it was something he did to calm himself when overwhelmed by emotions.

"I also don't want you feeling like we are square now that I beat you. It wasn't an equivalent to redemption."

Another half minute of silence passed before Alex spoke again. He took one last sigh. "You never did this to hurt me, so I don't want to hurt you. I just want to forgive you and forget you, like I have with Mom and Dad. I also thought you might like to know that the girls are okay. Well … better. Getting there. When we all got home I came up with a tentative explanation for why I hurt you, and we are all okay now."

More silence, like he was contemplating the next spiel.

"Maybe it'd be nice if you sent them a Christmas card next Christmas, or something small like that. Let some time pass. But please, because you owe it to me, take the money and just go. It's not out of my pocket. It's from … her life insurance. I hope the writing game works out for you, Owen. You deserve it. Maybe I'll even buy your book. But I don't owe you another word."

Alex slammed the receiver down. The sound of it, the scratches and the click, coursed through Owen's body like a jolt of electricity. He was taking in a breath as his brother said his last words, and ten seconds passed between his brother hanging up and Owen exhaling.

He laid down the phone on his bedside table and saw the cheque there. Twenty grand. Lillian must have laid it there when she brought in the phone. He'd feel criminal if he took the money, and yet he owed it to Alex to leave town. He'd take that money and spend some time in his father's old cabin near Terra Nova National Park, back in Newfoundland.

He started packing on the spot, and all his belongings fit in one large grey duffle bag that had belonged to his father. There was a time his father put him in that very bag and Alex in another and swung them around in circles like a carnival ride. He'd give them guns and tell them they were fighter pilots and make all the grunts and noises of gunfire, or he'd tell them they were caught in the middle of a tornado and sound out the gush of vicious circular winds. Owen thought of that as he packed the bag full, and it was hard to imagine that life now. And it was hard to imagine that a bag could be kept so long and witness such a change in the family it was servicing. And it was hard to imagine that he could once fit in a duffle bag. He found himself pressing the bruises on his ribs, accepting the pain to quiet his mind. He picked at the scab on his ear where Alex's foot had split his flesh.

In that moment, everything seemed inconceivable and hazy. Was his childhood, before the death of his family, really as magnificent as he remembered, or had hindsight glorified his earliest memories?

The act of packing that duffle bag was almost rejuvenating. There was a false sense of hope for something good in something new, because at least nothing worse could happen to him now. He put his laptop and Hannah's diary on top of the bag and decided he'd rather take a ferry back to Newfoundland than a plane. He wanted to feel the cold chill of the ocean. He wanted the trip to take a while, so that he could feel the distance he was putting between him and his brother. Between his past and his present.

# IN PLACE OF A GOODBYE

*November 13th, 2008,*
*From my bed, sinking again.*

*Two years ago today, you were born dead. I never did give you a name because it only would've made it all that much harder on me. See, if I named you I'd know who I miss, who I never got to know. But every November 13th you are all I think about, my only son, and for what it's worth I think a part of you stayed with me. It's as if your soul, since you died in my body, stayed within me. I still feel some connection with you, and I want to think that connection is more profound than a mere reluctance to let you go. So you may haunt me all you want.*

*It feels negligent and cold to mourn you only on your birthday/the day you died, but it's all I can muster, emotionally. I know there is a league of women out there who would agree with me that the hardest part of a stillbirth is having to go through with the labour in a silent, somber room. There is no crying baby, no relief followed by joy, no roomful of pink or blue balloons. There is just the saddest and most futile moment of your life.*

*One percent of pregnancies end this way, I was told.
One-fucking-percent, just enough to matter. One in a hundred
women never see this coming. One in a hundred pregnant
women will walk through life with the ghost of their child
stuck within them, never knowing what they look like, laugh
like, and live for.*

*My useless prude of a doctor says it might help to talk or write
about it so I will. I will say that the second worst part of a
stillbirth is the absolute lack of warning signs. There was the
shopping for cute clothes, the sporadic kicks from within, the
flipping through that baby name book I bought on a whim in
a line-up at some grocery store, and then there was nothing.
For days. I figured if something went wrong it would be
obvious, like a sharp pain or a lot of bleeding. Instead I felt
nothing and I didn't consider feeling nothing something to
worry about. I guess I knew something might be wrong, but I
waited, I lied to myself, I made up scenarios, like maybe you
were just sleeping. Does a seven-month-old fetus even sleep?*

*Owen was here with me today, thank God for that. He
doesn't know about you. He doesn't know that this stillbirth
was somehow, indirectly, the last blow for our sex life. Alex
wanted to surprise Owen with the news of our son-to-be. He
saw being able to hide a pregnancy as a perk of them living in
different provinces.*

*So Owen didn't know, but thankfully he acted perfectly today,
as perfectly as I needed him to, as if he did know. He didn't
want sex, he didn't talk too much. We lay on opposite ends of
the couch and he tangled his legs into mine in a way that
shared the pain, and in a way that the girls wouldn't read too
much into.*

*We watched stupid reality TV shows and Oprah. She talked
about the top ten healthiest foods and how to age gracefully. I
would have preferred tips on how to start again. He made us*

*lunch and fixed my tea just right. He had to run out to the post office at four and called on the way home to see if I'd rather him pick up a pizza than cook. I couldn't even eat today, let alone cook. Why is it harder this year?*

*I am glad no one called to acknowledge it today. I wasn't in the mood to act strong. And I am glad that Alex either forgot or chose not to say anything about it at breakfast this morning.*

*I find myself more engrossed by kids' shows these last two years, and more able to relate to children, and I wonder if there IS some ghost of you within me, and that is why. I sound crazy, I know, but I had to finally say that out loud, or write it out anyway. And I am sorry. I am sorry if there was something I did wrong, or if I could have prevented this somehow, like going to the doctor more often than I did or sooner after I felt you stop moving. For what it is worth, I made them check again and again for any sign of life in you. I made them wheel me into a different room so we could use a different machine in case there was something wrong with the first one. I even asked two different nurses to operate those machines in case one of them was overlooking something. And then I made Alex try out both machines. By the time I gave up everyone thought I was insane, and I could tell by their faces and the way the held their bodies that they wanted to yell at me for my frustrating persistence, but they were too polite to scold a grieving mother.*

*I remember, painfully, how on the second attempt to hear you in there, I heard a thumping noise and shrieked. I thought it was your heart beating, but it was my own. The nurse was right, it wasn't the typical swooshing noise I'd heard before. The swooshing noise of an ultrasound for a healthy baby. That sound wasn't there at all, there was only the sound of my own broken heart thumping away. Do-dah, Do-dah, Do-dah, KKSSHHhhh…*

*Placental malfunction. I don't know. All those stupid medical terms I heard that day go way over my head. You'd have to ask your father what the real problem was termed. My placenta failed us, so it was technically my fault. It separated from me and you weren't getting enough blood, which meant nutrients and oxygen. How did my womb support two eight-pound girls, and not you? I carried you for seven months. I imagined you into existence. Then I had to explain to your sisters that they would never get to meet you. They never really understood and don't seem to remember. Maybe I am a little jealous.*

*I love Callie and Lucia, but you were going to be my little boy. I had a few names ready and I was going to choose the one that came to me the moment our eyes met. I was going to give you the name I saw myself calling you for the rest of your life. The name I would write on all your birthday cards and Christmas gifts, or what I'd yell when I scolded you for getting into trouble at school.*

*During the seven months we shared my body I developed an idea of who you might be. A month before you died we moved into a new house so you could have your own bedroom, the one Owen has been sleeping in. I think that maybe you'd have liked animals, nature, been an environmentalist and guilted us into composting and recycling everything possible. I think you'd have the presence and dignity not seen in men these days. I think your words, because of their sincerity and your nobility, could convince anyone you were right, even if you were wrong. You'd have all the strengths of your father and uncle combined, and without their wretched weaknesses and childhood scars. I think that you would have had only serious long-term relationships and treated those girls like they dreamt of being treated. You would rebound from heartbreak with a lesson learned, not a wound carried along into the next relationship, like your father or his brother. Hair kept short so it wouldn't tease your forehead or your ears, corduroys would feel more comfortable than denim. I picture you telling me all about your important job and using words I don't understand, but I'd nod my head to keep you talking to me, just because I love the sound of your voice.*

*And now I'll never know what that voice would have sounded like. Now I'll never get to hold you, feed you, comfort you. I never even got to take you home. All I ever did for you was sign your death certificate. The one with no name on it, just Baby Collins.*

*As they took you away from me, your arms swung from your body like a hypnotist's pendulum. I couldn't bear to look at your face. I wanted instead to keep my own image of you, to at least not have that shattered too. But I saw those little hands of yours, perfectly formed and ready to touch life. And now. Now those little hands will never hold anything.*

*I first felt you kicking in my belly while standing in line at Toys R Us. I was buying a car seat. Alex was at work of course, but I called him, thriving with excitement. He was in the middle of a surgery. The memory and sensation of that firm little kick is all I have of you now. Alex called me back a few hours later. He wanted to name you Ross, after some uncle of his he admires, but I wouldn't have it. You wouldn't have been a Ross. I could tell from the way you kicked me. Like you were trying to communicate, asking for companionship, ready to come out because you couldn't wait two more months to meet me.*

*They stuck a black ribbon on the door to my room so everyone would know I was a grieving mother, not a happy one, not a new one. They sent a grief counsellor who encouraged me to cry and name you, even though I was already crying and couldn't name you because I never got to look in your eyes and see who you were. The counsellor was a nice man, but who can really help someone in a situation like that, and in one brief* meeting? We were given the option to let the hospital deal with your "disposal," and I am sorry to say we did. I regret that now. I wish you had a headstone. I wish I could go visit you like Owen does his mother, if only to be alone in the world and clear my head sometimes. But there is no headstone, just tears falling from my aged face onto the bright white sheets of this childish diary. And don't worry, none of these tears help shed the memory of you.

Happy Birthday, and goodbye for another year. I love you. And even if it makes me crazy, I miss you. I hope you are happier than your mother is right now, wherever you are, and I hope you are smiling and laughing and not even thinking of me.

# NO STEADIER FOOTING

SUNLIGHT WAS FUNNELING IN THROUGH the ferry's circular windows like spotlights, illuminating its dated, vomit-orange carpet. Carpet that had been trampled by thousands of feet, by thousands of people heading in thousands of different directions through life. Not many of them, Owen imagined, had sat alone in the bar, waiting for someone to serve them at 11 a.m. He thought of helping himself to the whiskey, only an arm's length out of his reach, because the world at least owed him that much. One free glass of Glenfiddich to wash down a life thrown away. The glasses were there, right beside the whiskey no one had an eye on.

He limped away from the bar. He hated knowing that the bartender wasn't simply in a washroom or out for a quick smoke. There just wasn't a bartender in the bar at 11 a.m. He hated what that said about him, sitting there expecting one. A little surprised there wasn't one.

He hadn't rented a room, and decided to spend the rest of the ride on the deck, leaning into the railings, watching the black water, waiting to see land in the distance. Leaning over the rail and watching the water was calming, pacifying. It lulled him into a meditative state.

It wasn't the idea of dying that enticed him, of suicide, but about halfway back home, he wanted to be surrounded by one thing and one thing only: cold, black, salty water. To feel himself sinking deeper and deeper into cold black nothingness. He wanted to be consumed by it, disappear into it, forget about everything but it. It was a brief and fleeting moment, but in it, he simply felt that drowning would feel like escape, relief, and redemption all at once. There would be no fear or guilt or pressure to survive, just his lungs filling with water. There would only be those final thoughts, and he wanted to know what they'd be. He was thinking of Virginia Woolf, his father's favourite writer, who filled her pockets with stones and walked stoically into a river. It seemed romantic, fitting, everything at once. The right balance between right and wrong. He didn't have the courage or conviction to jump and he knew it. He could only hope the railing he was leaning against, with all his weight and strength, would snap and drop him overboard. That nobody would see him fall, that the sound of the boat would drown out the sound of his splash, and that it would be as tranquil a death as he imagined.

He took a step back from the rail, shook his head, and looked around to see if someone was watching him.

He'd originally walked outside onto the platform of the ferry to watch it approach Port aux Basques. He wanted to spend the last hour outside so he could watch a tiny, insignificant dot in the distance become Newfoundland, his home, the place where he belonged.

His hands were buried in his pockets but still numb from the cold, and his face and tongue were drying out from the salty air off the Atlantic. Normally he would notice the salt on his skin, and as a compulsive writer he would normally take out his notepad and write out some metaphor about how the salt was exfoliating his *old* skin, his *old* self. The metaphor could've been good – the rejuvenating return to home. He could've lent it to one of his characters, but Owen had spaced out too much to notice any of this, including the fact that the ferry was docking and he'd missed the hour-long approach. He'd been staring into the ocean for exactly one hour, as if it was a wishing well and he was rich.

He'd been spacing out like this often enough lately to be concerned about it. It was like he was awake and dreaming, and only certain elements of reality, someone's voice or a sudden unfamiliar sound, could wake him from his daydream fantasies.

❧

Owen was *still* forgetting about his limp. When he'd sit for too long it would slip his mind and he would try to stand on his leg as if his tibia and patella weren't full of screws and still healing. The flash of pain and ground teeth never helped to prevent a subsequent lapse of memory. When he woke up in the mornings, he'd roll out of bed and absentmindedly put all his weight on the bad leg and fall back into bed, clenching his jaws. The occasional pain he felt reminded him of Hannah, and the newfound inconvenience of stairs reminded him of his brother.

As he descended the wobbly metal staircase that bridged the boat to Newfoundland, he took in one long exaggerated breath of that famous, fresh, Newfoundland air. He flung his father's duffle bag onto a weathered bench and searched through its contents until he found the tattered, blue-and-yellow bus information guide. He read the bus schedules with a false sense of optimism. The bus he was looking for was the one heading to Port Blandford, where his father's cabin was, but he let himself consider it the bus that would take him from his old life to his new one, from the past to the future. The idea of rejuvenation felt better than the alternative, and it gave some vague sense of purpose to his return home.

He had an hour to waste before the bus would arrive, so he sat on the bench to put another dent in his novel, but was distracted by a woman's concerned shouting. "Jacob, too close to the water! Jacob, don't chase your sister, one of you'll trip and fall!"

The kids, like any kids, were absolutely fearless because their mother was there, so nothing bad could happen. They peered out over the wharf, throwing snowballs into the ocean, and running away from the water each time, as if a shark might leap up to exact some biting revenge. He liked the devilish kid in the baby-blue jacket, laughed at him. He peeled open a granola bar and found himself watching the red-haired mother of two. She had freckles, the type the sun would draw out, and the sunlight was doing something beautiful to her face, the right balance of light and shadows highlighting all her features. She had a magazine crumpled up in her mittened hand, the pages buckled and blowing in the wind. She looked a little too cerebral for the magazine, but with two kids, maybe she was just looking for fluff to turn her mind off, something to glance at in between watching out for her kids. Not *her*, not necessarily this woman in particular, but someone like her, and he could let go of his past. Move on. There was hope in that much.

She glanced briefly at Owen, saw the deep red cuts embedded in yellow bruises, the ones his brother had left there. She looked equally wary and sympathetic, and stepped closer to her children.

He found himself hoping the redhead and Jacob and his sister were waiting for the same bus. Maybe he'd sit behind them and pretend. Maybe it only felt like an uncanny notion, the innocent vicarious experience.

A man in a lime shirt and black peacoat walked into his field of vision, hoisting ice creams over his head. Jacob and his sister came running, all smiles, towards him. They grabbed air trying to get them, laughing at their father's teasing them by keeping the ice creams just out of reach. "C'mon, kids, take your ice creams, c'mon." The redhead laughed. It was in her smile how much she loved him. The way she smiled at him when he wasn't even looking. He gave the kids their treats, and then slid an arm around his wife, knew right where to lay it.

The father yelled jovially, "Jacob, stay away from that wharf! If you fall in you'll lose your ice cream!" And she hit him with the rolled up magazine, laughing, okay with their good cop, bad cop parenting routine.

∽

The bus stopped at an orange-and-white North Atlantic Petroleum gas station directly off the highway and at the entrance of the amiable town of Port Blandford. It stopped so abruptly that everyone was jolted forward. An old lady gasped, a kid laughed, and Owen snapped out of another daydream.

As he descended the four steps, limping, the bus driver recommended the French fries in the restaurant attached to the gas bar. He spoke with a smile in his words. "You'll wanna make it an extra large, Chief!" He winked, to promise Owen he'd love those fries, and Owen wanted to be able to care that much about something as simple as French fries. He smiled and let himself wink back. Laughed at himself for winking. But Owen couldn't even be social enough to utter a word to the bus driver and try the fries. He headed straight for his father's old cabin with his head down, squinting from the sun glaring off banks of snow.

All the houses he passed were comfortably modest, with their shrubs wrapped in brown burlap for the winter. Clusters of tall and slender aspens functioned as fences to separate the houses. With the exception of two short roads leading from the highway down into the town, Port Blandford was essentially one long street running parallel to a calming body of water, with nothing but hardy spruce trees beyond the blue bay. The water was a stone's throw from the backyards, and it was calm and spotted with gulls and the white crests of gentle waves.

He didn't want to rush to the cabin, and he didn't know why. Halfway there, he stopped to watch a red squirrel hop along a woman's yard and raid a bird feeder, almost laughing at its quick paranoid movements: it moved its head, not its eyes to watch all angles. He walked on for another few minutes, watching a man in a green-and-black flannel coat chop wood, and loved the crack of it echoing in the cold winter wind.

Long before he was anywhere near his father's place, Owen fished through the change in his pocket and dug out the loose key scattered among pennies and dimes. It was Lillian's copy, and the lettering on a grimy taped label, in faded black ink, read, *Roger's Cabin?* Ever since his father had been admitted to the Waterford Hospital, Lillian had had the only spare key. She'd spend time there whenever she could. Maybe a week a year.

There had been a time when his family spent at least one weekend a month at this cabin, but when he and Alex got to junior high, they'd lost interest in spending the weekends with their family. There were girls now, and parties and video games. The cabin was old, boring, and, relative to those parties and their elating cheap thrills, a form of prison.

He regretted that now, as he approached the old cabin. The swing set was left there to rust in the rain, and grass had grown over their sandbox. It had morphed from a family cabin to one man's getaway. After they'd lost interest in the place, Owen's mother never had any desire to spend time there either, and the cabin was considered his father's retreat, as if it were as silly and childish a retreat as a kid's treehouse. His father spent the weekend there every three or four weeks. He'd take up some big project of his to work on.

Considering the delusional nature of his father's "projects" last going off, Owen was a little scared about what he might find lying around in the cabin, maybe more of those flyers with certain letters underlined to spell out delusional claims. Because Owen was only in his teens when he'd lost his father to schizophrenia, parts of his father's falling ill were still hazy, but he never forgot the day his father's psychiatrist gave him a Polaroid camera and told him to take a picture of his supposed employer next time he saw him. Owen never forgot those three blank Polaroid pictures his father had taken when he *thought* he was seeing and talking to "Mr. James." There was one of a black, *empty* office chair, one of a wall, and one of a street full of cars but no people. Mr. James was in none of them. Those photos meant it took his father three futile tries to be shocked enough to give up and realize he was sick. His father could describe that man, right down to his mannerisms and how he talked too loudly. Sadder still was the Polaroid picture he took of Owen and Alex the next day, to make sure his children were real. It wasn't too long after that picture that his father went catatonic and never spoke again.

The key felt like a crowbar now, like he was about to break and enter some foreign place. He wanted that feeling to disappear before he stuck the key in the door. The town looked nothing like how he remembered it. It was more of a *town* town when he was a kid, people lived there all year round. Now, all the new cedar A-frame houses, and B&Bs, and all the closed-down convenience stores made it feel like a cabin town, a seasonal place. He liked that though. The seclusion.

He had made it to Port Blandford, but couldn't ignore how many symbols of his past had come along with him. He'd loot from them, make use of them: the lack of distractions here would help with the writing, and he had been sketching out the male protagonist for weeks now. He took out his notepad:

> *The main character has a limp, like mine, that is a reminder of something horrible from his past. Maybe every time the pain flares up, he remembers a different aspect of that horrible accident. Have him walking into his new town with a duffle bag flung over his shoulder that used to belong to his father, so that he is symbolically carrying some piece of his past along with him. The same sun that is shining down on him is feeding the grass above his lover's grave in his old town. A large premise of the book being this: there is no escaping ourselves, our pasts. So how does one really let go and carry on? Or does one? Have him meet a single-mother redhead at the ferry terminal. As battered and broken as him, and she has a great, captivating backstory. Maybe her kid falls in the ocean and he dives in and saves him.*

# WAITING FOR DECEMBER, FOR SOMETHING THAT NEVER COMES

*November 26th, 2008,*
*In my giant bed, a solemn slut beside my husband.*

*Alex sleeps in the same position every night: on his side, in the fetal position, hugging a pillow as if it were a teddy bear. He looks like a man who spent his childhood lonely. He has tried so hard to build himself a perfect life, an obvious attempt at compensation for his sad childhood, and now I've become the flaw in those plans that might topple everything he has stacked so neatly in place. He at least deserves an ideal adulthood. He put his faith in me, gave me two children, and look what I've done with that trust.*

*I feel guilty. I feel guilt in my gums and teeth and core. And since guilt is the result of an act of greed, I was greedy to want Owen, even if Alex was neglecting me. The fact I feel guilty must mean I still love Alex. Whatever "love" means. I swear to God we invent words sometimes. Grand concepts with undefinable definitions. I believe there are many forms of love, and they ought to be named individually so we can get it* right. There are men out there who truly love their wives, but burn for another woman. What is that burning called, when it isn't just hormonal? There are women out there who dearly love their husbands, but get swept away by the sweet new man who wanders into her world as a reminder that life is full of other options. What is that temptation called?

The comfort and routine of my and Alex's relationship is a wonderful thing: that bond years together creates is a beautiful thing, and knowing someone so well: when he's going to laugh during a movie, or cry; what he's going to do, right away, when he wakes up. But that kind of love is different than what I have with Owen: enthrallment, and _not_ knowing everything but wanting to, and noticing everything about the person: the way his mouth rises before a laugh, or how truly kind he is. And desire. Desire is again its own form of love. The fleeting one. The one that gets all the attention in poetry and Hollywood.

I've fucked up. I can't keep them all straight, and share them all with the same man.

I spend every autumn falling apart like this, and in November it peaks. I am a mess, from the first miserable memory of my thieved childhood (his hot breath on my face like an upturned ashtray, his hands sculpting me from an innocent child into a lost cause) to my most recent memory of this desolate adulthood (flipping my husband's pillow to hide the semen stain his brother left there because I was too lazy to do laundry yesterday). You'd think depression/anxiety wouldn't make you lazy, you'd think you'd feel better distracting yourself with mundane chores like laundry.

I know November breaks me down because it was a November when I spent that time with Tommy. Lately, when I think of it all, I blame my parents. Then I feel wrong for that, for the need to place blame. Dad's brother's family had to move to our city *and build a new house because Tommy was expelled from the school in the town where they lived. Fine. That wasn't Dad doing anything wrong. But then, does Tommy sound like the kind of kid you want in your house? With your daughter? And then I feel evil for blaming him, even though I've read that it's normal to misplace blame, intially, as you try and deal with it all, years later. It says so in the book Alex bought me. After he realized he couldn't "fix me" himself.*

*That "short stay" turned into four months. The longest four months of my life. There may be only sixty seconds in a minute, and seven days in a week, but how we feel that time pass has nothing to do with numbers. It has everything to do with how we experience the world during those moments. We remember our lives through isolated memories, not in a serial manner, not minute by minute.*

*He was an ugly, zit-faced, sixteen-year-old reject, too much of a bully to be bullied or befriended, and a piece of shit like that doesn't deserve such a prominent role in my life. But he took it anyway. I hate leather because he wore an ugly, black, fake leather jacket, even in the summer. It creaked when he moved and it smelled of shoe polish. The smell of his jacket masked his natural scent of bacon grease and pimples. They'd been staying with us a week before he summoned the nerve to make his way into my room. Coward. Was he just bored? Desperate? Sick? What makes someone an incestuous sociopath?*

*It was dark, but I knew it was him because of the sound of that jacket squeaking whenever he bent an arm. I was seven. I knew nothing about the world or how I fit into it, I knew nothing about my body or his. By the time he left my house fifteen weeks later he'd taught me what my body was for.*

*I couldn't process the horror he put me through. I was too young to know what was happening. I only knew I didn't like it and it hurt. The brain doesn't know what to do with shock and things we aren't prepared for. All I had to try and piece it together with was his words. He covered my mouth, his big hands almost blocking off my nostrils too, and whispered in my ear, "This is all you are good for. Don't tell anybody or they'll get mad and stop loving you. Nobody really loves you anyway. This is what you are for, so don't complain about it. Don't tell anyone you've been bad." I believed him until I was old enough to understand what had happened to me. By then it was too late: I understood love only as something physical, not emotional, and I gave my body up to feel wanted.*

*So tonight I have to wonder, Is this what happened with me and Owen? Was it love or merely our pasts that made us cross that line months ago on that hot, splintery wharf at the cabin? Do I not know how to feel appreciated and noticed by someone like Owen without whoring myself out to them because of those four months and everything that did to me? Is there more to Owen and me than that?*

*Sometimes I think this happened because we both found each other at a mutually vulnerable time in our lives — him crawling back from rock bottom, me in the lowest point of my marriage. Since the miscarriage, it's been … hard.*

*Owen and I just happened to fill each other's empty spaces at a time when we were both feeling empty. In each other lay all the answers to all the questions we had about life, all the proof we needed that life could be electric and electrifying, and then we crossed a line. Is that beautiful or sad? Right or wrong? The sex happened only to convey all the things words never could. At first, it was never a physical thing. At first the sex was a kinship, it was something spiritual, for lack of a better word. Does that make it necessary, excusable? We just needed to be that close to each other. The intimacy of it, not the cheap thrill of sex.*

*Those four months with Tommy changed how my life turned*

out. Growing up, I mistook horny teenagers fumbling over my bra straps and belt buckles as love. I never even had the confidence to really push myself at university, to apply myself to anything but motherhood. As an adult my identity is still shaky, all I know is that I am a mother of two and a doctor's wife, and now here I am jeopardizing all I know of myself by sleeping with Owen.

In the years since my marriage died, it has been my two little daughters that keep me together, the mightiest of bridges rest only on pillars. And this year, at least until the guilt of it all set in, there was Owen. A new support. But as of this week, any joy he brings me has to contend with all this guilt, and it's a pretty even battle. So it's all just one more tight knot in my belly. He did postpone what I am feeling like tonight as I write this, and because of him I almost got through November without falling apart, but...

BUT!

Of course there is a but. Every time we fall in love with someone new, we fall in love because we feel like there will never be a but with this person. We genuinely feel like things can only get better or at least stay at the same electrifying peak with this person. Sometimes, they say, it stays that way. But this I know: Owen is distant lately and that distance hurts. That distance puts me on the other end of loneliness, looking in on the world.

I am starting to feel like he is around less when I am on my period. I know an affair is a physical thing, so I guess I understand, but I feel it makes a whore of me. I want to think there is more to our affair than sex, and I know I love it more when he kisses me on the forehead in passing than I do when we just fuck. He used to hug me and give my shoulders a little squeeze as he hauled himself from me. I felt safe and happy and pretty and wanted. I felt giddy.

*Now I don't.*

*Now I feel dirty, guilty, silly. What was I expecting out of this affair anyway? Escape from my reality? A new life? Was that even possible? This is so wrong and so unrealistic, and so many other things too.*

*Things with me and Owen kind of feel like me and Alex all over again, and I am not going through that twice. I remember with Alex, his lack of interest in our sex life coincided with a tendency to dart his eyes on other, more attractive women when we were out somewhere. A cashier in the grocery store, a waitress. Friends. I tried so hard to keep him interested in me that I felt pathetic and lost any self-confidence I once had. I felt so pathetic and unattractive that it stuck with me. One week I bought lingerie and sexy pajamas, but he looked at me no differently than if I were wearing a turtleneck and overalls. I read all those tips in girlie magazines about spicing things up in a marriage: "the three things every guy wants to do to you but is afraid to ask." The magazine advice failed me. One by one, the articles failed me. I told him I would let him do anything he wanted, and all he said was, "I'm not into all that, Han. Straight-up sex is fine with me." But weeks would pass between being intimate. Then months, then infinities. Then Owen. He made me feel beautiful again.*

*But now it is dissolving between us too. The emotional aspect of our affair feels absent, and the rest of it, the sweaty fumbling and grinding, isn't worth losing my family over. Especially since he won't even want that soon. The connection I have with Owen, it is true that I don't feel it with Alex anymore, but we have two children that keep us together. Maybe that is enough, our past, our children. As for Owen, I can't say the connection is totally gone, because some days it's there and as obvious as the sun, but I can also say it has been two days since we kissed. I don't think he has noticed this yet.*

*Blah.*

*What does it mean that two men, that both brothers, are neglecting me? It means I am a useless, ugly wretch! That's what it means. Greedy for attention I don't deserve. Worn-out, over with, undesirable. It means Tommy was right, I am a mess, a whore. He'd love this, me screwing one man in this bed by day and sleeping next to his brother at night.*

*I'd hate me too if I were a man. That last ten pounds I can't drop, these deflating tits, this aging skin. I look in the mirror in the mornings and I want to smash it. I want to go back ten years and stay there. I want love to liberate me, and I want to know it is real, not just what Tommy promised me it was.*

*I wish Alex would wake up and win me back, love me like he used to. Was I just one more thing he collected and ticked off his to-do list while he was building his fallacy of a life? Look at him there, so defeated, who is he fooling?*

# LIKE FATHER, LIKE SON

THE KEY SLID INTO THE door with ease. This inexplicably surprised him; he expected some rust, some resistance. Instead the house welcomed him in as if it was expecting him.

It was a bungalow, a red bungalow with black trim. A patio surrounded the entire house, giving it the appearance of a UFO. At the back of the house was the kitchen, with a view of the ocean through its patio doors, and in the front was an oversized living room, with a fireplace and a well-stocked bookshelf built into the stone above it. The view from every window was so pristine the poetry wrote itself. Even the sounds made the place somewhere worth living: the distant gush of waves off rocks and the sounds of songbirds not present in a busy city.

But what he last read in Hannah's journal erased it all, pulled a curtain around it. He'd take it all in later. After he processed that entry. He read it on the bus, sitting straight up then slinking down, again and again, laying the book down over his knee, then picking it back up. His lungs felt too full of air. He never cried, but his eyes burned for her. She had it all wrong, and he could never tell her the difference now – that the sex was a byproduct of their kinship, not the purpose of it – and that impossibility hurt like being burned alive. She died never knowing what she meant to him. How she hollowed him out, softened his bones, every time she laughed or touched or kissed him. Like nothing or no one before her. How he loved the way her slender arms bent at the elbow. Her bellybutton. The two lines that formed brackets around her mouth whenever she smiled. When he thought of her, sex was the last thing on his mind. It was more about her being how he fit into the world.

He opened a bottle of wine he found in his father's wine rack. A Barolo, a wine that could last the twenty-five years since the bottle was stamped. *1984.* He blew dust from his father's old wine glass, rinsed it, poured the wine, and brought the bouquet to his nose: cherries, licorice, leather. He poured it down the sink after one sip. First the glass, then the whole bottle, mourning the clugging sound he missed so much. He walked into the living room, fell into a brown leather chair, and coughed on the cloud of dust that recoiled back up at him. *First thing to do is find all the light switches and clean up a little, check the plumbing.* Lillian told him she had already called about the electricity.

He sat in the chair for twenty-five minutes, staring at a photo on the fireplace of him and Alex holding up two dead rainbow trout by their tails. He remembered the moments before that picture was taken, how it took about ten shots to get the picture because he kept dropping the slippery fish. In the photo, his father was standing between him and Alex, holding up the fishing rod he'd caught them with, an arm slung around each brother. In the moments that followed the photograph, Owen could remember Alex being fascinated by the anatomy and morphology of the fish. *Dad! Why do fish have tails?* Owen was more interested in the iridescent colours of the fish, what purpose they served, what the fish might have been doing right before they caught it.

It was one of many memories captured in the plethora of

photos on the walls surrounding him. His father had the walls and every ledge in the cabin plastered with photos. He always had a camera on him, "collecting moments." Everywhere Owen looked he saw memories of what felt like another life, another time, another planet far away from this one. He remembered when and where every photo was taken, and yet there was something hazy about each one. Like they were all false or constructed memories.

At least one weekend every month, his family came to this cabin. Every Sunday morning before they'd head back to the city, their father would take them fishing or hiking over in Terra Nova National Park, explaining the relationships between plants and animals, sun and soil, and how insignificant people are in the grand scale of things. He'd always fuse a biology lesson with a contempt for human ignorance that even a ten-year-old could pick up on. "We are here solely and simply because of these plants at our feet. They can use energy from the sun and make their own food. No grocery stores necessary. And then we eat them or the animals that eat them. That's how we get our energy. Understand?" He always waited for at least one nodding head to carry on. "And if that wasn't enough, without them, there'd be no more oxygen on earth for us, because they breathe out what we breathe in: oxygen. Imagine! And yet every day, in every place on earth, we're pouring cement over forest! Keep that in mind when you two grow up to be leaders of the world, okay?"

Two nodding heads. "Okay!"

His eyes shifted to another picture on the wall. One of him and Alex chasing a red squirrel through a field of daisies and *Solidagos*, their hands full of peanuts they wanted to feed the squirrel. Moments after his father took that picture, Owen asked him why daisies were white and the *Solidagos* were yellow. His father smiled and said that the answer didn't matter.

"What matters is that you asked." He sat his kids down,

one on each knee, and carried on. "There might be a long, complicated, scientific answer, but it is just someone else's guess. What's your guess, Owen?"

The brothers came up with theory after theory on why some flowers were different colours than others, and their father laughed at their childhood wonder.

He spoke so confidently, like a god. "There are answers for everything, kids, but they don't mean a thing. Because every time you go searching for an answer it ends with more questions, and the questions chase the answers like a cat chases its tail. Do you want to get dizzy like the cat or enjoy this day?"

It was a metaphor for life he said, the one thing he hoped his kids would remember him teaching them.

"Life isn't about finding the answers to questions; it's about not needing those answers," he said, standing up.

Owen sat up from his chair, plucked a few photos off the wall, and threw them in the bottom of the linen closet. He had always felt that his father lost his mind looking for something more meaningful than him, Alex, and their mother. That he'd lost his mind to cope with his not being a pre-eminent journalist, respected worldwide. A changer of lives. And that made his father a hypocrite. *A man who needed something more.*

He limped over to the kitchen window. All he could see was the black ocean and the endless blue sky streaked white with cirrus clouds. He leaned into the windowsill and sank his chin onto his arms and stared, waiting. All he needed now was a sense of what he was waiting for. He tried to imagine the cabin filled with the patter of a child's excited footsteps running from room to room, and a wife, sitting out on the patio with a book opened over her thighs. A good book. Maybe she'd feel the need to share some of the lines, or insist he read it when she was done. She'd have a cup of tea on the arm of the chair, but be so engrossed in the book it would get cold before she drank it. He'd entertain the kids, and make supper, just so she could finish the book and tell him everything she loved about it later, when they were in bed together, because he loved the sound of her voice. He'd dedicate all his novels to this woman, because she'd be the one who read every chapter as he wrote them. And then again as he rewrote them.

⤚

He checked all the appliances. The fridge, the stove, the microwave, the toaster full of rock-hard ancient breadcrumbs, and anything else with a cord attached. Everything was still working. He searched the closets for a broom, mop, and cleaning supplies and found them. He dealt with the expired food and made a list for some basic needs he could buy up at the gas station.

When he got to the station, there was a black truck parked in the parking lot, a handmade for sale sign on the windshield. He'd need a vehicle of some kind. The truck would do. He didn't know where else he was going to find a car for sale in that little town and didn't have the money for anything worth more than a few thousand dollars anyway. There was no proper grocery store in Port Blandford anymore, but Clarenville was only a fifteen-minute drive and had everything he could need, including a Walmart and a hospital. The sign, handwritten in black marker on a piece of loose-leaf paper, was stuck to the windshield with a needless fury of tape: *For sale, 2000 bucks or so.* Clearly there was room for negotiation. *Ask the lady in the gas station.* So he did.

"Keen on Clyde's truck, are ya? You knows your fadder was buddies with the owner of it?"

Owen was confused by the father reference. He didn't know the woman.

"What? I knows you must be one of Roger's two boys. Not much gets by us that lives here, b'ye. I seen ya gettin' off the bus earlier. See, my husband's been watching over Roger's place since your fadder, you know, got sick in the head or whatever you wants to call it. So he called to say he seen ya goin' into the house earlier on. Besides, we seen ya growing up, and then there's all the pictures on the walls down at the house. He used to have us all over for a laugh, for a feed, and once he got a few drinks in him, he'd crack out the pictures of his two boys. 'What's they gonna be,' he'd say, 'by the time they're an old feller like me?'"

Owen didn't know what to say, or how to compose himself. He darted his eyes onto a hangnail, into her eyes, and back down to the hangnail, flashing his most friendly smile maybe too much. She was talking to him with such familiarity for a stranger. He felt like he should be shaking her hand maybe, and explaining he'd be living here now, for a while at least.

"Look at ya there, right confused. Sure, I probably changed your diapers, me son! Which one is ya? Owen or Alex?"

He laughed, perplexed and yet charmed by the lady. "I'm Owen." He was surprised by the warming effect of the smile glued on his face, how it wouldn't go away.

"We all used to call him Mr. Know-It-All, a real smarty pants, he was. Could do it all, fix your truck or talk your ear off about all them books and that. We teased him for being the townie who wanted to be a bayman. Some sweet man he was. Shame what happened. Sometimes I got to wonder why God chooses certain things to happen to the good ones, ya know? Because your fadder was for certain one of the good ones."

*How rude would it be to tell this sweet woman God is folklore?*

"S'pose you thinks your fadder used to come up here all those weekends to be alone, do ya? Truth is, he used to host most of the weekend parties. Few drinks in him and he was the life of the party!" She laughed and started to organize the tray of Nevada tickets, smiling like she was reliving a great memory.

"And when he'd flick on Debbie's karaoke machine, well look out, Owen! The tears from the laughter would be rollin'! Half the town'd be all jealous he was married. Had his way with the women, your fadder." She winked at him and sized him up, shamelessly.

"He didn't even have to try, they was just drawn into him, and I'm s'posin', just from lookin' at ya here, it's the same way with you, I bet! How many women ya got yourself, wha? Three or four?"

Owen was speechless.

"Yes, I tells ya, all the ladies up this way thought quite highly of Roger Collins. His missus, your mudder, she never saw the fun in it out this way. Townie, see."

Owen couldn't picture this, he couldn't summon this image of his father. His family collectively assumed his father came out here to relax. To be alone. To work on his hobbies and articles.

"Last going off though, he kept to himself. Right, I dunno, right retreated he was. Right withdrawn. Always working away on something, almost suspicious of people that used to be his friends."

She was visibly uncomfortable now, and changed the topic. "Anyway, dear. That's Clyde's truck you're asking about. Do ya know where Clyde lives?"

He smiled and shook his head. No one used street names or house numbers. There's just Clyde's house, or Maude's, or the Noseworthys'.

"It's that one there." She pointed out the dirty, postered window. "The yellow one, with that beast of a white truck parked out front, okay?" She smiled, waiting for a nod.

"And I doubts you got much of a supper planned for tonight, so if ya don't, that's me and Tim's house right next door to Clyde's. You're more than welcome for supper, love!" She grew even more excited as she remembered. "Sure, Clyde's coming over for supper too, if ya wants to wait til then to talk about the truck. I sorta looks after him a bit, ever since his wife passed. So maybe we'll see you later, dear!"

Strangers cooking strangers supper. He felt like going home to absorb that conversation, to process this new image of his father, but he headed over to Clyde's to ask about the truck.

A kind, weathered man opened the door. His grey eyebrows were freakishly long. They swept up onto his forehead as if they were a clothing of some sort, and his forehead was scoured by deep, fleshy wrinkles, like maybe they sagged a little differently every day. His yellow cardigan was far too big for him, as if he'd lost a lot of weight very quickly. He seemed more interested in who Owen was than in selling the truck.

"Collins? Any relation to Roger Collins?" He pointed down the street to Owen's father's place.

"I'm Roger's son, Owen." He extended his hand.

"Well, my Jesus, look at ya! Sure, I should've guessed it, ya sorta looks like him! Roger's son, hey? Well, for that, the truck is yours for fifteen hundred. How does that sound, boss? Come in, Jesus, come in, b'ye!"

He did. The porch smelled like baked potatoes. He took one shoe off, but before he started in on the other, he was told, "Don't be silly, leave them on. There's no women in this house to worry about!" Shoes on, he followed him down a hall and into a floral wallpapered living room.

"You want a drink of tea, or a drop of scotch? A water? I knows if you're your father's son, you'll want a drop of scotch. He loved his scotch, your father. Some people said he never knew when to stop once he started, but what odds when you can handle it, right?" He laughed. "I'll be right back, Owen, take a seat. You're at home in my house, and don't you forget it, for as long as you're going to be staying with us here in Port Blandford!"

"Only if you're putting the kettle on, I'll have tea." He could almost taste the scotch. The burning satisfaction of it.

Owen could only hope the next question wasn't, *So, what brings you here?* Someone was bound to ask eventually, if everyone was so friendly and curious about *Roger's boy.* Would he lie, or villainize himself so quickly? *Well, I kinda slept with my brother's wife, and if we weren't sneaking around behind his back, I wouldn't have hydroplaned and killed her. So, you see, I'm here because I'm banished and belong nowhere else. I don't even have a profession, or any motivation, I lost all that when ...* It almost sounded surreal, or darkly comedic.

"I'm gonna go flick on the kettle and grab a plate of cookies for us, and we'll square up with the truck. Let me grab the key from the shed, hey? Be right back, make yourself at home, boss."

Owen nodded, staring at his hands, and Clyde disappeared.

Owen was glad Clyde had to go find that key, he needed a minute alone. He knew his father was a kind, benevolent, and lovable man, but never saw him as the life of a town. A man who sang karaoke and loved scotch. He never really seemed to *love* anything. Owen just got twenty-five percent off the price of his truck because of his last name. Did these people know a different side of his father, or did they just know him better? Maybe his father came up here to be a different man for a few days a month. To escape himself, to live a double life.

~

Clyde had been out in the shed for maybe ten minutes, and his sudden and animated re-entry into the room startled Owen out of a daydream.

"Nice man he was, you should know it's an honour to carry his name. He knew a bit about everything, Roger did, and he could talk the ear off of you if you talked to him about something he was passionate about." Owen never knew his father as a talkative man. He was a kind man, a sensitive man, a man with all the right words, but more than anything, Owen remembered his father as a man of few words.

"He taught me an awful lot myself, actually. I was looking at the world the wrong way, my whole life, but it only took a few conversations with your father to fix that. I thought Roger was a quack at first, Owen, but it turns out I was."

He laid a plate of brownies on the table then and bit one in half. His teeth were brown now as he carried on. "And my wife, Cassie, she loved lit-trature. We never got out of this town much, certainly not Newfoundland anyway, and she used all those books your father has down there, in that monstrous bookshelf of his, as a way to vacation, to hear about other people's lives, cities, and worlds."

He grabbed another brownie then, and picked up the plate to extend it to Owen, visibly confused as to why Owen wasn't helping himself to the brownies.

"Thing is, she couldn't read, or write, and I never really knew how to teach her. I mean, how do you go about it, right? Point to every word and tell her what it is? Your father though, he had that way about him. He could help people see things in the simplest and easiest way. A born teacher and preacher, I called him. I s'pose you know that already, hey? How your father had that way about him?" He waited for a nod before carrying on, so Owen felt compelled to nod. A lie.

"So Cassie would go down there when your father was around, and he'd read to her. She hated having to wait two or three weeks for him to get back and finish the stories they started last time he was in town. I s'pose in hindsight, I could've read them to her, but I never cared for fiction, and I stumble too much when I read out loud. Listening to me read is like listening to some kid in kindergarten still unsure of his words." He laughed, and quickly turned in on himself and collapsed a little in his chair.

"He was teaching her to read and write just before she got the cancer. Esophageal cancer, no hope with that one, they say. She's dead now, died just before your father got sick. It was a bad year, I guess."

He pointed to a picture on the mantle, and they both stared at her. She was absolutely beautiful, and reminded him of Hannah in a way, how her eyes seemed not to see the world, but to project it. Everything around her in the picture, the sky and the trees, they seemed to be there solely to accentuate her. She had dusty blonde hair that curled up and off her shoulders, and a coy smile that seemed so unsure of itself, of why she was smiling. From the picture, he could tell she was always smiling. He could tell that she always wore a long summer dress like the white and blue one she was wearing in that picture. Flashy, yet casual.

"So what is it you do, Owen? You got your father's brains?"

"I've been leading a modest life as a starving writer—"

"Oh!" he cut him off. "For the papers and that, like your father?"

"No, no. I lack my father's persuasion in my writing, or for that matter, his gifted way with words. My father's diction could've been used by the military as weaponry, it was really that powerful."

Clyde looked a little confused, so Owen carried on. "I write fiction, mainly. I embed my own life into fictitious stories, or build fictitious stories out of things I see in everyday life around me. If I overhear an odd conversation in a grocery store, I find a way to plug it into a story. If I like some mannerism I see in a waitress, I'll build a character out of her. I don't care much about plots, because I think real literature is about more than just telling a story. The story should just be a way to comment on the world somehow, on the human condition and what it means to be alive in today's world. But I guess I'm just babbling here now, am I? Sorry."

"No, not at all. And good for you, boss." He reached out to slap Owen's knee. "Because that is a profession that comes from the heart." He tapped his chest with a closed fist as he said the word heart.

"Not many people are working from the heart nowadays, Owen. They're just burning themselves out so they can buy more stuff and things and lose their identity trying to be like everyone else, and exist in a world whose only goal seems to be to stay on top of your bills and make ends meet. Your father would be proud of you, *I* think. He'd rather see you poor and happy than on top of your bills, trust me there, kid."

Clyde stopped talking for a minute. He stared at Owen, *into* him, and smiled. A sympathetic smile like, *I am sorry for your loss.*

"To be honest, I couldn't get the names right, because it was so long ago, but I do remember your father joking about how he was fathering one Einstein and one Thoreau. I've got three kids of my own, so I know a parent doesn't have a favourite, but we both know who your father would be more proud of, and I'm guessing you were the Thoreau."

There was another pause, not awkward, just a moment of silence and some shuffling of feet. Owen appreciated the comment.

"It's a goddamn shame what happened to your father, Owen, and we all heard about your mother too. But for what it's worth, you're still intact, and seem like a man your father would be proud of."

*You don't know me, old man.*

He jammed another brownie into his mouth. His sixth. "I got to confess, I didn't know much about schizophrenia, but when the neighbours told me that's what it was that got your father, I had to go over to the library in Clarenville and get myself some books on the topic." He pointed to the left, in the direction of Clarenville.

"What I was more interested in than anything was the treatment process, whether he could be cured or not. I mean, how does a man just lose himself like that? And from what I read, most people are diagnosed by their mid-twenties, so how did your father escape it so long? One of the books I read, Owen, was more like a novel than a textbook, and I read it twice. I'd recommend it as a good read to anyone. It was a bunch of case studies by different doctors, and they put an interesting spin on the disease." He grabbed another brownie then. Every time he licked his teeth from brown to white, he'd grab another brownie.

"The way they portrayed some schizophrenics, and in a way schizophrenia itself, was that it was just as much an escape from reality as it was a disease. In certain cases anyway. I mean, like any disease, it comes down to physiological causes, but some of these schizophrenics had created people, like imaginary friends, I suppose, out of a subconscious need for something they were lacking in their real life. These imaginary people helped the schizophrenics feel safer, happier, saner, or whatever. Whatever the schizophrenics were needing, they came up with delusions and hallucinations to fill that need."

"Yeah, well, in my father's case, I guess it was a need to feel more relevant in his field. Last going off he thought he was working for some top-secret newsp–"

"Oh, I don't know about that. I s'pose we'll never know. Any of us. All we can ever do is assume things about each other, boss, we can never really know each other. Because I think we wake up as a different person every day, based on what happened in all the days before the one in which we are living. You know what I mean? We're an ever-changing product of yesterdays, not rigid, static people. At any given moment who we are can change. Hell, to a degree, every new person you meet changes you, every conversation. So, I don't think anybody knows anybody." A few seconds of silence. "I don't think anybody knows themself, either." He laughed. They both did.

They sat in silence for a few minutes, letting that mutually agreed upon statement bond them. Clyde caught Owen staring at a bottle of scotch and a look of acknowledgement was exchanged. A lot was said in that look, a lot more than either of them was willing to say, yet. Clyde had clearly seen a dark past in Owen, and to have seen it so quickly and so easily could only mean he had one of his own.

"Anyway, we can talk anytime, Owen, but I got to head over to Clarenville before dark and pick up a few things at the Walmart. I don't trust my eyes in the dark anymore."

He shot up out of his chair, pressing a wrinkle out of his pants. "Clyde Noseworthy is the name, and you know where I live if you need anything, or have any problems with the truck."

Turning towards the window. "My eldest son, Bradley, he bought me a new one." He pointed out the window at a new white Ford pickup. "He lives up in Alberta now, like half of us Newfoundlanders, I s'pose. He's an electrician. Anyway, the tank should be full in your new truck, Owen. We can square up about the damned paperwork next week sometime. It's been nice meeting you and chatting a little. I don't know how long you're staying, and I know better than to ask a man about more than he's offering, but isolation is good for nobody, your father taught me that much, so if you get bored or need something while you're here, a cup of sugar or a game of pool, we're neighbours and I'd love to chat."

He followed Owen to the porch. "Don't ever assume an old, lonely widower doesn't want to hear about it!"

⁓

The town talked of Roger Collins, still, as some kind of legend. It distorted Owen's view and knowledge of his father, but it was all good, all praise, and that made up for Owen's declaring him a hypocrite earlier, when he saw that picture of him and Alex and remembered his father's words. *Life isn't about finding the answers to your questions, it's about not needing them.* The man this town described sounded like the kind of man who would utter those words to his children, and mean it.

He put his supper in the oven: a bag of McCain French fries. He hadn't taken the truck over to Clarenville for groceries yet. Leaving them to cook, he headed for his father's office, with hesitation in his step, afraid he'd find a room full of "coded flyers," or something even worse. He flicked on the light and leaned on the door frame. He took the room in; it looked exactly as he remembered it: red walls, white borders, and an absolute mess, yet neurotically organized. There were piles of papers and boxes everywhere, but similar things were bunched meticulously together. He had to choose his steps carefully to walk through the room, or he'd trip over one of the stacks. There were piles of his father's publications, piles of old, yellowed newspaper articles he liked, piles of literary journals, piles of photo albums, two "miscellaneous" piles, and a pile of his father's prose.

*You wrote too?*

To scour this room was to learn about Roger Collins, the man, not "Dad." He made his way through the maze imposed by the stacked piles of paper, and sat at his father's desk. It was a mahogany desk, covered in a thick film of grey dust. Owen sat and looked around the room, out the window. He traced *Roger* into the dust with his finger, not realizing he was doing so until he was rounding the top of the second r. There was nothing on the desk except for a monstrous, ancient, army-green typewriter. There was one piece of yellowed paper tucked into the typewriter, bowing back down over its keys. He tore it free from the grip of the typewriter and read what his father last typed. What were essentially his father's last written words: *If I could go back in time, what would I take to this day and what would I leave behind? What would I take to this day, and why?*

Owen nodded, he would borrow it. He would start his new novel with that as an opening line. The new novel he'd been trying to start since Hannah died.

The desk had two drawers, each locked and the key nowhere to be found, so he ran out back to the shed, still remembering the combination to the lock, 3-6-9, and got a crowbar. The aged locks snapped with surprising ease: the crowbar seemed like overkill, like using a hammer to crack an egg, and he laughed at himself. In the first drawer, he found two time capsules. One labeled, *Owen, ten years old*, the other, *Alex, ten years old.*

Ten years old, before the world had terrorized them and broke their big, red hearts, back when they were who they were and not who they are. Time capsules from a time when they were their truest selves: unmoulded and omnipotent. There was a picture inside each capsule. A photo of each brother at ten years old, taken at the very desk Owen was sitting at. There was a Memorex cassette tape in each one too, but he stared, dumbfounded, at those two pictures. The innocent, mischievous looks on their faces, like nothing could go wrong, bedheaded in matching Spiderman pajamas. Like life was all laughter and games of tag and being able to hang upside-down on the monkey bars longer than your brother. He studied the smiles on their faces, the gloss in their eyes. He hadn't realized how much the world had beaten out of him and his brother until he saw those two photographs.

The cassette tapes were thirty-minute interviews their father had conducted with each of his sons. He sat in front of the stereo in the living room and he lay down on a large, brown, oval rug, stared at the white ceiling, and learned all about who he *was*. The tape was intended to capture who he wanted to be when he grew up, but as he listened to it, it had the opposite effect. It was a tape of who he wanted to be again. A kid who saw the beauty in a sunny day, who played dinkies with Alex, and that was enough. To find a simple joy in feeding a red squirrel with his father there, and his brother right beside him.

"So, Owen, tell me. What do you want to be when you are my age?"

"Um, what did Alex say?"

(laughter)

"He said he wanted to be rich, like your Uncle Ross."

"Oh. Well. I want to be a hero. Can I be a hero?"

"That's up to you, my son, and remember that. But tell me, what kind of hero do you want to be?"

"You know, a hero, someone who saves the people other people hurt."

"That's nice, so maybe a doctor or a police officer?"

"No. I don't want a job. When I grow up I am just going to get a cheque book like Mom's. I won't need a job then. I'll just pay for everything with cheques."

(laughter)

"I'll let you think it's that simple for now, kiddo."

❧

By the time he finished listening to both the tapes, an hour had passed. The fries he'd put in the oven and forgot about burned black and set off the fire alarm, right in the middle of

Alex's interview. His father asked Alex why he loved his brother.

"Because he is always there, we are always together, so if one of us gets hurt, like when I fell off my bike last night, he'll help me. When I got lost at the museum during last week's field trip, Owen was the one who found me, remember? That's why it's good to have a twin, you're never alone when you get hurt or lost. You don't have to wait for the bus alone, and he's good at the parts of video games that I can't figure out. Most people only see their best friends at school. Mine is always around, and always will be."

Owen made some toast, because the fries had burnt and all he had in the house were fries, bread, tea, and butter. He took it into his father's office to open that second drawer. There was nothing in it except a wooden jewelry box about the size of a carton of eggs. He shook it. He slid the lid off and hauled out a note from Cassie, Clyde's wife, the woman his father had taught to read and write. The note thanked him for much more than the English lessons and was signed, *Love Cassie.*

Love.

Beneath the note, there was a strip of joined, black and white photos, those strips of four photos from old photo booths in shopping malls. In the first photo, they were caught off guard and ill-prepared for the flash of the camera. His father was just about to sit – looking behind him with a hand on the seat – and Cassie was standing, still taking off her jacket. In the second photo they were laughing at themselves for missing that first photo opportunity – their faces side-on and their mouths wide with laughter. Her hand was on his father's knee in a way that suggested she was familiar with his body, that she'd wandered its landscape in a darkened room enough to know his body with her eyes closed. In the third picture they smiled and faced the camera, their heads resting together. This one was their attempt at a nice photo of the two of them. She was wearing the same blue-and-white dress she had on in that photo on Clyde's mantle. In the fourth photo they were kissing, their faces pressed together in a way that suggested they knew exactly how to kiss each other, that they'd been together enough to know exactly how the other one liked it.

On the back of those photos, his father had penned a message: *Here's to loving someone so much there is no such thing as time anymore. Just when we are together and when we are not.*

Owen was speechless. A little pissed off, and, surprisingly, a little touched at his father's sincerity. At least Clyde wasn't his brother. Maybe that's all it was: justification of what he'd done with Hannah. Like father, like son. Breathing a little slower, he dropped the photos back into the box and closed it, thieved of even more of his sense of family. *So that was your big project up here, was it, Dad? Another man's wife?*

And then he remembered Clyde saying that Cassie died shortly before his father went mad. His father lost his mind shortly after Cassie died. So he had to wonder, Was her death a contributing factor to his father giving in to schizophrenia? Was it the death of his father's beloved mistress, a woman Owen knew nothing about, that finally sent his father over the edge? His Port Blandford life was the life he ran off to, to escape his reality, to escape his life in the city. This was the place where he was happiest, where a whole town talked of him as an ethereal saint. When Cassie died, he lost all that. He had nothing but a wife who never understood him, two children who actively avoided spending time with him, and now he had nowhere to run off to. All he had was his profession, and then his newspaper failed. It was a glorified, simplified explanation, but it helped Owen understand things a little more. Or he let it explain things a little more.

He gazed out the window. The view out the window from

his father's office was the rusted swing set and the grown-over sandbox he and Alex once loved. They used to dump sand in each other's hair because they liked the sensation of picking the sand out of their scalps. Alex said it was like scratching fly bites.

# A MOTHER, NOT A LOVER

*December 4th, 2008,*
*Fumbling Towards Farewell.*

*Love might be beautiful, but it's a vicious sort of beauty.*
*Vicious in that it forces you to act. Possesses you. You can't*
*ignore it. Not for sure anyway. Not always, or for convenience*
*or wedding vows or a clean conscience. Yet we try and*
*entangle love with all the laws of morality, even though*
*morality shatters like glass when love swings a fist. We've all*
*done something we shouldn't have in the relationship*
*department, or we at least thought about it and deprived*
*ourselves, and that is really no better.*

*What is love anyway? What are we separated from, as human*
*beings, that we are so desperate to find in someone else? I*
*thought Owen was all my answers. Maybe in another life he*
*could've been. Now I see that we are only complicating each*
*other's lives. I mean, maybe if I wasn't married to your brother,*
*Owen, maybe then we could've kept this feeling alive. Instead*
*we're hiding it, hiding a fire. A fire between us can only burn*
*us. It can do nothing more. It can light up no brighter life. It*
*can only destroy my family, my children, your brother.*

Juliet never listened to her mother, maybe she should have, but she didn't. That's the point of her and Romeo's story, of mine and Owen's: love is bigger than us, it decides for us, so why do we shit ourselves and apologize for what it does to us? How can we even pretend that who we want in 2008 will be who we want in 2018? Who wears what they wore a decade ago? Who doesn't change over the course of a decade? We change. What we want changes. It's only natural.

But I am a mother and this is a selfish way to think. And I am sick to death of thinking anyway. I've thought it to death, and here's why I am sorry I've had an affair: family is enough. A great family like mine is far more beautiful than love itself, I think. Or at least I have chosen to believe, for the sake of my husband, my children, and my own consience. For the sake of alleviating the sensation that my organs are tied in knots growing tighter every day.

Because last Wednesday was too much. The scene hasn't left me, the wicked and savage dishonesty is ripping me apart. Alex called and left a message on the answering machine as his brother was bucking against me on our bed. It felt vile. I was a monster. I died, right there in our bed. My skin was throbbing, it's the only way I can describe it. I cried. Alex called to say he was craving my potato-leek casserole for supper, that he'd love me for life if I could make it for him. I died, I sank right into the bed with guilt and remorse. I was afraid he'd somehow hear us there in the bed. Through the machine. Somehow. But Owen, he just kept on thrusting and moaning away. He didn't even react. He just kept on panting, eyes closed, raising then slowly lowering his head, over and over.

Owen Collins is missing something human. It was so unnerving. He isn't insensitive to how this could crush Alex. It's not that, it's that he's missing something human. It's hard to explain. He's indifferent to his very existence, to everything *and anything that could happen to him. You could shoot the guy and prod the wound and he'd just sit there, unflinching. I know he cares for Alex, but today when Alex left that message, he didn't even react. Indifferent, not cold. It's like the world is a movie he's watched so many times it bores him now. I remember maybe the third or fourth time we made love. I just burst into tears. I pushed him off of me then hauled him into me for a bear hug and wept wildly on his shoulders. He comforted me, but I don't think he got it. The guilt. I mean he got it. Three weeks later I was kissing him again, guiding him onto the couch, and he mustered up a "Are you sure, are you sure?" He got the guilt, but I don't know if he <u>felt</u> it.*

*It was beautiful what we've shared. It was love. But it has to end soon. We are kidding ourselves to think it can evolve. It's not so much guilt that I feel now, it's a crushing sadness and a feeling of futility in being with Owen this way. We will never have a house and children of our own. We will never see the kind of kid we could create, a precious little girl with curly locks and freckles, or a devilish little brown-eyed boy, and we will never have a house with walls to paint and railings to accidentally ding up. We will never be able to have a proper relationship where we can project ourselves into the future, so what's the point in what we are doing? If there is no place for something in the future, and time is always dragging us into the future, what is the purpose of what Owen and I are doing? Besides, I don't have the strength to leave Alex or the desire to destroy my family. You can't raise your daughters with your brother-in-law while their father is still alive. That goes without saying. Not that I haven't thought about it. Pictured it. Pictured us spooning before bed every night, him rocking me to sleep, rubbing my palms with his thumb like he does.*

*Just after Alex left that message, I turned into a mad ball of tears and snots. I lost it. I pushed Owen off of me and gathered my clothes up off the floor. By accident, I'd pushed him into the lamp on Alex's night table, and it smashed off the wall behind him. I thought I got all the glass, but I never thought to check the sheets. Alex crawled into bed that night and a slender knife-like shard, the same colour as the sheets, sank deep into his back, right behind his heart. How's that for guilt? We are villains. We both agreed we've gotten too casual. No more sex in that bed, no more assuming Callie and Lucia won't pick up on our closeness. They are far from naïve, and years beyond their ages.*

*Last week, last Thursday night, Alex surprised me with tickets to a Hayden concert. He knows I love him, knows he is my default music and accepts the crush. And Hayden was great, and funny in between the songs, and played the trumpet part of one his songs with his mouth, because he was playing alone, and it was cute and funny and perfect. How do you not love a guy who wrote a song about his cat? After the show, Alex took me out for supper. It was nice. We laughed a lot, he even pulled my chair out for me to boot. He is a gentleman, if only because people are watching. He hates most restaurants because the seating is too crowded and most people can hear his conversations, and that makes him feel like he should be saying something special. He's always so worried everyone is judging his appearance, because he is either over- or under-dressed. And he worries that he'll mispronounce something on the menu and seem uncouth. It's so vain of him, but if you know him, like I do, it's kind of cute. It's kind of sad, because you know why he is the way he is. My point is that it was a nice night, and I know they don't happen enough, but I also know we'll have many more nice nights, and maybe moments are enough? Maybe I can let moments be enough. For the sake of my children.*

*Owen gives me every minute, makes me feel like a beautiful, interesting, and worthwhile woman. Unique. Like I am me*

*and no one else is. He makes me feel like a giddy little teenager.
Sometimes I don't even know what to do with my arms and
legs, he excites me that much. He points out the things about
me I never think of or notice, like how I hold a mug, and they
all make me feel so distinct and noticeable. But we both
know that will fade. I'd rather cut it off now, before it does
fade. Because all of this guilt and shame won't have been
worth it if it does fade. All this risk and anxiety. All this
jeopardizing my children's childhoods. I have one duty as a
mother: keep my children safe and happy.*

*So this week was it for us, or at least the beginning of the end.
I relished and exploited every moment of it, and now I intend
to end this affair in a beautiful, courteous way. I will tell
him it is over and he needs to move out. For the sake of my
beautiful, innocent family. And he will have to understand.
Our relationship is a dead end for him, a bomb in waiting for
my family, and emotional suicide for me.*

*I am a mother first, not a lover. I am at least a better mother
than I am a lover, and Callie and Lucia are more important
to me than Owen is. Period. And my own life for that matter.
I would deny myself food, air, and water for my daughters – I
would readily die for them – and so I will deny myself Owen.
For them.*

# WORDS LIKE SHRAPNEL

HE FINISHED READING HANNAH'S LAST journal entry. The writing in the last paragraph was shaky – she'd written it in the car. The rest of the pages were empty. There was no more left to read. No more left to say. And he'd started drinking again.

He was half-drunk as he read it. He laid it down, finished the bottle, and walked over to a window. Put his forehead to it, felt the cold there, the winter against his window, the condensation, wet and slippery. A slight squeak. There was a pine grosbeak in a tree, not a rare bird but a notable one, with its grey body speckled red in a way that looked like blood splatter. It was clinging to a branch, trying to hide from the wind. The branch floating up and down, swaying left to right. He could've sworn the bird was staring him down.

He sat back down, brought steepled hands to his face, stared at her journal, then flung it across the room like a Frisbee. Sparks shot out of the fireplace and logs cracked from the blow and rolled over each other. The smoke from its pages burned a darker black than the smoke from the wood. Toxic smoke. The paper was gone in seconds, and then the cover slowly seared, twisted, curled in on itself, and turned to ash. The diary was gone, and yet burning it never changed a thing. Those pages, her words: they were an inextricable part of his life now, another tragedy to live with, and why bother? What for? Who'd notice if he was gone? He could've crawled into the fireplace and burned with those pages and felt no pain at all.

He'd walked back up to the North Atlantic gas station, the only place in town that sold wine. The selection was shit and he sighed about it. He brought three bottles up to the counter, dropped them down, and they clanged off each other loudly. One fell over. The cashier was scared. She took a step back, but he saw a look of sadness that overwhelmed her fright, so she looked confused to him. She tried to diffuse the situation. "Heyya, Owen. Heard ya bought Clyde's truck after? Had a grand ol' chat with him? He's chatty. He's like a woman that way, but fun as they comes, re–"

"How much is the wine?" He hated himself for the irritibility, she was a sweet woman, but he just couldn't pretend. "Sorry, just ... in a rush."

"Company coming, dear?"

He shook his head and she looked down at the three bottles.

He came back the next night for more. It was the kind of town where the amount of booze he'd bought couldn't go unnoticed, so he hated being *Roger's boy*, knowing that meant someone was going to intervene. Clyde had the obvious *in* with Owen: the sale of the truck and the conversation over brownies.

Owen was washing a week's worth of dishes when Clyde knocked on his door. "Hey, Owen, I found the driver's manual for your truck in my shed just now! Thought you might want it." He held it out to Owen. It was yellowed and buckled and spotted with brown residues.

Clyde squinted a little, his crow's feet tightening, as if he barely recognized Owen's face behind the patchy beard he'd grown. Owen looked down, took himself in. He looked disheveled, if not unhygienic: black-and-white pajama pants, dotted red in various places by what was obviously wine, and a plain black golf shirt that needed an iron. Hair like an old wig he'd found balled up in a closet somewhere and pulled on his head. Frizzy and bedheaded. He watched Clyde stumble, improvising a plan to get some one-on-one time with *Roger's kid.*

"Listen, I was thinking, if you're not too busy ... maybe you could join me for a game of pool later? Don't worry, I'm not going to become that annoying neighbour you hate, but it's been a long week, and I could use a few beers. Besides, it gives me an out from another social obligation. My goddamn neighbours are going to ask me over for a game of cards again, I know it, and if I see another goddamn deck of cards this week I'll puke my guts out!" He rolled his eyes and raised his eyebrows.

"So what do you say, boss? Feel like helping an old man out or what? Let me show you where the local pub is, huh? It's just up the road, and if you show up with me, Patsy'll trust you enough to set up a tab for you. C'mon, spare me that game of cards with my dimwit neighbours!"

Even though he liked Clyde, Owen hated the idea of it. But his whole life he'd been unable to say no to social obligations. If someone asked, he obliged, willingly or not. Saying no to someone, especially someone like Clyde, felt so rude. He said yes, hoping a night out of the house for a few hours could distract him from the incessant, gnawing melancholy he'd felt since reading Hannah's last journal entry. What she said was brutal, devastating, and entirely true. But more importantly it meant he lost his brother for no good reason. He had lost his brother for sex, not love. He was here alone because of sex. It seemed so pathetic, so wrong. He'd burnt her journal, but he felt like maybe he should have kept it, just to re-read the way Hannah talked of him on those first few pages.

"Yeah, sure, Clyde … but give me a few hours, hey? I'm right in the middle of writing a turning point in my novel. The rest of the book, the direction I take with it, sort of hinges on what I write today. I got a few ideas in my head I don't want to lose. I kinda need to run with them and see where they go, you know? Give me a few hours?"

Clyde nodded, even though Owen's hands were still dripping wet from the dishwater.

As he watched Clyde walking away, Owen thought maybe he could get some material for his new book out of him, maybe even base a character on him. Maybe even create some kind of exaggerated story about the triangle between him, his father, and Cassie. The notion made it easier to go out for that game of pool. Two weeks ago he deleted a novel he'd started. He was five chapters into it. He started a new one, but had only the opening line: *Love can never be wrong, and that can cost you everything.*

It's hard to pull off using an aphorism as an opening line, but Percy Janes did it, among others. He liked it. It all depended on the second sentence, the story that followed, and if he didn't know for a fact Alex would hate him for it, he'd write his life's story with enough fabrication, altered specifics, and exaggeration to call it fiction.

&#x223d;

It was a small, sports pub style bar, but the space was used well. It felt bigger than it was. Owen wasn't interested in what their stares insinuated they wanted from each other, but he caught himself eyeing a girl, all night long. She sat at the bar, alone, on the same stool, watching a hockey game on mute. He could tell she wasn't really interested in the game, she was probably just cheering for the team whose jersey appealed to her the most. The bright red and blue one. She was just passing time, or amusing her eyes and brain as she drank herself drunk to forget about something, like Owen was doing. When the Montreal Canadiens scored a goal, and the rest of the bar raised their drinks and hollered, and clapped the palms of their hands off the sticky tables, she sat there indifferently, shoving another handful of peanuts into her cute little mouth.

He wasn't attracted to *her* so much as he was attracted to her indifference, because he identified with it. She was attractive, his kind of woman, but she could have just as easily have been a man or a child, and he'd have been watching her for the same reason: to identify with someone else who was feeling like a ghost before death.

At one point he lost himself in her, and Clyde had to smack him back into consciousness with the thin end of his pool stick. The blue cue dust from the stick flaked off onto Owen's shoulder and sat there like dandruff.

"What are you lookin' at, boss? You're up, and I'm kicking your ass somethin' fierce! You missed my bank shot. You're no challenge! I'm only playing with you so you'll compliment me, and here you are missing all my good shots! Pay attention, boss, maybe you'll learn a few things from me and make an old fellah feel useful. Maybe I'll make a pool shark out of you, and we'll hustle the town poor. Whaddaya think?"

It was an unspoken rule in the pub that to play any more than two games of pool in a row, if someone else wanted a game, was rude and not tolerated. So four games of pool and a dozen beer later, when two men slapped their loonies into the slots on the coin-operated table, Clyde and Owen yielded their pool cues to the newcomers and sat at a table. It was a round, black table, sticky from spilled booze and the sugar residues of mixes. The chairs could be used as rocking chairs, one or two legs a little bit longer than the others. The wobbling seats accentuated their inebriation.

"That's Rodney and Kent," Clyde explained. "They're probably the best players around. But a few more weeks of me teaching you my ways, and I'd say we could take them in a game of doubles."

Owen laughed. He was drunk enough to be happy and pleasant company now. "I think those were the only games of pool you'll be getting out of me, Clyde. Pool's not my thing. First game I've played in maybe a decade was tonight."

When Owen caught himself laughing, he wondered if it was just the booze. Maybe it was just Clyde. Clyde was a man with so many implausible stories that it was hard to believe that much could happen to one man in sixty-seven years. It was also hard to believe he was sixty-seven. He was too liberal with his eyes towards the women in the bar, too electric and witty, too *something* to be sixty-seven. His stories were endless and captivating, the type you'd come play pool with him just to hear. Owen laughed out loud at them and jotted some of them down to use in his writing, sure he could fit them into a story or two, and the idea excited Clyde.

"Oh, if you need some fuel for your writing, I'm your man. I'll make you a bestseller and won't even charge ya. You'll just have to play the odd game of pool with me."

He got up then, to fetch another round of Honey Brown. He started another story as he laid the drinks on the table and slid into his chair. He knocked the table with his hip, tipping both beer on their sides, and Owen caught both bottles before too much had spilled. They laughed like giddy drunk nineteen-year-olds.

"Good catch, boss. Drunk as fuck and still swift as a fox!" He wiped the beer bottle with the sleeve of his thick, grey, cableknit sweater. "Your father ever tell you about the bear incident? When we was hunting bear that time?"

Owen laughed. *Bullshit.* He could swallow most of Clyde's stories about his father, but not this one. Picturing his father out hunting bear was as funny an image as picturing his father doing ballet in a tutu.

"The bear was well off in the distance, but I took her down in two shots. It was a ten-minute walk down to the bear then, up and over hills, around deep bogs. When we got within ten feet of her, the bear stood up!" He laughed, slapping a knee and leaning forward. He saw all his memories so vividly. "Your father jumped back against a tree so hard he really hurt himself. I mean, he gave himself a good thunk in the head and bloodied his ear. The bear, well, the bear was even more frightened. They're near blind, black bears, and gets quite a fright when people sneaks up on them. Luckily they're pretty meek animals, unless they got a cub. Anyway. We was baffled after the big old bear got up and run off! And then we saw the dead one, over in the distance! What's the chances of a live bear napping not far from the one we'd shot, right?" Eyes widened, head nodding. "Right?"

A night out with Clyde couldn't have come at a better time. He was a good drunk. He was wild, but harmless, and totally unpredictable. His arms flailed off in every direction as he spoke. It was dizzying. And his words flew out of him with enough fervour to chip his teeth. It didn't matter whether he was laughing at him or with him. He was laughing. And Clyde was a good man, a funny man, and so full of life.

And then there was that girl at the bar. Maybe he wouldn't have cared about her so much if Clyde hadn't shared some of that liveliness. He needed her story. If he couldn't get it, maybe he'd write an imagined account of her, like he had that day at his mother's grave during Thomas Brooke's funeral. That fictional, imagined story of a real person *was* his last windfall. Maybe this girl would be his delayed follow-up.

She was so stoic, she wore stoic like a flashy accessory. Her mouth looked so out of place on her face, like it had spent a lifetime smiling but then, unexpectedly, had run out of things to smile about. Now it felt out of place on her rendered-sullen face, being so perpetually unmoving. Her mouth was now just a place to shove in peanuts in a dingy bar, or swallow alcohol. It spoke to some sudden and recent tragedy she must have endured.

Her nose was tiny, cute. It probably had to overexert itself to pick up a scent from anything. Her eyes were arrows: he felt their pierce every time she looked over, even if his back was turned. They were a hazel brown that glowed, even under the dim lights of the bar. They were eyes that had seen something too tragic to be able to take in anything beautiful anymore. A sunset was no longer stunning for her; it was just a too-bright orange sky she wished would just turn back to blue, so she could stop squinting. Any strain was too much strain for her now, including squinting at a sunset. A man staring at her from across a bar was just a man who wanted something from her she wasn't ever going to give him. Owen was drawn to her for that reason.

Every time he stared at her, Clyde waved a hand in front of his eyes. "Earth to Owen, you listening to me? Here's a quick little story about your father. You'll wanna jot this one down for that book of yours."

At some point that night, well after midnight, he tuned into one of Clyde's stories, and when he looked up the girl was gone. The bartender rang her last-call bell, and Owen tried to help a far-too-drunk Clyde into his jacket. Patsy, the bartender, offered Clyde a ride home and relieved Owen of the responsibility of dealing with him. She seemed used to Clyde getting so drunk she had to drive him home. She slung his arms into his jacket in a way that seemed rehearsed, and then she scooped him up by grabbing the armpits of his jacket. It was like watching a mother dressing a baby. She didn't seem to mind doing so, as if it was only a slight setback to having such a big spender in the bar all the time. Clyde winked at Owen when she wasn't looking, like, *Yeah, we have a "special" arrangement, me and this girl. Not bad, hey?*

"You mind if I run to the washroom before you lock up?"

"Sure, go ahead. We'll take off, just make sure you turns the lock on your way out and pulls the door to. I knows where to find ya if you steals anything." She laughed. She could tell her trust surprised Owen. "Only in Newfoundland, right?" Owen smiled in agreement. "I knew Roger enough to know he couldn't spawn no thief! Have a good night, Owen."

She turned back around to face Owen, holding Clyde up like a wounded soldier. "It was nice of you to give this old fellah some company tonight, Owen."

He leaned against the wall of the stall for support as he relieved himself. Clear urine shot out of him like an orgasm, and he moaned, just as relieved. Being on his feet for a few minutes stirred up the dizzying consequence of all those drinks. The bathroom felt slanted, and wherever he shifted his weight, the world seemed to tilt in that direction. On the way out of the bar, he flipped the lock and pulled the door shut behind him. He pulled on the door exactly three times to make sure it was locked. And then he heard the flicking of a lighter. It was the girl. She was sitting on a tree stump behind the bar. He looked in her direction. In the dark of the night, the smoke from her cigarette looked blue.

"Geez ... you step out for a smoke around here and they lock you out!"

"Well, if I had the key, I'd let you back in. Thing is, it's not my bar."

Owen had spent years concealing alcoholism, so he was able to not slur his speech or slip on the ice underneath his feet, but his social etiquette had drowned in the beer, and he approached her as if he knew her. He was stumbling towards her, and she was sort of giggling about it. "I'm Emily ... Emily Grace." She extended a pack of cigarettes. "Care for a smoke, stranger."

"I'm Owen, and I'll pass on the cigarette, thanks."

"Yeah, I'm a dying breed. Funny thing is, I only picked up smoking last year."

He realized he'd just walked over to greet an absolute stranger. She hadn't called him over, not directly anyway, and within a minute they'd run out of conversation. He fidgeted with a hangnail, made a dimwitted comment about the shape of a tree to fill a silence, and she pretended she never heard him.

"Don't suppose there's another bar around?"

"Not that I know of."

And more silence poured itself in between them. There was only the sound of waves coursing over pebbles, massaging them into sand, about twenty feet from where they sat. The stars shone so brightly, being so far from city lights, that Owen almost expected to hear them sparkle up there, in that deep purple night sky. They were both staring up at the stars, as if to seem preoccupied and fill the silence with action, not words.

"So, Owen, you live here in this quaint little town?"

"Yes and no. As in, I just moved here for an indefinite amount of time. Long story."

"Aren't they all? The good ones anyway."

She looked right into him as she said that, as if she knew, as if she knew exactly why he was there, drunk, in Port Blandford that night. He didn't want to share that story, not yet anyway.

"What about you, Hannah, what brings you to Port Blandford?"

"Emily."

"What?"

"Emily … my name is Emily. You called me Hannah. Who is Hannah, and what makes you think I don't live here?"

"Jesus. I am drunk. Sorry. Hannah is an old … girl … friend of mine, and I have no idea why I assumed you don't live here."

"Well, I don't live here. I'm just spending a week or so here. I had to run away from my life for a while." She sized him up and down with squinted eyes and a playful grin. "You seem like a man who could understand that need for isolation and time alone. I'd say if we had a few more drinks in us, we could lay some pretty heavy stories into each other's laps. Because, no offense, Owen, but you look like a man with the weight of the world clung onto his shoulders."

She sucked in and blew out a few more clouds of blue smoke. "But I won't pry. I hate when people pry. It's why I came out here for a week, to avoid people prying, sympathizing, baking me dry cakes and tasteless casseroles, as if it were food I needed." She turned and tuned into a noise in the trees behind her. She startled easily.

"I live in Corner Brook. I'm staying in the B&B down the road there." She pointed to it as if it were visible. "But I got myself in a jam here. The lady says she locks the doors at midnight and doesn't want people traipsing in after twelve and waking everyone up."

"So, what are you going to—"

"So, I remind you of an ex, hey? Of Hannah?"

"No … well … yes and no. Why? You kind of look like and act like … her."

She was still smoking the same never-ending cigarette. Either he'd lost his sense of time, or there was something wrong with that cigarette.

"So, what are you going to do?"

"About what?"

"About being locked out of your B&B?"

"Good question. What would you do if you were me? Sleep down on the beach there, or go knocking on her door and feel like a wild bitch for the rest of your stay in this little town?"

He was drunk, and everyone and everything about this town seemed harmless, especially her. So he spoke without thinking of how it sounded. "Well, I'm living in that red house there." He flung an arm in its general direction. He was so drunk that the sudden shifting of his weight almost toppled him over. "I'm going to pass out in my bed, instantly, and I guess it would be harmless if you took the couch."

Her jaw dropped, and right away he felt like she'd misinterpreted his invitation. He waited for the harsh decline.

"And here I was thinking you'd never ask! Only in Newfoundland, right?"

"And with the right dose of alcohol."

"Yeah." She laughed and held out her hand for him to help her up off the stump. "The only way this works is if we get rid of the awkward right here and now. I have no intentions of sleeping with you … or … otherwise being with you in any way. Okay? Now you say the same thing. That's how this works, Owen Collins."

He hadn't told her his last name yet.

"And I want you to know, as a matter of personal intergrity, that this is an act of circumstance. Me going back to your house. This is not something I'd normally do. But I am having the kind of month where I just don't give a fuck. You understand this, right? And you still haven't reassured me you aren't going to try and pull anything with me."

He wanted to joke and say, *Is that why you were making eyes at me all night? You needed somewhere to sleep?*

It all seemed so surreal, drunk and lulled by a 3 a.m. fatigue. Living in Port Blandford. Heading "home" with this Emily girl. And he was so inexplicably desperate to connect with her. He liked not having to worry that she'd judge him for the state of his house. They were both in that town for reasons similar enough that she wouldn't care about the unwashed dishes and unswept floors. The grey lines of dirt running along the baseboards.

⟋

When he got back to the house, he couldn't find an extra blanket and pillow to offer her, so he just tore the pillows and comforter off of his own bed and brought them out for her. He'd just ball up his sweater and use it as a pillow. He'd slept on worse in similar drunken states in the past.

When he walked back out to the living room, she was sitting on the couch and staring into the fireplace.

"So." She pointed at the black mass in the unlit fireplace. "What book was so bad you had to burn it?"

"It wasn't a book. Long story. It was a journal, Hannah's journal."

"*My* Hannah, the girl you think I look like? You didn't like what she had to say?"

"Yeah. Something like that. And you don't look *too much* like Hannah, it's just that something about you reminds me of her."

"So?"

"So what?"

"What did she have to say?"

He laughed. The way she was asking was friendly, not nosy, not annoying or too forward.

"And if you don't mind me asking, why the limp? An injury?"

"Well … how interested would you be if I told you the limp and the burnt journal were related?"

"Very. I'd say pop the popcorn and tell me the story! Or,

better yet, we can substitute that bottle of wine over there for the popcorn."

He laughed as he lit the fireplace. "And what do I get out of it, besides the pleasure of entertaining you?"

"Well, let's face it. We're the new cats in town, just visitors, and we don't feel like telling our stories to everyone else. So why don't we have a lay-it-on-the-line, brutally honest relationship with each other? We're perfect strangers, and that makes us perfect shrinks for each other. Consider me a pair of curious ears and nothing more. I won't know all the people you're talking about, so I won't be biased, and I won't know the other sides of the stories you tell me. It's kind of perfect, isn't it? Consider me a sponge, lay it all on me, try and shed some of that weight on your shoulders. Or is it guilt? What do you think? Want to abuse this situation, make the most of our acquaintance for the next week?"

And he did. He told her everything. And she did too. All she left out was why she needed only a week, or maybe less, to deal with all her problems, whereas Owen was there "indefinitely" to deal with his. They never interrupted each other's stories, not once, and sympathies were exchanged in looks that said more than words ever could have anyway. Their giant shadows shrouded the walls, dancing in concert with the fire's flames, and accentuated their ample hand gestures. By the time they were done, the sun had come up and the same Sigur Ros album had replayed four times. The fire burned out around 4 a.m., and they'd polished off two bottles of wine. She preferred white, but drank his reds without complaining too much about the tannic snap of them.

# UNDONE

OWEN AWOKE THE NEXT MORNING feeling like a lion was biting into his wounded knee. It felt like there was glass under his skin, and he scratched at it, helpless to do anything with all the pain but clutch it between two hands. For five long minutes he thought maybe it was glass, that they'd left some in there by accident during the surgery. He'd seen things on the news about doctors leaving just about everything in their patients: towels, tools, gloves. A shard of glass seemed entirely plausible. Stumbling back into consciousness, he accepted that there were screws in his bones now.

He thought of the shard of glass in Alex's back, the one that Hannah had written about, and he thought about all that glass in the car that night, the sound of it smashing and changing everything, as it spilled into the car between them. He thought of how it massacred her beautiful, angelic face. The disjointed eyebrow. Then he thought about Emily on his couch. *How did that happen? Did it really happen? Was I that drunk?*

He dressed and checked his reflection in a mirror to make himself somewhat presentable. The more he contended with his bedhead, the worse it got. The hair on the left side of his head was as flat as a wall; the hair on the other side of his head spiked out at a ninety degree angle. He ventured out to offer her breakfast, knowing he'd first warn her that the B&B would likely have more to offer in the way of a decent meal. A quick little joke might be a good start to the day, considering the topics of their conversations the night before. He tugged his pajama pants around so his bulge was less noticeable, or maybe the lack of a bulge, then decided to change into a pair of jeans and pull on a respectable shirt.

But when he got out to the living room, the pillow he'd given her was resting on top of a perfectly folded blanket, and she was gone. She was pretty vulnerable and laying it all out there, maybe she left upset? Maybe she was an early riser, and, sober, felt weird on a stranger's couch. Maybe she left to get some food or had somewhere to be. He'd swing by her B&B later to check in on her. His pang of hunger demanded his immediate attention. He still hadn't made that trip to Clarenville for groceries, so all he had was that same loaf of bread, and as he reached for it, he feared it would be spotted green with dots of mould.

Her story had taken as long to tell as his.

"My shrink always told me that's just the way it is. We will spend our adult lives as we spent our childhood. And I'd say, 'So what then? I'll spend my adult life getting fucked? Feeling useless, used, and not in control?' 'Well, yes,' he said, 'unless you get a lot more receptive to this therapy ...'"

When she poured a glass of wine, she poured her glass as full as Owen did, and drank it just as fast.

"As if that's my problem. My being skeptical of my uptight shrink's tactics. A man who seems like he's barely lived a life but thinks he can understand everyone else's. He acts like I'm a puzzle put together all wrong, and if I'd just let him, he could undo me and put me back together all right. It's bullshit! Putting me back together would require cutting out half my memories, and he can't do that. So I skipped my session this week, and came out here to Port Blandford with a new plan for myself."

She never did share that *plan* with him. They had agreed not to interrupt each other with contrived condolences, or fruitless words of wisdom.

"The thing is, for me to feel better, I would need to go back in time to undo things, not just talk about things. It kind of makes psychotherapy a sham, at least in my case. I'm sure there are some people out there who doctors mentally rewire with cognitive therapy, but I'm not one of them. Not statistically."

There was a long pause, a hesitation. She looked at him to gauge his level of interest before moving on.

"I may seem fine to you, Owen, but you only think you know me, and I can guarantee you I will wake up tonight crying and screaming and kicking my legs, as if my father was invisible and in this living room with me. That invisibility makes him, and my past, inescapable. Helplessly inescapable. The constant presence of the past in my life makes life a constant struggle."

Their stories were different, but it was like he was talking to himself.

"I survived it all though. I escaped my childhood, at least physically, and I saw having my own child as a way to start again. A clean slate, all mine to fill out. I figured being a mother granted me a new identity, a new life, a new role, and the responsibilities would drone out the depression, the memories, the night terrors. It worked, to some degree, but ironically, I felt even more robbed of my own childhood every time I cradled Andrew, lovingly in my arms, because I knew I would give him everything. I could and would do anything to keep him safe, and as a kid I never had that. I had a mother, bedridden from gross obesity, and a vicious mule of a father. *Don't scream, don't wake your mother or you won't get your supper.* Not that my mother would've cared if she knew. She was too embittered by her condition. Her rage-filled eyes, God! She just stared at people, no words, and watched TV twenty-four seven, but not really even paying attention. Just gazing at the TV like a complete idiot. A completely apathetic idiot. At some point, I couldn't even bring myself to look at her anymore. She looked at people as if it were all their fault. Like I deserved that cloak of unhappiness she saw me in, because she was in it too."

By now they were uncorking their second bottle of wine, and the fire was dimming. The intensity of the stories they were sharing made it okay for them to sit on opposite ends of the same couch, toes touching, because a little physical contact helped them unload those weighty memories.

"The contrast between how I raised my son, and how *I* was raised, made me realize how I was denied the purpose of childhood: to feel like the world is infinite and assembled just for your happiness. For at least a few short years, children should be allowed to think that they can take what they want from the world. As a kid, I was only ever trying to escape my life, trying so hard to ignore the perfect lives of all the other kids that it wore me out. I entered adulthood too exhausted to handle it."

*Entering adulthood too exhausted too handle it.* She was exactly what he was hoping she was when he saw her sitting all alone on that barstool. And so uncannily similar to Hannah that he felt he knew her. Knew things he couldn't possibly know, like she probably brushed her teeth too hard and wore slippers around her house. Expensive, functional ones.

"When Andrew was born, I was reborn with him. When they passed him to me in the hospital, he looked at me with an instant, unconditional love and need for me. I knew that I was going to be the door through which he walked into the world, and I promised us both that I was going to lead him into the best world possible. No matter what. Because Andrew was going to be how I found meaning in my life. He gave me exactly what the world had taken away from me. Love is amazing like that, maternal love anyway. Love creates something that never existed before, a new world to live in. It makes the past a little less present."

The smile left her face. Her tone changed. She curled up into a tighter ball.

"Seven months ago, when Andrew was three weeks into the fourth year of his life, I was dying a scarf for a co-worker. I work in retail, but earn most of my money on the side making textile art, scarves and bags, whatever. I was just putting on a surgeon's mask and opening a bottle of dye when the phone rang. I thought of letting it ring, but I never, and now that single decision, that one irrelevant phone call, cost me my life. Tragedies are so much harder to accept when we can pinpoint the exact moment where it all could have been avoided. Normally, I'd have just let it ring, but I was expecting a call from the girl I was making the scarf for. It wasn't her on the phone though, it was another co-worker, Jocelyn. I hate Jocelyn, and I always have. She's a desperate, lonely annoyance, and she calls me to talk because she has no one else in her life. It's always boy trouble. She wonders why she can't keep a man, why they all only use her for one-night stands, and then tells me all about her wild sexual escapades, as if I cared about her disgusting, elaborate details. I had music on, Brian Borcherdt, so I didn't hear the first few rings, and had to make a mad dash to the phone. In doing so, I'd left the baby gate opened, and Andrew ... he ... wandered into my studio, so silently, as I talked on the phone. I'd left the bottle of dye on the floor, within his reach. It was MX 808 Crimson Red. I can see that label in my head: the tacky red-and-yellow butterfly cartoon and the comic sans font. I see it every day. I cry tears that feel more like fire than water. The dye was in a small bottle, about the size of pill bottle, and full of dried, concentrated, toxic dye crystals. He ingested the whole bottle.

When I found him, his saliva was running red, like blood, all over his shirt. I knew exactly what went wrong. Indirectly, I'd killed my son. They pumped his little stomach. They stuck tubes down his nose and throat as I watched, but it was too late, his body had absorbed it. I read afterwards that what I should've done before rushing him to the hospital was make him throw it all up. It could have saved his life. Apparently, most poisons get thrown up before they are absorbed into the body. Most, but not this one. Not the one I was using that day, the one and only time I left that gate to my toxic studio open. Now, every day, it's just too much without him. It's just hour after hour of guilt and loneliness. I hear noises at night, and know it *isn't* just Andrew stirring about. And losing a child, so young and so unexpectedly, is losing everything but your heartbeat and instinct to breathe."

Owen nodded, wanting to say something, but stuck with their pact of silence. He reached an arm out, but drew it back. Where would he lay a hand on a perfect stranger? What would his touch really change?

"Andrew lifted me up and out of my dreary life, and when he died I was slammed back into it, and … just cannot readjust. I don't even want to. Every day I drive myself crazy wondering: What if I never made bags and scarves? What if I never left that gate opened? What if Jocelyn hadn't called? What if I never worked where I work, and had never met Jocelyn, or the girl I was making the scarf for? What if I never used chemical dyes in my studio? Why did he swallow all those crystals? How much did it hurt, did it burn like fire in his belly? Where is he now? Is he thinking of me? Can I really live without him? Is there even a one percent chance that heaven is real and we'll meet again, so that I can say I'm sorry and see his beautiful face one more time, his cute buck teeth and freckly face? If I tried to make him throw it all up before I rushed off to the hospital, would his body still have absorbed the dye and made his blood toxic? Jesus, Owen, he was so beautiful, so innocent. And I killed him! I ... killed him."

It was the most guttural, heart-stomping crying he'd ever witnessed.

"If only some of this left me every time I cry! If only these tears shed something, cleansed me. Instead, they just remind me, make a mess of me, and I'm afraid, and I don't know why. I'm afraid I can't go on without him, and afraid I'll forget all the little things if I do. He wore glasses, Owen, and hated them. He was always pushing and pulling at them. How long until I forget all the little things?"

∽

Owen hopped into his new truck to head over to Clarenville. He could've gone another few days without some substantial groceries, but he really needed a bottle of Drano for the kitchen sink.

As he drove past the B&B Emily had pointed to and claimed she was sleeping in, he saw a huge black sign placed in front of it. Its oversized yellow words declared *CLOSED UNTIL JUNE*. All in capital letters, and it was January twenty-eighth. There was no way Emily was staying there, unless she knew the owners, or they had made an exception for her. Maybe they needed some extra cash, and Emily seemed the type who could be pretty convincing.

Or maybe she lied. He never wondered why, because he knew people like her – and him – had their reasons for lying. Maybe she made up the story about not being allowed back in after midnight so that Owen would invite her back to his place, so that she wouldn't have to be alone. Maybe she just valued her privacy and didn't want him knowing where to find her. Invisibility was half the reason they'd both come to Port Blandford.

# WITH ALL THE JEALOUSY
## OF A FLIGHTLESS BIRD

AS OWEN WAS PULLING BACK into Port Blandford, he saw Clyde running frantically towards his truck, bootlaces untied, flailing his arms. He pulled over, ready for some bad news.

Catching his breath. "Just wanted to warn you, there's some weather coming. Twenty to thirty centimeters of snow, and some pretty high winds, then she's gonna turn into freezing rain." He peered into Owen's truck. "Looks like you got some groceries, you're good there. Got yourself a flashlight? I got an extra one if you needs 'er."

Laughing. "Okay, thanks for the heads-up, Clyde. I got some food and candles. I'll survive it all, I'm sure."

Clyde, nodding and smiling, possibly drunk. "It's not like in the city here, kid. If the power goes, she's liable to be gone for a while. And it could be a while before the roads get cleared off."

He peered into Owen's grocery bags and screwed up his face.

"So, I had a good time the other night. Maybe you'll want another pool lesson next week?"

"I'll schedule it in."

"Okay, well, I won't keep ya." He patted the truck as if it were an old pet. "You look good in that truck, boss."

Owen beeped the horn as he pulled way. He liked Clyde, but he was fascinated by Emily, and wanted to see her again. To be around her, and feel that radiant comfort she exuded so effortlessly. She made him feel something he couldn't feel without her. Part of him suspected that Emily wouldn't come around to visit if Clyde was around. She was shy like that, and would only want to be around Owen, someone who could understand her. So he was avoiding Clyde in hopes she'd come back that day, and he felt bad for avoiding the poor old man.

&#x223D;

By 11 p.m. there was a full-on Newfoundland blizzard outside. Blowing snow hung like white blankets outside all of his windows: the town disappeared. Not even the lights of a neighbour's house were visible. In the darkness of his living room, the sounds of the storm were amplified rather than muffled. A vicious wind repeatedly threw itself at the house, trying to break in. Wet snow beat off the windows, maliciously, as if it were trying to smash the glass and get inside.

He sat to write a note, a letter to Callie and Lucia. He would give it to his Aunt Lillian for safekeeping. His idea was that she could give it to them when they started university, or graduated high school, or turned eighteen, or at some life-defining moment that indicated a stumbling into adulthood. They would be ready to understand what had happened between him and their mother then. The story needed to be told, and their mother needed to be absolved, and he would work on that note until they couldn't blame her for it. But he kept losing focus. There was a splash of red wine on the bottom left-hand corner of the page.

As he lapped up the wine with a paper towel he took out of a trash can under his desk, he heard a hurried, urgent knock on the back door. *Clyde?*

It was Emily. He felt his cheeks rise, felt the dumb smile there on his face.

"So, the storm made me feel like curling up next to a fireplace with some tea and chatting, but the thing is, the place I'm staying in doesn't have a fireplace, and I have no one to chat with. Do you mind if I invite myself in?"

She smiled, eased her way into his porch, and twirled her scarf off her neck. It was a red scarf, blood red. She took off her black peacoat and stuffed the scarf down into it.

"Where *are* you staying, Emily? I drove past that B&B you pointed to the other night, and the sign said the place is closed until June."

"Does it really matter where I'm staying, Sherlock?" The way she said it made her declaration seem true. It was sharp enough that it stated: *Back off. Are you stalking me? Drop it.*

"Fair enough. I thought you'd gone back to Corner Brook is all."

"Gone back? I can't go back now. I'm sick of everyone tiptoeing around me. I'm sick of getting away with being late for work, or not coming in at all. I get the same goddamn looks from everyone. They smile at me, a smile of condolence, but they can't even look at me, so they stare down at their feet as they pass by me. No words are shared, ever, and I feel deaf and mute. It's just as well I was. I'm sick of being poor old Emily. I was invisible before Andrew died. I liked being faceless in a crowd, but now I'm *that poor woman with the dead kid*, or at least I used to be, now I'm *that women with the dead kid who is drinking too much. The poor soul.* Their careful words, nervous glances, and obligate condolences make me feel like a ghost. Besides, there are too many happy mothers running around that town, and I cannot help but look at them with all the jealousy of a flightless bird. I see a mother scold a child too harshly, or get impatient at their never-ending curiosity, and shake my head at their not realizing what they have, how lucky they are, what they are taking for granted."

Realizing she'd trailed off, she reiterated her point, "There's nothing left for me back in Corner Brook. I'm not going back to that. Why would I?"

"Well, okay, I was just—"

"Nobody knew me before Andrew died. Now I have celebrity status. It's odd how a tragedy makes the invisible more apparent, don't you think? You could argue that compassion unites us, or you could argue that tragedy turns us on. Look at the headlines on all those magazines next time you're in a line-up at a grocery store. They're all about who is getting divorced, who is in rehab, or slitting their weak wrists, you know? It's never good news."

She shook the snow out of her hair, then dried her hair in the sleeve of her black cardigan. Owen lit the fireplace and put Eric Bachmann's *To The Races* in the CD player. She explored the living room, took in the family photos he was living amongst.

"You know, you kind of look like your father, or, at least in ten more years you will. Same eyes, like you trust nothing!" She laughed a little, like, *I'm kidding but I'm serious.*

"It's sad the way you lost him, Owen, but at least you can still love him. I don't even have that, if it makes you feel any better."

Owen said nothing: she was more or less talking to herself, perhaps nervously rambling, since they didn't really know each other well enough for her to show up like this, unannounced at that. She walked over to the bookshelf and ran her fingers along the spines of each book, each a porthole into a different world. Her finger lingered on some titles longer than others as she read them.

She sat and joined him on the couch as he opened a bottle of wine. "What's it like, Owen, living amongst all these photos and your father's affairs? I ask because I know I found it unbearable living in my apartment after Andrew died. I could've boarded up his room, but there were reminders of him all over the place, like the pencil marks on the porch door where we measured his height every birthday, or like the stain on the living room carpet where he laid a red popsicle he didn't want while he watched *Scooby-Doo*, or like the pictures of him I couldn't take down, because they made me feel less alone. I could've gutted out his room, or moved, for that matter, but I knew I would always still picture that room in my head, you know? Me laying him in his crib and flicking on the baby monitor, or us baking cookies together and him dusted white with all the flour. He loved helping me with things, it made him feel more grown up. I wonder why that is? Why do kids reach three or four and have a sudden desire to be grown-ups? It's ironic that parents and children want to swap lives, don't you think?"

Owen nodded.

"So, I can imagine it's both nice but heart-wrenching to live amongst all this stuff, Owen? The photos of your mother, Alex's time capsule, all of your dad's belongings–"

The power flickered, almost violently, and each time, the room went blue as the lights dimmed, then orange as they flared back on. The way the lights flickered made it clear that the power was just about to go out, not that it might, as if the power lines were clairvoyant or the weather was kind enough to warn people things were about to go black.

And then they did. The fire flickered on, but the room felt colder and less inviting under that darkness. The sudden silence was jarring, unwelcomed. The music had created a warm atmosphere; their words sank into it and their emotions revolved around it. Both Owen and Emily looked at the silent, powerless stereo. There was only a faint crackle from the fire now, each other's faces barely visible, and oranged by the fire.

"We could go out in my truck and chat, maybe take a few CDs out with us and flick the dome light on. I've got some Mark Kozelek. I think you'll like him, and The Great Lake Swimmers."

She smiled, no words of confirmation, and bundled herself up in her scarf. She jammed on her boots, mittens, and jacket.

Clapping her mitted hands. "C'mon then."

If he hadn't remembered where the truck was parked, he might not have found it. It was like pushing his way through endless white curtains, and if Emily hadn't been walking right in his footsteps, she might've lost him. The wind burned. Stung. Snow pelted at his eyes so he kept them mostly shut.

He waited for her to reach out a hand, onto his shoulder maybe, so that he could guide her. He would've liked that.

He started the truck, to heat it up a little, and when the stereo cut in, it filled the truck with the melancholy, un-mistakable sound of Nick Drake. When Owen went to eject the CD, he felt the slap of Emily's hand off his.

"Don't! I *love* this man, and I haven't heard him in so long now. It's a shame he killed himself before he was even thirty. Can you imagine how big he could've gotten?"

Pulling a glove back on. "I didn't know he killed himself."

"Pills. Like all the great artists. It's always either a bottle of antidepressants that wouldn't work for them or a bottle of narcotics they were hooked on. But, I guess it's not always pills though. Hemingway and Cobain went the shotgun route. There's no way to go wrong there."

"Yeah, really hey? Personally, I could never quite wrap my head around Elliot Smith's suicide. He took a knife and drove it through his own heart. He couldn't have even questioned it, you know? Or Sylvia Plath, she stuck her head in an oven! Or that poet, John Berryman, who was reportedly so calm during his suicide that he waved to a passerby as he was falling through the air after jumping off a bridge!"

"I'm jealous of people with the courage to kill themselves. Me, I'll just live a long miserable life writing sullen, repetitive journal entries about Andrew. Besides, if I did get the courage to kill myself, people would only thrive off of it, and reduce me to someone too weak, definitely weaker than them, to carry on. As if they knew me, what made me this way. I'd be reduced to someone too weak, and nothing more. So I won't give them the pleasure."

Owen was jolted by the casual way she talked of suicide.

"But I am afraid that if I linger on feeling this way, I will forget about that beautiful life I used to have, you know?"

⌒

The conversation lightened as the storm raged on. They sat there so long the seats had moulded around their tiring bodies and started to feel like beds. They'd reclined them all the way back, and as Emily drew fish and flowers in the condensation on her window, Owen fell in love with her hands: the soft lines in each knuckle, the hue of pink, the fingers so adorably tiny.

The gaps between their conversations got longer, and the silence was soothing. The sound of the wind was hypnotizing, like waves on a beach. The snow eventually stopped, and just before he fell asleep, Owen looked straight out of his windshield and saw Clyde's house, the chimney still going at 4 a.m. Maybe the old man had fallen asleep, drunk, or maybe he was still awake and drinking, lonely, wishing Owen was there and listening to him relive his life through another slew of memorable stories.

When he awoke, Emily was gone. And she must have been

gone a while, because there weren't any footprints in the snow. Cold, tired, and hung over, he fell asleep again, throwing his feet up onto the passenger seat where Emily had been just a few hours ago, convincing him of things he needed convincing of. There was an empty bottle of wine in each cup holder, no glasses, and the dashboard was covered in CDs, empty bags of bite-sized pitas, and a tub of hummus.

At ten in the morning, Clyde knocked his large, leathery hand on the driver side window. Owen jumped out of his seat, and the sudden burst of sunlight on his retinas was agonizing. He raised a forearm like a shield against the sun.

"Jesus, Clyde! What the hell?"

"What the hell, *Clyde?* Sure, you're the one sleeping in a goddamn truck. So you tell me, what the hell, kid?"

Owen rolled down the window so they could talk more reasonably, instead of shouting at each other through the glass. "I dunno, it got cold inside and I came out here to turn on the heat, and I wanted to hear some music. It was oppressively silent in the house, and boring, so we came out here."

"We? Who's we, boss? I've been watching ya since dawn, don't be so foolish."

"Me and Emily."

"Who … is Emily?"

"The girl from the bar the other night. After Patsy drove you home, we kind of met outside. We've been talking a little ever since."

Clyde raised an eyebrow and laughed. "Talking, hey? That's whatcha calls it now, is it? *Talking?*" He walked around the truck and hopped into the passenger seat. "So where is Juliet now, son?"

"Good question." He didn't know, but he did know that she wasn't going to come back if Clyde was around. He felt bad for wishing the sweet old man away.

His tongue was a pile of sand, and his stomach was rolling with hunger. Where he wished Emily was, was up to the take-out buying them some greasy breakfast.

"She must be staying down at the golf lodge. If there was an Emily running around this town out of the tourist season, trust me, we'd all know about her. Was she that redhead you were eyeballing all night?"

"Me? *You* were the one stumbling over her all night. It was embarrassing, man! And no, Emily is a brunette, short messy hair, cute enough to marry." He laughed as he recalled Clyde, the sixty-seven-year-old man, flirting with that young redhead all night like some college kid. As miserable as he felt that morning. He could force a smile in Clyde's presence.

"Well, whatever." Clyde slapped his knee. "Get up and get inside, b'ye. You're making a spectacle of yourself sleeping in your truck like this, never mind that the day's half over."

Something about the comment tasted sour to Owen. He resented it. He caught himself about to lash out at Clyde. *Like I give a fuck what this town thinks of me, old man, and it's only 10 a.m. yet,* but he caught himself, calmed down, a little surprised by the vicious rush that coursed through him. By now, Clyde had gotten out of the truck and was opening Owen's door and extending his hand to him. His limp evoked this courtesy from people, including strangers, even though it was a limp symbolic of guilt and callousness. He was sick of walking on that leg. Both the pain, and what that pain represented, had grown too unbearable, too unforgiving.

He grabbed the two empties and the corkscrew. The rest he would clean up later. He scratched the stubble on his chin with the handle of the corkscrew, and as he looked down at the corkscrew, he remembered giving that very corkscrew to his father for a birthday present over two decades ago, when he was so young that he never actually bought it himself, his mother bought it for him to give to his father. He stared at the corkscrew now, as the memory of that birthday replayed itself, thinking of how his father never knew him as an adult, as an alcoholic. He never really knew him at all. He left when Owen was just a child who could've become anything.

The loud squeal of a gull snapped him back into consciousness. He stared out at the bright blue ocean, at the gulls that hovered above it. He watched a bird, an indistinct bird he'd never seen before, dive deep into the water and disappear. He nodded his head.

～

He approached his front door, noticed it was already open, and saw Emily's black peacoat coiled around her boots like a snake. He saw her red scarf hanging off the porch doorknob. He laid the empties down and yelled out to her. Something felt wrong, urgent, the house felt filled with silent screams. Adrenaline, for no reason, was tugging at his muscles, contracting them. His heart was kicking off his ribcage.

"Emily?" He checked every room.

He found her body on his bathroom floor, contorted and folded over itself like a dropped doll. Her forehead pressed into the base of the toilet looked raunchy and wrong. He grabbed her body and rolled her over. She felt lighter now. Her body unfolded as Owen laid her on her back – her limp arms slapping off the floor as they fell against it – and she looked like she was sleeping. More peaceful than vulgar now. She looked ethereal, and beautiful – her face up close like that, their bodies touching. He felt hollow, and cold. He was shaking now as he stared at her. Of all the things he could feel, he felt riddled with fear.

As he looked down on her body there, it wasn't sad. She looked pristine. Pristine, not beautiful. Restored, not dead. Pure.

He saw not defeat or surrender, but courage and release. Not depression, but liberation. He saw her smiling, almost coaxing him to be as brave. She was dead, with a smile on her face, as if she died thinking of Andrew and nothing more. She looked exhausted, but liberated now. Released from any guilt, or any sense of failure. Free, she looked as if death had freed her from everything.

He took a deep breath, checked for a pulse, and felt nothing but cold on her neck. He needed to call the police, or an ambulance. He needed to dial 9-1-1, but he couldn't drag himself away from her body. Couldn't let go of her. Of her soft skin and flacid little hands.

He stumbled into the kitchen, his mouth too dry to speak into the phone, and grabbed a near-empty glass of water that was resting on the countertop. Emily must have left it there when she came back in the night before, before she did *that* to herself. He swallowed the water in one desperate gulp: and it burned like all the fire in hell. He felt an acidic searing in his mouth, a scouring in his throat. He felt claws tearing at his esophagus, and ripping up his stomach. His lungs burned now too, and wouldn't fill with air, so he grabbed at his shirt and beat on his chest. The inside of his mouth was covered in a chalky substance, and he lifted the glass into the light by the window. He saw a white powder, and on the counter he saw a slew of empty bottles of household cleaners, over-the-counter medications, and an empty can of Drano. He dialed 9-1-1 and tried, screaming whispers, to give his address.

He didn't want to live and he didn't want to die, he just wanted the pain to stop. By the time the ambulance came, Owen had toppled over and was face-down on the living room floor. The fall into the coffee table broke his nose and chipped two teeth. He wasn't entirely unconscious as he lay on the floor, and behind his closed eyelids was not darkness, but light. A cloudy whiteness. His head felt enormous, and his body was sinking into the floor beneath him.

In that whiteness, he saw him, Alex, and their father at the firepit out back. His father was hooking marshmallows onto sticks for them. They were laughing. Alex would always char his marshmallows, get his mother to tear away the blackness, and then eat the gooey middle. Owen took the time to roast his slowly, over the coals, not the fire itself. The image was slowly fading. Their father was impersonating their mother, and all three of them laughed, excessively. Then there was nothing but whiteness. Whiteness and the sound of laughter.

And then the sound of sirens getting closer and louder. And then no sirens. He heard them burst through his front door, their urgent footsteps and shouting, and the sound of the stretcher's wheels along the hardwood floor was a deafening rattle. They found him retching on the living room floor. Revolting dry heaves.

"Sir, have you ingested something? Are you choking?" A man twice his size knelt down and plunged two fingers into Owen's mouth and wrestled against his tongue to check his airway. It hurt and he gagged. It felt like a stick in his mouth. The man looked at the other paramedic and shook his head.

"Can you speak? Nod if you can hear me."

Owen threw his head up and down, but he could only mumble incoherently, it hurt too much to talk. He was pointing frantically to the next room and the smaller paramedic stormed off to the kitchen.

"Jesus Christ, Frank ... get out here and look at this! Drano ... and ... there's a whole caustic cocktail out here!"

# I AM MY FATHER'S SON

OWEN WOKE UP IN A bed and felt like he was back in rehab. It was a small green room with cement walls, and his bed was the only one there. One of the four walls was all windows, with two thick, dust-covered red curtains blocking out the sun. He woke up as Clyde was parting them to let the sun in. One strip of sunlight dove through the room and threw itself across Owen's bed, illuminating his left knee and his left knee only. He turned his head and saw Lillian clutching his hand.

As he turned around and their eyes met, Clyde shook his head, his mouth an upside-down half moon, like he had horrible news for Owen that he didn't want to share. Lillian saw her nephew awake, kissed his forehead, and hurried off to find a doctor, her chair still sliding across the floor. A sense of safety followed her out of the room.

Clyde, benevolently, as if he was looking at his own son. "Are you feeling all right now, Owen? Can I get you something?" He came closer and sat in the chair Lillian had abandoned.

It hurt to talk. It didn't seem worth the effort to form a whole sentence. "Thirsty, water?" The pain surprised him more than waking up in a hospital.

"I dunno, my son, you've got your throat and stomach all torn up. We'll have to wait and see what the doctor has to say about food and water." Clyde motioned to the IV bag draining into Owen's arm. "He shouldn't be long now. Lillian is off to get him."

Owen couldn't argue. Instead he looked at Clyde, perplexed and a little pissed off. *What's that supposed to mean? You've got your throat and stomach all torn up? Emily poured this goddamn Drano-Comet-Aspirin cocktail I drank. It was an accident.* He calmed himself. "Me? I didn't–"

"Shh …" Clyde put his index finger to his lips. "Your aunt will kill me if she sees me letting you talk with your throat gone like that."

They both fell silent when they heard Lillian's unmistakable voice whispering loudly outside the door. The second voice was male, quivering, and familiar. *Alex?* He shot an inquisitive look in Clyde's direction, and Clyde put his head down and walked out of the room as a doctor walked in.

The doctor poked and prodded Owen, adjusted some of the machinery, the tubing attached to him, explaining how the morphine drip worked, and asked him everything except how he was feeling. He had an obvious, unmistakable contempt for Owen, like he felt attending to an attempted suicide case was a waste of time better spent saving a life, not postponing a death.

Owen looked to his left and noticed the dialysis machine. His eyes followed the blood-filled tubing leading deep into his arm. He almost threw up when he saw it: he audibly heaved. The doctor explained everything they had done to keep him alive and how long they'd have to keep him under observation, to keep an eye on his stomach and kidneys and liver. But Owen wasn't really paying attention to the doctor, he was too disturbed by the sight of the tubing running into his arm. When the doctor left him alone, Clyde and Lillian swooped back into the room as if they were his parents.

Lillian sat in the chair next to him, and Clyde sat in the windowsill, with his head down. Owen knew Alex was out in that hallway. He could feel him there, the same way he could feel hot or cold with his eyes closed. He heard that clicking sound his brother made his whole life, by nervously plunging his tongue down into the floor of his mouth, over and over. He wasn't going to mention that he knew Alex was out there, and he wasn't expecting Alex to step into the room. It was enough that he flew back home with Lillian.

Lillian and Clyde were clearly trying to summon the courage to share some bad news with him. Lillian would take a deep breath – her chest puffed up – and purse her lips to speak, but then she'd just exhale, slowly. Like she was deflating, like she was rethinking her wording. Like the words on her tongue were bullets and she refused to shoot him point blank. He assumed the bad news was about Emily, that she'd died. What they didn't know was that he was already expecting this news. He'd held her cold lifeless body, and he'd checked her pulseless neck with his own two hands before he called the ambulance.

He tried his voice again, limiting his sentences to as few words as possible, every word like vomiting up a razor blade, "Emily okay?"

Clyde looked at Lillian and their heads slung down in unison, their eyes closing for seconds before re-opening.

"Lilly ... is Emily okay?"

Lillian looked up at him, biting her lip, one eye not able to hold a tear back and it fell straight down onto her lap. She looked back down at her lap, at the wet spot, ran a thumb over it, like she didn't want to be the one to finally break him beyond repair. Clyde jumped down off the windowsill and made his way over to Lillian. He laid a sympathetic hand on her slumped shoulders. Exhaled slowly.

"I can do this if you want, Lillian. Why don't you go buy us a round of soft drinks and bottled waters?"

She shook her head, and Owen watched Clyde walk out of the room and shut the door behind him. Turn and pull it to.

"Owen." She grabbed his hand and held it in a show of support. She was letting him know that she was there, and going nowhere without him. "There is no … Emily. You did this to yourself. You are sick, Owen, like your father. Do you understand what I'm saying?"

She was talking to him differently than she usually did. Long drawn-out words spoken a little too loudly, as if he was stupid. He shook his head.

"What do you *mean*, there is no Emily? How would you even know about her?" The intensity in his long, sharp sentences cut into his throat like a meathook. He sank back into the bed. He almost turned on her, blamed her for the pain.

"Owen, don't talk, not until your throat heals. Just think about what I am saying, let it sink in for a while. I'll be right back, sweetie. You are not alone, okay? We aren't going to leave you to go through this alone. Don't worry about that. You can come up home with me, or I will come back here to be with you."

Desperate for more of an explanation, he was terrified. "Lillian! I didn't do this. I drank whatever Emily drank. By accident." He felt frightened now, inexplicably frightened, like he was in a tank full of sharks. He wouldn't contemplate what she was implying. He felt exposed and unaccountably humiliated.

She sat back down. "If there is an Emily in your life, then where is she now, Owen? Why wasn't her body found with your body … sweetheart?" She cupped his hand in hers again, and he felt weak. He felt dizzy.

"Owen, on the morning you did this to yourself, Clyde caught you talking to yourself in your truck. He assumed you were just drinking, heavily, and having it out with yourself. But when he came down and talked to you, you claimed you were talking to someone, a girl named Emily, who no one in town had ever seen or heard of, or knew anything about. He stayed calm. He asked around, asked the staff at every B&B and the golf lodge about her. He tracked down your brother. He had no idea about you and Alex's falling out, so he called him out of concern, because he knew about your father's illness and suspected it in you long before you started talking about this Emily girl. He wanted to be sure he was right before he contacted us. He left you in the truck that morning, and he ran home to call us. By the time he got back to your house to check back in on you, the ambulance had taken you away and the neighbours filled him in on what you'd done to yourself. He was devastated. And what you need to know, Owen, irrefutably, is that only one body was loaded into that ambulance, and that body was yours. Only one person attempted suicide in that house that day, and that was you."

He refused to believe it.

They'd go back to his father's cabin, her and Lillian and Clyde. They'd find Emily there on the bathroom floor. Why would the paramedics, or anyone else, think to have looked in there, in the bathroom, where he held her cold, solid body in his arms, felt the weight of it. Saw the hair bend where it hit the floor. Saw his tears soak into her shirt and dissolve into the shapes of stars.

His heart was thudding off his ribs and his mouth felt filled with salt. Still, he shook his head. Maybe Emily got up and out of there before the ambulance came, or maybe her body was still there, undiscovered. It was too much, all at once. The room got smaller, darker: it spun a little. He felt every breath he was taking in, felt it against his teeth and his raw throat, felt it slide along his gums, cooling his saliva, and he was breathing faster, and faster. His heart was beating so unsure of itself, questioning its function.

He could deny it all he wanted, like he'd watched his father do, but it wouldn't change anything. And that's when he noticed the bottle of pills on a table next to Lillian's purse, and a pamphlet titled "Caring for a Schizophrenic Loved One." He remembered the day he opened the medicine cabinet in his parents' bathroom and saw the clear orange bottle of CPZ next to a green can of shaving cream and a pack of disposable razors. It caught him off guard, like he'd opened the cabinet and a bird was in there. And then he just stared at it: a bottle full of little yellow discs that might or might not save his father.

The doctors had already diagnosed him. Probably medicated him. There was likely CPZ in that IV bag right now, if that was possible. Maybe they were right, or maybe Emily was still lying on the floor of his bathroom, or maybe she was up and wandering aimlessly around town looking for him. And this was all a horrible mistake, an accident.

"And if you didn't do this, Owen, if this was an accident, how do you explain the note? That scatterbrained apology to your nieces we found on your father's desk in the office?"

He pictured Emily in his mind now, and realized she had looked exactly the same *every* time he saw her. She was always impossibly exact in her appearance. Her clothes were always the same; they were even wrinkled in the same places, and folding around her in the same way. Her hair was always a mess in the same way, covering half of each ear like that. He thought about all those things she knew about him before he'd told her about them, like the names of everyone in his family, or where to find that bottle of Drano and all those pills. And he thought of Hannah now, and how similar her and Emily's stories had been. How they were *too* similar.

He sank back into what was essentially his deathbed, and stared at the white ceiling tiles, the infinite constellation of dots in them. He lay there in an unnerving silence. Too much existed in that silence. His thoughts were too loud and frightening. He would end up like his father, he knew it, despite the optimism Lillian had.

"This is a lot to take in, sweetie. I need you to relax, let it all register. They say you are lucid and coherent and intelligible and that's a good sign. It may be a high-functioning form of schizophrenia. So let's start with that for now."

Lillian caught him staring at the bottle of pills, the pills that couldn't save his father. "You can't take these now, but you'll have to ... later." She smiled feebly. "I'll hold onto them for you." She tucked them into her purse.

He felt like a slave to something, and rabid with fear. He felt cheated by life: always waiting for something to happen, and now this. So suddenly.

According to Lillian's logic, nothing he'd known was definite now. Was Clyde even real? Was he actually in the corridor? Some of his life had to be real, for him to exist and be physically present in the room, he knew that much. He knew some things where unquestionable, like the definite consistency of his mother's chicken and rice casserole, the sweet-salty smell of it. The way he felt when he watched her body topple over and convulse that day, in slow motion, and the way his breathing skipped that night in the hospital when he fell back against that wall and watched her body recoil against the defibrillator after each shock. The fingers threatening to snap out of their joints. Her dead, but her body still there.

He knew his betrayal of Alex was real, because he could so easily recollect the way his head cracked off Hannah's gravestone that day, the sharp burn of the kinked neck, the pinch of it, and the grip of stone as it tore flesh from his face.

He thought of the signs of schizophrenia in his father in the beginning. How had he not seen them in himself? The desire for seclusion, for one, to be so utterly alone. Away from it all. *Social withdrawal*, the doctors would call it. He knew the psychological toll of losing his father was real though, the crushing hope his father would conquer it, fight it off like a flu. He knew that was real by the hundred different ways it tortured him as the schizophrenia tore his father further and further away from him, further and further out of reach. He knew his father was real because of the bits of unprompted advice he would dole out after too much wine. The flashes of conversation that came back to him at random throughout his life. Mere sentences he couldn't place, couldn't attribute to a when and where.

*Know one thing,* his father had promised him. *And the rest of it doesn't matter.*

But what about when that one thing is gone, absent, unavailable, forcefully ripped away from you, died right in front of you, maybe because of you? The rest of it mattered then, the crushing sadness that he'd never see her again. Never catch Hannah at an angle he hadn't seen her in before, never kiss an inch of her he hadn't kissed before, never see light accentuate some minute feature of her: the curve of her forehead, unique to her, the diamond-shaped knuckles separating finger bones. He'd never loved a woman so deeply before, to see the skeleteon that carried her. Never saw the kink of a woman's hair in a way that made the world make sense.

He thought of that piece of paper he'd found in the typewriter, back at his father's cabin: *Regret, what you've wanted and denied yourself, is the only way to put your life into perspective. The only way to know what has mattered.*

His one comfort, lying in that hospital bed, ready to lose himself, was an utter lack of regret.

# ACKNOWLEDGEMENTS

I am forever thankful to Rebecca Rose and Breakwater Books for so fully supporting an emerging writer. I thank Annamarie Beckel for her diligent and open approach to editing, and for her patience in allowing painstaking structural changes at the last minute. I thank Rhonda Molloy for making this book look the way it reads; I was worried no one would understand the "mood" I wanted, then was shocked at how easily she did. I thank Anna Kate MacDonald for her pep, patience, and insights regarding this novel, which all bettered it, and I thank Jackie Pope for her enthusiasm to sell this novel, and for sharing her mother's top-notch baked goods.

I thank Peggy Tremblett for her contagious faith that I would be a published novelist by thirty if I kept at it, and for being the first set of eyes on anything I write (every draft of it).

I thank the entirety of my elaborate family for obvious reasons, but my mother, in particular, for supporting such a quixotic passion long before I got any recognition, and my father for passing along the character required to churn out a novel and my step-parents for their support. My brother, Scott, for supporting my obsessive habit in the ways he does, and my sister-in-law, Kim, who has been so great about my long haul to publication. Ashley MacDonald for being so supportive when it matters the most, Marlo and Geoff for your sustained interest in and conversations about my writing career, Joel Upshall for being my in-family affirmation that people should only be doing what they want to be doing (as I type this you are opening for Kiss), Beverly has been particularly sweet, and my grandparents for actively keeping informed about my writing (even if I hope they never read this blunt novel).

I also thank The Writers' Alliance of NL for the services they provide local writers, particularly since a rough draft of this novel won entry into their Emerging Writers Mentorship Program. I thank my mentor, Mark Callanan, because I still cringe when I think of that first draft. Instead of running from the book, he stuck around, honed in on a few things, and made me a better writer so that I could go back to the manuscript and make a book out of it. I suppose now is as good a time as any to apologize for all those long, panicked, incoherent emails?

Obviously, thanks go to Kathleen Winter, M.T. Dohaney, and Kenneth J. Harvey for taking the time to read and endorse this novel. Kathleen's writing is a crash course in modern creative writing, M.T. Dohaney's *The Corrigan Women* made me fondly jealous I didn't write it myself, and the *Globe and Mail* said it best about Ken Harvey: "Shout Harvey's name from the rooftops ... There is no other writer like him." I am grateful to Michael Crummey, because during his time as MUN's writer in residence he read the first few chapters of a rough draft and showed me the power of language without lazy modifiers. Nothing has improved this novel more than replacing 95% of its adverbs and adjectives with dug-deep-for descriptive and evocative sentences. Speaking of MUN, I still appreciate Iona Bulgin's support and interest in my writing, and I have certainly benefitted from Larry Mathews' unpretentious and deft pointers, as well as everyone I sat around that table with in Larry's creative writing course.

My sincerest gratitude to the following people for reading old manuscripts of mine before anyone should have been reading me, and still encouraging me: Mary Beth Collett, Samantha Smith, Megan Mullaly, Kaylen Hill, Clay Badcock, and Kim Bragg. And, for long-standing encouragements and showing up to my first reading: Mark Shallow, Carla Myrick, Devin Rose, Isobel O'Shea, and Christine Champdoizeau, because nothing satisfies an author more than seeing a reader's hands and eyes glued all over their work when it matters the most. I know I am forgetting people, but look how long this is getting. I will financially reimburse you for any snubbery.

CHAD PELLEY is an award-winning writer from St. John's, NL, and sits on the board of directors for the Writers' Alliance of Newfoundland & Labrador (WANL). He works in editing and sells photography. *Away from Everywhere* won entry into WANL's 2008 Emerging Writers Mentorship Program. His stories "Subtle Differences" and "How Far is Nowhere" are featured in *The Cuffer Prize Anthology*.

He enjoys writing fiction and music, most red wines, and everything about books. Visit his website at http://chadpelley.wordpress.com.

# ...after thoughts

# AWAY FROM EVERYWHERE

## SPECIAL FEATURES

## AWAY FROM EVERYWHERE
## ORIGINS AND UNEXPECTED OUTCOME

∽

### AWAY FROM EVERYWHERE CAME OUT ALL WRONG...

Not all wrong, just not as planned. Originally titled *The World Before Now*, my goal was to have a jaded man rediscover himself in small-town Newfoundland, away from the complexities of his busy life. It was to be a serious novel, but with a seriously comedic edge as well; I had some ridiculous characters sketched and ready to go. Also, the "journal chapters" were never supposed to be Hannah's; the sister-in-law was originally not to be a major character. My idea was that, at first, it wouldn't be known to the reader who was writing them, until Owen meets the woman: a forlorn art teacher who just lost her child. She and Owen would meet and sort of bring each other back to life, but not in the generic Hollywood way – I was thinking a unique friendship with a comical one-way crush. I never had to worry about avoiding the cliché though, because by the end of the first chapter, what I had planned for this novel faded away as the characters of Owen and Alex started to come to life, and the "why" of Hannah's affair as well. I found myself letting go of all my plans, and every time I sat to write I was writing paragraph to paragraph, not knowing where I was going with the story. I wrote about twenty-five different drafts of this novel, each one a different story with different intentions.

### THE STORY STARTED TO WRITE ITSELF, REALLY...

The first chapter of *Away from Everywhere* has never changed. I knew it was the right first chapter for a novel because I was four chapters into another novel, titled *Your Crooked Smile*, but found myself more and more fixated on this opening chapter, and eventually abandoned *Your Crooked Smile* to write this novel.

Incidentally, somewhere between thinking about this first chapter and sitting to write it, I had a near-death hydroplaning experience myself. I remember thinking, *Great, now I can accurately describe the feeling of losing control of a car!*

I thought the exposed affair was a great way to get an already shaky character shunned and shipped out of his family's life to a small town in Newfoundland. Originally, Owen was to be an alienated and depressed English professor on sabbatical, going to spend the summer at his father's old cabin, to sort of come to terms with Hannah's death and a few other troubles in his life. That was supposed to be chapter two, but in the final draft, Owen doesn't head back to Newfoundland until the novel is nearly over, because I had to ask myself, Why is there a family cabin he can go use, and do I want to explore the brothers' childhoods, just a little? I did, and that *just a little* turned into "part two" of this novel, the longest part. I'd turn on some music and just string sentences together, and the next thing I knew I was writing about a mentally ill father and a dead mother, and alcoholism, and the brothers coming out of it all as two very different men. For a while, I found myself purposefully trying to have the brothers represent two different and costly approaches to modern life. I played that notion up originally, but then toned it way down. I think an element of that has remained in the novel.

WHERE THE SCHIZOPHRENIA CAME IN...

I needed a reason why there was an abandoned family cabin for Owen to run off to in part three of the novel. I thought dead parents would explain the abandoned cabin, but then I thought that wasn't original enough, so I had the family succumb to dealing with schizophrenia. I can't imagine the exhaustion and pain of losing someone this way, because, as with the Collins family, there's no real closure: a schizophrenic can get better and worse and better again. But then life's never the same. I think some of the most potent scenes in the book are the ones with Owen watching his family fall apart, and the toll it took on his mother. Owen and his father had a real bond too, so Owen lost a really valuable connection with his father: a man who saw and lived life the same way. Initially, this notion was the origin of the title, as in the two of them talking of getting away from that world they perceived as having no meaning, only to ironically disappear to wherever it is a schizophrenic goes. The title later took on a multitude of meanings.

I researched the disease, of course, but relied more heavily on ten specific case studies I read online, because I feel like individuals are better to study than sweeping, textbook generalizations about a mental disorder. I didn't want it sounding like I was cutting and pasting symptoms into a character, and I tried to avoid "teaching" readers about schizophrenia and bogging them down with terms they'd need a glossary for, because my intention was to show the *effect* of schizophrenia on the Collins family, not to prove I did my homework.

## THE ORIGINS OF HANNAH'S "JOURNAL CHAPTERS"...

Once the childhood was explored and I got to writing part three, the "return to Newfoundland" bit became a smaller portion of the book and I ditched the cast of eccentric characters I had planned, because the tone of the novel had gotten too grim for them. I also ditched the lonely art teacher who was to be Owen's salvation and the one writing the journal entries.

I decided the "journal chapters" would be a good way to tell the story of the affair through *Hannah's* eyes, so she could be kept alive in the book, and so she could also provide insight into who Owen and Alex are, and to bring up what I see as one of the solid motifs in this novel: the flipside of love. The complexities of it. The blows and lows a relationship can take and the conundrum of denying yourself what could be a truer love. I started making

Hannah a more and more complicated character to add more layers to this conceptual element of the book. In doing so, Hannah also became what I consider the saddest character in the novel, and from what I gather, her journal entries get the biggest reaction from readers: they love her or hate her, or both. They identify with parts of what she says, or they think she is naïve; they get uncomfortable with some of the truth in what she has to say, or think her opinions are unfounded. I guess a reader's reaction depends on that reader's life experiences and who they are? That's an ideal character, in my mind.

I think most people shy away from acknowledging the wavering nature of love and buy into the Hollywood portrayal of the happily ever after. I always joke that if the movie kept going, half those couples would end up divorced. Sounds bitter, yes, but I'm a romantic as well, and that's no better, we expect *too much* from a relationship. Relationships are naturally volatile things with highs and lows, and the people sharing them change over time, and sometimes outgrow each other. I mean, ultimately, relationships give life meaning, but inevitably, they get tested by time. So I wanted to write a book that cast a light on that. It didn't come out as I planned though, through Owen and Abbie. Instead it came out through the mind of a complicated married woman. I found myself, as a writer, having fun with this notion, and her character, and next thing I knew she was the voice of ten chapters and, later, almost dictating where the story was going, not only thematically, but plotwise as well, when Owen starts reacting to what he reads.

I'm sure as a male writer I'll take flak for embodying an unhappily married woman too. But I didn't. I embodied Hannah Collins, a very complicated woman. I had her character endure much, and I hope it didn't seem like me exploiting serious tragedies for gripping writing. The miscarriage, for instance, was only there because she and Alex never really dealt with it, and sadly, psychologically, a miscarriage can affect intimacy and interpersonal relations for a couple who go through one. I didn't want to scream stuff like that at readers though. I wanted it to be true to life. Hannah, in the end, wasn't sure what her and Alex's biggest problems were. Most couples on the rocks don't. She struggled to understand the "why" of the affair herself. In the end she chose Alex, or did she just settle? I don't know.

## THE TWO ABANDONED ALTERNATE ENDINGS ...

Originally, I toyed with the idea of having Alex become schizophrenic. I thought, How gripping would it be to have the girls calling Owen about their father muttering to himself and "acting scary," and Owen *knowing* but unable to help because he can't go near them, and everyone else telling him to back off, "Alex is just grieving," until one of the girls get hurt by his schizophrenia-induced negligence or delusions. Can you imagine the salt in the wound of Owen taking custody of the girls? A trustworthy source felt that would have schizophrenia overwhelming the story, and I decided some warped version of this could be material for another book. I tackled a lot in this novel, and needed to save something for future ones!

I moved on to this idea: Emily was initially "real," and she killed herself, as in the final draft, but Owen *accidentally* drank that glass of water while waiting for the paramedics. *Accidentally*, and then everyone assumed it was a double suicide. I had Owen have a redemptive epiphany about life while holding her dead body, which insinuated he'd be okay now. But that ending felt like it simplified all the complexities of the novel. It was too preachy, my own thoughts on the world came through too obviously, and I would rather make a reader think than listen. That ending interfered with letting the reader judge Owen, Alex, and Hannah, and all of their actions, for themselves.

## SETTLING ON THE ENDING ...

I never planned on having Owen share the same fate as his father, but in the end it seemed appropriate on many levels. I went back through the story and laced it with clues – obvious ones, like the hints Emily was a delusion, and subtle ones, like his being so socially reclusive. The whole depersonalization disorder bit was a misdiagnosis; I wonder how many readers will realize that? I also foreshadowed the suicide attempt ten different ways too, like his train of thought on the ferry back home, so it wouldn't come out of nowhere.

This schizophrenic, delusion-assisted suicide ending I settled on seemed fitting. So fitting it sort of wrote itself out, and I like when a final chapter has a reader flipping the pages, but it feels genre-defiant. I am worried having a "spoiler ending" of "he goes mad" might overwhelm the rest of the story and make this a novel about a man who went insane. That is not what the novel is about. I'd let a reader muse on whether or not his losing himself was symbolic and fitting. On many levels. It was certainly not just a gimmicky ending, and now I am worried a reader might hear how the story ends and think there is no point reading the book, knowing the ending. This is a multilayered novel with a handful of "themes," but I will leave "what it's about" up to the reader, because it will hopefully strike a different chord in everyone who reads it. That's what a good book does: raises questions instead of preaching an author's opinions. It took me years of writing to embrace that.

I do know what my "intentions" were with this novel, but that shouldn't affect what questions *Away from Everywhere* raises about life for any given reader. I like that, so far, everyone seems to react to a different element of this book. I like that there are different elements to like, or dislike, for that matter. It's like this book reads differently for everyone who reads it. I let myself stop worrying that some audiences might like one chapter and hate the next. It's that kind of book. It's like life that way.

# BOOK CLUB QUESTIONS

1. What was this novel really about? What questions did it raise for you as you read it?

2. Now that you are finished the novel, what do you think about when you reflect on *Away from Everywhere*?

3. Why might the author haven chosen to end the novel this way? Did the ending overwhelm the rest of the story? Is it what lingers for you?

4. What does the title mean to you?

5. The author contends that this novel, in part, explores "the flipside of love and the complexities of relationships." Did this really strike your as a major element of this book?

6. Consider Hannah's line, "Love makes us weak so we will succumb to it, give into it." Is this "weakening effect" of Owen on Hannah a test of the strength of her relationship, her own will, or was it nature's way of telling her that Alex was no longer the right man for who she'd become in her thirties?

7. Are there any indications that Hannah's affections for Owen are moreso a result of her and Alex's troubles than her feelings for Owen? Is it a mix of the two? Is she even sure herself? Is this true to life?

8. Consider Clyde's sentiment, "We are an ever-changing product of yesterdays, not rigid, static people." Is there any truth to this? In what ways is this a novel about the plasticity or instability of identity?

9. Was Owen justified in claiming Hannah's journal to "spare" Alex from having to read about the affair? Ultimately, which brother would have benefitted the most from reading it? Been crushed the most by it?

10. Is Alex villainized in the first half of this novel? Are Owen's and Hannah's opinions on him a fair assessment of his character? Where in the novel is his character most redeemed? Most flawed?

11. On page 149, Hannah says "I feel trapped in the world before now. Fenced in by it. Caged in." How much of life are we not in control of? To what degree are we to be held accountable for our actions?

12. What is similar about how each section starts on pages 19, 22, 59, and 258. What might be the intention here?

13. Which parts of the book were the most compelling? What was the biggest lull in the book that lost your attention?

14. What part of the novel turned you off from a character the most? What action redeemed a character the most?

15. Who did you find your opinion of shifting the most? Which of the characters did you like the most, dislike the most, and what would you like to ask one of them?